Praise for the novels of JoAnn Ross

"Moving… This engrossing and hopeful story will hold
readers from start to finish."
—*Publishers Weekly* on *The Inheritance*

"Family secrets, complex characters and a glorious setting
make *The Inheritance* a rich, compelling read… JoAnn Ross at
her best!"
—Sherryl Woods, #1 *New York Times* bestselling author

"A wonderfully uplifting story full of JoAnn Ross's signature
warmth and charm."
—Jill Shalvis, *New York Times* bestselling author,
on *Snowfall on Lighthouse Lane*

"The connection between a deeply conflicted man slowly
coming to terms with loss and a woman who understands
him adds strength and intensity to a perceptive story that is
more than the average friends-into-lovers romance… Verdict:
An excellent start to a promising community series with a
stunning Olympic Coast setting."
—*Library Journal* on *Herons Landing*

"*Snowfall on Lighthouse Lane* is another deftly crafted gem of a
romance novel by an author who is an impressively consistent
master of the genre."
—*Midwest Book Review*

"A widower gets a second chance at love with his wife's best
friend in this…sweet first book in Ross's Honeymoon Harbor
series… Fans of cozy small-town romances will be willing to
read further in the series."
—*Publishers Weekly* on *Herons Landing*

"It's a cause for celebration when a favorite author gifts us
with a new series… Seth and Brianna are a delicious couple."
—*All About Romance* on *Herons Landing*

JoAnn Ross

Second Chance Spring

HQN

ISBN-13: 978-1-335-47998-3

Second Chance Spring

Copyright © 2022 by JoAnn Ross

Just One Look

Copyright © 2019 by JoAnn Ross

Recycling programs
for this product may
not exist in your area.

For questions and comments about the quality of this book,
please contact us at CustomerService@Harlequin.com.

HQN
22 Adelaide St. West, 41st Floor
Toronto, Ontario M5H 4E3, Canada
www.Harlequin.com

Printed in Lithuania

MIX
Paper from
responsible sources
FSC® C021394

CONTENTS

SECOND CHANCE SPRING

To Jay, whom I married twice, the second time
during our own real-life second-chance spring.

CHAPTER ONE

FROM THE FIRST time he'd walked through the door of 30 Rockefeller Plaza as a twenty-one-year-old, wet-behind-the-ears, first-round rookie draft pick, the building had been Burke Mannion's favorite in Manhattan. The name had changed to the Comcast Building, and despite the huge LED NBC peacocks lighting up the New York skyline, to him, the building that had embodied a dream he'd been working toward for as long as he could remember would always be 30 Rock. Where his adult life had begun.

As the Gotham Knights' quarterback, he'd entered the American pantheon of NFL players. Because, as Sinatra had sung, if you could make it in New York, you could make it anywhere. Even all these years later, as he walked beneath the large, art deco sculpture of *Wisdom*, he felt a surge of energy. He'd grown accustomed to that. But today it was crackling with extra tension.

When he entered the suite of offices on the fifty-sixth floor, the receptionist greeted him with a chirpy "good morning" and a dazzling smile. A moment later, one of several minions immediately appeared to ask if he wanted coffee, espresso, a latte, perhaps? Water? With the team's blowout Super Bowl win over Washington last season, the Gotham Knights had become football royalty, and he was their tall, ripped, handsome king—not his words, but those written in a gushing *Sports Illustrated* editorial.

Burke knew that the headlines and the appearances on the morning talk shows—where he'd flirt, just a little, with the female anchors, talk jive with the men, and help prepare the dubbed-every-year "best ever" Super Bowl dish for the viewers at home—were all hype. As were the radio and late-night show interviews, where he'd have no shortage of stories to make audiences laugh. Because if there was one thing he'd realized, even going back to his high school days, it was that people liked their sports heroes to not only be the best at what they did, but also be funnier and shine brighter than other mere mortals. He'd always been sure to give them what they wanted.

The Knights had a dynamite publicity and social media group that sent out a blizzard of highlight reels after every game. While various sports shows might show the sacks, interceptions and blocked kicks from weekly games, the videos coming from 30 Rock were always positive. Narrated by Morgan Freeman's deep, vibrating baritone, they showed off dazzling long pass receptions into the end zone that had fans holding their breaths, or QB Mannion dodging an onslaught of opposing attackers only to pull off a play no one saw coming.

And if that weren't enough, nearly every game there'd be a touchdown he'd run in from the red zone when he couldn't find an open receiver. More than one sportscaster had begun referring to him as a human highlight reel. Burke knew that he'd be making headlines as soon as word of what he was considering leaked. Hell, he might even break the internet. And not in a good way.

"You've got to be freaking kidding me," Sam Otterbein, the team's general manager, said. It was exactly the reaction Burke had been expecting.

"No. I'm not. We've had this discussion before, Sam. Several times over the years."

"And we've been working on the problem." From the way the guy who'd changed his life so many years ago was glancing down at the bottom drawer of his desk, Burke guessed he was thinking of that bottle of Henry McKenna Single Barrel ten-year bourbon he kept in there.

"When you picked me first in the draft, you promised a front line that would protect me."

"I've been trying. But the cap..." He shrugged, as if proclaiming himself helpless when it came to the annual payment limits of the league.

"The cap didn't stop you from signing Curt Washington." The team had traded two years of first picks and three other players to be named later to get the Heisman Trophy running back. "Not to mention the kid's twenty-million-dollar signing bonus on top of the twenty million for four years."

"What can I say?" Another shrug. Another furtive glance at that drawer. "Mel had his finance team run the numbers and decided he'd be worth it in the long run." Mel being Mel Montgomery, the billionaire owner who'd made his fortune in finance and trading. To him, the Knights were like all his other investments. It would always come down to the numbers.

"Because Vince wants another running back," Burke said. Vince Jones, the team's head coach, had come out of an SEC university renowned for winning national titles. Not all coaches could make the transition from college to the pros, and he and Burke had both been rookies here their first year. The guy was good. Better than good, he was brilliant. But despite the team's winning record, their styles had never meshed as well as Burke felt they could.

"You knew when you accepted the offer to come here that Vince likes a running game."

"I did. I was also told that I'd been acquired to shake things up. Because not only can I throw the long ball, I can do it from out of the pocket on the fly."

"No one's better."

"Yet you're not letting me do that as often as I could if you'd just give me a damn front line that can keep me from getting sacked. We both know that Vince is never going to change. He came from college with a game that won for him."

"As you also knew. And you can't deny that it hasn't proven to be a winning pro game, too. We haven't had a year without a postseason since you arrived. Vince brought the game. You provided the magic that lifted it to NFL level."

Burke had been through this conversation so many times he could have it in his sleep. Which he had. More and more lately.

"Do you know how many concussions I've had?"

"Not exactly. Not off the top of my head." And didn't that question cause yet another glance at the drawer.

"Neither do I, because concussion protocol wasn't a thing when I was playing in high school or college." There were admittedly times during those years, even after he'd gone pro, when he'd been younger and thought himself invincible, that he hadn't told his coaches or trainers about times he'd gotten his bell rung hard enough that he'd have no memory of plays he'd catch later on the highlight reel. "All I know is that I've been getting sacked an average of forty damn times a season."

"And what *I* also know, and what Vince has suggested, is that the average would improve if you adopted a less sack-prone play," Sam countered with a flare of heat. "Hell,

Burke, the days of you having to carry the entire team are behind us. You've got some of the best guys in the league who can gain yardage on the ground. There's no reason for you to invite pressure by leaving the damn pocket."

"Which I need to do to buy time to make the plays that win games. And championships." He was proud to have received the NFL's Walter Payton Man of the Year award, granted to a player for their impact on their community. He'd been to nine Pro Bowls, including in his rookie year. He'd won three MVP trophies, including one in the season he'd been sidelined by a concussion that prevented him from playing in the championship game he'd earned. That caused a loss when all the oddsmakers had the Knights as Super Bowl champs. But he'd made up for it the following year, when he'd achieved his lifetime goal of winning the shiny Vince Lombardi Trophy and a big-ass gold-and-diamond ring that looked like it could be seen from space.

But after a painful one-point loss due to a sack in the red zone with twenty seconds to play this past January, sports reporters who'd once fawned all over him had spent the last few months reminding football fans that Burke Mannion hadn't joined the elite group of quarterbacks who'd won back-to-back Super Bowls. And with the team the Knights' management was building, membership in that club was looking as elusive as Bigfoot.

"Look, I'm not blaming anyone here," he said, dialing down the temperature of the conversation. "But we've been in the bottom fourth of the league in offensive line expenditures the past five seasons. Our front line can't effectively block the other guys' defense. Which leaves me having to scramble to conjure something out of nothing. If I stayed more in the pocket, there'd be a lot more sacks." And injuries. "With the money the front office is paying me, you can't want me warming the bench."

Sam literally threw up his hands. "Hell, Burke, I know that. You know that. But the damn cap—"

The discussion was cut off by Burke's phone dinging a text. Deciding to deal with that later, he reached into his pocket to silence the phone when he saw a CALL ME NOW text from his brother Aiden. A former LA vice cop who'd taken the job of Honeymoon Harbor's police chief after being wounded in a shoot-out that had killed his partner, Aiden was not one to ever use all caps. Unless it was an emergency.

"I've got to take this," he said. "It's from my brother and looks important."

"Sure. It'll give me time to call Mel and set up a meeting for the three of us." That alone assured Burke that he was valued. Not many players got a meeting with both the GM and the team's owner. "You're our guy, Burke. We realize with your contract expiring, given that you're an unrestricted free agent, we could lose you to someone else. Believe me, we don't want that to happen.

"I've been thinking it'd be a good idea for you to have more input in how the team builds. It only makes sense that dialogue between you and the front office should happen more frequently. You say you want a better opportunity to win a second Super Bowl. That's what we all want. So let's see what we can work out."

"That's all I'm asking," Burke said as he left the room to call his brother.

Aiden answered on the first ring and didn't mince words. "It's Mom," he said. "She's been in an accident."

Burke's career woes fled his mind as his blood turned to ice. Aiden wouldn't have called for a fender bender.

"How bad?"

"I don't know, but it's not good. She was T-boned by a truck at the crossroads right in front of Blue House Farm. Fortunately, the impact was on the passenger side, but the force spun her around into the borrow ditch on the side of the road. Jim Olson called in the wreck, said she was unconscious when he reached the car from the farm. He couldn't get to her because she was tipped sideways in the ditch and the other door was smashed in. She was still unconscious when I arrived, about four minutes after Jim's call."

"Damn."

"The good news is that she *had* regained consciousness by the time the fire department arrived to cut her out with the jaws of life. But the EMTs asked the usual head injury test questions, and she doesn't have any memory of the crash. Or what she was doing before impact. She also didn't know what day it was. But did get the president's name right. Although she stumbled a bit on coming up with it."

"I'll be there as soon as I can."

Aiden didn't mince words. "That's why I called you. I figured you'd want to come home, especially with it being the off-season."

Burke's head was spinning and foggy, the same as he felt when he'd get those concussions his mother worried about. Visions of her being cut out of her beloved red Prius swirled through his mind.

He stuck his head into the doorway. "I'm sorry, Sam. But we'll have to take this up some other time. It's my mom. She's been in an accident. Her car was T-boned. My cop brother says it was bad."

"Go." The man he considered both his boss and a friend waved his hand. "I'll call and have the Gulfstream waiting for you." The team was one of a handful in the league that traveled on their own 767 to and from games. The smaller

Gulfstream was for the team owner, his family, and his one-percenter pals.

"I appreciate the offer, but you pay me enough that I can charter one myself."

"The hell you will," Sam said. "That'd take time you don't need to waste. And just in case the thought occurs to you when you're in the air, I'm not doing it to win points or pressure you into signing. This one's personal."

Despite their differences, Burke knew that to be true. "Thanks."

After racing back through the bronze revolving doors and out of the building, he grabbed a cab and stopped by his apartment just long enough to throw some clothes in a bag. On the way to the airport, he prayed to the God he hadn't thought about all that much since his youthful prayers of a pro football career had been answered.

He decided not to call Aiden, who was probably busy doing cop things to find out more details. He didn't want to call his dad, who'd undoubtedly be an emotional mess. His parents had fallen in love as teenagers. He couldn't imagine one of them without the other.

No. Don't go there.

Brianna, his sister, would be busy comforting everyone, bustling around, using her former hotel concierge skills to find out information and do whatever it took to make the situation less horrific. Then there was his brother Gabe. But he had his own family he'd be dealing with. The foster kids he'd adopted with Chelsea Mannion were like John and Sarah Mannion's own blood grandchildren, and having spent so many years in the foster care system, the last thing they needed was to have their lives turned upside down again.

So he called the most logical brother. The rock. Quinn, the eldest, who'd given up a high-paying law career in Seattle to return to Honeymoon Harbor, open a craft brewery, and reestablish the family pub that had been closed down during Prohibition over a century ago. Quinn had brought it back to life, and Burke had figured part of the reason for its success was the eldest Mannion brother's superpower: an uncanny knack for listening. Burke couldn't count all the times growing up when he'd go off on a rant, losing his temper over some undoubtedly trivial thing, and Quinn would nod his head, listening until Burke wound down. And most times, Burke would figure out his own solution to whatever grievance he'd been mad about in the first place.

His brother answered on the first ring. "Just a minute," he said. Burke heard him speak again, undoubtedly to other family members huddled in some waiting room at the hospital. "It's Burke," he told them. "I'll be right back." There was a buzz of conversation in the background, then silence, suggesting Quinn had left the room.

After what seemed like a lifetime, but was less than a minute, he said, "Where are you?"

"On the way to LaGuardia."

"What airline and flight number?"

"It's the team's private jet. I figured I could save driving time by flying into Port Angeles instead of SeaTac."

"Good plan." Quinn didn't question it. Perhaps he thought private jets were the usual mode of flying for the most famous Mannion brother. Or more than likely, it was simply that he'd always been a man of few words.

"How's Mom? Aiden didn't get into details."

"Still too early to know. Apparently she was coming back from a meeting with a design client out at the lake, and her car was T-boned at that four-way stop by Blue House Farm."

"Aiden told me that much. That had to be hard for him, taking that call."

Burke knew that his brother had dealt with a lot worse while working undercover on LA's mean streets. Hell, from what he'd heard from Brianna, the shoot-out that had killed his partner had sent him spiraling into a dark place for a time. But none of the victims of the crimes he'd investigated had been their mom.

"No shit, Sherlock. Someone—Aiden suspects kids—stole the stop sign. The delivery truck that hit her blew through the intersection. Reports from some people the driver passed said he'd been speeding, which, if true, will show up on the EDR the company puts in its trucks. It's like those airplane black boxes, reporting speed, impact, and brake pedal data. Of course, knowing that won't make what happened to Mom any better. So..."

His voice drifted off. Burke heard what sounded like an inhaled breath. Then a long exhale. "Jim saw it happen and called it in," he said, repeating Aiden's account of the accident. "Which was lucky since the road to the farm doesn't get all that much traffic. Did Aiden tell you that they had to cut her out of the car?"

"Yeah. And that she was unconscious when he got there but had come to by the time the EMT arrived."

"Which is a positive. The paramedic and EMT said the airbags and seat belt did their jobs, but she has some fractured ribs." Having experienced such an injury himself when a linebacker had plowed his helmet into his chest, Burke winced. "It's her head everyone's worried about," Quinn said. "They did a CT scan and didn't find any skull fractures, so now it's mostly a waiting game."

That was one game Burke would give anything not to play. "They didn't airlift her to Seattle?"

"The surgeon's former military. Wanting a quieter life after so many war-front deployments, after leaving the Army as a major, she transferred from Madigan military hospital in Tacoma to here. If there's one thing she knows, it's trauma."

Trauma. Over the years, Burke had witnessed a lot of rough, even career-ending injuries on the field. But never in his wildest nightmares would he have imagined his mom suffering something so brutal.

"Better yet," Quinn continued, "during the doc's service, seeing so many TBIs—traumatic brain injuries—"

"I know what they are," Burke broke in.

"Yeah. Sure you do." There was a long sigh. Burke could imagine his brother dragging his hand down his face. A seemingly inborn habit he shared with their dad. It was one of the two men's few tells of stress. "Anyway, along with her being a board-certified surgeon, the Army sent her back to school for more training, so she's a board-certified neurointensivist, which, from all the hospital jargon we were given, sounds like a neurologist on steroids."

"And she set up practice in Honeymoon Harbor?" The small, two-stoplight town on Washington State's Olympic Peninsula that Burke had been hell-bent on escaping was a quaint, picturesque place that could've been painted by Norman Rockwell or Grandma Moses. It wasn't the type of place where a surgeon who could practice in the most prestigious hospitals in the country was likely to settle.

"She winter-trained on a joint mission with some Navy SEALs in the Olympic Mountains a few years ago and apparently fell in love with the place, so when she left the Army, we were lucky to get her. Brianna looked her up online. She has patients from all over the peninsula and has admitting privileges in hospitals around the state."

"Lucky," Burke echoed.

"Yeah." Quinn's tone flattened, suggesting that things sucked when you had to look that hard for a bit of luck.

"How's Dad?"

"You know him. Outwardly, he's as calm as one of those Tibetan monks he lived with in Nepal during his twenties. Inside, I suspect every atom in his body is firing."

"They've been together nearly forever. If anything happens—"

"Don't say it," Quinn warned in his quietly dangerous eldest brother's voice. Burke hadn't heard it since his teens, when he'd been caught coming home from a party drunk and reeking of pot.

Having planned a long career in the pros, Burke had typically treated his body not so much like a temple, but as something to take care of if he wanted it to achieve NFL, then Hall of Fame status. But that night, the Honeymoon Harbor Sea Lions had won the state championship. Again. And it had all been because of his ability to throw the long, game-winning pass to his now brother-in-law Seth Harper.

"I need to get back to the others," Quinn said. "I'll call you on the plane if there's any news. Keep me updated with your ETA, and I'll pick you up."

"No. I don't want anyone having to drive me around. I'll arrange to have a car waiting at the airport."

"That's not necessary. Between us all, we have enough vehicles that there'll be one available for you. Dad bought a new truck for the farm last season." There was a long pause. "Damn, I wish Mom had been driving that." Burke heard him blow out a breath. "Anyway, see you in a few hours in Port Angeles. And, hey, bro, don't beat yourself up for not being here."

With that, he ended the call, leaving Burke wondering how his brother always seemed to know what he—and seemingly everyone else—was thinking.

CHAPTER TWO

BURKE WAS NO stranger to private jets, but deep inside, he still got a kick out of being welcomed aboard by a crew whose jobs were solely to make his flight as comfortable as possible. The pilot, he remembered, was former military who had flown jets off carriers in the Persian Gulf. Once, after being invited into the cockpit, Burke had asked him if he found ferrying rich guys around the country boring after that. He'd told him that while there were times he missed the rush of landing on a deck that was being pitched by ocean waves, the payoff was knowing he'd be coming home to his wife and three kids, something they hadn't been able to count on during his Marine pilot days.

"So the trade-off was worth it?" Burke had asked.

"Absolutely." The guy had glanced over at Burke, who'd been studying the cockpit's complex controls. "You're not married."

It hadn't been a question, but Burke had answered anyway. "No."

"Then you can't fully understand. I was a typical hotshot pilot, playing the field when I met my Amy. She's a pediatrician. She was out at a club with her girlfriends to celebrate her thirtieth birthday. I was there with some guys, doing what guys do at clubs."

"Drinking and picking up women."

There was a time, not that long ago, when that had been

Burke's second-best sport. The tabloids had even started showing him out at clubs with various models, actresses, and pampered, rich society girls who were living lives as empty as their heads on Daddy's dime. Burke never did drugs or got drunk in public. He understood that he had a reputation to uphold. Not only for the team and all those kids who saw him as a role model, but for his parents back home as well. Brianna had told him that their mother kept a scrapbook of his exploits on the field and his charity work, but had left out the part of his life that had landed his face on the covers of tabloids and gossip magazines, not just in America, but even in Great Britain, where the Knights played a game every preseason.

"It got so we couldn't go to the market without seeing your face," she'd told him. "Always with some new woman. Mom and Dad didn't say anything, but back when I was working in Vegas, I could tell they were worried from the way they'd ask if I'd heard from you."

Brianna was not the only one of the siblings to have passed on that information. Except for Quinn, who'd only texted once, asking if Burke was all right. And reminding him that he was always there to talk.

I'm right as rain, Burke had responded at the time, even adding a stupid umbrella emoji for emphasis.

Great, Quinn had texted back. But Burke knew the eldest of the Mannion brothers had known he'd been lying. Because Quinn always knew everything.

Always true to his word, his brother was waiting when the jet landed at Port Angeles's William R. Fairchild Airport.

"How is she?" Burke asked as they drove to Honeymoon Harbor, a small Victorian coastal town located on one of the world's largest inland seas.

Situated between the volcanic chain of the Cascade Mountains and the Olympic Mountains, encompassing Puget Sound, and the Canadian waters off Vancouver, British Columbia, the sea had four hundred islands, including the San Juans. Surrounded by lush, mossy old-growth forests and home to majestic orcas, the Salish Sea was a crown jewel of the Pacific Northwest.

"Her chest X-ray showed two broken ribs. And, unsurprisingly, she's got a helluva headache, dizziness, and some nausea."

"It's scary," said Burke, who not only didn't know how many concussions he'd had, but had lied about his condition just to get back in the game. But that was then, and this was now, and more importantly, it was his mom they were talking about.

"Yeah."

"It's lucky she wasn't killed. Like I told Aiden, I don't know what Dad would do if he lost Mom."

They'd been together since their high school years, when, according to family lore, they'd sneak out and ride the ferry out of town together because their mom's parents didn't want her dating a town boy for fear she'd get stuck in Honeymoon Harbor. She was the first Harper to go to college, and they'd had "higher" plans for her. Which was how she'd ended up out East for school. But even that hadn't stopped them from seeing each other, because John Mannion had lived on a shoestring while at UW, saving his money to fly back East every few months to be with her.

"I don't know what any of us would do," Quinn admitted. "She's always been the heart of this family." He braked to let a herd of Roosevelt elk cross in front of them. The magnificent animals had always inspired a feeling of awe in Burke. Not today.

"You said the doctor was good."

"Supposedly the best in the state. In addition to Brianna's googling, I made some calls."

Of course he had. "Well, then, we'll have to count on that."

Neither spoke the rest of the way to Honeymoon Harbor General Hospital. As they got into the elevator, Burke was surprised when Quinn hit the button for the cafeteria. "I ate on the plane."

"Good for you. There's someone you need to talk to before you come up to the waiting room."

"Brianna?"

"No." Quinn had returned to his typical closemouthed self. "Someone else you apparently know," he said cryptically. The doors opened. Quinn stayed where he was. "I'll see you in a bit. We're on the fifth floor. The nurse at the desk can point you to the waiting room."

Still not knowing what he was doing besides experiencing the same sense of icy dread he felt whenever he knew he was about to get sacked, Burke stepped out of the elevator. Hearing the doors close behind him, he followed the arrows painted on the wall down the hall to the cafeteria, where, as if attracted by a powerful magnet, his gaze was immediately drawn to a woman, seated alone at a table by a window that overlooked the harbor. She was holding a cardboard cup in her hands. A box of additional cups sat on the table in front of her. The impetus for his spiral into that reckless club life didn't look any more eager to see him than he was to see her.

It didn't make any damn sense. What the hell was Lily Carpenter doing in Honeymoon Harbor? What were the odds that of all the towns in all the world, she'd end up in his?

He'd once dated a psychology professor from Columbia who'd talked him into attending a retreat in Northern California where you were supposed to "get in touch with your true spiritual self."

He'd put himself through a weekend unplugged from the outside world, taking tai chi classes at dawn and eating all-vegan meals. Yoga had twisted his athlete's body into pretzel shapes and left him grateful for the saltwater hot tub. Workshops on "mindfulness" led to him pissing off his date by constantly referring to it as "mindlessness." The weekend ended with everyone walking barefoot on hot coals. Which was how he felt now as he crossed the room to her table.

"Hello, Lily," he greeted her, saying her name out loud for the first time in nearly two years. Not that he was counting. Why the hell hadn't Quinn given him a heads-up?

"Hello, Burke." Silence strung between them, long and tense. "I'm so sorry about Sarah."

"You know my mother?"

Lily shrugged even as her knuckles turned white from tightening her hold on the cup. "It's a small town. And Brianna's one of my best friends."

"My sister?" Burke asked, surprised Brianna hadn't mentioned making friends with the woman who'd turned his entire life upside down. Then again, unless Lily had told her, she would have no way of knowing the two of them had even been together. Lily had insisted on keeping their relationship private.

"She doesn't know about us," she confirmed, as though she'd heard the question that had exploded in his mind. Then she released her death grip on the cup long enough to run her fingers through her shoulder-length honey-blond hair. Which, damn, reminded him of how it'd felt on his bare chest after making love.

No. Not love, he'd learned. Sure, she'd been the first woman he'd given his heart to since Ms. Howard, his second-grade teacher, but in turn, she'd trampled on it as if the red-soled high heels she'd been so fond of wearing had been the cleats of an entire opposing defensive line. That was when he'd realized that she'd meant it when she'd told him she didn't do relationships. Apparently he'd simply been a diversion. Hell, sex with a pro athlete had probably been on one of those to-do lists she was always creating.

"What are you doing here, Lily?" Somehow, even over the olfactory assault of alcohol, disinfectants, and overly scented cleaners, along with questionable aromas coming from the cafeteria line, she still smelled like sunshine and the wildflowers that turned the spring mountain hillsides around Honeymoon Harbor into an impressionist landscape.

"I told you. Brianna's my friend. Where else would I be at a time like this?"

"Not *here*." He swept his arm to encompass the cafeteria. "In Honeymoon Harbor."

Her hand took another swipe through her hair. Her nails were short, shiny, and painted the color of a ripe peach. "Would you mind sitting down? It's difficult to have a conversation while you're towering over me."

"Funny. I don't remember you thinking we needed a conversation when you broke up with me. By text."

Color rose in her cheeks, reminding him—dammit, yet again—of how flushed and beautiful she'd look after sex. "That wasn't my best moment," she admitted.

You think? Realizing that they were drawing attention to themselves but wanting to get the conversation over with before he went upstairs, he pulled out a chair and sat across the table from her.

Those peach-hued nails began drawing little figure eights on the table. He could remember them doing the same thing on his bare back. ... *No. Don't go there.*

"I told you from the start that I wasn't looking for anything long-term or permanent. That I was pretty much a rolling stone," she said. "You told me you weren't in any position for a relationship, either. That football was pretty much your life. And after the Pro Bowl, you were spending six weeks in Mexico with your performance team and one of your receivers."

What he hadn't told her was that he'd been about to ask her to go with him. First to the Pro Bowl, and although he realized she couldn't take six weeks off work, he'd figured that she could fly back and forth to Mexico on weekends. Although he was known for one of the toughest training regimens, traveling with his own trainer, physical therapist, massage therapist and chef, even he couldn't work 24/7.

"That doesn't explain how you ended up in my hometown," he said evenly, his voice belying the fact that his heart felt as if he'd been running wind sprints.

"It was the way you talked about it. You always made it sound like a Hallmark holiday movie."

Which, although they weren't his thing, he'd watched with her in bed instead of his annual viewing of *Die Hard*, which she'd refused to accept as a Christmas flick. "Just because all that shooting, murder and mayhem takes place during Christmas does *not* make it a Christmas movie," she'd insisted. He'd been about to argue that point when she'd climbed on top of him and covered his mouth with hers, and her taste caused all the ways he was going to prove her wrong to escape his mind.

"Those Hallmark movies aren't real," he said now.

"I realize that. It's hard to explain, but it sounded so appealing at the time. New York hadn't suited me the first time I'd moved there from Hawaii after college. It was too busy. Too loud. Too, well…brash, I guess."

He leaned back in the metal chair and folded his arms. "Yet you'd returned." Where it had been his bad luck to meet her.

Revealing nerves, or perhaps to avoid meeting his eyes, she began arranging the sweetener packets on the Formica table by color. Pink. Yellow. Blue. White. "I'd been working down in Atlanta when I was offered that opportunity to work at a foundation focused on food insecurity. I decided maybe, being ten years older, I'd find the city different."

"But it wasn't."

"No." She glanced briefly up at him, then began carefully putting the packs back into the bowl. "I didn't leave because of you."

How many times had he given that *It's not you, it's me* excuse? Although it had always been true, it sure as hell felt different having been on the other end of it. "If that's true, then there wasn't any reason for you not to tell me in person when you planned to leave the city."

"It's complicated."

"Apparently. So, you came here directly from New York?"

"No. I flew to LA because it was the first open ticket I could find at the last minute. I rented a house in Malibu for six weeks, and as much as I enjoyed living on the beach, I kept thinking about this town. I initially came out of curiosity, because of how you'd always described it. Call me jaded, but I didn't believe a place like this still existed. Yet the minute I stepped off the ferry, I felt an inner click. As if I'd finally found where I belonged. Honeymoon Harbor is the only place that's ever felt like home."

She looked up, her moss-green eyes finally meeting his gaze. "Except for a few years in a Swiss convent school, and some time in Paris as a child, this is the longest I've ever lived in any one place. I'm happy here."

The convent school was a section of her biography he hadn't known. As was the fact that she'd spent part of her childhood in Paris. But then, he'd never known much about Lily Carpenter's backstory. Whenever he'd brought up the past, she'd always deftly shift the subject back to him.

She'd been good at that. Making him later wonder if he'd merely been yet another in a long line of guys she'd dumped over the years. Scattered from place to place like the clam shells abandoned by seagulls littering their beaches.

"Good for you." He pushed the chair back and stood up. "And now that you've made yourself clear, I've got to go see my mom."

"Of course you do." She paused, glancing down at her watch. It was a Lady Rolex, with tiny diamonds taking the place of numbers behind the face's protective crystal. "I told Brianna I'd be back in ten."

He shrugged. "Don't let me keep you. Like you said in the text, and repeated just now, whatever our relationship was, we both agreed going in that it was never meant to be permanent."

Having seen how difficult professional sports could be on families, Burke had decided early on that marriage wasn't in the cards for him. Being single allowed him to concentrate solely on the game. And he mostly had since his Pop Warner days, although his teacher mother had never let him get away with not doing his homework before going to bed. But Lily Carpenter had gotten him thinking that perhaps, maybe...

"It was just convenient, no-strings-attached hookup sex," he said.

Color rose again in her cheeks. As she began stirring her coffee, her hand trembled. Not enough for most people to notice. But just as his eyes were capable of taking in an entire football field in action, he'd always been hyper-attentive to this woman. He'd known she'd built walls around herself, but he had been chump enough to believe she'd lowered the drawbridge for him because he was special to her. Not just because of the sex, which had been off the charts, but because they'd had a strong connection from the moment they'd met at that charity event she'd organized.

"I didn't put it that way." Unable, or unwilling, to meet his stony gaze again, she was staring into the depths of the cup.

She may not have written the words back then. But the meaning had come through loud and clear, along with the pain. He'd thought he'd put it behind him, but it still felt like a scalpel to the chest, plunged straight into his heart. "Like I said, I've got to go."

"I am so sincerely sorry," she said, following behind him as he headed back toward the elevator. Her voice was so low, he wasn't certain if she was talking to herself or to him, but he glanced back over his shoulder. "About your mom," she continued. "And, well, everything."

"Mom will be okay." Burke could not, *would* not, allow himself to think otherwise. In middle school, he'd gotten a book from the library on the power of positive thinking. He'd followed those tenets through high school, college and into the pros. It was why he'd been voted the offensive team leader his second year on the team.

"Of course she will," Lily agreed. "As for Brianna, it didn't seem necessary to tell her about us because you haven't been home since I've lived here. Not even for Thanksgiving and Christmas."

"Which would've been a bit difficult considering both occur during football season." And she damn well knew it, too, given that one and only time she'd been willing to go out in public with him, that Christmas Eve they'd gone skating at the Rockefeller Center rink while the iconic Christmas tree, trucked in from some farm in Maine, towered over them, ablaze in white lights.

"It wasn't meant as criticism."

She followed him into the elevator, standing as far away as the small closed-in space would allow. There was a guy on the team, a safety, who was severely claustrophobic and preferred to take the stairs rather than an elevator. Although some of the guys ragged him for this, Burke never had. But he'd also never fully understood his teammate's seemingly irrational fear of not being able to escape confined spaces. Until now.

"Could've fooled me. As for us—" he hardened his gaze "—it's a bygone. In the past. Forgotten." He shrugged. "Like you said, it wasn't anything real or serious anyway."

Because she hadn't let it be.

Burke had gotten over Lily Carpenter. Moved on with his life. At least, that's what he'd been telling himself. And now, finally, he needed to believe it. Because he had someone far more important to concentrate on.

CHAPTER THREE

BEFORE RETURNING HOME to Honeymoon Harbor to turn a dilapidated Victorian house into a bed-and-breakfast, Brianna Mannion-Harper had worked as a high-end resort hotel concierge in cities all over the country, the last one in Las Vegas. One of the reasons for her success was her ability to sense a guest's needs at times even before they knew what they wanted.

Sitting in the expansive private family waiting room that had been assigned to them (thanks to her dad being mayor and her über-wealthy brother Gabe having helped fund the children's trauma center), she sensed tension between Burke and Lily Carpenter as her brother sat waiting for his turn to see their mother. To keep the stress level down, the medical staff had strict rules about only two family visitors at a time.

Now that she thought about it, something was off. Quinn, who'd gone to pick up Burke at the airport, had returned to the room alone. When she'd asked where Burke was, before going back into the hospital room to join his father, Quinn had explained he'd stopped to get some coffee in the shop.

Yet Burke had arrived empty-handed. It was Lily, who appeared moments afterward, who held a box of drinks from the specialty shop that Cops & Coffee had opened in the cafeteria. After handing them out, she'd sat down next to Brianna.

"What's between you and my brother?" Brianna asked at a near whisper. After they'd hugged and she'd welcomed him home, wishing that his return to Honeymoon Harbor had been under better circumstances, the moment Lily had entered the room, Burke had given Brianna another quick hug, then moved to the far end of the room. His attention was now directed toward the TV, which was showing an episode of *The Great British Baking Show*, the tension that had followed them into the room was like an electric wire strung between them, sparking in the morning fog.

"Which brother?" Lily's attention was drawn to a watercolor painting of Mirror Lake that, ironically, Sarah Mannion had painted and donated to the hospital. It was the lake at sunset, a wash of blues and pinks and gold, meant to instill calm. Unfortunately, it was not working.

"Burke," Brianna said. "Why didn't you tell me you knew him?"

"Who said I did?"

"Lily." Brianna was atypically tense and not at all in the mood to play games. She narrowed her eyes and lowered her voice again. "It's obvious. You came into the room and didn't even ask who he was. Or seem surprised that he was here."

"We ran into each other briefly downstairs. In line for coffee."

"He doesn't have any with him."

"The woman between us was taking forever to make a decision. He didn't want to wait because he was in a hurry to be up here with you all."

That made sense. Except for one thing. "But how did you know who he was?"

"You can't live in this town without knowing who he is, even if you've never watched a football game. The athletic department at the college has a framed photo that's larger than the school president's. And wearing a Burke Mannion football jersey on game day might as well be declared Honeymoon Harbor's official uniform. Besides, we came up in the elevator together."

"Yet you didn't come into the room together." Brianna glanced toward Burke, who now appeared intensely interested in a choux pastry competition. Their attempt to avoid looking at each other had become more than a little obvious.

Lily sighed. "All right, since it's bound to come out, we've met before. At a fundraiser for child hunger."

"In New York?"

Brianna thought it was a good thing Lily didn't play poker, because she was not good at hiding the color that rose in her cheeks. And her eyes shifted again to that same painting Burke was now studying so intently.

"Yes," she said on another resigned sigh.

"But you said you'd left the city after deciding you weren't suited to that lifestyle."

"That was when I was just out of college, coming from Hawaii, and it proved too overwhelming. But then, a few years ago, I was working in Atlanta's tourism department when I got recruited by a headhunter to be an event planner for a New York–based nonprofit. Because it was for a good cause, and since I was a bit older, I figured I'd give the city a second try. I enjoyed the work, which was for a charity I care deeply about.

"When I met you and realized that the Gotham Knights' quarterback was your brother, it didn't seem important enough to mention. I did so many events, and there were other, more high-profile New York celebrities taking part that night, including Robert De Niro, Taylor Swift, Leslie Jones, Hugh Jackman, Justin Timberlake—even Jay-Z and

Beyoncé. So, quite honestly, your brother was only one of the crowd."

She'd ticked them off on her fingertips in a way that, if Brianna were a suspicious person, might've had her thinking Lily had come up with that reasonable-sounding answer in the elevator. "That's quite an A-list company you were both hanging out with."

"As I said, it was for a good cause. And those I named were only off the top of my head. Everyone I reached out to didn't hesitate to help."

Personally, though admittedly biased, Brianna didn't think that any of her brothers—especially Burke, who'd appeared to slip so easily into fame after preparing for it since childhood—could ever be just one of a crowd. Even in a star power group like that.

Whenever Lily had casually brought up her globe-trotting past, Brianna had wondered why, of all the places she'd lived in the world, she'd chosen to move to this small town in the upper northwest corner of the country. When asked, she'd simply said that it had been a random choice; plus, she couldn't resist seeing if it was as idyllic as its name implied. When it had turned out to be even better, she'd decided to stay.

That had always made sense. On the surface. But now Brianna had questions. Especially given the way Lily and Burke were acting. There was something more than a mere casual meeting at a charity event going on.

"Burke's always had the most positive attitude of any of my brothers—well, with the more recent exception of Quinn, who's been seemingly living in zen mode since returning from Seattle. But I'm getting seriously negative vibes from Burke today." Even his hug when she'd greeted him had been stiff, and his mind had seemed somewhere else. "He seems unusually tense."

"Of course he is." Lily covered Brianna's hand with her own. "He's worried about your mom, the same way we all are."

"She's going to be okay," Brianna said, putting the question aside for now when she had far more important things to be worried about.

"I've not a single doubt of that," Lily agreed as she linked their fingers together. "Sarah is the strongest woman I've ever met. No way is she going to let a stupid car accident keep her down."

It was the same thing Brianna had been telling herself since Aiden had called with the horrible news. She could only hope it was true.

Sarah Mannion had always been a force of nature. After studying at Sarah Lawrence College, and getting a master's degree from Oxford, she'd gone to Japan to teach a course about the works of Jane Austen, because—who'd have guessed?—nineteenth century English romance novels had been very popular over there at the time.

She'd been offered a position at Oxford, where her plan had been to get a PhD in literature, and eventually become the head of the English department at a prestigious university. Or, at least, that had been her parents' plan. Her father's family was from a long line of fishermen, going back to the founding of the town. Starting out working for others, Jerome Harper had his own small fleet of boats, but Sarah had been their only child, and while they'd established a good living, they'd wanted "better" for her. As it happened, their daughter had a mind of her own, and rather than spending her life in some ivory tower of academia, she married her teenage sweetheart and got a job teaching at the local high school while raising four sons and a daughter on what would become the Mannion family Christmas tree farm.

She'd stayed in education, going on to become a principal until her retirement, after which she'd returned to school herself, taking design classes at Clearwater Community College.

"I'd better go talk to Burke," Brianna said. He looked strangely lost, which she supposed wasn't surprising, given that he was undoubtedly accustomed to controlling things as an NFL team captain.

"Go. I need to run to the restroom anyway."

Something in Lily's behavior still seemed off, but again, this was no time for in-depth questions, so Brianna moved across the room and sat down next to her brother as, one by one, the contestants took their plates of chouxnuts to the judging table. "She's working on her semester design project," she told Burke. "That's what she was doing out at the lake. Every time you look, there seem to be more McMansions being built out there by wealthy tech people from Seattle and Portland, and she's working with a family to turn one into something more closely resembling a comfortable home than the current video arcade decor. I suppose that makes sense since it was originally built for some single guy who designs computer games."

"Why the hell couldn't she have just retired, like everyone else her age?"

"Hello?" Brianna waved her hand in front of his face. "Showing that you've been away from home too long. May I remind you that you're talking about our mother?"

"You're right. She's always been a dynamo."

"It's going to be okay," Brianna said, taking hold of his hand and lacing their fingers together.

"And you know this how?"

She briefly closed her eyes. Then her gaze drifted out

the hospital window to the forest and beyond, to the jagged, snow-clad peaks of the Olympic Mountains. "Because it has to be." Because anything less than okay was unthinkable.

"I'm with you on that," he said. "How are Gram and Gramps doing?"

"As well as can be expected. They're both tough and elderly enough that unfortunately they've lost friends and family. Gramps's older cousin, Sam, had a fatal heart attack last month while marlin fishing in Florida."

"That's tough. But it's got to be different when you're worried about losing a child. Especially your only child."

"You're not going to get any argument from me. It was hard to get Gram to put her rosary beads down long enough to eat something. Finally, Dr. Kim sent them home. She said Mom was keeping her busy enough. She didn't want to have another family member become a patient. Kylee's with them at the farm. Although you never showed much interest in my girlfriends, surely you remember her. She was my best friend in high school and like the sister I never had. I told you she got married, right?"

"Yeah. To another photographer she met when she was taking photos of World War II vets' graves in France."

"Her wife's name is Mai. They adopted an adorable baby girl, who's now a toddler. Kylee will be happy to see you."

"And you're wrong about my not having any interest in your friends. I had a crush on her back in the day," Burke said. Despite the seriousness of their situation, his lips curved in a faintly reminiscent smile. "When I asked her out, she told me that I was a nice guy. And hot. But she played for the other team."

That was a surprise, and for a second, Brianna was grateful to have something other than worrying about their mother to think about. "She hadn't come out then. She must have really trusted you."

"I guess. Mostly I think she wanted to shut things down to keep me from asking her out again, which I probably would've done."

At the time, being the star football quarterback who'd unanimously been voted prom king, Burke probably could've had almost any girl at Honeymoon Harbor High. But he hadn't dated that much, saying that he didn't want to risk falling in love and getting sidetracked on his way to playing professional football. He'd always been so single-minded that Brianna had never doubted he'd achieve his goal. Just as he'd never doubted her plans to become a concierge at some of the country's best hotels.

Like birds flying from the nest, they'd left Honeymoon Harbor. And now all but Burke had returned home to make new lives. Aiden, the former family bad boy, was the town's police chief, proving that God indeed must have a sense of humor. Wall Street wizard Gabe was building boats while continuing to run a nonprofit investment foundation; Quinn had left a prestigious law career behind in Seattle to brew beer and run a pub; and here Brianna was, settled down with the man who'd once been married to her best friend. The man she'd loved since elementary school.

"How long can you stay home?" she asked. Not that this had been Burke's home for several years now, and from the casual way Lily had listed all those celebrities he apparently hung out with, he was unlikely to ever want to return to Honeymoon Harbor.

"As long as I need to."

"But—"

Her question was cut off by his father and Quinn entering the waiting room, accompanied by a woman wearing a white physician's coat.

CHAPTER FOUR

JOHN MANNION HAD always been a strong, robust man. Growing up, Burke had heard stories about his dad's two years in Nepal, hiking over the high-altitude mountains for miles and helping the people alter their food supply by planting a variety of trees that would provide a nearly year-round harvest.

Instead of working in the family bank, as his father had expected, when he'd returned home, he'd bought a Christmas tree farm, married his high school and college sweetheart, and over the years, the Mannion Christmas tree farm had grown to the point where it was now shipping to dealers in thirty-eight states. The people who took the trees home probably didn't realize that the evergreen brightening their dark winter days didn't automatically grow in that perfect, conical shape, that Christmas tree farming was a year-round business. It took a lot of economic planning, the hard work of planting, then shearing to shape. The selling season was spent dealing with shippers and the always popular holiday festival, only to start all over again with new plantings. There was also the stress of dealing with forces outside your control, like weather, pests, markets, and the ever-changing style demands of buyers.

Even in the rainy Pacific Northwest, his dad's face had always borne a tan from whatever sun managed to make it through the cloud cover, but now, his complexion was as gray as a February peninsula sky.

"Hello, son." His welcome home smile didn't reach his eyes. "I'm glad you were able to get away."

"Where else would I be?" Burke asked as his father drew him into a hug. Not a one-armed pat on the back, but a full-out one. Growing up, Burke had felt sorry for friends whose fathers were more distant. Everything his dad was thinking or feeling was revealed in his face and gestures. Especially when any of them had gotten into trouble, like the time Aiden had been caught swiping a twelve-pack of Coors from the back of a delivery truck parked outside Marshall's Market. The punishment that was the hardest to take was their father's disappointment.

"Your mother will be glad to see you," he said, as if this was any ordinary visit. As if Burke had just arrived at the farm, and any minute, his mom would come running out the door accompanied by Mulder and Scully, the energetic Australian shepherd mixes who herded Burke and his brothers and sister as if they were sheep or cows.

"How is she?" he asked.

"Holding her own and insisting on going home." He stepped back and introduced the white-coated woman. "This is Dr. Hanna Kim. She can explain better than I can. Doctor, this is my son, Burke."

"The star quarterback." She held out her hand. "I've heard a great deal about you since moving here. Although I never attended football games in high school or college, I've joined the crowd watching the games at Quinn's pub. You've definitely made me a fan." Her brown eyes warmed in a way that had Burke thinking that while she had to be super intelligent to practice her specialty in medicine, she also seemed to be a kind and caring person. Having had a great deal of experience with medical issues himself over the years, he'd come to realize bedside manner was often as important as a doctor's medical knowledge.

"My brother told me that she was still unconscious when he arrived at the scene," Burke said. "Which means she has a level four concussion."

Despite the seriousness of their conversation, the corners of her mouth quirked in a slight smile. "I'm not surprised you know the levels, given your occupation."

"I've had my share," he said with a shrug, not wanting to make this about him.

"So I've read. And yes, being unconscious for longer than a minute did put her at a level four. But we did a CT scan immediately upon arrival, and her speech now seems normal, as does her memory for everything except the moments before and during the accident, so for now, her prognosis for a full recovery is very positive—if she stays quiet and allows her brain to heal. She can't expect to go back to work for at least two weeks."

"I'll sit on her if I have to," John said, folding his arms. He'd always been the quiet parent, but if you paid attention, he was every bit the force of nature as his wife. Aiden had always said that while their mother was like a velvet steamroller you could see coming from a mile away, their father had stealth ninja skills, which had you agreeing to something before you knew what hit you.

"As her physician, I wouldn't advise that," Dr. Kim said with another of those near smiles. But her eyes lit up a bit with humor. "There's also her fractured ribs to deal with." She glanced toward Burke. "As you undoubtedly know, fractured top ribs need immediate critical care because they have the possibility of causing more serious damage. The good thing is, they almost never break. The bottom ribs are also troublemakers, being located around the diaphragm.

"The middle ribs, which are the ones she injured, are the sweet spot for most rib fractures, and fortunately, although they cause pain and some difficulty breathing, there's usually not risk of further injury. If she takes it easy, as I've prescribed, those should be feeling better in a week or two. And, given that she has such a large, involved family, and since the CT scan looked clear, I don't feel the need to prescribe professional home nursing."

"So you're letting her go home?" Burke could hear the hope in his dad's voice.

"It's already getting toward evening," she said, glancing down at her watch. "I'd rather err on the side of safety. I'm keeping her here overnight. Just in case."

His dad blew out a breath and dragged his hand through his hair, which had more silver in it than the last time Burke had been home. "I was afraid you were going to say that," he said. "And I was equally afraid you wouldn't. Although she wouldn't have been left alone a minute."

"I've no doubt of that," Dr. Kim said. "But if any symptoms suggesting a problem suddenly occurred, none of you would be able to do anything about it other than call 911 and have her brought here."

"Which would take valuable time," Burke said.

"Exactly. Whenever you're talking brains or hearts, every second counts," she agreed. "If she doesn't present with any problems tonight, she'll be having breakfast at home tomorrow morning. Besides," she said, skimming a look over John's haggard face, "you look as if you need a good night's sleep."

His dad squared his shoulders. "I'm fine." His jaw

firmed, and Burke could read the determination in his blue eyes. "I'm staying here."

"Fine." She did not seem surprised by his response. "I'll have a chair, pillow and blanket brought in for you. So," she said decisively, "if she gets through tonight without incident, I'll sign the release papers in the morning."

"You'll be the one to tell her she's spending the night here, right?"

Finally, she allowed a full smile at that question, revealing that she already knew it was not the news Sarah Mannion was waiting to hear. *Tough*, Burke thought.

"That's part of my job," Dr. Kim said.

"She's going to be okay." Burke repeated what had become a mantra.

"Of course she is." His father took a deep breath, and this time, swept both hands through his still-thick hair. "But I'm damn glad I'm not the one breaking the news to her," he muttered as they went into the room.

Except for some abrasions and bruising, she looked the same as always. Burke felt a rush of relief flood through him, stronger, more powerful than he'd ever felt when completing a deep ball pass into the end zone.

She shook her head, which sent silver-laced red curls bobbing, then flinched at what he knew firsthand had to be a throbbing pain. "I told them not to call you," she greeted him a bit crossly, instead of the warm welcome he was used to receiving whenever he returned to the peninsula. "A few broken ribs and a concussion are no reason for you to rush all the way across the country."

"You had to be cut out of a car, Mom. And you were unconscious when Aiden arrived."

"I'm sorry I caused such a fuss and scared everyone," she said, then gave him a smile capable of brightening the dreariest of the Pacific Northwest's gray skies. "But looking on the bright side, now you and I are in an exclusive Mannion family concussion club."

"That's not exactly a club to be proud of belonging to, love," Burke's dad pointed out.

"Oh, don't be such a worrywart." She airily waved away his concern, then looked up at Burke. "I can't hug you because of my stupid ribs. Did you know they don't really tape broken ribs the way they do in books and movies?"

"I do."

"Of course you would," she said. "You chose a career that invites weekly injuries. Dr. Kim said the compression of taping makes it more difficult to breathe deeply, which increases the chance of pneumonia."

"Which you've already had," Burke's dad reminded her.

If Sarah Mannion had a flaw, it was that she too easily brushed off her own problems, including health concerns, like the time, before vaccines for pneumonia had been available, she'd insisted her coughing was merely annual spring allergies due to the state's invasive Scotch broom. Every spring, when the yellow flowers burst into bloom, even people not typically susceptible to allergies would go around sneezing with reddened eyes. When his mother's cough worsened after the blooms had passed, she'd finally agreed to go to the doctor and had been diagnosed with viral pneumonia.

"And you needn't worry about me getting it again, because I'm fully vaccinated, and my ribs aren't taped," she pointed out briskly, sounding like the former principal capable of controlling a high school. "Now, bend down so I can at least give you a kiss," she instructed Burke. "Then I'm going to get dressed and we're going to, as my father would say, 'blow this pop stand.'"

Burke and his dad exchanged a look, which, having eyes like a hawk, she didn't miss.

"Except for a headache and sore ribs, I'm feeling fine," she said, addressing her words to the doctor.

"That's good to hear. And we'd like to be certain you stay that way," Dr. Kim responded. There was a thread of steel in her easy tone. "It's only for one night." She held up a hand when Burke's mom opened her mouth to argue. "Let me suggest a different scenario," the physician said. "What would you want me to do if my patient in this situation was your husband?" She looked at John. Then Burke. "Or one of your sons? Or daughter?"

His mother blew out a breath. "That's not fair," she complained. "Using my family against me."

"It's only for one night, Sarah. And I'll be staying here with you." His father reached over the bed and ran the back of his hand down her cheek.

That was another thing about his parents. They'd never been hesitant about showing affection in public. Burke remembered a time when they'd been chaperones at a school dance, and even the usually tolerant Brianna had been embarrassed when they slowed danced closer than any of the other parents. Thinking back on that night, Burke realized they'd looked a lot like the teenagers they'd been when they first fell in love. From the way their eyes met and held now, they still did.

Burke had never thought seriously about marriage. He'd seen plenty of pro athletes get divorced, in large part because their partners were left to handle family life alone for most of the preseason and regular season.

It wasn't an easy life. He remembered a Sunday barbecue at the home of one of the players. The wife of a running back had laughingly said she'd learned early in her marriage not to use the good bedsheets during the season.

They'd always get stained with blood from the battering her husband took.

Now, as his father bent down, and his mother leaned up a bit so their lips could brush, it occurred to Burke that another reason he'd never been tempted to get married was that he'd only ever met one woman he'd thought he could, just maybe, see himself spending a lifetime with.

And look how that had ended up.

"I'm still annoyed everyone has made such a big deal of this," his mother complained. "But I can't deny that it's wonderful to see you in person instead of on TV."

His mom had never been one to play the Catholic guilt card often, so he doubted that's what she was doing now. But it sure triggered that knee-jerk feeling in Burke.

He wanted to apologize, but then she'd feel the need to assure him that wasn't necessary. He knew firsthand how badly her head was aching, and there was no point in dragging this conversation out. She needed to rest so she'd be able to go home tomorrow morning, where he knew every one of them was going to watch her like a hawk.

Because, although he might have been missing in action a lot over the years, Burke's ties to his family remained as strong as ever. He had no idea what would happen if they were to lose the best daughter, wife and mother anyone could ever wish for.

"There will be rules when you get home," Dr. Kim warned. "For at least the next week, not only do I not want you working, you're not to watch television, go online or on the computer at all, no playing video games, or any other type of games for that matter. And no reading."

"No reading?" she asked incredulously. Burke had seen that protest coming the minute he heard Dr. Kim give the instruction. "What do you expect me to do?"

The other woman folded her arms and straightened to her full height of perhaps five-foot-three in a way that reminded Burke she'd been an Army major and expected her orders to be obeyed without question. "Rest and recuperate. That's nonnegotiable. You've had a serious concussion, and often, symptoms of more dangerous problems don't show up right away, but within hours or days. It's imperative that your brain be given a chance to heal itself."

Burke's father took her hand and laced their fingers together. "I'll read to you." He glanced at the doctor. "If that's okay."

"That should be fine. Just perhaps no thrillers. We don't want her excited."

"Excuse me." Sarah raised her hand. "*She* happens to be right here."

"I was merely answering your husband's question," Dr. Kim said equably. "But let me put it directly to you. I don't see a problem with your husband, or anyone else, reading to you."

"Thank you." Sarah nodded, then winced a bit, revealing that she was still suffering from that concussion headache.

"The goal here is to keep you from having any further problems," the doctor said, softening from her earlier stance.

"I realize that. I truly appreciate it. And I apologize for seeming difficult, but I have this project due for my design class final, and all I need to do to finish it up in time is—"

"Whatever it is will have to wait." Dr. Kim glanced up at Burke's father. "Is she always this impatient a patient?"

"Hello, again," his mother said. "I'm still here. And no, to answer your question, people have always found me very agreeable. I've been an educator since I was twenty-one years old and have always gotten very high likability scores from students, parents and colleagues. And I'm not accustomed to being a patient because, except for giving birth to five children and a case of viral pneumonia decades ago, I've never had any health issues. I've only been in this hospital for a fundraising drive and the times I've brought my sons into the ER for adventurous mishaps. My daughter," she said, shooting Burke what appeared to be an accusing look, "never caused me a moment's concern."

Sarah Mannion had never possessed a temper. But Burke could tell she was coming to the end of her patience. He exchanged a look with his father, who seemed to be agreeing with his thought that was a good sign. Although it did cross Burke's mind that a sudden change in personality was one of the concussion danger signs.

"I'll call the college," his dad said. "I'm sure they'll give you extra time to get the project in, given the circumstances, and the fact that you're a star student who's never been late with a project. Not to mention all the money you've raised over the years for the scholarship foundation. Even more so since Lily Carpenter started planning events. She could probably pull some strings for you."

Burke schooled his face into a neutral expression to hide his surprise at that statement. So Lily really had settled in. But for how long? Would the president of the college someday receive an out-of-the-blue text saying that his director of marketing and publicity had taken off to greener pastures?

"But the project is part of the work I'm doing for a client. A paying client," his mother stressed.

"I'm well aware of that." His father took her hand again. "And we both know that they'll understand. After all, they came to you after seeing the work you'd done to bring Herons Landing into the twenty-first century while keeping its early nineteenth century charm." Since that didn't sound like something his father would typically say, Burke guessed that's what her clients had stated after visiting his sister's B and B. "A couple weeks' delay isn't going to matter."

"I hate being late," she muttered. Which was true. She'd always been the punctual kind of person who'd arrive at an event at exactly the time stated on the invitation. "Being late shows a disrespect to whoever's waiting for you to arrive," she'd always say as she'd round up her five children every morning to get them onto the various school buses. There'd been a time, given their staggered ages, she'd had one in elementary school, two in middle school, and two in high school. All with slightly different pickup times. It was only later, after he'd grown up, that Burke had realized why so many considered her Honeymoon Harbor's own Wonder Woman.

"You know all those medical papers you've sent me over the years?" Burke dared enter the conversation. "And the warnings you've given me about not playing too soon after a concussion?"

"That's no fair using my own words against me," she muttered. Then sighed. "Though you're all right. I think it's my headache and seeing my lovely new dream car all smashed that has me out of sorts."

"Totally understandable," the doctor said, her own apparent frustration now easing. "I get grouchy with a cold."

"I don't get colds," his mother stated correctly. She'd been right about hardly ever getting sick. Which again had Burke wondering how she'd managed that since a summer cold could spread through the house like wildfire when they'd all been kids.

"Then you're a fortunate woman." The doctor's smile soothed the last remaining bit of contention in the room.

"The insurance company will cover the car," his father said. "Then we can go shopping for a new one."

"I liked the one I had." Her eyes, for the first time since Burke had come in the room, moistened. She lifted them to him. "They had a pretty sea-glass-colored one, along with pearl, dark blue and oyster-white at the dealership. But I decided to give myself a retirement present and get the supersonic-red one that was waiting to clear the port up in Seattle. Every time I looked at that car, it made me happy."

"We'll get you another one just like it," Burke's father promised. "I'll start working on that first thing tomorrow once we get you home. So, you'll have it for when you're able to drive again."

She lifted a hand to his cheek. "Thank you." And in those two words, and her soft voice, Burke again saw the love that had kept the couple together for nearly forty years. And acknowledged they were a hard act to follow. Yet Brianna, Aiden, and Gabe had each managed to find their perfect person. He and Quinn were the last two single Mannions standing.

"I'll go arrange for that chair," the doctor said, drawing the conversation to a close. She turned toward Burke. "It was lovely meeting you," she said. "But for your mother, visiting hours are now officially over."

"Right." He bent and brushed his lips against his mother's cheek. "I'll see you in the morning, Mom. And we'll blow this pop stand."

She laughed at that. Then he saw the flash of pain.

As he returned to the waiting room, he saw the chair Lily Carpenter had been sitting in before leaving the room when Brianna had come over to talk with him was still empty. It appeared—no surprise—that she'd taken off. Again.

CHAPTER FIVE

WELL, WASN'T THIS a fine mess she'd gotten herself into? Lily asked herself as she hid in the restroom. When Brianna had told her he was on his way back to Honeymoon Harbor, she'd first considered coming up with some work excuse to leave the hospital. But the fact was, there wasn't anything as pressing as being with a friend at a terrible time like this.

Lily wasn't used to having friends. She never had any as a child, and since her eighteenth birthday, she'd avoided getting too close to anyone for fear that she might slip and allow her secret to come out. Which was why she'd become a drifter. Or, to put a more positive spin on it, an international globe-trotter.

That life had worked well for over a dozen years, until she'd found herself caught in the middle of two life-altering events. The first had been meeting Burke Mannion at that fundraiser. The chemistry between them had been instantaneous, and although she knew the risk of getting involved with such a high-profile man, one who couldn't walk down the street without people calling out to him or snapping photos, she hadn't been able to help herself. She was relieved when he seemed equally willing to keep their affair private. At least in the beginning. The spotlight of fame had left scores of celebrity relationships shattered, and theirs felt too special to allow outsiders in.

What she hadn't told him was her true reason for not wanting to go out in public. That being seen together would undoubtedly land them on the covers of tabloids in bodega magazine racks all over the city. Not just New York, but across the country.

Being seen with the team's star quarterback would inevitably bring up questions about the unknown "average" woman's identity. Although she thought she'd done a good job of hiding her tracks, invariably, some enterprising reporter might dig a little deeper and find out that Lily Carpenter was not who she claimed to be. And that until she'd legally come of age and taken her life into her own hands, it hadn't been anything resembling average.

There had been one close call, when she and Burke had nearly been caught on the street outside her building one morning, not by one of those paparazzi types who roamed the streets looking to catch famous people going about their daily lives, but by a family of tourists. Since he'd been leaving for the West Coast for an away game, instead of his usual disguise, he'd been wearing a black cashmere overcoat over sport coat, shirt and slacks.

The father of the three little girls that morning had turned out to be an avid sports fan, and Burke, being Burke, had stopped long enough to sign an autograph. When asked by one of the daughters who she was, Lily had smiled and simply said, "I'm no one special. Just a friend visiting from out of town."

Which had drawn a sharp, curious look from Burke, but the family had been too caught up in their brush with fame to notice. And Burke had to rush for his flight. Afterward, fighting an all-too-familiar panic after meeting with a group of bankers, who'd promised a hefty donation, she'd gone to her office and, apologizing for not having given sufficient notice, claimed a personal emergency, and re-signed from her job.

Then she returned to the furnished apartment that had been home for the past fifteen months, packed up enough clothes and shoes for a week, her cosmetics and hair-styling tools, and arranged to have the rest of her clothing, books, and the very few personal possessions she'd packed in a box air-shipped to a storage location at her destination. She'd done this so many times over the years, she had it down to a science. Except for an admitted addiction to shoes, she wasn't one to acquire a great deal of possessions anyway.

Once seated on the first flight she could get on such short notice, as the other passengers were boarding, she texted Burke that she was sorry, but as much as she truly cared for him, she couldn't see any future in their relationship, so it would probably be easier for both of them if they just ended things now.

Oh, and by the way, she'd left the city.

Just the memory of that thoughtless behavior had her cheeks flaming with shame. Thankfully, hiding in here while Burke was with his mother kept him from seeing it. She'd told herself at the time that it'd be easier. But now, remembering back, she'd felt guilty as she'd written that text. She'd wallowed in that guilt as her escape airline had flown over the country to Los Angeles. By the time she'd reached LAX, she'd emerged as she always did, appearing as free as a bird, planning to slide into life in her new town as if she'd been born there.

But this time, something had been different. For the first time in her life, she'd left behind the one man she'd never been able to forget. Unable to get him out of her mind, she'd relived all their conversations and belatedly realized she'd always talked about her work. Although his life for the past years had revolved around football, he'd never talked about it all that much. Mostly his conversations were about the town he'd grown up in, and had, he'd admitted, always planned on escaping. He had talked fondly and openly about his family. So much so that by the time she'd actually met them, she'd felt a familiarity with them that was another uncommon thing. She'd always carefully kept her distance. But as soon as she'd met Brianna, it was almost as if they'd been friends all their lives.

She'd known it was a risk coming to Honeymoon Harbor. As she'd told Burke, she'd only been curious, and yes, skeptical, and had wanted to see for herself if it had lived up to his description. She hadn't meant to stay. But from what he'd told her, it was remote enough that she could hide out for a few weeks, preparing for her next life. Burke was, after all, in Mexico, doing his off-season training, though there was always a chance he'd cut it short and return to his hometown before preseason began in August. Intellectually, she knew that due to Sarah's accident, she was on the verge of being found out to be a liar. Perhaps she hadn't exactly lied to Brianna. But she certainly hadn't been truthful about her past with them. Which at the very least made them lies of omission. And if she were to be perfectly honest, just as she hadn't planned to fall in love with Burke, she'd fallen for this small town in the far northwest corner of the country.

For the first time in her life, she had friends. Not just Brianna, but also the town librarian, Chelsea Prescott, now Mannion, having married Gabriel Mannion, the former hotshot Wall Street titan. He definitely didn't fit the stereotype, but according to Brianna, he once could have been the poster boy for a workaholic, take-no-prisoners corporate raider. Now he was happily settled down with Chelsea and their two adopted, former foster children and had become a much in-demand wooden boatbuilder.

Then there were Kylee and Mai. And Jolene, who'd married Aiden Mannion, another of Burke's brothers. Damn. If Burke were to say anything to Brianna about their affair and her behavior—and as coldly distant as he'd seemed downstairs, he just might've—she was definitely going to have some explaining to do.

Or she could do as she'd done for over a decade. Run from her past. But that was no longer a possibility, because this time was different. She'd found a home. Made friends. Connections. Years ago, when she'd changed her identity, she'd been excited to be starting a new life. But as a therapist had pointed out, she'd continued to drag her demons along with her. They'd controlled her life every bit as much as others had for her first eighteen years.

Wasn't the often-quoted definition of insanity doing the same thing over and over again and expecting a different result? And hadn't that been exactly what she'd been doing?

So the only answer was to change that behavior. Right here. Right now. But how? As she imagined the final *Jeopardy!* "Think" theme song playing in her head, she splashed cool water on her burning-hot cheeks, wondering whether it would be better to open up and confess the truth to each of them. Mai and Kylee, being married, could be told together. So that left Chelsea, Jolene and Brianna. And, hardest of all, the steady, down-to-earth Sarah, who'd become like the mother Lily had never known but had always dreamed of. A member of the board of Clearwater Community College, Sarah had taken her into the Mannions' tight-knit circle, as if she were part of the large, sprawling family. Something else she'd never known. How could she possibly tell the woman the truth when her life could be in danger?

Sometimes Lily imagined she knew how Chelsea and Gabe's children must be feeling, former foster kids stunned by their good fortune to have landed in this noisy, warmhearted family. Even as she had initially worried about Burke showing up back home and blowing up her world. But as the days, weeks and months went by, she'd foolishly allowed that concern to fade into the background.

Then there was Quinn. Who, in his typical fashion, hadn't asked any questions when, on learning that he'd be driving Burke to the hospital from the airport, she'd asked him to send his brother to the cafeteria when they arrived, instead of taking him directly upstairs to the waiting room. Which he'd done.

Lily hadn't expected a *hey, happy to see you again, babe* reunion. But Burke's cold distance had cut more deeply, more painfully, than the anger she'd expected. Had she been the only one who'd felt as if she might have found The One? The one who, unfortunately, was also the very worst one she could've fallen in love with?

If only she'd hit it off with that CPA who'd done her taxes. Or the IT guy who'd fixed her computer when it had died while she'd been writing an important proposal to the city council. Or the ER resident who'd stitched up her finger after she'd sliced it to the bone following a *YouTube* video on how to spatchcock a chicken for roasting. All had expressed interest, and she'd even gone out with the resident a couple times.

On their first date, dinner at a neighborhood Greek place, he'd explained up front that a resident's life didn't allow for relationships. It took less than a month of him showing up late, or skipping a date entirely, for her to realize he'd been telling the truth. Which had, honestly, been a relief because as nice as he'd been, there hadn't been any sparks between them, and she couldn't envision herself as a doctor's wife.

But Burke had been different. Lily wondered how long he planned to stay. How she'd be able to keep from running into him while he was in town. And worse, how she'd deal with the fact that she wanted to, even as she was forced to acknowledge that he hadn't given her a single sign he was open to ever talking to her again.

Since she hoped he wouldn't reveal their past to anyone—other than, perhaps, Quinn—she might not have to worry. As people tended to say, the eldest Mannion brother held secrets tighter than a priest hearing confessions at Peter the Fisherman Church.

Putting that concern away for now, she returned to the sticky problem of how to come clean to everyone. Maybe she should gather them all together as a group and just get it out. "Like pulling off a Band-Aid," she murmured as she reapplied her lipstick, which she'd eaten off. That would probably be easier. But she'd have to wait until Sarah was home and well enough to hear such a revelation.

"She has to be okay," Lily told herself, as if saying the words out loud could make them true. Then, tossing the paper towel into the waste container, she left the restroom, returning to the waiting room, relieved when Brianna told her that Quinn and Burke had left for the farm.

"So," Quinn said as he and Burke drove back to the Christmas tree farm, where Burke would be staying in the room he'd once shared with Aiden. "What's up with you and Lily Carpenter?"

Quinn's superpower was not only listening, but observation. Which he hadn't exactly needed in this case because Lily had apparently decided that they should try to clear the air before going up to the waiting room where his family had gathered. And since Quinn was the one driving him to the hospital, he'd been the obvious choice.

After being initially stunned to find that she'd landed here in his hometown, Burke wasn't all that surprised that she and Brianna had become friends. Although they'd worked in very different fields—Brianna catering to the needs of the rich and famous, Lily working to improve people's lives—they both were, each in their own way, people pleasers.

"Nothing," Burke answered. Which was the honest truth.

"Then you want to tell me why, when she heard I was picking you up at the airport, she took me aside and asked me to bring you to the cafeteria before you came upstairs?"

"I thought you'd given up law," Burke muttered.

"I have. For the most part. I did keep my license and bar association membership so I can help out family and friends from time to time."

"Then why do I feel as if I'm up on some witness stand being cross-examined?"

"Beats me." Quinn shrugged. "Unless you have something you're hiding? Something you're feeling guilty about?"

"I'm not the one to have anything to feel guilty about. Because I'm not the one who broke up with someone by text."

That caught Quinn's attention. He glanced over at his brother. "You and Lily were a thing? Mom never mentioned that. And she has Google alerts set for your name."

"Tell me you're kidding."

"As a matter of fact, I'm not. Once I got home, I found out that she had them set up for all of us while we were living away from here."

Still keeping track of her kids. "Geez. That's like when she told us that moms have eyes in the backs of their heads, which is why we could never get away with anything."

"That's what I thought when Aiden told me. Not that I have anything going on that she probably doesn't know about, since I'm living here in the fishbowl that is our hometown. But that still doesn't explain how the two of you kept a relationship beneath Google's and Mom's radars."

"It was more of a hookup."

"I've never been a player, but I do know that hookups aren't usually *relationships*."

"That's my point. I wasn't in any position for a real relationship. My life doesn't lend itself to one."

"Yet lots of pro football players have wives. And families. Hell, the TV in the pub is tuned to the Pro Bowl coverage every year and with all the wives, parents and kids, it looks a lot like summer camp..." His voice drifted off. Burke could practically see the wheels spinning around in Quinn's former legal eagle brain.

"That was the reason for your crazy partying phase," he said, hitting the nail straight on the head. "After the text breakup."

Burke knew enough not to lie. "Yeah. I guess I overreacted a bit," he admitted. He didn't mention that he'd been surprised more than his ego had gotten wounded. It had hurt. Deep, deep down. A lot.

"I suppose the only positive was that since no one knew we were seeing each other, I didn't get a reputation as that guy who got dumped. By text."

"I went out with a woman for a while in Seattle who was hooked on *Sex and the City*, so I ended up watching a lot of episodes. One of the characters got dumped by a Post-it. I suppose a text is the 2.0 version of that."

"I guess so."

Neither one of them said anything for a while as they drove along the waterway to the road leading out of town to the farm. Quinn had the radio tuned to an old-time blues station, and Burke thought it kind of prophetic when B.B. King started singing "The Thrill Is Gone." He was feeling relieved that he'd escaped the subject better than he'd expected when Quinn proved him wrong.

"It does seem that your wild time might have been overkill after getting dumped by a woman with whom you only had a hookup deal going. How long did it last?"

"Three months. But it was during the season, so we weren't together every day."

"That's still a long hookup. I'm surprised it didn't get out in public."

"That's the way she wanted it."

"Huh." Quinn fell quiet again. Then he said, "I hadn't given it any thought before, but she's always kept her life pretty close to the vest. I don't know anything about her other than she's head of marketing and publicity at the college. And does a lot of social work stuff. Like volunteering at the library and reading to the elderly residents of Harbor Hill."

"I can see that. She was working for a nonprofit when we met. I was one of the city's 'celebrities'—" he put the word in finger quotes "—brought in for a charity event for food insecurity. There were other names a lot bigger than mine, and we raised a bunch of money for community gardens to be built in vacant lots in low-income neighborhoods for residents who don't have easy access or the dollars for fresh vegetables."

"She and Brianna are close," Quinn mused. "I'd guess that our sister may know more details."

"If she does, and Lily had asked her not to tell anyone, she wouldn't." Brianna was as trustworthy as Quinn.

"That would be true. So, what are you going to do about it?"

"About what?"

"The woman you're still carrying a torch for."

Terrific. As if on cue, the song changed, and now Muddy Waters was standing around crying over a lost love. "Did I say anything about carrying a torch? I'm here for Mom. That's all. As soon as she gets the all clear from the doctor, I'll be going back to New York. Training camp starts the third week of July."

"Which is two months away."

"And he can count, too. You always were the smartest brother," Burke said without heat.

Unlike Gabe, who'd had seemed competitive where Quinn was concerned, Burke had never had any problem with Quinn's continual string of successes while they'd been growing up, having only cared about sports, football in particular. Quinn had definitely epitomized the first-born overachiever stereotype. Though now, here he was, running a craft brewery and pub. Which had Burke thinking that of all his brothers, Quinn would probably be the best one to help him make a decision about what to do with his life. Of course, then there was Gabe, who'd given up his high-flying Wall Street trading gig to return home and build wooden boats. Go figure.

A very strong part of him wanted closure with Lily Carpenter. She'd told him, that very first night, when he'd asked her to join him for an after-event drink, and she'd invited him to her apartment instead, that she wanted to keep their private lives to themselves. So they could get to know each other without being in the glare of spotlights and avoid turning up in the *Page Six* gossip column that was like catnip to all the New Yorkers who would never admit they read it.

"She hasn't dated anyone since arriving in town," Quinn volunteered. "Or if she has, she hasn't come into the pub or shown up at any events with anyone. She might have gotten away with having a secret life in New York, but things are a lot different here. Everyone pretty much knows everyone else's business. Which is why I started buying condoms online."

Despite the weight of the day's events, Burke threw back his head and laughed. "At least you're getting some."

When Quinn didn't say anything, Burke glanced over at him. "The fact that you didn't respond to that means that you must be going out of town for any recreation. Or you're going through a dry spell." Which Burke could relate to, having burned himself out after Lily had walked, or more precisely, flown away.

"I've got my eye on someone," Quinn said. "But I'm taking my time."

"Why?"

Quinn blew out a breath. "It's complicated."

This time, Burke's laugh held no humor. "What the hell isn't?"

Burke had realized that at some point, between his Pop Warner days and that meeting in the team's GM's office this morning, while he wasn't paying attention, he'd somehow grown up. And so far, from what he could tell, adulting sucked.

CHAPTER SIX

JIM OLSON WAS still shaken the morning after the crash. Yesterday, he'd been out in front of the house, plucking off spent flowers from the daylilies his mother had planted when he'd been in middle school. At the time, he'd told her that daylilies weren't very practical since each flower would bloom in the morning only to die at sunset. And not only that, the daylily *Hemerocallis lilioasphodelus*—a flowering plant in the genus *Hemerocallis*—wasn't even a real lily, despite its common name.

"That they only bloom once a day is why they're special," she'd blithely commented as she placed another plant in one of the holes she'd had him dig. "Besides, the plants have so many blooms, they'll give us flowers all season long. And most importantly, they'll make me happy."

Although he now understood that he should have left it at that, his twelve-year-old self had informed her that the daylily was reputed to represent the beautiful but fleeting nature of love. Refusing to be deterred, she'd laughed and responded that whoever thought that foolish notion up hadn't ever truly been in love. Hadn't she and his father been in love for decades, going back to when she'd transferred into his elementary school when her family moved from Portland?

Still in love, they were now living in Arizona, where his farmer father had taken up golf, and during every one of their weekly calls, she'd tell him that the over fifty-five retirement community they'd moved to was like living at a resort. She'd joined a dance group and a tennis team, and had taken up something called Zumba, which he'd had to google.

Personally, when he'd visited them last Thanksgiving, he'd found the place buzzing with so much activity, he couldn't imagine living in such a beehive. But it had certainly seemed to suit them fine. His mother was literally glowing with health, and whatever was in that blindingly bright Arizona sun seemed to have taken a decade off his father. Tom Olson was normally a quiet man. His dinner conversations had once been focused on worrying about some farming problem. Of which there could be many.

"Farming has never been an easy occupation," his dad had warned him over a weekly Monday dinner of meat loaf, peas and mashed potatoes when Jim had been in high school. "Just because I stuck with it after inheriting it from my father, who'd inherited it from my grandfather, doesn't mean you have to. You have a unique, brilliant mind, son. You could work at any of those tech companies in Seattle or Silicon Valley and make a fortune working with people you have more in common with."

Which had been a nice way of saying that he'd fit in with people who were considered to have Geek Syndrome. Having originally been diagnosed as having Aspergers—which later had been changed to considered as being on the Autism spectrum—Jim had researched his condition and discovered that his father had a good point. That in the world of technology, no one cared if you were different, as long as your code worked. Jim knew his father had only been trying to help, but he'd explained that he must have inherited some farming gene not yet discovered, because that's what he cared about. What he loved doing. Especially the creation of hybrids.

They'd never brought it up again. Partly because now his father's conversations were filled with a dizzying amount of energy, including a senior group bus trip to the Grand Canyon, which Jim must see some day. And he couldn't count the number of times he'd heard about that hole in one that had required his father to buy drinks for everyone at the club. He still believed it was highly illogical that there would be such an expense involved after achieving something supposedly very difficult, but from the way his father beamed every time he brought it up, Jim had the good sense not to share that thought.

As he'd finished deadheading the plants yesterday, being careful not to wound any of the buds while discarding the crumpled buttery-yellow flowers, he'd been deep in thought, pondering the idea of love. He'd wondered if anyone other than his parents could ever love a guy like him, and if so, what it might feel like to be in love, when a sudden loud sound had shattered the morning quiet.

Racing to the crash on the road in front of the house, he'd dialed 911. The car was on its side, the passenger door smashed in, so he couldn't open it. Seeing Mrs. Mannion in the driver's seat, Jim felt his blood turn as cold as winter sleet.

Back when he'd been fourteen, he'd been worried about transitioning to high school; although he'd been mainstreamed since preschool, he was uncomfortable with new situations. And afraid of being bullied. Which he had been occasionally, though Mrs. Mannion had made it clear to one and all that she would not tolerate such behavior in her school. During those four years, he'd come to love her nearly as much as his own mother.

He'd been calling out to her, not sure she could hear him because the car windows were all closed and she appeared to be unconscious, when Aiden Mannion, Honeymoon Harbor's chief of police and one of Sarah Mannion's sons, pulled up in his black SUV, lights flashing and siren blaring. Moments later, Jim heard the whoop, whoop, whoop of the ambulance.

Aiden thanked him for calling the accident in, and getting the license plate number of the truck he'd seen speeding away. Jim stood back and watched as the fire crew pulled out three heavy tools they used to lift the car roof, spread open the door, cut through the heavy steel door post, then push the entire dashboard and front of the car forward, making room to extricate the former high school principal.

Even as his heart had felt as if it were about to pound through his ribs and out of his chest—something he knew wasn't medically possible—Jim admired how they'd worked in unison, as a team, staying calm and collected in a way he never could have been under such circumstances. She seemed to stir as they put a yellow collar around her neck and carefully carried her to the gurney the ambulance crew had waiting.

"You did good, man," Aiden Mannion had said. "Thanks to you, we're going to get Mom to the hospital within the golden hour."

"Will she be okay?" Jim couldn't imagine what it would feel like to have his mother die.

Aiden's jaw had clenched at that question. His eyes, which Jim had forced his own to meet, were flint. "She's got to be," he said with a conviction that suggested if he believed it hard enough, he could make it come true. Which was, of course, totally irrational, but as admittedly lacking in social skills as he was, Jim understood that this was no time for logic.

"Gotta go. Thanks, again." Aiden gave Jim a *well-done* pat on the back. As the other man walked swiftly back to the SUV, Jim hoped the police chief had been too caught up worrying about his mother to notice his instinctive flinch. Some people were touchers. Jim was not.

He only briefly considered going to the hospital to be there for her, knowing that there was nothing he could do to help. Ten years, four months and three days ago, his mother had had her appendix taken out. When he'd visited her in the hospital, all those blaring code announcements coming over the loudspeakers, the doctors, nurses, and other staff buzzing around with intense purpose, had made him anxious.

Jim had not slept well the night after Mrs. Mannion's accident. The next morning, he could still hear that crash in his mind. After going out to his greenhouse, he put in his earbuds and tuned to Frédéric Chopin's Nocturne Op. 9, No. 2 as he worked on cloning plant tissue samples. He considered Chopin to be one of the masters of the Romantic era, and while many of his pieces were relaxing, the fact that he could write this stunning nocturne that overflowed with beauty at only twenty years old—ten years younger than Jim was now—had him wondering if the composer had also been on the spectrum. Not that people knew about such things back then. Which, he supposed, was why the musician had been declared a genius without having to suffer any of the cruel labels Jim had been taunted with while growing up.

When he'd been younger, those words had wounded, but he'd learned to let negative words and looks slide off him like water off a duck's back.

When he felt the tap on his shoulder, rudely jerking him from his thoughts, he spun around, annoyed at the interruption, until he saw the woman standing in front of him. Suddenly, as if he'd landed in a Disney movie, he could envision the annoyed words that had been on the tip of his tongue flying away like a cloud of butterflies from a *Monarda didyma*, a perennial wildflower commonly known as a bee balm plant.

"I'm sorry." She was backlit by the morning sun. "The woman at the house told me that I'd find you out here. But you're busy."

"That woman is Anna. She works for the Clean Team. She and Brenda come in once a week to spruce things up." That was what Megan, the owner of the cleaning company, had called it when he hired them after his parents had moved to Arizona. "And yes, I am busy."

"I'm sorry."

"You've already apologized. It isn't necessary to repeat it."

"Okay." She blew out a breath and turned as if to leave. Then, apparently changing her mind, turned back toward him.

"I promise not to take up too much of your time. My name is Sage Fletcher."

"That's a very pretty name," he allowed, realizing that he might have sounded rude before.

"Thank you. My mother had a baby naming book. She's Wiccan, and a big believer in signs, and listening to the universe and all that, so she opened to a random page, closed her eyes, and pointed at a name. Which turned out to be Sage. Which was lucky, because if she'd gone down the page one more line, I would be Sagitarios. Can you imagine going through life named for a zodiac sign? Even one that means an optimistic, enthusiastic extrovert. Which I am, maybe because I was born under that sign."

"Sage is an herb typically used during the preparation of a Thanksgiving dinner," he inserted. She was talking so fast it was hard to keep up. "But astrology is a pseudoscience. Ever since the adoption of the scientific method, researchers have challenged it on both theoretical and experimental grounds and have shown it has no scientific validity or explanatory power."

He realized, too late, she could have taken that as an insult, but she smiled. "That may be true, though certainly a lot of other cultures have followed astrology for a very long time. I'm not really into it, but I do enjoy reading my horoscope every morning on my phone. Though I also ignore negative predictions."

"Which does validate the optimism description," he allowed.

"It does, doesn't it?" She flashed another of those sunny smiles.

"Your actual name, Sage, is botanically known as *Salvia officinalis*, from the Latin word *salvere*, meaning 'to be saved' or 'to be a savior.'"

"Well, isn't that a coincidence? That's why I came here today. Because I think we can save each other." Her voice was as pretty as the rest of her, reminding Jim of morning birdsong.

He put her height at average for an American female, approximately five-feet-four-inches. She was slender with a tumble of brown curls that would have been *beaver* in the box of crayons he'd enjoyed as a child. It was also Oregon's state animal. The curls surrounded a face free of makeup. Full lips curved in the warm and friendly smile he'd heard in her voice. They were the pink color of the peonies so popular for weddings that provided a good deal of the farm's income.

He was hit with a sudden curiosity to observe the color of her eyes, which never, ever happened because meeting eyes had always proven a struggle. Jim had never understood why "normal people" insisted on gazing into each other's eyes. Why not a hand? Or foot? Her feet, he noticed, were as pretty as the rest of her, with her toenails, clearly visible in a pair of red sandals, painted a pure sky blue.

Jim had often thought that if he could only create a rose that color, he'd become wealthy enough to achieve his plan to expand Blue House Farm. Although no amount of hybridization could currently produce a blue rose, because there was no gene for blue, the Japanese had found a way to insert a blue gene from a viola and an iris into a red rose. But even then, it had resulted in a purple-blueish rose rather than pure blue. Which was what Jim was determined to develop.

He belatedly realized that the pretty Sage had been talking. "What did you say?" Before a doctor in Seattle had diagnosed him as being on the spectrum, Jim had been misdiagnosed with ADHD. Which had never made any sense to him. It wasn't that he possessed attention *deficit*. He had attention *overload*. Forcing his mind to focus solely on this conversation, he decided that watching her lips would help.

"I came here about your booth," she was saying when he dragged his currently disordered mind back to their conversation.

"The booth at the farmers market?" He also had an honor stand at the gate that led to the farmhouse with a sign asking buyers to put their payment in the metal box on the counter. Some might find that unwise, but his parents had begun the practice before he was born, and there'd only been three times in all those years that the money had been stolen, or that a buyer hadn't left the proper payment. On the contrary, often there was evidence of overpayments.

Watching her lips wasn't helping, because he kept wondering what they'd taste like. He'd first been kissed one afternoon during his freshman year in high school. Marianne McCarthy had come up to him at his locker and suddenly, without warning, pressed her lips against his. Fast and hard. While his head was still reeling, she ran back to a group of girls standing by. They were laughing, and he'd overheard that she'd done it on a dare.

"That's the one," she said, pulling his mind from the memory that still, after all these years, stung. "I was wondering why you don't have someone working at it and decided to use an honor box instead."

"No one has ever stolen the money or cheated." Possibly because his booth was next to that of Cops & Coffee, which was manned by former police officers.

"It's good that people are so honest. But I buy flowers there every weekend, and sometimes I wish I could make my own arrangement."

"My sister, Jessie, who lives in Sequim, usually creates the arrangements. But I could make you whatever you'd like now," he offered, wondering why he'd initially wanted her to go away.

Although he preferred sticking to his routine, there were occasions when plans required changing. He could, after all, take his tissue samples later. It wasn't often a pretty girl showed up in his greenhouse. Actually, never. Unless you counted Chelsea Mannion, but she only came to bring him textbooks she'd found for him. And they were just friends. Almost like cousins, or even a brother and sister. Not someone you'd ever kiss, but she would give him a little peck on the cheek from time to time, which had made him uneasy at first. But now he'd not only gotten used to it, he'd come to enjoy it.

"Thank you, but that's not necessary," she said. "I already picked one up last weekend, and the flowers are still in great shape. My suggestion is that if you were to also keep a few buckets of loose flowers along with the already made-up arrangements, which—don't get me wrong—are lovely, people could choose exactly the flowers they want arranged."

"If I did that, I'd have to be there." And be bombarded by all the music, noise and conversations that buzzed in his head like angry wasps.

It had taken Jim years to learn that conversation with other people involved give-and-take. A person would say something, like, "Nice day," and instead of responding, "Tissue cloning is superior to traditional cutting because it generates thousands of plants in a very short time and square footage," which he might be thinking at that moment, the proper answer would actually be, "Yes, the sun is out."

But when surrounded by chaos like the crowded market, that acquired skill would too often desert him. The only reason he'd agreed to allow Chelsea's library adventurers tour the farm each summer was that she'd promised him all he had to do was explain some basics to her, and she'd take over from there.

"I understand," Sage said, as his mind flashed back to all those children descending on his property every summer. He liked children. In small numbers. For small periods of time. Like his two nieces who loved visiting the farm every week when Jessie came to make the arrangements. They were always well behaved.

But he'd also seen the crowds of children, chasing each

other around and laughing and shouting at the crossroads in front of the farmhouse while waiting for the morning school bus, and then, in the afternoon, bursting out its yellow doors in an explosion of pent-up energy.

"I don't want to be rude, but no, you don't. Understand, that is."

"As it happens, I do," she corrected him. "At least somewhat. I have a cousin on the spectrum. He's been playing the piano since he was a toddler. One day, he climbed up on the bench and began playing, 'The Wheels on the Bus Go Round and Round' after hearing it one time on *Sesame Street*. But I'm sorry, I promised not to take up too much of your time, and you didn't need to know about my cousin. Anyway…"

The hand that pretty Sage ran through her curls had long fingers, which glinted with rings. "So, here's my idea." She paused for a long moment, making Jim wonder if her mind had wandered the way his tended to do. "I can do it."

"Do what?"

"I could help you with the farm. Lily Carpenter, who's head of marketing at Clearwater Community College, where I'm taking marketing classes, suggested I come here. She said that you've been super busy working on a cloning project."

"I know Lily. She's very nice, and she's right about me having been busy. Cloning makes it possible to grow many more flowers more quickly, which is why I want to expand the number of greenhouses, to have room for additional cut flowers to sell year-round to the wedding industry, which is becoming more and more active in the summer. That would also allow me to begin shipping them around the state. And perhaps, someday, across the country, so long as I could ship enough to make the cooler container costs reasonable.

I'm also considering starting a seed business. Seeds would be much easier and inexpensive to ship."

"That sounds both sensible and ambitious. But to get through the clutter of all the businesses these days, especially those targeting organic customers, you're going to need a marketing plan. Which I could do for you."

"I doubt I could pay you enough to make it worth your while until I become more successful. The best way to make a small fortune in farming is to start out with a large one," he quoted the old saying his father had used many times.

"That's a joke, isn't it?"

"Yes." He'd meant it as a true statement, but because she seemed to enjoy it, he'd let her think that's what he'd intended all along.

"It's a good one." She ran her fingers through her curls again. Jim had never been good at picking up social signals, but he sensed she was nervous. "Here's the thing… I still haven't nailed down a class project, but last weekend, when I was at the market, it occurred to me that if you let me try my idea, and we did some marketing, we could compare the profit you've been making now, and in the past, to what you would bring in by having someone there to sell the flowers, and even offer on-site arranging. I could do that during the time of the comparison testing. But I wouldn't charge you.

"Anyway, although Lily can vouch for me, let me tell you a short backstory about me that hopefully will explain why I want to pass this course so badly. I came to Honeymoon Harbor last summer to be a bridesmaid at a sorority sister's wedding. Which, as a side note, was more than a little embarrassing because nearly everyone there had been at *my* wedding last year."

"You're married?" Among her many rings, he didn't see one that resembled a wedding band.

"No. Unfortunately, the intended groom bailed and left me at the altar."

"I'm sorry." This time he didn't have to think of something appropriate to say because that was the truth.

"So was I. Not so much because he was obviously a jerk, and I was well rid of him, but he ran off to Bali with our wedding planner. Whom I'd already paid up front. And there were also vendor bills I thought she'd taken care of that I had to pay, which was even more embarrassing because I was, in my former life, a CPA, and should have been more vigilant about ensuring that she was sticking to the budget we'd agreed on." Her sigh ruffled her curly bangs.

"But, leaving all that in my rearview mirror, I fell in love with this town and, deciding it was the perfect place for a new start, I stayed. I'm currently waiting tables a few hours a week at Sensation Cajun, because of all those bills, including the reservation deposit on the honeymoon at that beachfront hotel in Bali that she'd found."

"They stayed at your intended honeymoon hotel?" Even Jim, who admittedly wasn't up on current social norms, found that to be very wrong.

"Yes. All my friends said I should sue, but that would've taken time and attorney fees, and I just wanted to move past it." She shrugged, drawing his attention to tanned shoulders bared by her bright yellow sundress printed with poppies. "Although I'm not as woo-woo as Mom, after deciding that my mess of a wedding was a sign that I should entirely change my life, I started taking courses at the college to see if something fit that I could make a living at.

"Watching Bastien create his magic at the restaurant, I tried a beginning-level course in the culinary program and discovered that I apparently lack the cooking gene. My brown butter always turned black, and I accidently set a dish towel on fire while learning to flambé."

"But you didn't burn the kitchen down."

Her smile lit up the greenhouse like summer sunshine. "That's true. I like people who can find the good side of a situation. I've always tried to be like that, but many people seem to be so negative…

"Anyway, after failing at nursing, because just the sight of needles and blood makes me dizzy, I took a marketing class from Lily and discovered I'm really, really good at it. Especially social media. Which, not casting any aspersions, you could use help with."

"The definitive word is *social*." Jim knew that his lack of socialization, and his near hermit life here on the farm he'd grown up on, was undoubtedly why he'd never met Sage Fletcher. He also felt a strange tinge of something that felt like regret about not having been at his booth all those weekends she'd bought his flowers.

"Again, that's why you need me."

He dragged his gaze from her shoulders, which were scattered with freckles, to her eyes, which were exactly the brown-and-gold color of the agate stone he'd found back in elementary school while walking on Sandpiper Point beach by the harbor. He'd spent the rest of that summer searching for rocks and polishing them in the tumbler his parents had bought him for Christmas.

They were still in a dish on the wooden coffee table his grandfather had made with lumber harvested on the property to make room for more farmland.

"Maybe I do. Need you," he clarified, when he realized his mind had wandered yet again. Which rarely happened in the solitude of his greenhouse.

"Great. Why don't we go in your house, where we can sit down and start making plans?"

"Now?" He belatedly realized that several minutes had passed while they'd been talking. Which had thrown him off his schedule. "In eight minutes, it will be time for lunch."

"Even better. Do you like burgers?"

"Yes." Though they were not the tuna fish sandwich he'd intended to make today. He always had tuna from Kira's Fish House on Wednesdays.

"What would you say to talking business over burgers at the pub?"

That was *not* in Jim's plan for the day. Burgers and going to a noisy pub at lunchtime was not on this week's schedule. It was *never* on the schedule.

"Here's another idea," she suggested when he didn't immediately respond. "We can get takeout and eat at the park on the lake." Her hands were on her hips, drawing his already unsettled attention to her slender curves.

"All right," he heard himself say. "But I am buying the burgers."

He'd learned from movies that when on a date, a man paid for the meal. Not that this was a date. It was a business meeting, although he found Mirror Lake an odd venue for such a discussion. Also, typically, the man was the one to ask the woman out for a meal. Sage Fletcher was so far outside his comfort zone, she might as well have landed here in a spaceship from another planet.

But she was correct about one thing. While researching business plans, he had reluctantly realized that while he might be the one horticulturist who could actually someday hybridize a true blue rose, he was decidedly weak in the area of sales and marketing.

"You're on," Sage said. She reached out a hand to shake his. Then, as if realizing he'd take that as an invasion of his space, she dropped it to her side. Oddly, a small part of him regretted that she'd stopped herself.

"You're very pretty," he said as they walked out of the greenhouse. Once again, his mouth had seemed to take on a mind of its own, exposing his thoughts.

"I know," she said on another of those musical laughs. "But I'm also smart as a whip. And, as you've undoubtedly noticed, extremely persuasive."

As Jim settled into the passenger seat of Sage's sunshine-yellow car and considered all the important work he was leaving behind in order to eat a burger at the lake with a pretty stranger he'd just met, as irrational as the situation might be, he found he could not argue her point.

CHAPTER SEVEN

THE MORNING AFTER the accident, when they brought his mother home, Burke wasn't surprised to find that Brianna was already prepared. She'd changed the sheets and towels, dug out the old bed tray his mom would use to serve them meals when they were kids and got sick, and had several newly released books Chelsea had brought from the library on the bedside table. Their father, unsurprisingly, was not about to leave his wife's side. Also, not surprising, since Burke knew firsthand how difficult it was to sleep at a hospital, his mom had fallen asleep almost the moment she'd gotten into bed.

Since there'd been a paperwork delay in her being released (again, no big surprise), it was lunchtime by the time his mom was settled in and able to sleep. Luca Salvadori showed up with pizza and antipasto for lunch, along with a pan of lasagna and a container of minestrone they could heat up later. He assured them not to worry about grocery shopping or preparing meals because Diego Chavez was covering Mexican tomorrow, with Bastien Broussard from Sensation Cajun next up, followed by a meal from Leaf, the town's vegetarian restaurant. Luca had brought menus from all the restaurants in town, assuring them that anything they'd ordered was on the house because of various debts owed to Sarah for her advice—and often intervention—with various agency hoops they'd had to jump through in establishing their businesses, which were now a vital part of the town.

After being told they'd just be in the way, since Quinn had been away from the pub for the past two days, Brianna sent Burke and Gabe off with him. There was nothing they could do at the house anyway.

"I still have trouble envisioning you running a pub," Burke said as they entered Mannion's Pub & Brewery, located on the street floor of a faded redbrick building next to Honeymoon Harbor's ferry landing. The former salmon cannery had been one of many buildings constructed after the devastating 1893 fire that had swept along the waterfront, burning down the original wood buildings. Jacob Harper, one of the town's founders and Burke's brother-in-law's ancestor, had built the replacement in 1894 for Finn Mannion, who'd served as the town's mayor along with running a pub that mostly catered to local loggers and fishermen.

Unfortunately, with Canadian alcohol flooding into the state during Prohibition, Finn had been forced to close, effectively putting the Mannions out of the pub business for nearly a century. Until Quinn had walked away from a high-profile law practice in Seattle, returned home, and hired Seth Harper, whose family still ran Harper Construction, to reclaim the abandoned space. There were five choice tables next to the windows, offering a dazzling view of both the harbor and the mountains beyond. A second row on risers behind the first row also allowed a prime view. Other heavy wooden tables, which Quinn had custom-built from reclaimed wood, took up a good part of the floor. In a far corner were two pool tables and dartboards.

They sat at the long wooden bar Seth had located at a reclamation place in the old Nevada gold rush town of Virginia City. Behind the bar, above the glass shelves holding a variety of liquor bottles and awards won in craft beer competitions, a baseball game was playing on one of two flat-screen TVs. It was the bottom of the seventh and the Seattle Mariners, playing at home, were trailing the Yankees by five runs. When Judge hit a grand slam, putting New York ahead by nine, Burke felt torn between the team he'd grown up with and the one he'd adopted while living in Manhattan.

As the announcers, seeming to realize that the game was looking dire for the Mariners, enthusiastically reminded viewers that win or lose, at least the first ten thousand fans would be going home with retro jerseys, Burke decided that a jersey giveaway beat potting soil night. Turning away from the game, he glanced up at the ceiling. "I like the stamped tin. It looks like it's original."

"That was the point. I wanted to modernize the place while trying to keep it as close to the original as possible. Fortunately, the Harpers apparently never throw anything away regarding their work, so Seth was able to find the original plans. He replaced all the wiring and plumbing to bring the place up to code, added AC, and put in the windows looking out over the harbor, which had originally been a back brick wall."

"It's a great view," Burke said, looking out at the sailboats skimming across the blue water. The shoreline, sand in places and rock in others, was backed by towering Douglas fir trees. "You'd think Finn would've wanted to take advantage of it when he first built it."

"Seth said that glass was difficult to make in sheets during the Victorian days, which would've made it too expensive."

"Or perhaps they made it brick to allow the male customers to hide from their wives," Gabe suggested.

"That makes as much sense as anything," Quinn agreed as Jarle Bjornstad, a red-bearded giant who made Sasquatch look like a preschooler, appeared from the kitchen to take their orders. After years of cooking for fishermen out of Dutch Harbor, Alaska, the Norwegian, who sported a full sleeve tattoo of a butcher's cow chart, had gotten tired of freezing his ass off during winter crabbing season, and ended up in Honeymoon Harbor cooking for Quinn.

Burke ordered the barbecue ribs and wings, while Gabe decided on the blue cheeseburger and fries. Quinn, who'd gone to work behind the bar as the lunch crowd started to come in, said he'd eat after the rush settled down.

"Your cook could've played a marauder on the History Channel's *Vikings* series," Burke said as Jarle lumbered back through the swinging doors. "I don't think there's a team in the NFL who has a linebacker his size. Thank God."

"Especially considering you've been getting hit a lot the past few seasons," Gabe said. "You need a better front line and some pass receivers with the speed to get down field."

"Gee," Burke drawled, his tone thick with derision. Not so much for his brother's comment, but the situation. "Why didn't I think of that?"

"Jarle's six-foot-seven," Quinn said, deftly redirecting the subject before it got out of hand. He paused to take an order for three Bloody Marys and one virgin from a server. "Seth had to take out four rows of bricks to keep him from banging his head going in and out of the kitchen."

"You know," Burke mused, having watched at least two tables of women observe the cook with interest, "if you cleared that wall space enough to make an open kitchen, you might even draw in more customers just to watch the guy cook."

"I've thought the same thing," Gabe said. "I've been ob-

serving him since I got home, and he's proven a chick magnet. I've even seen women ask to thank the chef in person
after a meal just to get to talk to him."

"We do get a lot of women from the courthouse during
lunch," Quinn said as he pulled a beer from a tap and placed
it in front of Gabe. "But his heart—which is, beneath that
rough, burly exterior, as big as the rest of him—has been
taken. Which was a relief, because he tended to fall instantly in love a lot with women who'd come in. Thankfully,
he never did anything about it. Until one special woman.
We knew it was serious when he ran over to Leaf—this
vegetarian place that's opened up since the last time you
were here—to get some flowers to put on her Dungeness
Crab Louie salad."

"I would've paid to see that," Burke said, looking at the
tap tag on the keg Quinn had pulled his brother's beer from.
"What's that one?"

"It's my new summer brew. Catch a Wave. It's not officially out yet, but I test new ones here, and it's selling well.
It'll go on sale more widely the first day of summer as I've
done in past years. That way people can look forward to it.
I've already got preorders from various restaurants along
the West Coast."

"Showing that you learned a lot from those gazillionaires
who used to be your clients," Gabe said. "I wasn't here for
the Good Vibrations launch, but just like Surfin' Safari, it
tastes like summer and goes great with barbecue."

"That's the point," Quinn said. "As for my former clients, some of them had good ideas, which is partly how
they made it into the one percent. I've stayed in touch with
a few who've continued to give me good advice. One's offered to be a silent partner if I want to expand nationwide."

"Are you considering that?"

Quinn shrugged. "I don't think so. I'm making a good living, and I don't want to be like some of those brands that start out as a regional craft beer with a good reputation and suddenly have executives on the seventy-third floor, like my old office in Seattle's Columbia Center, making decisions that change the way I do business, or worse, change the beer."

"I was going to order the Captain Jack Sparrow," Burke said. "But I'll try Catch a Wave."

"It's his third homage to the Beach Boys," Gabe said. "Dad told me that people came from all over to buy cases of Good Vibrations to take back home. And then last summer, Surfin' Safari caused a bigger splash, pun intended, with the craft beer crowd. I think this will easily top the first two." Gabe turned back to Quinn. "Which the old me would've told you was the time to expand. Even go public. Maybe franchise."

"And have stock prices set by algorithms determining what I make? That may be working out for a lot of brewers, but it's not the reason that I got into the business."

"That's why the new me agrees that you're better off sticking to your current business plan," Gabe said. "Because this way, your beers have a mystique. They're a novelty because people can only get them out West. And more importantly, you're living the life you left that high-priced law firm for."

"I sense a disturbance in the Force," Burke said. "When you're not pushing our brother to go for the big bucks."

"I said that was the old me," Gabe said. "The new me is all about living your best life."

Burke exchanged a look with Quinn, who pulled two beers for the Cops & Coffee guys sitting down at the end of the bar, then began blending a pitcher of frozen strawberry margaritas for a table of women who, from the one wearing a glittery silver Bride-to-Be tiara and the other four sporting pink glittery tiaras reading Team Bride, Burke could tell were indulging in the town's wedding industry.

"What are you going to do when you run out of Beach Boy hits?" he asked.

"I should live so long," Quinn said easily. "It's been sixty years since 'Surfin' Safari' came out, and as far as I'm concerned, their California Sound is still a damn good summer soundtrack. And I must not be alone, because last year's beer outsold all the others over the course of the season.

"While I was up in Seattle, there were times, especially during February's Big Dark, when it seemed like the sun would never shine again and the rain would never stop, that I occasionally considered moving down the coast to LA or San Diego."

"With all those California girls," Burke noted, referencing the group's signature song.

"A guy can always dream," Quinn said. For a moment, Burke thought he'd spotted something in his brother's eyes that suggested he might have one California girl in mind, but it had come and gone so quickly that he decided he must've imagined it. "I decided I'd just be in the same old rat race and changing directions, and that coming back home would be a better fit."

Burke took a drink of the ale Quinn placed on the bar in front of him. It really did taste like summer and was tailor-made for a backyard barbecue. "Damn, you're good," he said. "If you moved to New York, you could triple your price."

"And at least quadruple my cost." The high-powered Seattle lawyer Quinn had once been could've fit right into New York's power scene. Brianna, who'd always been at the center of the Mannion siblings, called each of them on a regular basis to catch up and had mentioned how zen the eldest brother had become since his return to Honeymoon Harbor. She was right; his attitude seemed to have taken a one-eighty from the way he'd been before, going back to when he'd been a success-driven Honeymoon High valedictorian. But there was one thing that appeared not to have changed. And that was Quinn's quest for perfection.

"This just may be the best beer I've ever had," Burke said.

"Our big brother's always been an overachiever." Gabe's tone lacked the edge it had back when they were growing up and his need to best Quinn had been obvious to all. It had occasionally escalated into fistfights, causing its share of friction in the Mannion household. "He's been winning competitions since his first Captain Jack. I'm betting this one's going to make you have to add some shelves behind the bar for all the new awards."

"No point in doing something if you don't do it right," Quinn said easily. "Like your boats. Which you have to stop by the shop and see," he told Burke. "After he finished that Viking boat, he built one for me. Not a faering. It's a cruiser, for the chance I might have time to spend a night on the water. But I still take it out on nice weather Mondays, when we're closed."

"I remember that sloop you built for Seth back in high school," Burke said to Gabe. "We had some fun times in it."

As they each grew quiet, thinking back on memories of those halcyon summer days of their youth, Jarle brought out their orders, then paused to strike a pose that showed off his ink for a nearby table of twentysomething girls who'd asked to take a selfie with him before he disappeared back into the kitchen.

"He's a bit of a tourist attraction," Quinn said as they all watched. "Especially with the women. But, like I said, he's off the market." Jarle put a half order of ribs with a baked potato and coleslaw in the kitchen window, which Quinn took to an old man down at the opposite end of the bar from the Cops & Coffee guys. Burke recognized the customer as someone who used to come to his gramp's weekly poker games. He must be about a hundred years old by now. He and Gabe exchanged a few words. Then Quinn was back.

"He wanted me to know everyone is town was pulling for Mom," he said. "I assured him she was fine."

"She was lucky," Burke said, "that Aiden and the ambulance got there so fast." New York City was constantly under construction, and he'd seen more than one ambulance tied up in snarled traffic.

"Let's hope she stays that way," Gabe said.

There was another moment of silence as all three brothers contemplated the alternative.

"She's got to," Burke said, knowing they were all picturing the accident, which only Aiden had seen. "Thank God for Jim Olson."

As if on cue, the door opened, and who should be standing there, backlit by the sun, but the owner of Blue House Farm with a pretty brunette.

"Well, that's a surprise," Quinn murmured as he saw the couple standing in the doorway. "But it saves me having to drive over there to thank him after I get off work."

"I don't think I've ever seen him in here," Gabe said.

"He doesn't like crowds." Burke remembered how Jim had a permission slip from the school nurse to skip Friday afternoon pep assemblies in high school.

"Well, we'll make it easy on him." Quinn left the bar, wove through the tables, and had a brief talk with the couple, who then turned around and left the pub.

"I told them I'd bring their order out to their car."

"Is Jim on an actual date?" Gabe asked.

"Apparently they're talking business."

"It would be cool if it turned into a date," Burke decided. As his brothers agreed, it crossed his mind how much courage it must've taken for the guy to leave the farm and go out in public, to a busy pub during the lunch hour, no less. He wondered, with a familiar twinge of frustration, why the hell he'd never been able to get Lily to even have a damn drink with him out in public.

Quinn put in the order. Then things got too busy to talk any longer. As he made trays of drinks and delivered them, along with helping the servers take the orders Jarle in turn was rushing out to tables, Gabe and Burke finished their meals, waved goodbye and left the pub.

"I'd better get over to Kylee and Mai's and pick up the girls. Chelsea and I are concerned that after having lost their parents in a car crash, they'll worry Mom's going to die," Gabe said. "She's been their grandmother since we adopted them, so this has got to be weighing on their minds."

"Go pick them up," Burke said. "I'll hang around town awhile longer. Check out what's changed."

Burke was glad that he was able to redirect defensive linemen better than he could his own brother when Gabe followed his glance over to the pier, where Lily's hair shone like a bright sunny beacon.

"Yeah, checking out what's new, maybe who's moved to town since you were last here, is a good idea. We've got a new bakery. Why don't you pick up a cake for Mom? After you're done checking things out."

Burke shot his brother the middle finger, then turned and headed over to the pier.

CHAPTER EIGHT

MOTHER NATURE HAD gifted the peninsula with sunshine the day after the accident. With a still brisk breeze coming off the water, Lily hoped that a walk would help clear her head. Her thoughts had been ping-ponging back and forth between worrying about Sarah Mannion and wondering how long Burke was going to stay in town and how she'd be able to avoid him.

After his cool remoteness at the hospital, she'd gotten the message. Loud and clear. He didn't need her to keep apologizing because he really hadn't cared. Which had been what they'd agreed on that first night. Sex without strings.

Since it was still a bit early for full tourist season, which would begin after Memorial Day, the pier was empty. She walked her newly adopted dog and cat out onto it, pausing when the dog, whom she'd named Chance, sniffed at one of the posts, lifted his leg, and left his mark. She stopped when they reached the end, and as she stared out over the water, her thoughts drifted back to that damn text she'd sent.

"What were you thinking?" she asked herself out loud. The dog looked up, his brow furrowed, his expression appearing worried by her sharp tone. "I'm sorry." She patted the golden head. "Your mom's just mad at herself."

Having lived with chaos for her first eighteen years, she'd realized at an early age that when thrown into tumultuous waters, you had to either sink or swim. She'd learned to survive under pressure and had always prided herself on her ability to adapt and keep a cool head, whatever the situation. Until the moment she'd met Burke Mannion, when that lifelong self-control had flown out the window. The truth was, she hadn't been thinking. At all. Just feeling things that she'd always believed herself incapable of.

Lily was so deep in thought, mired in memories and what-ifs, she wasn't aware she was no longer alone until Chance began wildly wagging his furry butt. When she glanced over her shoulder and saw Burke, her first instinct was to run, which was impossible because one, she'd already done that, to her shame, and two, if she went any farther, she'd have to jump into the icy water, taking the dog and cat with her. So she held her ground and met his eyes, which, at the moment, were impossible to see, given he was wearing a pair of dark-lens Oakleys.

"Do you have a pink harness on that cat?" he asked. Not the opening she'd been prepared for.

She glanced down at Zendaya, the black-and-white tuxedo cat, who had a perfect white heart on her black nose.

"I can't let her run loose. She could get away and be eaten by coyotes or wolves. Or an eagle, owl, or even one of those great blue herons that nest behind Brianna and Seth's B and B." The peninsula was known for its natural wildlife, which was wonderful to see in the actual wild, but wasn't very pet-friendly.

When he took off the shades, hooking them into the pocket of the button-down black shirt he was wearing loose over jeans, her unruly heart, which apparently hadn't received the *stay cool* message from her brain, took a leap. "Adopting pets suggests you really have settled in."

Oh, God, she loved his voice! It was deep, with some sexy gravel that had other unruly body parts, undoubtedly remembering the things he'd say to her in bed, waking up. "I told you that I had. They're a pair of rescues."

"What's the dog's name?"

"Chance."

"For him getting a second chance at the good life."

"Exactly." She looked down at the dog, who'd dropped to the wooden planks, displaying his male bits as he wiggled on his back, offering his new friend the honor of patting his stomach. "Cam Montgomery, the vet who runs the shelter where I found him, thinks he's part corgi, part golden retriever. But he's not one of those designer dogs people are breeding, because his naturally docked tail and one blue eye suggest Australian shepherd in his ancestry." Chance was, admittedly, an odd-looking dog with his golden coat, short stocky legs, wiggly butt where a tail should be, tall, pointed ears, one dark chocolate eye, and one icy blue eye. It was part of what she liked about him. He was one of a kind.

"The corgi and Aussie should make him perfect for herding squirrels." Burke crouched down to pet the dog between those decidedly corgi ears, which caused him to wiggle even more.

Was the fact that he'd made a joke a sign that he was getting over his admittedly deserved anger at her? Or was he merely making fun of her dog?

"He's not much of a guard dog, and he sheds enough to make an extra dog, but he's already proven his loyalty and heart by taking responsibility for the kitten." She stood up for Chance, who was currently moaning in canine ecstasy as Burke's broad hand moved to his stomach. "I hadn't intended to get a dog," she said conversationally, hoping to avoid the topic she was going to have to talk about if he stayed in town very long.

When she'd been fifteen, attending a court-ordered girls'

boarding school in New Hampshire, she'd seen a notice about an Al-Anon group for students that met in the town library on Saturday mornings. She'd gone to one meeting, but the moment she'd walked in, she could feel a change in the girls who'd been standing around talking, piling cookies and other baked goods onto paper plates. It was as if the air had shifted, and the friendly chatter came to a sudden stop, like a water tap being turned off.

The notice had assured her that the group was anonymous and that everything that was shared was kept secret—what happened in group stayed in the group—but nothing about her had ever been anonymous. Her entire life, for as long as she could remember, including the truth, rumors and flat-out lies, had been covered by journalists worldwide. Deciding she'd give the members even more to talk about if she turned and walked out, she put a chocolate chip cookie on a plate, then sat down on one of the folding chairs, determined to keep quiet, sit through the damn hour, then leave and never return.

The meeting operated in much the same way as AA meetings did on TV and in movies. People introduced themselves, and when all the heads turned toward her as they moved around the circle, she inwardly shrugged and stated her name. But everyone already knew that. Prompted by the silver-haired woman leading the group, everyone, including girls who'd never spoken to her at school, welcomed her, though none of those voices held the true welcome she'd heard given to the others.

She knew she'd changed the dynamics when the group that had previously been chatting like close friends essentially shut down. When apparently no one had had anything happen that week to talk about, the leader surrendered and began talking about this week's step, step number ten, instructing members to take a personal inventory, and when wrong, promptly admit it.

She'd realized that what she'd said in the hospital cafeteria, about that text not being her best moment, did not come close to living up to the spirit of the rule. It was something she was going to have to address. But out here in public, when his mind was undoubtedly on his mom, was neither the time nor place.

"I'd gone to the shelter for a cat because I thought it'd be a better bet, because they're supposed to be more independent," she said, in an attempt to fill in the silence that had stretched between them like the Grand Canyon. "After all, dogs need to be housebroken, trained not to bite mail carriers, and behave well in public places."

He'd stood and looked down at Chance, who was now sitting up on his haunches, looking up at him as if hoping for more loving. Or a treat. So far, she'd discovered he was fond of any food that wasn't tied down. Which she attributed to his former life as a stray.

"He doesn't seem like a dog who'd bite a mail carrier," Burke said.

"True. But one day I was passing the park and stopped to watch dogs going through an obedience class. They were beautifully behaved, and I was thinking that it might be nice to get a dog when one black Lab failed an assignment by breaking free of his 'stay' command to chase a squirrel. So, after reading several online pet message boards, and weighing the pros and cons of dogs versus cats, I decided a cat would be simpler. All I'd need would be a box, kitty litter, kibble and toys.

"The vet, Cameron Montgomery, who you wouldn't know since he's fairly new in town, set up a no-kill animal shelter, partly because so many people were dumping animals at his clinic during the night. It's gotten to the point where if you ever want a dog, or cat, or even bunnies, he's the place to go."

"I'll keep that in mind." She thought she'd detected a hint of his dry humor, but perhaps that was merely wishful thinking.

"He recently married Megan Larson, who owns a cleaning company, the Clean Team."

"If that's the same Megan who dated Gabe for a while, I thought she ended up marrying Jake."

"She did. But he turned out to be a jerk—"

"Which anyone in town could've told her."

"I'll take your word for that. After he cleaned out her bank account and ran off with another woman when Megan was three months pregnant, she went back to school, got her Associates of Arts degree and set up her business. Cam was one of her first clients, and he, as the story goes, fell in love with her at first sight."

Fearing he might think she was comparing Cam and Megan's instant attraction story to theirs, which they both knew had nothing to do with love, she steered the topic back on track.

"Anyway, he told me that I'd know which cat was the one for me. But none of the ones up for adoption that day really spoke to me, so I was going to ask him to help me choose, when I saw this dog and cat, far removed from the others. Cam told me that they were a bonded pair, and since the dog upset the cats in the cat house, and the dogs in the kennel scared the cat, he'd given them their own private suite, so to speak. Apparently they'd both been dumped in the park, either together or separately, no one knows, where they could have been eaten by wildlife.

"Rangers and campers had seen him scrounging for

food, but it took a while to catch him, because he's really smart. And wily. When they did manage to track him down, they discovered that he'd been taking care of the kitten, keeping her warm at night, and apparently feeding her. Even though I hadn't been prepared to adopt a dog, I knew they both deserved a forever home. Besides, their story sounds like a Pixar movie. How could I not rescue them?"

"Makes sense to me." Zendaya, apparently deciding that Chance was getting too much loving, started head-bumping Burke's leg for attention. Easily scooping her up, which had Lily releasing the leash, he began scratching her behind her velvety ears. They made quite the contrast, the tall, buff athlete, and the tiny kitten that could have fit in his hand. *No!* Lily warned herself sternly. *Do. Not. Think. About. Those. Hands.*

She drew in a breath. Blew it out. Which earned a raised eyebrow, suggesting he'd recognized her mostly unconscious technique for controlling her nerves. "Anyway, after I got them home, I discovered that she screams bloody murder if I try to take him outside without her. Which is a moot point, because he sits his butt down and refuses to go outside without her. I suspect that along with being her self-designated protector, he's also afraid that he'll be returned to the shelter. Or, worse, sent back into the park. So she comes with us on walks."

"That explains the harness."

"Yes. As I said, they're very bonded. He doesn't look all that big, but he's strong when he decides he's not going anywhere. So I took Zendaya, that's her name—"

"Like the actor in those Spiderman movies? I thought you weren't into the Marvel universe," he said, reminding her that she'd never gone to a movie with him.

"I'm still not. I gave her the name because she's a tuxedo cat, and Zendaya rocked a tuxedo on the red carpet at the Grammys."

She was not surprised by his blank stare. She recalled he felt the same way about award shows as she did superhero movies. They were so different in so many ways. Yet somehow, they'd fit. Until, even with his frustration over the restrictions she'd put on their relationship, they'd grown too close for comfort.

Controlling her breath this time, she pushed on. "As I was trying to carry her out to the car, she was doing her best to rake the back of my hand open." The kitten didn't seem to feel the same fear/anger with Burke as she had that day, because she'd closed her bright green eyes and was purring like a small engine. "As soon as Chance jumped into the car, she stopped fighting, snuggled up against him, and immediately fell asleep. She does, despite her size, snore like a lion.

"To make an already long story shorter, I drove back to the veterinary hospital and bought this tiny harness from their retail section. A toddler we passed in the pier parking lot certainly got a kick out of it."

"The pair would undoubtedly get some high Instagram hits."

"I don't do social media. Except for my job."

"I know." His tone, which had started to sound, if not warm, at least cordial, turned crisp. He put down the kitten, who complained with a sharp meow, handed the leash back to Lily. Then, instead of walking away as she'd thought he might, he stood beside her, his hands on the railing as he looked out over the blue water, brightened by dancing sun sparkles. "Dad would bring us crabbing here when we were kids."

"That sounds like fun."

"It was. And another thing Quinn excelled at. He was the poster child for high-achieving elder sibling. Looking back, it drove Gabe, who was as competitive as I am, crazy. Especially since Brianna, being more in the middle, was also seemingly perfect at everything she did."

"She hasn't changed."

"I've noticed. Though she obviously changed her goals when she left her high-powered job in Vegas to come back home."

"I may not have known her before I came here, but I've stayed at some of the luxury hotel chains she worked at, so I have a sense of how much it must had taken to reach that level. I've also seen before and after photos of Herons Landing before she and Seth restored it, so it's my guess that she took that drive and put it into turning the old ramshackle Victorian into a bed-and-breakfast.

"And she's still catering to people and making them comfortable and happy. She's booked year-round except for the two weeks she closes after Labor Day." And that brought up another thing she'd been worrying about since he'd shown up in the hospital. "How long are you planning to stay?" she asked.

He shrugged shoulders already broad enough to block out the sun before he put on those weekly game pads. "I don't know. At least until Mom's out of danger. I don't have to return to New York until July 21st, when training camp starts."

"So you *are* returning?"

Lily had never read the sports pages before meeting him. These days, she couldn't help scouring the *Seattle Times*, the *Honeymoon Harbor Herald*, the *New York Times* online, and various sports social media threads, following the rumors that he might be leaving New York for another team.

Some even suggested that he might retire, though from the comments, they proved to be a minority opinion. He had, after all, won a Super Bowl, and was making millions per year playing in the city with the most media coverage in the country. Fans wondered who in their right mind would walk away from all that?

"That's up in the air," he said.

Lily was curious for so many reasons but reminded herself that what Burke Mannion did or didn't do in the future wasn't any of her business. Not any longer. Not after what she'd done. Taking a deep breath, while they were still looking out over the water, she went for it.

"I owe you an apology. What I did was horrible. And I'd like to say that it wasn't the person I am. But to be honest, in taking a serious inventory of my behavior, I have to admit that perhaps it is. Or at least, the person I was back then. And I don't want me being here, being friends with your sister, to make things more difficult for you." She paused, gathering up every last ounce of courage. "So, I was thinking we should talk about it. Hopefully get it behind us. Brianna has already sensed something, although I'd told her we just met briefly at that event."

He looked down at her, not with the hot desire she'd been accustomed to seeing, but with disapproval. His eyes, a sharp contrast to his jet-black hair, were an icy blue surrounded by a dark blue ring. "You lied to my sister." His deep voice had turned as chilly as the water lapping against the posts of the pier.

She couldn't deny his accusation. Having grown up caught in webs of lies spun by so many others, Lily had always attempted to be truthful, choosing to be purposefully vague about her past.

"We were waiting to find out how badly your mother

had been injured," she reminded him. "It didn't seem like the time or place to bring up our past relationship."

He shrugged again and jammed his hands into his back pockets as he turned his attention back to the water, toward an iconic green-and-snowy-white ferry chugging toward a nearby dock. Seagulls followed in its wake, loudly squawking and diving for any fish the heavy wooden boat might churn up. "Don't worry about it. After all, you were right about us not really having a relationship. Like I told Quinn, it was more a hookup deal."

"You talked with Quinn about us?" Of course he had. Didn't everyone talk to Quinn? If the lawyer-turned-pub-owner started charging therapy rates, he could probably make as much as he had in his Seattle law practice. Old habits kicked in, and Lily felt the walls she'd built over so many years, stone by stone, rising up to protect herself.

"Only after you dragged him into it, asking him to divert me to the cafeteria when I arrived," Burke countered. "And it's not like he's going to tell anyone…" He paused. Then he stunned her by asking, "Are you involved with him?"

She looked up at him again. His face was hard. Distant. It was his game face, the one that was always shown close-up on her TV screen, that made him looked as if he was going into battle. Or like Russell Crowe in *Gladiator*, about to face off with tigers in Rome's Colosseum. "Involved? If you're talking about dating—"

"You and I weren't dating during those three months we were burning up your organic thousand-count sheets," he reminded her.

As what he was implying sank in, Lily couldn't decide whether to be angry or to cry. Or maybe angry cry. She began to cross her arms over her chest when she remembered that she was still holding two leashes. She did lift her chin and looked a long way into those now inscrutable blue eyes. "They were four hundred count." Just because she happened to have money didn't mean that she was willing to waste it. "Once you get into those higher numbers, they have more threads per square centimeter, which makes them heavier and less breathable. And if you're asking if I'm sleeping with your brother, the answer is no."

"Yet you're close enough to have told him something about us."

Was he actually jealous? "Being his brother, you should know how easy, and safe, Quinn is to talk with. And I didn't tell him anything specific about us. I was trying to avoid you being blindsided when you saw me at the hospital."

"I'd already been blindsided by you once," he reminded her, folding his arms, drawing her attention to his rock-hard biceps. "How would a repeat make that much difference? Since you obviously knew I was coming, you could've left before I arrived."

"No, I couldn't have. Because Brianna and I are close friends. Maybe not as close as she is with Chelsea or Kylee, since they grew up together. But there was no way I could take off and leave her while things with your mom were still up in the air." She felt her eyes filling, blinked furiously and took a deep breath. "Look, it's obvious that we really do need to talk."

"I thought that was what we're doing."

The passengers were disembarking from the ferry, several headed toward the pub. What if one of them was a football fan, recognized him, and took a photo?

"I owe you an explanation."

"You already gave me one. That you couldn't see us going anywhere. That pretty much sums it up in a nutshell."

"No." It was time, she'd realized during long hours spent

tossing and turning. "There's a lot you don't know about me. About my life before you."

"That's only because we were so busy screwing like rabbits, we never talked."

"We did talk. I knew about your parents, about their forbidden teenage romance, how they'd ride the ferry just to be away from prying eyes so your grandparents wouldn't find out. I knew about Brianna traveling the world, being one of the few women allowed into that top concierge group. And Aiden nearly getting killed when he'd been a cop in LA. I knew about Gabe doing your summer reading book reports for you. And Quinn always being the perfect older brother you, Aiden, and Gabe sometimes resented. Which is honestly surprising, since he's the nicest, most easygoing man I've ever met."

"When you're fifteen, sibling rivalry comes with the territory. And, for the record, Quinn definitely wasn't always the laid-back guy he seems to be now. But you've just proven my point. You know nearly everything about me. But I don't know a damn thing about you. And here's the weird part: when I googled you—"

"You googled me?"

"Hell, yes. After you left and the sex haze faded from my brain enough, it dawned on me that I only knew your current life. And the strange thing is, after scrolling through all the stuff you were doing for that nonprofit, the next mention of you shows you working as an intern for an ad agency in Manhattan after graduating with a bachelor's degree in creative arts from the University of Hawaii. But there's no bio. You're not on LinkedIn, and except for that honors mention in the graduation program another student posted online, you seem not to have existed before graduating college. It's like you were in the witness protection program or something. What's with that? Were your parents mobsters?"

She tilted her head. "I never realized you had such an active imagination." Except in bed. Which Lily knew better than to bring up again.

"You didn't answer my question."

"No, my parents were not mobsters. And I'm definitely not in any witness protection program."

"Were you CIA?"

"Again, no."

"Then what the hell are you hiding?"

It was her turn to shrug as she turned her gaze back out over the water. "It's complicated."

"That's what you always used to say. Along with some vague comment about your parents not being in your life. So, were you orphaned? A foster kid? Born beneath a leafy green vegetable like a Cabbage Patch Kid?"

As uncomfortable as this situation was, Lily couldn't help smiling. Just a little. "No to all of those."

She drew in a deep breath. Blew it out. The wind off the water was ruffling her hair, blowing strands across her face, and when she went to tuck them behind her ears, he was there first. Just that touch of his fingers on her sea-air-chilled cheek caused a spark. Looking up at him, she knew he'd felt it, too. And was remembering that night they'd met.

"I know you need to be with your mother," she said. "But we can't have this…thing…hanging between us without people noticing. Especially since it'd be weird if I didn't visit Sarah."

"So, what would you suggest?"

"I'll tell Brianna that I need to get back to work for a few hours. Which I actually need to do. The college is taking part in the Heritage Day celebration, and I still have to create media copy and a video for the college and local TV station to run. That will give me an excuse for not being at the farm today. And tonight, I have an adjunct class I teach on marketing."

"This is a small town," he reminded her. "We can't keep coming up with ways not to run into each other for the next two months, if I end up staying until camp."

"I realize that. Maybe you can tell your family you're going to run tomorrow morning. Then come over to my place for breakfast where we can talk in private."

"Now you want me to lie to my mother?"

"No." She dragged her hand through her hair, causing the wind to pick it up again. "Not exactly. There's a strip of beach not far from my house. I'm just out of town past the lighthouse on Sandpiper Point. A lot of people run and walk there, especially in the morning and evening during low tide when they can find sea glass and agates. You could park in the lighthouse lot and run to my place. Then your story wouldn't be a real lie. More of a white one."

He shook his head. He'd cut his hair shorter, which only accentuated his blue eyes, the wide, high cheekbones, and strong jaw. "It sounds as if you have a lot of experience walking that razor-thin line between full-out lies and white ones."

She met his gaze, which had turned hard enough to cut glass. That wasn't at all encouraging. Then, feeling as if she were driving off one of the coastal cliffs into the icy, dangerous waters of the Pacific Ocean only a few miles away, she went for the absolute truth. "More than half my life."

She saw the surprise move across his face, followed by another of those heavy silences stretching between them.

"What time?" he finally asked.

"Whatever works for you. Tomorrow's Saturday. I don't have to be at work."

"Seven."

If he thought he was making it early to inconvenience her, he'd be wrong. That was an hour after Chance would wake her up to go out.

"I'll see you then." She glanced down at the cat and dog, who, obviously bored with their conversation, had gone to sleep, curled up together in a slanting ray of spring sun. Calling Chance, who immediately jumped up, waking Zendaya, who in turn complained with a scratchy meow, she began walking toward the lot where she'd parked her car. Although she could feel him watching her, Lily did not look back.

CHAPTER NINE

ALTHOUGH SHE WAS both physically and emotionally exhausted between the stress of Sarah's accident, and her ensuing conversations with Burke, for the second night in a row, Lily found sleep to be an impossible target. It was as if every nerve in her body was on high alert. She spent a long time staring up at the ceiling, listening to the lonely call of an owl somewhere out in the forest, the whistle of the midnight ferry, and the wind whispering through the boughs of the Douglas firs and Western red cedars in the woods behind her cottage. Her mind kept rerunning all the times she'd spent with Burke. That nagging voice in her head had warned her, the first night they'd met, that he'd be trouble. That it would not end well. But like that Selena Gomez song, even as she could list a million reasons why she should give him up before she got in too deep, the heart wants what the heart wants.

Finally, sometime before dawn, she'd drifted off, only to dream of flashbulbs blinding her as she was led through crowds of reporters with their cameras, along with hundreds of people gathered behind the orange-and-white-striped barricades the police had created to hold them back. They'd all come to witness the nightmare of a circus that her life had inexplicably become. In her turbulent dream, slow-motion scenes—swirling like facets of a dark kaleidoscope—flashed through her mind. In addition to the man who'd ridden in the long black car with her, two uniformed officers walked in front of her, two others behind, as she climbed the high courthouse steps, keeping her eyes straight ahead, struggling to shut them all out.

That was the morning the first stones of her walls had been laid down to protect her from the shouting crowd of strangers and the blinding glare of camera lights. In contrast to the chaos out on the sidewalk, the inside of the courthouse was hushed. So quiet she could hear the sound of her shoes along with the police officers' polished black dress ones echo in the marble-walled hallway.

No one, not even the tall man wearing a suit several shades darker than the police officers' blue shirts, said a word. On the drive there, in the back seat, her hands clasped so tightly together in her lap that her short nails had left half-moon indentations in her skin, she'd been reminded, yet again, that if she did exactly as instructed, did not waver from the precise, legal plan, everything would be all right.

Finally, after what had felt like forever, they'd reached a tall, dark, eight-paneled wooden door with a transom above it. The shiny brass plaque beside the door read Judge James L. Freeman. Just as one the officers ahead of her reached for the doorknob, a high-pitched sound blared, jerking her from the all-too-familiar stress nightmare.

She grabbed for the phone on the bedside table, shutting the alarm off. Then she sat there, drenched in sweat, her nightshirt clinging to her trembling body as her heart raced. She hadn't had the nightmare since moving to the small town she'd never imagined would become her home. It was as if the stiff wind carrying a tang of salt she'd breathed in as she'd ferried into Honeymoon Harbor had blown it out of her mind.

"You should have known he'd come home someday," she

said to herself as she stood beneath the shower's powerful spray. "How could you possibly think you could hide away here?" The truth was, by the time she'd made the decision to stay, she'd also decided that she would face that problem when she came to it.

And now that day had come. It was time, she knew, to face the music.

BURKE WAS BACK in the bedroom he'd once shared with Aiden. At the time, the walls had been covered with Seattle Seahawks banners, along with posters of various quarterbacks from over the years. If Aiden had ever minded living in what was essentially a football shrine, he'd never complained.

Now the posters were gone, and the wall behind the queen-size sleigh bed had been painted a soft buttery yellow. It kept the gray wood of the bed from resembling the Pacific Northwest sky during their long rainy winters. The quilt on the bed was white with yellow-and-gray-striped throw pillows. The floor-length cotton drapes matched perfectly, framing a wall of bay windows that looked out over the farm's Christmas trees.

He took a shower, got dressed, and in hearing his mom's voice in his head telling him that she was his mother, not his maid, made his bed.

Brianna was sitting beside their mother's bed when Burke checked in on her. She put her fingers to her lips, then got up, came out of the room, and softly closed the door behind her.

"How's she doing?" he asked quietly.

"She woke up a few times, but still doesn't have any memory of the accident. She does, unsurprisingly, have a headache, and her ribs hurt, but Dr. Kim said the only thing she can have is Tylenol because anything else could cause bleeding. She's feeling guilty that we're staying awake to keep an eye on her and insists that's not necessary these days. Which, from all Dr. Google tells me, is true. But that's not going to stop us. I told her she shouldn't feel guilty, but you know her. Although we're all adults, she still believes that she's supposed to take care of us. Not the other way around."

She blew out a breath and folded her arms. "But she'll just have to deal with it." She swept her gaze over his lightweight black hoodie with the Knights logo, which he wore over a tight black long-sleeved T-shirt, ankle-length black compression tights, and black running shoes. "Are you off to audition for the next Batman movie?"

"No."

"Too bad. Because in that outfit, you'd give Christian Bale a run for his money."

"FYI, guys don't wear outfits. I'm going out for a run along the water. Gotta keep in shape, even in the off-season."

All of those statements were true. But the second was, as his mom might point out, a lie of omission. While his expression remained innocently neutral, inside, Burke was holding his breath. A lot like Quinn's superpower was listening, his sister's had always appeared to be the ability to read minds. Which, he supposed, was why she'd won all those high-end concierge awards, anticipating needs before clients themselves might realize they even had them.

"Well, have a good time," she said. "I was going to make Mom and Dad some French toast when she wakes up. Want me to make some for you, too? I can keep it warm in the oven until you get back."

"You don't have to bother. I'll just get something while I'm out."

"Okay. But for someone who hardly ever cooked, I've gotten really good at making breakfast."

"Good thing, since you run a bed-and-breakfast." He reached out and ruffled her hair, as he had when she was still a kid. "See you in a while. My phone's on if you need anything."

"We'll be fine." With her in charge, Burke had no doubt of that.

With guilt over sneaking around gnawing at him, he drove to the lighthouse, parked the red farm truck with the Mannion Family Christmas Tree Farm logo on the front doors, locked it with a click, and, pulling out the address Lily had given him, began to run through the fog that had drifted in from the water. Breathing in the salt air and looking at the crystal-blue water edged by towering dark green firs tipped with lighter spring needles had him thinking that he'd been wrong not to come home more often. Last year he'd even skipped his parents' annual barbecue. But he hadn't wanted his mother to know he'd been undergoing surgery for a dislocated shoulder injury from falling on his non-throwing arm after being sacked. He'd played the rest of the season wearing a shoulder brace beneath his uniform.

Sure, he had lots of reasons, with spring camp, the fall season, and then the late fall and early winter playoffs. And he'd always gone to Mexico with other players in the spring to train and keep in shape for camp in July before yet another season. And then there were all those commercial shoots for product endorsements... All excuses.

As she'd told him, Lily lived a mere five minutes beyond the lighthouse on the bay. Her house was a Folk Victorian, a prevalent style in the town, many having been built by a local mill in the nineteenth century to house loggers. It had been painted blue, with a white door and matching window shutters and porch railings, with a white picket fence in front. Instead of a lawn, the small front yard was a wildflower garden that had just burst into bloom.

The sidewalk was various shapes of flagstones, with moss growing in between. His hand had just lifted for the hand-carved Orca knocker when the door opened. "I was watching for you," she admitted, dispensing with any good-morning greeting. "I was afraid you wouldn't come."

"I told you I would," he said in a way that suggested he always kept his word while some people—not naming names—didn't. It was weird how he'd managed to convince himself that he was over her and had moved on. At least, until he'd walked into the hospital cafeteria and seen her sitting there, her long hair shining like gold from the gleam of a sunshower outside the window. Feeling as if he'd been hit by a helmet in his chest, it had been all he could do not to rub over his heart, which, despite what she'd done, apparently still hadn't gotten over Lily Carpenter.

Her cheeks colored a bit at that, revealing that she'd understood the unsaid part about her not being the most truthful person between the two of them. She took a deep breath, then moved aside to let him into the house. "I hope you like smoked salmon," she said.

"Having grown up in the Pacific Northwest with a fisherman grandfather, I'd probably be run out of town if I didn't."

"I was hoping that was the case. I'm not much of a cook, and more likely to stop at Cops & Coffee on the way to work for a breakfast croissant or one of their yummy cinnamon buns, but Brianna gave me some breakfast recipes a while back, and I thought I'd make you the smoked salmon, goat cheese and chive scrambled eggs that are popular with her B and B guests, along with some bacon, smoked on a local farm."

"Sounds great," he said. "But you didn't have to go to that much trouble."

"It's no trouble. I've never had anyone to cook it for, so..."

Her voice trailed off as she seemed to realize that she'd given a little bit of her life away. It didn't sound as if she was accustomed to making breakfast for some guy. Which in turn suggested that she hadn't had any men stay over until morning. She'd certainly always made Burke leave before the sun came up.

"It sounds great," he repeated, breaking the awkward silence that stretched between them again.

"Good. My menu isn't all that varied, though Bri also gave me a great recipe for French toast."

"She was making that when I left."

"She went online and chatted with other bed-and-breakfast owners who shared popular recipes with her when she was looking into starting one. She has a menu of eighty-five different dishes. Of course, she never offers them all at one time."

Though he still wasn't comfortable with this morning's stealth meeting, Burke smiled. "I'm not surprised to hear that."

"Why don't you come into the kitchen, then?"

As Burke entered the house, he heard the sound of nails clicking on the wood floor. Seconds later, Chance barreled into the room, moving pretty fast for a dog with such short legs. He slid to a stop in front of his new friend, his furry golden butt wiggling a happy hello. After bending to rub the mutt between his pointed, upright ears, which drew a low, happy moan, Burke followed Lily through the front room, which was painted in the same buttery shade his mother had used for his old bedroom. The couch was done in a garden of florals that echoed the outside, but the modern style kept it from being Victorian fussy.

Zendaya, who was lounging on a pillow on the couch, looked up languidly through slitted emerald eyes, apparently deciding that his arrival wasn't worth leaving the spot of sun she'd settled in. Two chairs, upholstered in blue, yellow, and white stripes, sat on either side of a white coffee table, anchored by a sisal rug.

"Nice place," Burke said.

"Thanks. I loved it at first sight. Seth had just finished remodeling it when Brianna told him I was in the market for a home. He'd planned to use it as a rental property but sold it to me instead. Your mother designed the interior, and I got the idea for the front garden from Kylee and Mai, who hired him to remodel a similar house from the same time period. The paintings over the couch are from your uncle's gallery."

Burke decided they must be prints, because unless his uncle Mike had deeply discounted them, those paintings would be super pricey. Michael Mannion's early work had sold at Sotheby auctions for mind-blowing prices. "You really have settled in." Which meant that there was no way, if he stuck around, their paths wouldn't be continually crossing.

"I told you I had."

"Yeah. You did." But he'd had a hard time believing it. Instead of a more trendy, open floor plan, the kitchen was through an arched doorway more suited to the period. It had been painted the same color as the front room, but here the cabinets were blue, the granite countertop a bright white.

She opened a refrigerator hidden behind blue cabinet doors and took out eggs, butter, a package of smoked salmon, and a container of goat cheese. "Brianna says sourdough English muffins are good with this."

"If my sister said it, it must be true."

"I thought we'd eat first. Then talk." She made some coffee, remembering that he took it strong and black, and added milk and sugar to her own mug. Then she put some yellow floral napkins on the table with forks. "If you have time."

"I'm making time," he reminded her. "This is pretty much your deal."

She didn't answer but turned and began to work as he sat there and watched her, somewhat surprised that the woman he'd first met looking sleek and sexy could also look so at home in a kitchen, wearing a frilly lemon-printed apron tied around her waist over light-washed jeans and a white T-shirt. She'd also lowered those walls, just a bit, giving him a glimpse of the real her, or of the new her she'd said she'd become. He couldn't tell which because she'd never opened up to him, so he wasn't sure he'd ever known who the old her was. Except in bed, the one place she'd never held back. Yet oddly, the two of them here in the kitchen, as she whipped up those eggs for him, felt as intimate as their lovemaking.

"Can I help?" he asked. His mom had never let him or his siblings skip kitchen duty.

"Thanks, but I've got it. I had everything ready to go. Brianna told me Julia Child's motto was that a few simple steps ahead of time make all the difference in the end."

"That's pretty much the same in football," Burke said. "Which is why, even after making the pros, you can't stop doing drills. I guess preparing for a game is like prepping meals."

"That makes sense."

She fried the bacon, scrambled the eggs with cheese, and toasted and buttered the muffins with an ease that surprised Burke, who'd never seen her eat anything but takeout on those nights they were together. They carefully kept the conversation to the subjects of his mother, local gossip, new businesses that had opened up since the last time he'd been home, and—always a safe topic in the ever-changing days of spring—the weather. As she plated the dish, she used a pair of kitchen shears to sprinkle the eggs with fresh chives.

Zendaya had, apparently, smelled the salmon and joined Chance, who was sitting beside Burke, both of them watching every bite that went into his mouth.

"That was delicious," he said when they'd finished.

"Thank your sister." When she stood up to clear the table, he put his hand on hers as she reached for his plate. Despite everything, the spark was still there. He knew she felt it, too, as her eyes widened.

"In our family, the person who cooked never did the dishes." He took the plate, gathered up hers along with the utensils, and within five minutes, had put the dishes in the dishwasher, cleaned the counter, and refilled their coffee cups.

At the same time, she'd put a few small pieces of smoked salmon and bacon into two bowls and placed one on a mat by the kitchen door, the other across the room. While Chance gulped his down as if he'd still been a starving stray, Zendaya studied, sniffed, licked, and finally deciding her rescuer wasn't trying to poison her, nibbled daintily at hers.

"If I'd known how entertaining pets could be, I would've

considered adopting one years ago," Lily murmured as they both watched.

"So you never had a cat or dog? Or parakeet? Maybe a goldfish?"

"No." Something flickered in her eyes, but it had come and gone before Burke could figure it out. "Do you want to go into the other room?" she asked, changing the subject.

"Sure."

When she sat on one of the chairs, he took the couch, putting the table between them. The easy, cautious mood they'd managed over breakfast grew taut as a drawn bow-string.

Since she'd been the one to suggest this meeting, he waited for her to break the silence.

She folded her hands in her lap. "I don't know how else to say it, but I have no excuse for what I did. I did honestly think that when you went along with not going out in public, you agreed our relationship was based solely on sexual compatibility."

Of all the things he'd been expecting her to say, he hadn't thought she'd put the limits to their relationship on him. "You're kidding, right?"

"No. I'll admit we had an attraction from the beginning, but I believed that we both knew it'd burn itself out eventually. So I thought it better to end it before things got messy."

"And you didn't think you owed it to me to discuss it first?"

"Looking back, that's what I should have done. But I was afraid of where we were headed. I'd realized you might not believe me, because I don't have a history of being entirely honest with you, but I'd never felt that way about anyone else before. Since our situation seemed impossible, although I'm not proud of it, I did what I've always done: I ran."

"We've already determined your parents aren't mobsters and you aren't in the witness protection program. Though under the terms of whatever agreement you and the Justice Department and US Marshals might've worked out, if you are, you'd probably have to lie about that."

"I was wrong in too many ways to count. And admittedly evasive about my past. But I never, ever, outright lied to you."

"The marshals probably would have created a fake past for you," he mused. "Which is one of the few reasons I can think of for you seeming to not exist until your twenties." He'd considered two other reasons. "Are you married?"

"No, I wouldn't have gotten involved with you if I were."

"You could've been hiding from an abusive ex." Burke had spent a lot of time in hotel rooms on the road, which gave him the opportunity to watch multiple *Dateline* episodes in which boyfriends or husbands of missing women usually turned out to be the killer.

"I'm not."

"Are you running from the law?" That would've surprised him, but he'd been forced to consider it.

"No." She sighed. "I'm running from my past. Which I realized I have to tell you about."

"Whatever it is, it can't be that bad." Not enough to change how he'd felt about her. "And you had three months to tell me."

"It didn't seem all that necessary. And it wasn't entirely three months, since you were away a lot."

"It was during the football season. My job isn't a nine-to-five office one."

"I knew that going in and didn't expect to have a normal dating relationship. So it made sense that our relationship was all about sex."

"Do you honestly believe that?"

"That was the deal we'd made."

"It was the deal *you* insisted on. Which I only went along with, thinking that eventually you'd change your mind. Hell, Lily, as good as things were in bed, if I'd only been after sex, I wouldn't have had any trouble finding it. Did you really think I'd put up with the conditions you set for anyone else? Not ever being able to tell the guys about you? Not any sex stuff," he said quickly, in case she thought he was one of those men who had to share conquests in the locker room. "Though you can't deny that it was off-the-charts great."

He saw her hesitate. Her expression softened, and a small smile appeared at the corners of her lips, which, dammit, as frustrated as he was with her, he still wanted to taste again. "No, I can't deny that. But great sex alone doesn't make for a relationship."

"I remember saying the same thing. A lot. Whenever I wanted to take you out and do normal stuff together. Which was when you'd reminded me that you don't do relationships."

"I don't."

"Which, in turn, had me wondering if you made every guy you ever slept with hide out in your apartment?"

"I went out," she allowed. "But those men weren't famous. They were anonymous outside their own circles. You can't walk down a street or into a bodega or restaurant without someone, a cabdriver, a construction worker, or a tourist, recognizing you."

"Like road trips and practices, that goes with the job. It's not that I need, or even want, the attention."

"I'm not accusing you. What I'm saying is that you're a celebrity. Which is why, I have to point out, I asked you to take part in the charity event in the first place. But you're not just a big name in New York. I saw that bit when you and Jimmy Kimmel went out on the street in Hollywood, the one where he asked people how they thought the Knights were doing in the Olympics."

"Kimmel's Lie Witness News is a thing he does, stating outrageous situations to see how many people will pretend they know about it."

"I know. He's an auto-record on my DVR, which is how I saw it. Even aside from the people his crew stopped to interview, you couldn't get more than a few feet without someone stopping and asking you to take a selfie. Some didn't even recognize Jimmy. But they all knew you."

Burke couldn't deny that. In the beginning, he'd gotten off on being recognized. It was, after all, the fame he'd been wanting for as long as he could remember. The first day he'd seen himself on the Times Square jumbotron in uniform with his game face on, posing as if about to throw a long pass, he'd felt like the king of the world.

But that thrill soon wore off, and by the time he'd met Lily, he'd learned to put up with fame as part of the cost of being able to continue to play the game he loved. And get paid more than people who did the important jobs. Like first responders, and all the medical workers who'd seen him through various off-season surgeries.

"No one recognized me when we went skating." In an attempt to instill some romance into their relationship, he'd talked her into going skating at Rockefeller Center, with the iconic lighted Christmas tree towering over them. He hadn't skated since he was a kid, when his family took a trip to Leavenworth, a cute little Bavarian town in the Washington Cascades. But then the night before Christmas Eve, while he and Lily had lain in bed watching the holiday classic *Elf*, after Jovie and Buddy the Elf shared their first kiss, he'd decided to try to convince her to do at least that the following night.

So, after some warm, deep kisses and long, stroking touches, which had led to another round of mind-blowing sex, he'd sprung the idea on her while her mind was still fogged from multiple orgasms. And sure, that might have been cheating, but sometimes a guy had to do what a guy had to do. Still…

"Even then, you made me wear that same disguise I had to put on whenever I came to your apartment. Dammit, Lily, you're an intelligent woman. How did you not realize that I'd never, ever wear a Jets jacket and cap out in public for any other woman?"

She lowered her eyes at that. "It's not as if I forced you to wear it."

"No, but you strongly suggested it in order to keep our affair, or whatever the hell it was, private. Which, in turn, also gave me the impression that you'd break if off if I didn't. Which would've been a deal breaker for anyone else. The fucking *Jets*, Lily? Seriously? Did you ever think I felt like a traitor to my teammates every time I put that damn jacket on? Especially during the season? Did you ever consider what would happen if someone with a phone had recognized me and taken a picture? Hell—" he thrust his fingers through his hair "—I'd have broken the internet. And not in a good way.

"Those people—especially local fans—you say call out my name? They'd have changed in a New York minute to shouting out every frigging name in the book and more." New Yorkers, he'd found, were admirably inventive when it came to cursing. "And how well do you think that would've gone over in the locker room? When the team I'm supposed to be leading, the guys who voted me captain year after year, and union rep, saw me wearing rival green-and-white colors?"

She turned back to him, her gaze meeting his, and had the grace to look embarrassed. "I never really thought about that," she admitted. "I simply wanted to keep our relationship private. So we could get to know each other without any outside interference." She sighed. "I figured that no one in the city would expect to see you in that jacket, so you'd sort of be invisible. Obviously, that was another mistake. When I first saw you in the hospital cafeteria, I thought you'd be furious."

"I damn well wasn't happy. Given that it was just one more lousy thing in a suckfest of a day." He rubbed his jaw, thinking back on her text to him. "Do you know the five stages of grief?"

"I'm not certain I could name them all, but I know the concept."

"I know it well, because I had a teammate, a cornerback who'd lost an identical twin brother in a boating accident. He talked about how his therapist had explained what he was experiencing. After reading your text, I went through every damn stage.

"The first is denial. I couldn't believe you meant it. I told myself that you were just upset about something and that it'd blow over, and you'd be back. It hadn't really sunk in that you could be gone for good without telling me what the hell I'd done wrong."

"It was nothing you'd done."

"Yeah. It's not you, it's me. I'm well familiar with that excuse."

She lowered her eyes again, unable to meet his. "As I said, it was not my finest moment," she said softly.

"You think?" He'd felt like he'd been sacked by some defensive lineman who'd hit him with every ounce of his three-hundred-plus pounds. He was no longer furious. But seeing her again had renewed frustration rising from wherever he'd stuffed it down inside him.

"Which brings us to the second stage, pain and guilt. Football is a contact sport. Even if you don't have some injury that lands you on the weekly highlight reel, after the adrenaline of playing wears off, you feel the pain. All season long. I admittedly don't get the hits the other guys get on any given game day. But last season, I had surgery to remove bone chips from my elbow, taped it up and played the next week. Mondays are 'get right days' where you enter the clubhouse and wait in line for a massage and the cold tub. Some guys can't even get out of bed.

"Injuries are a dirty part of the game teams keep secret from the press because if the other team knows a guy has an injury, that's where they're all going to hit him. To try to take him out. Hell, most of the guys on my own team didn't know about a lot of my surgeries, to ensure they didn't leak. There's a reason the Knights have thirty people on their medical staff."

"That many?" She was openly surprised, as he knew most people would be.

"Yeah. In the old days, before my time, maybe a team would have two docs and a trainer on the sidelines. We have an internist, an airway management physician, an EMT crew, an X-ray technician, an ophthalmologist, a dentist, a spotter in the press box who has the power to stop the game, along with one independent neurologist on the sidelines and a second in the control booth, who consult with the team doctor before the player can get back in the game, because concussions are being taken seriously these days. Even by the owners." Which brought Burke back to the decision he had to make, but right now he was far more concerned about his mom's head than his own.

"But I'm getting off track." As had so often happened with her. For a guy used to being in charge, calling his own plays, it had been hard to play solely by the other person's inexplicable rules, as he'd done for her. "My point is, I thought I'd known pain. But you taught me a whole new level. Then I kept trying to figure out what the hell I'd done to cause you to react that way. To disappear without any explanation, or even a proper goodbye."

"My behavior was cowardly," she admitted. "As soon as I was on the plane, I wanted to take it back. But by then it was too late, and I couldn't."

"Take back the text? Or whatever made you run off like that? Even the people at your office didn't know why you'd left. Or where you'd gone."

"You called my office?"

"I didn't call. I went there, and all I was told was that you'd handed in your notice, stating that it was for personal reasons, boxed up your stuff, and walked out of the building. The woman I talked with felt bad that they hadn't even had enough notice to throw you a going-away party. After that, I kept trying to call you. But the recording told me it was not a working number."

"I changed it." Because she'd been a coward. Afraid that he'd be able to talk her into changing her mind.

"Yeah. I figured that out." He took a deep breath. Thrust his fingers through his hair again. "The third stage is anger and bargaining. I didn't believe that bargaining would do me any good because, since you'd disappeared, there was no one to bargain with. So I went with angry." Burke flexed his fingers as he remembered his out-of-character reaction.

"I punched a hole in the wall." In the Tribeca penthouse that she'd never once visited.

Lily gasped at that. "You didn't. Did you injure your hand?"

During their time together, knowing how careful he was about avoiding injury to the hand and arm that had earned him the golden ticket to the NFL, it had become a game. While lying in bed, she'd place his hands on different parts of her body. "Does it hurt when you do this?" she'd asked as she bent his fingers to cup her breast. "This?" On the inside of her thigh. "How about here?" Between her legs. Which was usually as far as they'd get, because she'd be hot and wet, and there was only so much a guy could take.

He shrugged. "It was only a bruise." A bruise that had turned into a hematoma that had to be drained and nearly cost him a game. It *had* cost him a team fine for careless behavior. Another injury that fortunately hadn't made the news.

"Then we get to the hardest part. I'd never experienced depression. Sure, I'd be down after a loss, but it was nothing like what I was feeling. I began self-medicating with alcohol, and other stuff. Not pills," he assured her when he saw the concern written all over her stricken face. "By partying too hard." Fortunately, he'd hit that stage in late January, after the Pro Bowl, a time when he'd had to act as if everything was great while surrounded by the other players and their wives and girlfriends, all having a high old time.

"That part was hard to miss," she said. "Even all the way out here, I couldn't shop at the market without seeing you on the cover of every tabloid at the checkout counter. I'd never realized how many models and pop stars lived in the city."

"It wasn't the same," he said, still feeling shame that his mother would've seen those same tabloids. She'd never been one to flaunt his fame in order to have it reflect on her. He'd never met a woman more confident in her own skin. But he knew she'd had to feel embarrassment during that time. As it was in all small towns, gossip was a major currency, and he'd certainly provided enough. During her weekly calls, although his crazy nightlife was never addressed directly, he could tell she'd been concerned. "And I sure as hell wasn't having any fun.

"Then one morning I woke up with a complete blackout. I couldn't remember what I'd done the night before. And that's when I reached the upward turn. To reconstruction. To where I am now. At the acceptance stage."

Then, after the renewed surprise and annoyance of finding her living in his hometown had worn off, he'd discovered a second part of that final stage: *hope.*

He'd thought long and hard about it most of the night. And he'd decided, the same way he'd thrown those passes that had earned him the reputation of having the best long ball in the game, that he was going for it. What could happen? She'd take off again? She'd already said that she was in Honeymoon Harbor to stay. She even had a dog. And a cat. Not knowing why she'd seemed unable to stay in any one place for long, there was always the chance that she might run again. But this time he was prepared for the risk.

Although Burke was realist enough to know that he couldn't turn back time, he'd never believed the game was over until the last play and he heard that final buzzer.

"You must really hate me," she said softly, twisting her fingers together.

"I wanted to. But as hard as I tried, I couldn't. I realized that when I first saw you in the cafeteria." He been stunned and angry, but dammit, that inner voice he'd heard that first night said, *Here you are.* As if he'd always been waiting for her. Without even knowing he'd been waiting. "So, here's what I'm thinking… Why don't we try it?"

"Try what?"

"Dating the way regular people do. Really getting to know each other. Like, I ask you out, not at the last minute, not a booty call. But at least a day in advance. Like tomorrow, maybe. And we make it casual. Dinner at Luca's. Or the pub."

"Quinn's pub?"

"Last I heard, it's the only one in town. How about it? Dinner tomorrow night. At the pub. Unless you're still worried about people seeing us together."

He watched as those walls started going up again. What the hell was with her? "People will talk," she said. Zendaya, apparently deciding no more salmon was forthcoming, had jumped onto her lap. She began stroking the purring cat in a way he suspected was more to calm herself than the cat, who, if it had looked any more relaxed, would've been boneless.

"Probably. That's part of what people do for entertainment in a small town."

He'd once liked that part of small-town living on fall Saturdays, when he couldn't go anywhere without people stopping him to talk about the last night's game. His brothers were all off at college, leaving him to be Honeymoon Harbor's star Mannion. The one everyone had been invested in becoming famous, putting their tiny dot of a town on the map.

One thing Honeymoon Harbor had in common with New York City was that it had been built and populated by dreamers every bit as bold as the ones who'd built the sprawling metropolis. Originally named Port Vancouver, by the 1800s, with shipping and timber building the economy, the town had grown into a well-known, active seaport, banking on a rich future. A building boom had resulted in an abundance of ornate Victorian homes perched atop the bluff overlooking the port that was visited by vessels from faraway places.

Unfortunately, too much of the bustling port had been constructed on the shifting sands of speculation that it would grow to be not only a major city, but the state capital. Those dreams had been dashed when the Northern Pacific railroad, hampered by a deep depression that had gripped the nation, couldn't afford to connect the town to the eastern Puget Sound cities of Tacoma and Seattle.

Despite the boom being over by the late 1890s, which had caused the population to decline, those dreamers who'd stayed were handed a stroke of luck in 1910 when the king and queen of Montacroix, a small, wealthy Mediterranean monarchy, added the town to their honeymoon tour of America after learning of this lush green region from the king's friend, Theodore Roosevelt, who'd set aside national land for the Mount Olympus National Monument.

As a way of honoring the royals and hoping that both the national and international press following them across the country might bring more attention to the town, residents voted to change the name to Honeymoon Harbor. Later, Roosevelt's cousin Franklin visited, raising the monument to national park status.

Which gave Burke another idea.

CHAPTER TEN

"How about we begin easier?" he suggested. "Like dinner in the park at the Lodge at Lake Quinault? We'd be less likely to run into anyone from town there."

"But the tourists are beginning to arrive…" By Memorial Day, cars and RVs would fill the narrow roads, the shops and restaurants would be doing a brisk business, and his sister's B and B would be fully booked until the day after Labor Day. The visitors were already trickling in. "Surely they'd recognize you."

"That's possible," he allowed, still not understanding why that was such a big deal for her. Most women he'd gone out with had wanted to be seen with him. Some had even had their publicity people call their favorite paparazzi to make sure photos were taken to boost the women's social media profiles. "But also, I'd be out of place. So it'd be less likely."

"Don't you have to go back to New York once your mom is for sure okay?"

He shrugged. "Like I said, camp doesn't start until July. Meanwhile, I'm in contract negotiations, but that's what I have an agent for."

Since he'd decided to talk to Sam Otterbein and lay his cards on the table personally, both the GM and the team owner knew what he wanted. What he wouldn't back down on. So now things just had to be worked out—or not—in negotiations. The strange thing was, he'd come to the realization that he didn't really care. He loved playing, to look up in the stands and see thousands of fans rooting for him and the team. He couldn't deny that he'd also saved a collection of those highlight reels. Like his own personal hit parade.

But playing in the NFL wasn't like a real job where you could put in your years and retire with a gold watch at sixty-five, and unlike in the past, early retirements were rising. Burke had talked with a few players who'd walked away and found a good life after football.

One of the most talented QBs in the game had retired at thirty after a record-making season when he'd thrown for over four thousand yards and made thirty-nine touchdowns. Ironically, when news of his planned retirement leaked to ESPN before he could make a public announcement, fans booed him off the field in the third game of the preseason, showing that for all their enthusiasm when you were winning, even the strongest fan base held a what-have-you-done-for-us-lately attitude.

The guy had been a pocket quarterback who, even more than Burke, had depended on his line to keep him upright. After a four-year cycle of injury, pain, rehab, injury, pain, rehab, both in season and off, he'd decided to hang up his cleats to spend quality time with his family. He'd recently assured Burke that he'd make the same choice again.

Another had retired at twenty-six, just as he was hitting peak performance age for a quarterback, having decided the injuries weren't worth it. He didn't want to end up as one of those players who could never walk pain-free or play with their kids.

"Are you saying that you're going to be staying in town until then?" Lily asked, dragging Burke's mind back to their conversation. He wondered why he'd never realized how good she was at hiding her thoughts. He couldn't tell by her expression or her tone whether she believed that to be a good thing. Or a bad one.

"New York in the summer is miserable," he reminded her. "So, yeah, I was considering it before Mom's accident. Now I have even more reason to stay."

"You're that sure of yourself?"

"Sweetheart, I have never been sure of anything with you. It was only one of the things that made you different from any other woman I'd been with."

She arched a brow. That hint of a smile was playing at the corners of lips he'd spent too many nights dreaming about since she'd left. "You saw me as a challenge."

"No. I saw you as a woman I thought I might possibly have a future with."

"You didn't know me."

"I believe that's the point I've been trying to make. It was why I'd intended to ask you to go to the Pro Bowl with me. And I realized you couldn't take six weeks off work, but maybe we could have spent some time in Mexico on random weekends and during spring break."

"You were going to ask me to go to the Pro Bowl?"

"Yeah. Though I now realize you probably wouldn't have gone, we could've had fun in Mexico. Just think of it, Lily... Lying on a lounge chair with the sun shining down on you, toes in the sand, a mai tai in your hand, while dolphins frolic offshore."

"It admittedly sounds tempting. But I've read about your rigid training schedule when there, so I don't know how you'd fit me into your schedule. And now whenever I see a Miami Dolphins game. I'm going to be watching for the frolicking."

"Smart-ass," he said without heat. "I'm talking the real

sea mammal kind of dolphins. And as for my workouts, believe me, I would've taken time to do a different kind of workout with you."

He held up a hand, forestalling any argument. "But since we missed Mexico, the least we can do is spend this spring like regular people, really trying to get to know each other."

"It won't make any difference."

"Because you don't think you could ever fall in love with me?" He couldn't believe the *L* word had come out of his mouth. He'd always been careful to never say it. Then again, he'd never felt it might be a possibility. A long shot. But hey, he was a guy who'd gained fame and fortune for achieving long shots.

"No," she said. "Because I think I could."

"And that would be so bad, why?"

"I can't." She twisted her hands together.

"Why not?"

"Because… Dammit." She stood and began pacing the plank wood floor. Chance looked up, as if checking to see if a walk was on the menu, but when it appeared not to be the case, he went back to sleep. "I've managed to go my entire life avoiding anything close to love."

"Is it the concept you don't believe in? Or is it that you mistakenly believe you're unlovable?"

"It's—"

"Complicated," he finished.

"It is." She blew out a breath. "There's something I need to tell you. Before we're seen again in public."

"Okay," he said, deciding to let her call this play.

Lily looked around the room. She'd lived in so many places, in so many towns and countries over her life, but this was the first home she'd ever made her own. She loved it and, working with Sarah, had spent months decorating it. Which she'd never done before. After first changing her name, she'd lived in a dorm, then furnished apartments— not because she couldn't afford furniture, but because stuff tied you down. Even her New York apartment had come furnished and decorated, a perk offered by the developers for those who, like her, moved a lot, or who only used their apartments for a place to stay while in the city.

Every piece of furniture, every lamp, every dish, every towel—*everything*—in this house had taken her months to choose.

"Would you mind taking a drive?" She didn't want to spoil the peace and comfort of her home with a discussion that could turn out to be one of the most difficult of her life. Not only depending on how Burke would react, but reliving memories that she'd tried to lock behind those walls.

Talking in the car would also be a way to keep her hormones, which were currently battling with her anxiety, from misbehaving.

"Okay. How about up to Hurricane Ridge?"

Hurricane Ridge, in Olympic National Park, had been shaped by wind and snow. During the winter, winds gusting over seventy-five miles an hour buffeted the ridge, which is how it got the name "Hurricane." The paved, seventeen-mile road included several tunnels and was steep and twisting as it snaked up a mile and a half above sea level. Offering one of the best views in the state, it was also a popular tourist location, but having visited the park several times since she'd arrived in Honeymoon Harbor, Lily knew that the parking lot was large enough to offer some privacy.

She probably wouldn't be able to tell her story on the drive up, because she'd be gripping her seat's armrest, hoping that they wouldn't come around a blind corner to find one of the ubiquitous RVs taking up more than its share of the road. But since sharing her story was going to require pulling together every last ounce of courage she possessed, Lily decided that the white-knuckle drive was a perfect metaphor for what she knew she had to do.

"Brianna told me that while Zoe was deployed, Seth would drive up here every Sunday to keep her Mustang running," she said after they'd stopped at the Heart O' the Hills entrance station. "And continued to do that after she'd died."

The first five miles had been a mix of conifer and deciduous trees. But almost as if someone had drawn a line on the other side of the entrance, the trees jumped in size. When she'd accompanied Chelsea on a library summer adventure reader's group trip to the visitor's center, she'd learned that this was an old-growth forest made up of trees that had escaped those early lumbermen's axes.

"It had to be hard for Seth, losing Zoe," Burke said. "Especially given the way she'd been killed and the fact that the two of them had been together since high school."

Lily hadn't arrived yet when Seth had first been widowed, but she'd heard the story of his young wife, an Army nurse, being killed by a suicide bomber in Afghanistan. "But at least he had a second chance for a happily-ever-after."

Two years after that tragic event, Zoe's best friend, Brianna—who'd had a serious crush on him since second grade—had quit her job in Las Vegas and come home, and the two of them had fallen in love while working on Herons Landing together. They were now happily married.

"I'm a firm believer in second chances," Burke said mildly. "It's imperative in my business. If I spent the entire game angry about throwing an interception, I'd never get back in a winning mindset."

"That makes sense."

Lily fell silent, taking in the wildflowers that had begun to appear in open meadows between the trees. Although the temperature lowered as they neared the top, he'd opened the sunroof, allowing in the crisp scent of firs that always had her thinking of Christmas.

They continued driving in an unexpectedly comfortable silence, past the flowers, the trees, including a grove of old ones that had died and been turned silver by the mile-high UV rays, and snow left from winter storms. It occurred to Lily that this was the first time they'd driven anywhere together.

He continued on the loop behind the parking lot, which would give them privacy for their long overdue conversation, and stopped at the far end, next to several patches of snow that sparkled like diamonds in the sunshine. "Want to go for a walk and take in the view?"

Since she knew it to be one of the better of the amazing outlooks in the park and it seemed foolish to drive up here and not, she nodded. When they got out of the car, she zipped up the jacket she'd brought with her. Though it was the third week in May, a lingering chill of winter hung in the air.

As they walked behind the large brown wooden visitor's center, which she knew from previous visits housed an information desk, snack bar, gift shop, and theater for a park movie, they passed a couple coming back, hands entwined. They looked so comfortable together. So happy she could almost see the little hearts fluttering like butterflies over their heads. Which had Lily wondering if Burke was thinking the same thing she was. That they'd never done anything so naturally romantic as walking together, hand in hand, over the hills past a herd of grazing deer.

"It's just stunning," she breathed as they gazed out over

the panoramic view of jagged, deep blue, snow and ice-capped ridges and valleys, carpeted with profusions of wildflowers. In the distance, a dazzling view of the Strait of Juan de Fuca that led out to the sea. Beyond those deep blue waters, they could see Canada.

"You won't get any argument from me."

"I've been all over the world," she said. "But this is one of the few places that always takes my breath away. And not just because of the thinner air."

"I'd forgotten how much I missed it," Burke said. "Thanks for agreeing to come here to tell me your deep, dark secret."

He had no idea how deep and dark it was. "Thank you for suggesting it." And weren't they being polite? Until he took her hand and lifted it to his lips.

"As good as it's always been, it's even better, seeing it with you."

Even as she told herself that she should be relieved, knowing that the explanation would change nothing between them, she backed a little away. "We should get back to the truck. I think my cheeks are turning to ice." The chilly wind was strong enough to chap skin.

He didn't object when she reclaimed her hand. But as they walked back down the hill, past the visitor's center, she could feel that she wasn't the only one distancing herself. That uncomfortable gulf had begun to deepen between them. "Want to drop in and get some coffee?" he asked.

She hesitated, judging the chances of someone recognizing him. Or both of them. "That sounds good," she said. "But would you mind if I wait in the truck? I'd forgotten how cold it can be up here, even in spring."

He shot her a long look, his eyes giving away nothing. The same way his face would look on TV when he lined up for a snap. When he wouldn't let the opposing team know what play was being worked out in his head. Left unsaid between them was the fact that they both knew the visitor's center would be heated.

"Sure," he said. After seconds that had felt like an eternity, he reached into the pocket of his hoodie for the key. The truck beeped as he opened the doors. "I'll be right back."

She continued on to the truck, then turned on the heater. As she watched him walk into the building, her mind returned to that day long ago when she'd changed her name. People did it all the time, the friendly woman in the government office who'd given her the necessary forms and detailed instructions had assured her. Giving her a sweeping look, she'd lowered her voice and, apparently sensing Lily's nervousness, asked her if she was sure she wanted to do this. Then she mentioned times when teenagers, the same age as Lily's eighteen, would come in, change their name, then be back in as few as six weeks later to change back to the original when whatever disagreements they were having with their parents had cooled down.

"No," Lily had assured her. Her resolve apparently showed in her expression as she looked the woman straight in the eye. "I am not changing my mind."

"I hope it turns out well for you," the woman had said.

Lily had assured her, "It will."

And it had for over a decade, as she'd continued to flit around the world from place to place and job to job, unburdened by all the public scandal and pain that had come with her previously hyphenated name. Until she'd met Burke Mannion, who, unknowingly, possessed the ability to blow up her carefully constructed new life. Leaning her head against the passenger window, Lily felt like crying.

CHAPTER ELEVEN

WATCHING HIM WALK toward the car as he returned from the visitor's center, Lily couldn't miss the way other women's heads turned toward him. The same as they had that night of the event. There may have been bigger stars, ones whose names and films were known all over the world, but he was the one all the women had gathered around. At times, there was even a line to get his autograph, selfie, or a signed Knights T-shirt with his number seven on it. One night, she'd asked him why he'd chosen that particular number. He'd answered that it reminded him that every set of downs should end in seven points. She hadn't known all that much about football but had realized it was impossible. "It might be," he'd agreed when she'd shared the thought. "But that doesn't mean it's not a goal worth striving for."

As he got closer, carrying the tray of coffee cups, she was surprised all the women who'd turned to look at him weren't walking into trees. As hot as he'd looked in that Italian Brioni tux the night they'd met, those skintight black running clothes nicely revealed sharply defined muscles in a ripped body with only ten percent body fat. Having worked in press relations for the Arizona State athletic department for a short time, she'd put out enough preseason releases and profiles of player stats to recognize physical statistics.

As much as she tried to fight it, her mind flew back to that first night when they'd begun ripping each other's clothes off the moment they'd entered her apartment. She'd run her hands over every inch of him, and somewhere in her hormone-hazed mind, she'd decided he had the most perfect male body ever put on this planet. During six months in Florence, working as a tour guide, the single thing everyone wanted to see was the statue of David, carved from an enormous piece of marble, displayed in the Accademia Gallery. *Michelangelo*, she'd thought that night, *eat your heart out*.

As they sat in the truck, a silence not nearly as comfortable as their earlier one surrounded them. The coffee he'd returned with warmed her body, which was still a bit chilled from their walk, but the caffeine did not help nerves that were jangling like the bells the Mannions would put on the sleigh for the Christmas celebrations every year at the tree farm.

Lily knew he was waiting for what she'd promised to tell him. She'd gone over this conversation a hundred, maybe a thousand times in her mind last night, but had never come up with a good way to start. So, taking a deep breath that was meant to calm, but definitely didn't, she decided to just go for it.

"This is difficult," she said, continuing to look out the window. "But I haven't always been Lily Carpenter."

Burke turned toward her. "I figured that out from your lack of history before you landed at the University of Hawaii. Were you married?" Why would she have kept that such a deep, dark secret?

"No. I legally changed my name when I was eighteen."

"Okay. I guess this is where I ask why."

"Because I wanted a fresh start. One that completely broke all connections to my family."

Having grown up in such a close-knit family, Burke couldn't have imagined wanting to do anything like that.

She'd already nixed the mobster idea. What other reason would she want to hide them?

"Why?"

"They're rich. So am I."

"I figured that out for myself from those fancy red-soled shoes, diamond stud earrings, and the Chanel bag you were carrying the night we met. Not to mention your pricey West Village apartment that would be right at home on that million-dollar-listing TV show." Though, he'd always thought, it had been oddly under-decorated and impersonal, as if she were staying in a five-star hotel.

"Says the guy who lives in a Tribeca penthouse."

"Which you've never seen," he reminded her. "And having money isn't necessarily a bad thing."

Although his mother had insisted that she didn't need it, his signing bonus with the Knights had allowed him to pay for the remodel of her kitchen, which included a Sub-Zero fridge and a six-burner gas stove. When he'd been growing up, they'd had one refrigerator in the kitchen and two others in the garage to hold all the food he and his brothers would eat.

"I didn't say it was. But my family isn't merely rich. They're mega, one-percenters rich. My roots on my mother's side go back to an ancestor who was one of the builders of a railroad company that was, for a time, the largest in the world with a budget second only to the US government's. My father's lineage comes through a British baron who married a 'dollar princess,' which is what the American heiresses were called who were essentially sold off to pay the debts and reestablish the estates of impoverished nobles. They tended to be strategic marriages, exchanging American dollars for European titles.

"Moving forward a few generations, neither my father nor mother ever worked a day in their lives and were unbelievably self-indulgent. After their marriage, they both drank, had affairs, and came to hate each other. They would do whatever it took to hurt the other."

"Damn. I'm sorry. That sucks." And couldn't be any more different from how he'd grown up.

She shrugged. "I suppose dysfunctional families aren't that uncommon, whatever the financial situation. But having money allows people to get away with things ordinary people couldn't afford to do.

"They divorced when I was five, which set off a decades-long custody battle. I got caught in their cross fire and realized early on that neither one of them cared anything about me. I was merely a pawn that they could weaponize against each other. I can't remember much about that time, but I later read the papers, and they'd each hired private investigators to prove that the other was an unfit parent."

"Were they?"

She sighed. Deeply. "Unfortunately, although my father was the one who'd always paid the most attention to me, by the time I was in boarding school, he'd become a barely functioning alcoholic who went through a lot of women. I hadn't known about that, of course, but my mother always insisted that they were hoping to be his second wife. Not that any of them would've gotten all that much money, because he'd learned his lesson about not signing a prenup when he'd impetuously eloped with her to Turks and Caicos while they'd been partying with celebrity friends on a yacht in the Caribbean."

"Who was taking care of you while all that was going on?"

"I had a series of nannies, but none stayed very long. It wasn't," she said dryly, "a very peaceful environment.

"Although my mother wasn't an alcoholic like my father, just inordinately fond of champagne, she was too busy living a jet-set life to be burdened with a child, so she enrolled me in a Swiss boarding school run by nuns when I was six." Lily looked out at a mother doe and three fawns grazing in a meadow. From her next sigh, Burke guessed she was thinking back on those days.

"Didn't you have any aunts, uncles, grandparents, *anyone* who could protect you?"

"No, my mother's mother—who'd been widowed young when her husband died falling off his horse during a Palm Beach polo match—had a team of high-priced lawyers fighting both my parents for custody."

"She fought against her own daughter?"

"They did not get along," Lily said dryly. "While, admittedly, looking back, my mother was neglectful, the only reason my grandmother pretended to care about me was that she wanted to control my trust." Lily had continued to look out the car window as she'd related her story, but now, as she turned her head toward him, her eyes, rather than reacting to the emotional abuse she was describing, were expressionless. As if she was talking from behind that wall he'd watched her erect too many times. "She kidnapped me once."

She said it in the same matter-of-fact tone she might use to point out it was raining. He was stunned. "Really kidnapped you? Like, stole you and ran away with you?"

"Not exactly like that." Her faint, reminiscent smile was touched with sadness and didn't reach her moss-green eyes or warm her voice. "She'd offered my mother half a million dollars to bring me back to the States, and two hundred thousand dollars for each of two weekends every month and Christmas that I'd spend with her. That was another thing I hadn't understood until I read copies of the court documents."

Burke didn't know which was more appalling—that any mother would be willing to sell her child for two weekends a month or a holiday that had always been such a big deal in his family, or that a grandmother, who made the Wicked Witch of the West sound like Snow White, had that much dough to throw around every month. "Did your mother agree to that?"

"Of course. Her lifestyle required more than even her own hefty trust fund could afford, and it became even more expensive as she got older and her boyfriends got younger."

"So, she essentially sold you." Like a piece of property. A rage like Burke had never even experienced when being slammed by a cheap shot during a game rose hotly inside him. Realizing that anger was not what Lily needed right now—though it took every ounce of self-restraint he possessed—he shoved it down.

"I suppose you could say it was more like renting me out. It was after my father finally died of liver disease, conveniently taking him out of the custody equation. So, once we got back to the States, and the house my mother hadn't sold after my father died, she enrolled me in a private day school and pretty much went about living her life."

"Who was taking care of you?"

"Oh, we had staff who'd been taking care of the house until she'd decided what to do with it." This faint smile, at some distant memory, appeared warmer. "Dennis, the butler, used to drive me to and from the private school. He always told a lot of jokes, and we'd sing silly songs."

"You had a butler?" By now, Burke wondered why that would surprise him.

"Well, that's how Mother referred to him. He was more like the house manager, keeping track of things and making sure any work was done properly. Sort of like Mr. Carson in *Downton Abbey*." She paused at his blank look. "Which you never watched."

"I knew about it," he defended himself. "And I knew never to call my mother or Brianna on Sunday nights. When I was either playing football or watching a game."

She shook her head, but her smile finally seemed genuine. "At least, by me making us stay at my place, you and I didn't have to argue about which movies to go to," she said. "Because we'd probably never find one we agreed on…

"But, getting back to the kidnapping, the third assigned weekend, my grandmother wouldn't give me back. When my mother showed up to take me to our house, she refused to let her in and called the police. When they arrived, she insisted to the officers and the child services worker she'd also called, that she was protecting me from my mother, whose excesses were, admittedly, constantly making the news.

"My grandmother was awarded custody because socialites behaving badly aren't seen as all that maternal. Especially when it comes out that their child is being raised by house staff. After my grandmother was awarded custody, rather than risk having me go to school, where I might be snatched back by my mother, she hired a live-in tutor. Quite honestly, although it sounds like imprisonment, it was better than going to school, where I was bullied by mean girls and didn't have any friends."

"What about your father's family?"

"Oh, they've always been out of the picture. My grandmother on my father's side is a baroness who lives in Surrey, which apparently is known as the Beverly Hills of Britain. I drove by it once when I was living in London for a short time, but it's gated, so I couldn't see her house."

"Wouldn't she have invited you to visit if she'd known you were there?"

Lily's short laugh held no humor. "According to my father, she's a dreadful snob who considered my mother's family to be coming from 'trade,' despite an ancestor having established the world's largest railroad. So, along with not attending the wedding, she chose not to have any connection with my parents or me."

"That's pretty hypocritical for a woman whose family wealth had come from a rich American bride."

"The irony is not lost on me," Lily agreed. "I suppose she prefers living in her own special world of privilege."

Again, Burke contrasted Lily's story with his own, and couldn't imagine what kind of lifestyle she'd been surrounded by. It sounded like *The Great Gatsby* on steroids.

"My mother and grandmother spent years in court. On my ninth birthday, my mother bribed a maid to let her into the house while my grandmother was out at her Wednesday afternoon card club."

"She wasn't at home to celebrate your birthday?"

Lily shrugged. "Oh, she wasn't much for celebrations. But the cook had baked me a cake, and the staff sang happy birthday that morning. Anyway, Mother had a limo waiting outside, and we drove straight to the airport. She managed somehow to get me through French customs in Paris, where she stashed me in an apartment with a nanny and governess so she could continue to flit around Europe, go on safaris, yachting, all the things her friends did."

"What did your grandmother do about that?"

Another shrug. "I didn't know, exactly, because Mother wasn't there to be losing her temper and ranting over whatever legal machinations might have been taking place back in America, so I was pretty much in the dark. I imagine she had a lot of lawyers working for her to regain custody. But meanwhile, that was a good time for me. The best until

I turned eighteen. I had stability, learned French, and the nanny, being barely out of her teens, was more like an older sister. The governess, who had two children of her own, was like a surrogate mom, and although it may sound disloyal, I loved her more than my own."

"I don't see any reason why you'd need to feel any loyalty toward your mother." Burke imagined most feral cats treated their kittens better.

"Thank you for saying that. In my twenties, it took me a while with a therapist to figure it out. Anyway, while I was in Paris, we'd spend weekends riding on the carousels, going to patisseries, sailing toy boats at the Jardin des Tuileries, and watching marionette shows all over the city. My favorite was Guignol, in the garden of the Champs-Élysées." This time her smile was more fondly reminiscent.

Although it took an effort, because he was still honestly horrified, Burke smiled back. "How long did that last?"

"Nearly a year." Her walls, which had lowered for that brief moment, went up again. But not before he saw the pain from whatever came after those too-short childhood Paris days.

"You don't have to tell me any more," he said gently. "I've pretty much gotten the picture."

"Thanks, but I've gone this far. I might as well get it out, because it's part of my—well, not excuse, but explanation about my behavior…

"My grandmother hired a French law firm to work with an American one to have the courts there send me back to the States. One day I was studying fractions when a man and woman from the American embassy arrived at the door with some gendarmes and said I had to go with them. My mother was out shopping, and I asked if I couldn't wait until she got home to at least say goodbye. But they said that wasn't allowed, that there was a plane waiting to take me back home.

"I tried to tell them that this was my home now, but they wouldn't listen. Josette, my nanny, Anne, the governess, and Simone, the housekeeper, were all in tears. I'll admit I cried all the way to the airport, where two lawyers—a man and a woman—were waiting for me. I also probably annoyed everyone in first class by sobbing most of the way across the Atlantic until I finally fell asleep.

"Two days later, I had to go to court to talk to the judge when they were deciding who I should live with. My grandmother's lawyers had spent much of the flight coaching me on what I needed to say. They told me that if I didn't tell the judge I wanted to live with my grandmother, my mother would spend my inheritance, and I'd end up impoverished and maybe even living on the street.

"They didn't explain that the trust wouldn't release any money until I turned eighteen, when I would get a generous amount, and the rest on my twenty-first birthday. I kept imagining myself dying like the Little Match Girl."

"Christ. How old were you by then?"

"Ten."

Realization hit like the proverbial light bulb over his head. "Damn. You were the 'poor little rich girl' in the papers."

She appeared surprised by that. Surprised and annoyed, which he took to be a good sign. At least there were some sparks of emotion in her response. "Yes, and later, as I got older, I thought it was very lazy journalism given that the term had already been used for Gloria Vanderbilt. And how in the world would you know about that, since you wouldn't have been that much older?"

"Christmas tree farming doesn't generate enough revenue to send five kids to college," Burke said. "So, although we all got scholarships, we also had part-time jobs when we were teens. One of mine was a paper route, and although Gabe wrote my book reports for the summer reading program every year, I did read the newspaper every morning above the fold while I walked around town delivering it. You were on the front page for days."

He remembered that picture of the little blonde girl so bravely walking into the courthouse, surrounded by security, looking straight ahead as crowds of onlookers and photographers called out to her. Though he'd been older, he hadn't believed he could have handled it nearly as well.

Because he couldn't bear thinking of the little girl she'd been, he put his arm around her shoulder. Not to seduce, but to comfort. He took the fact that she didn't pull away as a positive sign.

"And thus we get to the heart of my problem," she said on another long sigh. "The day I turned eighteen, I legally changed my name and took control of my life. Lillian Taylor became Lily Carpenter, moved to Hawaii for college, and then, as you know, to New York for her first time. But I honestly found it too busy, too loud, too much after four years in Hawaii. So I left and moved back to Paris, where I got a job giving tours of the city. But maybe I was more like my mother than I'd thought, because just when I'd start to settle in somewhere, I'd begin feeling edgy, and like a tumbleweed, blowing off to a new country and a new job."

"And a new man?" Burke regretted the question as soon as he asked it.

"Not really." She shook her head and ran her finger around the rim of her now empty cup. "I dated from time to time, but nothing ever very serious because I didn't want to get tied down. I told myself that I was compensating for all those years growing up when I didn't have any choice where I lived. So I kept looking for somewhere I felt I could be happy for the rest of my life."

"Or perhaps you were running from that past."

She glanced up at him. "You're very perceptive. Where were you all those years I was paying two hundred dollars for forty-five minutes of therapy?"

He didn't want to scare her off, or cause her to run again, leaving behind what appeared to be a normal life with friends and a job she loved. But on the other hand, Burke realized if he'd laid his cards on the table much, much earlier, they might have been able to make things work.

"I was here. Then Seattle, getting a degree and playing for UW. Then New York." He paused, then decided to just say it. "Waiting for fate to have me meet you."

Her lips curved, just a bit, giving him the feeling that she was remembering that night when the world had tilted on its axis. "I'm not really a believer in fate. I'll admit to being a control freak—"

"You think?" he said dryly, with a half smile to take the bite from his words. From what she'd told him, it was only natural that she'd want to maintain control over the life she'd created for herself. Literally from scratch, when she'd left her first eighteen years behind her.

She laughed, as he'd meant her to, then turned serious again. "Meeting you terrified me. Because I was overwhelmed with feelings I'd never experienced before." She lifted her hand to his face, looking as serious as he'd ever seen her. "It was exhilarating and terrifying all at the same time."

"I terrified you? Funny. For me, it seemed as if that last piece of my life clicked into place, a piece I hadn't even realized I'd been missing."

"I know. For me, too. Which is what made it terrifying. Because it couldn't ever work out."

"Why not?" When she went to take her hand away, he caught it in his, and touched his lips to it. "Russell Wilson, the Seahawks' quarterback—"

"I know who he is. You can't live in this state without at least that much football knowledge. And are you now comparing our situation to football?"

"No, to life. He said something in an interview that stuck with me, about Edison having said that it took ten thousand light bulbs to get the right one. That's why you keep aspiring for the right light bulb. We found our perfect light bulb that night."

She closed her eyes. Shook her head. When she opened them again, they were shiny with tears. "Weren't you listening to what I just said? What I've never told anyone else?"

"Of course. And my heart aches for the little girl you were. I'm humbled that you shared what had to be an incredibly painful past with me. But, trying not to sound conceited here, that shows me you do care for me. More than any other guy you might have been with in the past."

"I did. I do," she corrected herself. "But that doesn't change anything."

Growing up, there'd always been a jigsaw puzzle on a table in the family room, and during days when the weather was too wet and windy to go outside and practice his passing, he'd worked on a lot of puzzles. He enjoyed finding that one special piece to complete the picture. In later years, he'd see every play in a game as a new puzzle to solve. But, although he may have felt he'd found the missing piece in his life when he'd met Lily, she'd turned out to be a puzzle wrapped in a damn enigma.

"Why not?"

"Because you're famous," she flared.

"We're back to that?"

His frustrated tone didn't seem to surprise or faze her. "Yes. Because it's important. It took me a very long time to move beyond my past, Burke. To find a place, and a life, that felt right. Like something I deserved.

"For years, because people who should have loved and cared for me had only treated me like a weapon in a war of attrition, you hit the nail on the head when you suggested that I might not believe I was lovable. Or that I deserved a happy life of my own. I admittedly messed up along the way while looking for that place, and my worst mistake was hurting you. But despite having found my perfect life here, which I owe to you for talking up Honeymoon Harbor the way you did, I can't relive those days. Or how I felt then."

"Why would you have to? Admittedly, my future's up in the air right now, but whatever it turns out to be, there's no way I'd ask you to give up the happiness and friends you've found here. Even if I end up continuing to play in New York, we could work that out."

"But don't you see? It wouldn't be just us. Because the minute our relationship became public, the press would dig into my past."

A thought belatedly occurred to him. "What backstory did you give Brianna? And anyone else who might have asked?"

"Only that I came from money. Brianna knows about the railroad, but things like that don't impress her. Knowing Chelsea's librarian information-gathering mind, she might have looked up the railroad's history, but there wouldn't be any Carpenter listed."

"Because you made it up. And despite having married Gabe, she's never seemed to care all that much about money, either. Except for what she can raise for the library.

You're right about them. But you do realize that you're not required to share your life history with anyone, Lily."

"I know that. But if anyone gets curious enough to do some digging, they'll notice the same thing you did. That Lily Carpenter doesn't have a past."

"I'm assuming the name change records were sealed."

"Yes. Fortunately, I could afford a very good attorney. But public records are maintained by public employees. It only takes one bribe to the right person and nothing's secret."

"Would that be the end of the world?"

She looked at him as if he hadn't heard a word she'd said. "I can't go through all that again," she repeated, her raised voice trembling with anxiety. "I don't want the paparazzi following my every move. And, it's not just me. It's you. I don't want you to have to deal with every article about you mentioning me. And any speculation that you married me for my money."

He almost laughed at that. But understood this topic was too important not to finish. "News flash, Lily. I don't need your money."

"I know that. And you know that. But things can always be twisted. If there's anything I've learned, it's that many people will believe anything they see or hear on TV, on the radio, or in the press."

"I have a suggestion."

"What's that?"

"That we lead such a normal, boring life, no one will want to follow us or write about us."

"If only." Skepticism dripped from those two words.

This time he took both her hands, which had gone unnaturally cold, in his. "We're not in New York right now. Sure, I'll probably get some local and state press this summer because of all the rumors about my career situation being in flux. But, not to sound arrogant, I'm betting that people are going to care more about who I'll be playing for next season, or even if I'll be playing at all, than take the time to dig into the past of the local small-town woman I'm spending time with who works at a community college.

"And not that I'm suggesting using her, which I'd never do, but my mom's accident would automatically be part of the story, because that's what brought me back home. So reporters will concentrate on the family stuff. About how long my parents have been married, maybe her days at Oxford and in Japan, and Dad's days in Nepal, which make for a good story. And everyone in town will be eager to talk about what a remarkable woman she is. Hey, maybe it'll even pull in some business for the Christmas tree farm."

"Now you're just being crazy."

"Maybe. Maybe not." He met her skeptical gaze and held it. "Give us a chance, Lily. And while I'm not here to play the guilt card—"

"Which you're about to do."

"Okay. Yeah. I guess I am. But don't you think, just maybe you owe it to me, to *us*, to see if what we had was real?"

It had been on his part. Her story, which must have been difficult to share, made him even more certain they belonged together. She deserved to be happy. He knew he'd do everything in his power to make her happy. So why the hell couldn't it work?

"We weren't living a normal life," she said. "Which I'll admit was my fault. But how do you know it wasn't just the sex?"

"Maybe that first night, in the beginning, it was a hormone surge," he allowed. "Actually, more like an explosion. But we were together, granted in a limited way, for three months. And you knew that I kept wanting more. Not just sex. But to be closer to you. The way we are now.

"You said you only knew about Honeymoon Harbor because I talked about it. I told you my parents' story, about my siblings. And my dreams of making it to the pros. I shared personal things that only my family knows. Things I'd never told any other woman. Hell, any other person. Can you honestly say that the sex was all it was for you?"

"No." She shook her head, studied their joined hands, which were on the center console between them. "It wasn't. Which was why I ran."

"To the one place you knew I'd show up again," he pointed out. "Where, that two-hundred-dollar-an-hour therapist might have suggested, you were subconsciously waiting for me. And even if that wasn't the case, if you honestly thought you could live in my hometown without me ever coming home, now that I have, you might be thinking about running again. But let me tell you here and now, that won't work anymore."

She looked up at him. "Why not?"

"Because if you run, I'll follow you. Wherever you go. To the ends of the earth, if necessary. Hell, you've got enough money to go into space. But so do I. Despite my fear of heights, I'd go up in one of those rockets. Just to be with you."

"That sounds a bit stalkerish. And you're afraid of heights?"

"There's a wooden bridge here in the park over the Hoh River Trail that serves as a literal bridge between the rain forest and Mount Olympus. Gabe and I were camping out on a scout trip when the scoutmaster took us on a hike there. It's a stunningly beautiful place, but the bridge is over a hundred feet above the river that's fed by mountain glaciers.

I got halfway across, made the mistake of looking down at all that rushing water, got hit with vertigo, and froze. I would've freaked out and maybe stayed there all day if Gabe hadn't been behind me to talk me the rest of the way across. I've never told anyone else that story. Until now."

"I promise to keep your secret. And although I don't have a fear of heights, I can appreciate your fear because I'm the same way with spiders."

"Thank you for understanding. But spiders aren't exactly the same as rustic wooden bridges high above rushing icy waters."

"You're right. It's possible to avoid high rustic wooden bridges, but spiders can suddenly leap out and come skittering toward you from nowhere."

"Point taken." He leaned across the console and touched his lips to hers. Softly, more of a whisper than a kiss, but Burke was encouraged when she made that familiar, soft little murmur in her throat that had always been all it took to make him hard. He wanted her. Here. Now. With every fiber of his being. But not only were they in a public place, he'd also learned back in college that a rush offense play was less likely to result in a big gain. So he reluctantly backed away.

"And to answer your question, no, I'd never track you down like a stalker. But like a man who was pretty sure he was falling in love with you and is willing to bet you won't send me away."

"You know my past now. But you still don't know *me*."

"I believe I do. Or at least, I now understand, as much as anyone who hasn't lived your life could. Admittedly our pasts inform all of us, Lily. But that doesn't mean we can't change. Like that poem about the two roads diverging in the woods, we can take a different path this time."

"You make it sound so easy."

"And you make it sound so difficult. We can resolve this. Give me a few weeks, Lily. For us to get to know each other, because I believe there's a good chance that we belong together. Like my mom and dad, who are definitely proof that a marriage can work between two very different people."

This time, a few tears fell, trailing down her cheeks like crystals. "You don't fight fair."

"By pointing out that most marriages are not the hell-scape you were unlucky to have been caught up in? Your parents sound like the most screwed-up couple I've ever heard of, even before you throw in your Cruella de Vil grandmother. And look how well you turned out.

"I saw the photo, Lily. Of you going up those stairs into that courthouse, and I didn't think I could've been nearly that brave. I'm just asking you to be brave enough to open up, come out from behind those walls you needed to build to survive, and give us this time before I have to go back to camp in July."

"From the way you argue your case, maybe you should've gone into law with your brother."

"Can I take that as a yes?"

She looked out over the mountains. He could almost hear her mind weighing the pros and cons. He'd watched her work over those three months, writing talks for local civic groups, lobbying politicians for money, planning fund-raising projects like the one they met on, and knew that she wasn't one to make snap decisions. Which was the opposite of what he did out on the field, where the ability to change course on a dime when a defensive line changed positions before a snap, or a planned play didn't work out, was a requisite skill.

"I have to ask one thing of you," she said.

"Anything."

"I need time to tell Brianna. And Kylee and Mai. And Chelsea. Oh, and Jolene. We've become friends, and I haven't exactly been honest with them. I mean, as I said, they know I have money, but it's never been a topic of conversation. But if you and I are going to be together, in public, I don't want them to find out about me from *Entertainment Tonight* or some trashy tabloid at the market."

"You've got it. I'm glad you've made such good friends." Deciding not to push his luck, Burke didn't point out that three of those women would be her sisters-in-law if they got married.

"Thank you." She blew out a breath. "I'll invite them to lunch at Leaf. Or maybe Luca's... No," she reconsidered, "those would be too public. I think I'll have them over for takeout and drinks at my place after work. But for now, I'd like to go back to town. Warning, I'm going to the farmers market to pick up some flowers for your mom. Then out to the farm, where we can't let anyone know about our past relationship. Yet."

"I won't give anything away. Mom was sleeping when I left the house. I'll take you home, check on her, and then, if everything's okay, maybe go over to the boat shop."

"That's expanded quite a bit since Gabe built his Viking boat."

"Just because he left New York doesn't mean that he'll ever entirely slow down," Burke said.

Unlike Gabe, at the moment his own future, both professional and personal, was up in the air. But the one thing Burke knew was that nothing was going to interfere with him coming up with a game plan to win Lily Carpenter.

CHAPTER TWELVE

THEY DROVE BACK to town in silence, as if Lily had talked herself out. Burke wondered how his sister and the others would take it when she broke the news that she'd been hiding in plain sight right here in Honeymoon Harbor. He suspected she was wondering the same thing. He could also understand why she'd been so reluctant to share her secret with friends after having not been entirely honest with them. As she'd done with him, she hadn't out-and-out lied. She hadn't made up a fake story about parents, or anything to do with how she'd grown up. He knew Brianna would never hold her omission against her. And hoped the others would understand.

Because his father had taught him to walk a girl to her door after a date—though the trip to Hurricane Ridge wasn't a date—not only did he not drop her off at the beach parking lot as she'd suggested, he drove her to her cottage. As they walked across the flagstones placed on a bed of moss through the colorful riot of flowers, he reached down and took her hand. It felt natural. Perhaps she was too drained from finally having shared the secret she'd been keeping for the past dozen years to object. But he wanted to believe opening up to him had caused enough of those walls to crumble that it felt as right to her as it did to him.

"Will you let me know when you tell them?" he asked.

"Of course. And I'll let Brianna know I've already told you, so she won't feel she's keeping a secret from you."

"You're right." As she looked up at him, he flashed those Mannion dimples he'd inherited from his father, feeling better than he had in over a year. "It *is* complicated. But we can work it out."

He saw the shadow of doubt move across her face but felt like he was making progress when she didn't insist that any relationship would be impossible. After she'd gone back into the house and he was driving away, Burke decided he'd take it easy. The key was to take things more slowly this time. They'd gone from *nice to meet you* to ripping each other's clothes off, and although he had told her about his family, she had never given him a clue about her past, nor had they ever discussed a future.

She'd warned him from the start that she didn't do relationships, which at first, had sounded like an attractive change from all the women who were more interested in him putting a ring on it. But since he hadn't expressed any thoughts about moving whatever they had to the next level, it was no wonder she'd mistakenly concluded he was only in it for the sex.

They'd made progress today. Maybe the next thing to do would be to shift things to the friends level. Give her time to get comfortable with the idea of them together.

And then what? a nagging little voice in the back of his head asked. While he'd been up on Hurricane Ridge, his agent had been playing hardball back in New York. He was what many considered to be the prime age for a quarterback, though Roethlisberger and Brady had managed to defy Father Time. After two tries, he doubted she'd attempt New York living a third time. And there weren't a lot of pro football teams on the Olympic Peninsula. Like, none.

The state didn't even have a community college league. He could do network game commentary, but if he had to travel around the country for months without playing, he'd undoubtedly miss the adrenaline rush and begin to doubt his decision to quit. But that was a dilemma for another day.

As he started to drive to the boat workshop, he changed his mind, turned around and went back to the parking lot, where he sat in the car, googling Lily on his phone, this time using her birth name.

She hadn't been exaggerating. He read through a series of front page stories touting her neglectful parents and Wicked Witch of the West grandmother. In the accompanying photos, the older woman was always shown draped in pearls, while Lily's mother obviously preferred the sparkle of diamonds.

Despite displaying a wealth beyond what most people could even begin to dream of, they appeared fairly normal. Somehow, they'd managed to keep all their greed and cruelty from showing, like Dorian Gray in the old black-and-white forties movie Burke had watched in some long forgotten hotel room, who'd sold his soul to remain eternally young and handsome while a picture of him showed all his sins. He imagined portraits in those mansions Lily's family had scattered around the globe turning increasingly hideous.

He opened a scratchy news video with a banner reading, *"Breaking News! Poor little rich girl Lillian Taylor arrives at the courthouse."* He turned up the sound and watched as the camera scanned the shouting crowd of onlookers and reporters as a black limousine pulled up to the curb in front of the huge stone courthouse. When the driver, wearing a black suit, got out of the car and opened the limo's back door, the noise level escalated to a roar as another man in a dark blue suit exited, followed by a young Lily.

Her blond hair, probably having been brushed to a sheen by one of the members of the house staff, fell down her back, nearly to her waist. She wore a green, blue and white plaid uniform that reminded him of a Catholic school girl, white knee socks and mirror-bright black patent leather shoes. With a uniformed policeman on one side of her and the blue-suited man Burke took to be her lawyer on the other, she walked, eyes straight ahead, past the crowd, all yelling for her attention.

The photo he'd seen that day on the front page of the newspapers he'd been delivering had been bad enough. But the TV coverage showed her walking up those tall steps into the courthouse. He heard the shouts, saw the crowd push against the orange-and-white barricades while unrelenting, blinding camera flashes went off. He wondered how such a young girl could possibly possess such composure.

Now he realized that she'd begun building those walls that had frustrated him at a very young age. To protect herself when none of the adults around her would.

"Damn." No wonder she didn't want to relive that day. He was about to call her and assure her that she didn't have to worry, that he'd keep her secret. Then, on second thought, he realized that she was right. She might be able to go on living the anonymous life she'd created for herself. But all it would take was one photo of the two of them together on Instagram, and reporters would dig up what they could on his latest girlfriend. Especially since she would be the first one he'd been seen with for months.

They had to be able to make it work. Burke didn't know exactly how, but they were both intelligent people. Surely there was a way.

THE NEXT MORNING, still thinking about that video and what she'd told him about building a home in Honeymoon Harbor, Burke got up, showered and shaved, and then left the house. The streets were quiet. The fishermen had already gone out for the day, the churches were holding Sunday services, and the tourists that had come for the park or outdoor activities were probably still on vacation time, sleeping in, if not already out on the mountain trails.

He drove to the pub, went around the back, and found the door unlocked, Quinn was inside the storeroom, holding a clipboard. Through an open door into the kitchen, Burke saw Jarle feeding a big chunk of marbled beef into a meat grinder. "I have a favor to ask. And I come bearing gifts." He held up the bag of bear claws and doughnuts he'd picked up along with a cup of coffee at the retired cops' shop.

"Good morning to you, too," Quinn said without turning around. He made a notation on a clipboard. "And gifts aren't necessary, though they're always welcome."

"I have a favor to ask."

"Sure. What's up?" Wasn't it just like Quinn to agree without asking what Burke wanted or needed? He'd always taken his role as big brother seriously, especially with so many kids in the house. Stepping in as a part-time surrogate parent eased the strain on his parents.

"I want to borrow your boat."

"No problem. Where are you going?"

"I was thinking, maybe, if it was okay with you, I'd live on it."

That had Quinn turning around. He arched a dark brow, which was about as close as he'd typically get to showing surprise. Though, Burke suspected, he hadn't been as cool and collected when he'd learned about their mom.

"For how long?"

"I don't know. No longer than July 21st, which is when I need to return to New York for training camp."

Quinn's only response was a faint hum.

"I can still bunk in my old room at the farm on Mondays. You can use it on your day off. Unless you stay open every day in the summer so you don't miss the tourist crowds?"

He'd sneaked a girl into his room a couple times after Aiden had left for college but had no intention of repeating that with Lily. And sure, her cottage was cute, but this time he wanted the option of going to his place. Fortunately, Quinn hadn't chosen to live on his boat. After having lived in an apartment above the pub for the first year he'd been in business, he'd bought a house out at the lake, a log one that had been built before all the tech money had flooded into the peninsula, thrown around by people looking for the solitude and serenity they couldn't get at home. Gabe had bought one of those McMansions. He'd told Burke the newcomers couldn't handle such a slow pace of life, so they unloaded the property at a loss and headed back to the cities.

His brother shrugged. "I stick to the Mondays-off schedule. When I first opened, before Jarle showed up, I worked seven days a week and was doing the cooking and a lot of the serving and bartending. It was helpful in those early days to get people accustomed to coming to a new place instead of driving to Port Townsend, Sequim or Port Angeles. But once we were running smoothly, I cut back to six days because, unlike the big chains, we don't have a big staff we can switch around. I've found that what I may lose in meals served, I make up for in atmosphere and good service by having a happier team."

"You've thought it all out."

"To tell you the truth, I'm working fewer hours than I did in Seattle, and my blood pressure's a lot lower. Plus, an unexpected side effect is that Tuesday's business has increased. It seems when people get a craving for ribs or wings, or one of Jarle's burgers, if they can't have them on Monday, they show up the next day. Which is a surprise because Mondays and Tuesdays are usually the slowest days in the restaurant business. But our Tuesday receipts are nearly as high as on the weekends."

He put down the clipboard and folded his arms. "Don't you usually go down to Mexico this time of year for off-season workouts with your army of a fitness team?"

"I have in the past. But nothing says I can't work out here." He'd spent yesterday running and doing wind sprints out at the lake. If he stayed until camp, he'd have to start working out at the new gym in town. Maybe pay extra for after-hours, so phone shots of him wouldn't flood the internet, giving him a glimmer of what Lily had been up against.

Another humming sound came from Quinn. "Does sticking around for a while have anything to do with Lily Carpenter?" he asked.

"Maybe," Burke hedged. There were two people in the family who possessed that steady, silent look that could cause you to squirm. His mother and his big brother. "Okay. Yeah." He put the bag on a table in the middle of the stockroom and jammed his hands into his back pockets. This was feeling a lot like old times.

"Interesting," Quinn said as he dug into the bag and pulled out an apple bear claw covered with cinnamon and sugar.

"It's complicated," Burke said, falling back on the statement that had driven him nuts when he'd get it from Lily.

"So it seems," Quinn said thoughtfully before taking a bite of the pastry. "She's a nice woman. A good one. You're not going to mess with her, then dump her, maybe as revenge for her dumping you with that text, are you?"

"Hell, no. How can you think I'd do that?"

Another shrug, which was one of his quiet brother's ways of communicating. That and those expressive black brows. "You've been away a long time. And last I heard, you were going through women like you'd been told you only had weeks to live."

"That was an aberration I've put in the past. And I'd never do that to anyone. Let alone her."

"Good," Quinn said as he picked up a jumbo-sized mug of coffee and continued to eye Burke over the rim.

"I'm pretty sure I'm serious about her," Burke said. "Correction. I *know* I am."

"Interesting," Quinn said again. "Though, not to shoot you down or anything, but Lily seems pretty settled in and happy here. From what I've heard, I don't think she'd be all that eager to go back to New York."

"Yeah. That's one of the things I have to work out. And not just for her."

The silence stretched out, making Burke think of those old gangster movies where the cops would shine a bright light into the eyes of the mobster they were interrogating. "Damn, you really would've been one hell of a lawyer in the courtroom. Because you've got that look down pat."

"I wasn't a litigator."

"So Gabe told me when you took that job." Burke had been surprised, since the kind of law their brother had ended up doing had never sounded like what Quinn had talked about when he first decided to go to law school. "Do you ever miss your former life in Seattle?"

"Like I told Gabe, not for a heartbeat," Quinn answered without hesitation. "Mostly what I did was push around mountains of paper, figuring out ways for the one percent to get even richer." He washed the crispy baked dough down with a longer drink of coffee. "After a few years, I felt as if I needed a shower when I got home at the end of the day.

"Then when I was home for the holidays one year, I saw this old, abandoned building and remembered stories we were told as kids about the Mannion who ran a pub and a speakeasy for a time. So, when I returned to Seattle, I started exploring craft breweries in the Ballard neighborhood. Which claims to have the most breweries in the city. It was a world I'd never really thought about, having decided on law back in high school.

"I spent a lot of time talking to the brewers, who were always happy to talk about beer. After deciding it sounded like a good fit, I came home and while Seth remodeled the place, I took classes in craft making, distilling, and cider making at Clearwater, where I learned brew stuff like fermentation temperature control and proper yeast management.

"Since I wasn't fool enough to think I could just jump in and run a business, I also took some business classes. Then, when I decided I was ready, I went for it. And never looked back."

He put the coffee cup down, dug into the pocket of his jeans, and handed Burke a key and a metal ring with the slip number on it. "Good luck," he said. Then, having probably said more words in the last few minutes than he normally would say in a week, he picked up his clipboard and went back to taking inventory.

CHAPTER THIRTEEN

SUNDAY AFTERNOON, Lily and Chelsea were at the market, eating fried clam strips and shrimp with fries at a table near the bandstand, while a Seattle folk singer performed her original composition, "One Brave Life." One line in particular, about no one getting through life without hurting anyone, particularly struck home with Lily. She'd definitely hurt Burke. And soon, she was likely to hurt a group of women who'd become her friends.

She bit into a clam strip and could almost feel her arteries clogging. Normally, she'd get a seafood wrap, or a Dungeness Crab Louie salad. But today, as conflicted as she was about Burke, and how she was going to break the truth to friends she'd been hiding it from for so long, she needed fried food and carbs.

After confessing her past to Burke yesterday, and being honestly surprised by his reaction, after picking up the flowers and having a brief visit with Sarah at the farm, she'd had a craving for sweets and ended up eating Tillamook Mudslide ice cream straight from the carton while she'd watched a K-drama about a heroine who, having grown up in an orphanage, wanted to be an independent career woman. Which supposedly explained why she kept resisting the charms of a wealthy, hot young businessman. It was basically a Cinderella tale, and like all romance movies and books, everything worked out in the end, but of course, that was fiction. Real life, Lily had learned, was a lot more difficult.

As she dipped another clam strip into the container of tartar sauce, she thought that if Burke stayed in town much longer, and she kept eating her feelings, she'd have to start buying bigger pants.

"So," Chelsea broke into her turmoiled thoughts, "how are things going with the college's participation in the Heritage Day celebration?"

"So far, we're having a food booth but haven't figured out the menu yet. As for the float, we're almost done with one along the lines of the Whistler ceiling mural in Herons Landing. One segment will show the peninsula's cliffs and crashing waves. Another will depict Mount Olympus, standing tall over Hurricane Ridge, the rain forest, fields of lavender farms, and the strait leading to Puget Harbor. The third will feature the indigenous first settlers, along with the fishermen, loggers, and builders, like Seth Harper's family."

"That's ambitious," Chelsea said.

"It hasn't been as labor-intensive as it sounds. The automotive and welding students created the frame, and Seth volunteered to build the platform. Then the art department students sketched the murals out, marking off different spaces, like one of those paint-by-number kits, and students from that department and other volunteers are filling them in. I think it's going to be really amazing. And the banner on the side is going to read, 'Education is a pathway to the future.'"

"I like it," Chelsea said. "We're going with a big rainbow as a nod to the show *Reading Rainbow*, then Snoopy lying on his doghouse reading a book, with other Peanuts characters all reading in various positions. I think we've probably bought up all the chicken wire and crepe paper on the peninsula," she said with a laugh. "Our banner is going to say, 'Reading is FUN'—with the *fun* part capitalized— 'damental.'"

"That will definitely be fun," said Lily. "I heard from Brianna, who heard from her dad, that the city council managed to book the *Lady Washington*. That always proves a big draw at the Wooden Boat Festival." The tall-masted ship was a replica of the original Revolutionary War ship named for Martha Washington. Docked at Grays Harbor Historical Seaport, it had appeared in various movies, including *Pirates of the Caribbean: The Curse of the Black Pearl* and *Star Trek: Generations.*

Honeymoon Harbor had a personal connection with the ship after Cameron Montgomery proposed to Megan Larson during a private evening dinner cruise. The new vet in town had been coerced into taking part in a bachelor auction to raise money for the animal rescue shelter, and he'd asked Chelsea, Lily, Brianna, Mai, and Kylee to bid on him.

He'd pay whatever it took, and then he wanted them to gift him to Megan as a birthday present. It had probably been the most fun Lily had experienced since arriving in Honeymoon Harbor. The night had gotten a bit raucous, possibly due to the free pre-auction margaritas, and the proposal aside, Lily's favorite part was when Brianna, of all people, marched over to a blonde who would not stop bidding and told her that the sky was the limit. Then she advised her to sit down because it was bound to eventually get painful standing on those five-inch stilettos.

"Speaking of Brianna," Lily said, "I was thinking that she, you, Mia, Kylee and I haven't gotten together all at the same time for a while."

"We've gotten busy with our own lives," Chelsea said.

"Too true," Lily agreed. "Why don't I check my calendar, then give everyone a call and see if we can find a day and time?"

"We'll want to do it before Memorial Day, so Brianna won't be too busy with tourists."

"The sooner the better," Lily agreed. Truer words had never been spoken.

IT DIDN'T TAKE long for Burke to move the small amount of stuff he'd thrown into a bag when he'd left New York onto Quinn's boat, which had everything a guy could need. The cabin had a curved bench around a table that folded up. The long part of the bench could be turned into a berth. The galley had a stove top, microwave, storage, and whatever dishes, and pots and pans Quinn might have hidden behind cherry cabinets, not that Burke intended to do much cooking. There was a head with a separate shower, and most importantly, as far as he was concerned, a bed tucked into its own alcove.

It wasn't a yacht like the ones owned by teammates, which he'd partied on from time to time, but all the finishes were high-end, from the gleaming cherrywood to the leather the color of winter rain clouds, with gleaming brass fittings.

That done, he headed toward Gabe's boat-building shop at the far end of the peninsula, next to the wooden boat school. Quinn had done the paperwork for Gabe to incorporate and hire boatbuilders who loved the craft but didn't want the headaches of running a business. Rather than one huge building, it turned out that he'd built a trio of different-sized metal workshops.

"This is quite the setup," Burke told his brother, whom he'd tracked down after the five-man crew working in the largest building had directed him to the smallest of the three.

"Thanks. I'll admit that even with all my planning, I didn't expect the business to grow so fast. Apparently, after decades of fiberglass, wooden boats are coming back in style. I decided that the work would run more smoothly if each project was built in a separate building. The one you just came from is the largest boat we've contracted yet. The guy's going to use it as a tourist cruiser on Puget Sound, going mainly for the high-end corporate trade.

"It's licensed for twenty-eight passengers, plus crew, and we're using mahogany, teak, yellow Alaskan cedar and red ironbark from Australia, a beautiful wood that's been used for over two hundred years. It's expensive, but not a problem for the owner. It's going to have oval windows along both sides, and the inside will be all finished wood, including the ceilings. There'll be a full bar with high-end Italian leather furniture. Aside from construction details, I'm subbing out the interior to a guy from Portland, Maine, who's designed yachts for the mega-bucks crowd.

"You're going to have to come back to town when we finally get it done. It'll be over-the-top luxury with all the deck fittings being twenty-four karat gold-plated. It's taking three hundred and fifty sheets of twenty-four karat gold leaf just for the vessel name and design on the stern."

"So, your client is Louis XVI?"

Gabe laughed. "No. He's a former client from back when I was trading. He's rich enough to have a yacht to get out to his yacht, which, of course, has the requisite mogul helicopter landing pad on it. He's Australian but has a son who moved to Seattle last year, saw the tour boats, and decided that would be a fun business."

"Daddy bought him a gold-plated boat. Must be tough."

Gabe shrugged. "Hey, don't knock it. It's providing some much-needed employment. The crew chief overseeing the guys you saw earlier grew up in a family that built luxury wooden yachts back during the 1950s. Times change, people get nostalgic, and what they're getting from Mannion Marine are custom-made boats. Chris-Craft built three-quarters of a million wooden boats between the 1920s and 1971, when the last one rolled off the line. But they were all mass-produced and a bitch to maintain. Our boats just need to be sanded and refinished every four to seven years and you've got yourself a one-of-a-kind family heirloom."

"I'm impressed," Burke said, thinking of Lily's mother off cruising on yachts instead of taking care of her young, vulnerable daughter. "What does something like this cost?"

"If we stay on budget, which I doubt we will because the owner keeps thinking of more stuff he wants, it'll come in at about three million five. I'm guessing, since we've got another year, at least, of work on it. He could go as high as ten mil once he gets an idea to gold-plate the john.

"And yeah, it's admittedly a vanity project, but it's already getting press in boat magazines and word of mouth among the cruising crowd. Now we have enough orders that we're booked three years out. I don't want to do anything we're not all proud of. And most importantly, enjoy making. One of our girls, Hannah, helped me work on the faering when she first started living with Chelsea and me, before we got married. She's here a lot and has started sketching plans of a boat she wants to make. I think we may be looking at a second generation."

"That's way cool," Burke said. Although they'd both been living in New York, Gabe had been such a workaholic that they were lucky to be able to get together once a month. It was a revelation to see him still super busy, but so relaxed. And, like their oldest brother—content. "I guess leaving the fast track has worked out for you."

"Although I wouldn't admit it back then, passing out at my old boss's funeral with what I thought was a heart attack scared the piss out of me. I was lucky that I got a smart-ass ER doc who didn't mince words about my condition. I thought I'd just take the summer off, get back in shape, and return to the New York hamster wheel. But then Chelsea had me rethinking my life. Which wasn't easy because it was what I'd planned since I was a kid."

"To make money," Burke remembered. In their own ways, they'd all been driven. Even Aiden, who'd been a top cop, had been working with the Feds and Homeland Security when he'd nearly gotten killed.

"Yeah. I wasn't sure how, but that was the goal. Which, once I made it, I realized that while it's admittedly advantageous to have and has allowed me to build this business, in the long run, money isn't what life's really about."

He looked down at the much smaller boat he'd been sanding. "This is going to be a custom eleven-foot, all-electric skiff. I'm making it for a mail carrier in Olympia who wants to go fishing with his eight-year-old grandson, who just beat leukemia." He stroked a hand over the mahogany shell. "It's a great feeling to be able to help the family get back to a normal life. And the fact that Chelsea lost her sister to childhood cancer when they were both young makes it extremely personal."

"I'm going to be staying in the boat you built for Quinn for a while," Burke said. "She's a beauty, by the way."

"Thanks." Gabe's arched brow echoed Quinn's. Apparently, they'd both expected him to take off as soon as their mom was declared healthy. Burke had come here today hoping Gabe could offer some advice similar to Quinn's on how he'd made that transition. Obviously he was happy about it. But for a guy who couldn't stop looking at his phone whenever they'd had dinner together back in New York, and who sometimes seemed as if his internal motor had been set to overdrive, such a vast change in lifestyle couldn't have been easy. Burke was about to dig deeper when there was a knock on the metal frame of the open door.

"I'm sorry," Jim Olson said. "I didn't mean to disturb you."

"No bother," Gabe said. "You probably saved my mother's life."

"For which we're hugely grateful," Burke tacked on.

He knew Quinn had already stopped by the farm to thank Jim personally, because Quinn and Brianna were the two most likely to think of things like that. Aiden had also thanked him when he'd gone to interview him for the police report. Thanks to Jim's quick thinking and photographic memory, the hit-and-run truck driver had been apprehended and charged with a class C felony, which, Aiden explained, could result in significant imprisonment and a hefty fine. Right now, the guy was sitting in jail, waiting for his court appearance.

"Mrs. Mannion was always very nice to me," Jim said. "I was happy to help. Well, not happy, because it was a terrible thing. But—"

"We get it," Gabe said. "So, what can I do for you? Are you in the market for a boat?"

"No. It's sort of personal." He glanced over at Burke.

"I'll leave if you want privacy," Burke offered.

"Oh, no!" Jim shook his head. "I didn't mean it to sound that way. I was just trying to decide if I should say something I've been thinking to you. Sometimes, actually, often, I'm told that I'm not very tactful."

"Well, now you've got my curiosity up," Burke said. "So, shoot. I mean, say whatever you were thinking," he said, remembering how literal Jim Olson could be.

"I would never shoot anyone," Jim said seriously, proving Burke's point. "I don't even own a gun." He paused. Burke could practically see the wheels working in that unique but brilliant-in-its-own-way brain. "That was an idiom, wasn't it?"

"It was."

"Well, what I thought this football season, actually for more than just this past one, is that you need a stronger offensive line to protect you. You can't win the game by yourself, and the defense is getting tired being out on the field so long, allowing the opponent to score."

"I ought to take you to New York and have you explain that to the team's owner," Burke said. "Just kidding about the trip," he tacked on quickly. "But I totally agree with your take on the situation and have been trying to make that exact point. I'm having trouble getting through to the GM and owner."

"Good," Jim said. "Not that you're having trouble, but that you didn't take offense, thinking I was criticizing your playing."

"I didn't think that at all," Burke said. Besides, he was used to it. There were already enough Monday morning quarterbacks who'd done that on social media, podcasts and radio call-in shows all last season.

"What can I do for you?" Gabe asked again.

The tips of Jim's ears had turned a bright red. "I was wondering if you could give me some advice about dating."

"Dating?" Burke exchanged a look with his older brother. That had definitely come out of left field.

"Did your date the other day not go so well?" Gabe asked.

"Date? I didn't have a date."

"We saw you at Quinn's," Burke said. "With some brunette."

"Oh. She's Sage. And she wasn't a date. We were having a business lunch at the lake. She's taking a class from Lily Carpenter at the college and needs a marketing project. Lily suggested that she talk to me about a campaign for Blue House Farm."

"If Lily suggested it, it's a good idea," Burke said.

"She had some very helpful suggestions. She's going to assist me in implementing them. But the thing is…"

Jim turned his head and took a deep breath, as if gathering his nerve to get to the point. "I like Sage."

"That helps if you're going to be working together," Burke said.

"It does. But the thing is, I *like*, like her. I think she probably only thinks of me as a partner on her project. But I'd like to take her out on a real date so we can maybe talk about something other than business."

"Sounds like a good plan to me," Gabe said.

"That's the problem." In contrast to Gabe's easy tone, Jim's voice was wavering with stress. "I don't have a plan." His gaze met Burke's. "I dated in college, which was a great deal easier. We'd go out for pizza right around the corner. And the girls were very much like me, so dating social skills were not necessary. I simply asked if they wanted to have pizza and they said yes or no. I never really cared if they said no. I'd simply ask until someone said yes. It was like working out a genome problem. I'd attempt different approaches until I received a positive result. And then we would spend the date talking about our studies. But Sage feels almost like a different species, so I need help. I don't know how to ask her."

"What are you thinking of doing on your date?" Burke asked.

"I don't know what she'd like to do on a date. I streamed some romantic movies, to study them, but the guys on them have a great deal more self-confidence than I do."

"That's because it's fiction," Gabe said. "In real life, guys are a lot more insecure about relationships."

"Scared to death of them," Burke agreed, speaking for himself. He still hadn't figured out how to get Lily to lower her damn drawbridge longer than their conversation had taken.

"Is that true?" Jim looked both surprised and, perhaps, a bit hopeful, discovering he wasn't alone in the female clueless club.

"My hand to God," Gabe said, lifting his right hand.

"A good bet for a first date is a movie," Burke suggested. "That way, you have two hours during which you won't have to think of things to talk about."

"But she's very interesting," Jim said. "I enjoy talking to her, although sometimes it's hard to get a word in. But that's because she enjoys her work so much. That's part of why I like her. That and because—"

Burke could practically hear Jim's teeth slam together as he cut the rest of that sentence off.

"She's pretty," Burke finished the sentence.

"She is, isn't she?"

"Very," Gabe said.

"Talking comes after the movie," Burke said. "Over dinner."

"A movie and dinner. I saw that on one of the Hallmark movies," Jim said, a touch of relief in his eyes. "But it sounds more stressful than pizza dates. And when I get stressed, I can't talk to people at all. Especially women."

"It's probably been a basic first date since silent movie days," Gabe said. He fell silent for a moment, clearly thinking. Burke and Jim waited him out. Then, after a moment, he said, "How about a double date? That way, you'd have other people helping you fill in gaps in the conversation."

"But who—"

"Wednesday is classics night at the Olympic," Gabe said. "Chelsea wants to go see *Casablanca*, which she's already seen so many times, I'll bet she could recite every line of dialogue. How about that? And if you like Italian, we can go to Luca's."

"Who doesn't like Italian?" Burke said.

"I like spaghetti," Jim said, hope lifting his voice. "I buy it in a can at the market."

"There you go," Gabe said. "But I guarantee Luca's is going to be a lot better than that. And here's another plus: the place has a private dining room."

"It's really private?"

"Yeah. We had a party there one time for my mom's birthday. We booked the room so our noise wouldn't disturb other diners, but also so we wouldn't be surrounded by a bunch of other people. There'd be just the four of us on our date. I know Chelsea and Sage get along because Sage volunteered to help with Chelsea's Zoom library reading hour for kids during the months the library was shut down."

"I'd like that." Jim's relief was obvious. "If I ask her tomorrow, when she's not scheduled to work at Sensation Cajun, will that be enough time to not look last-minute?"

"In some cities it might be more difficult to get a reservation," Gabe allowed. "But it's not like there's a lot to do at night here, so there's a good chance she'll be free and the room will be open. Also, how nervous are you going to be about this date?"

"On a scale of one to ten, at least ten cubed, " Jim admitted.

"Which will only get worse the longer you wait and think about it," Gabe said. "Believe me, I know all about anxiety. I ended up in the hospital after passing out on the sidewalk from an anxiety attack."

Jim paled. "I would not want to pass out. Especially in public."

"Then there's no harm in trying. Let me just check something." He pulled his phone out of the pocket of his jeans. "Hey, Luca, how's the private room looking for Wednesday night?" He waited while Luca checked. "It's not booked at all? Great. Could you book it in the name of Jim Olson?" Another pause. "For four."

"How about making that for six?" Burke asked.

Gabe turned toward him, lifting a brow. "Are you talking about yourself?"

"Yeah. I really like Italian. And judging from the take-out Luca dropped off for Mom, his food is Michelin-star delicious."

"Change that to a table for six," Gabe said. "Time?" He glanced over at Jim, factoring in the time it'd take for the movie to be over. "Around eight?"

Jim paled a bit, as if realizing what he was getting into. "That will be good," he said, not sounding all that confident, but he squared his shoulders, as if gearing up for a social occasion the way Burke might do before a game.

"Super." He turned back to his phone. "We'll see you Wednesday." After ending the call, he looked at Burke. "You just got to town. Where are you going to find a date?" Then he slapped his forehead. "Oh, wait! You're the big star pro football quarterback. You could probably walk into the market and find a bunch of women willing to go out with you." He paused a beat. "Of course, there's the problem that you've been gone long enough that most of the women who knew you have already gotten married. But you might have a chance with strangers who don't know all your flaws like we do."

"Ha ha," Burke said. "As a matter of fact, I have someone in mind."

"Who?" Jim and Gabe said together.

Burke crossed his arms, feeling pretty damn good about the idea that Gabe's suggestion could kill two birds with one stone. He would be helping Jim out, and even if Lily did try to weasel out of her agreement, he doubted she'd turn him down when she heard about Jim's dating dilemma. Besides, it wouldn't really be a date. There'd be two other couples. It'd just be a nice dinner out with friends. "Lily Carpenter," he announced.

"I did not see that coming," Gabe said.

CHAPTER FOURTEEN

ON MONDAY, Jim was sitting at a table in his home office, looking at a video on his laptop screen. "I like it," he said hesitantly. "But it seems very short."

"That's because it's a reel," Sage said. "For Instagram. I'm double posting this on my account. I have 200,000 followers. Admittedly, many are other marketing students or professionals, and a lot I picked up when I shared my left-at-the-altar story, but you never know how things will migrate.

"I've made some money from companies I feature, and also made a shorter Instagram story one for you. And a Tik-Tok, which is a better video platform but skews younger. I'm not sure what we'll get from it, but it never hurts to try. This is, after all, a tourist town, so spreading a wider net might work. Especially with the wedding business, which is why I started with that."

She was talking so fast, about so many unfamiliar things, Jim's head began spinning. "You shared your failed wedding story online?"

"Sure. I knew it would get me a bunch of followers," she said easily. "The more followers I have, the more I can be considered an influencer and get paid to feature things, so even with all the bills I had to pay, I still made money off a bad situation. But don't worry. As I said, I'm not charging you for handling your account."

"I have an account?"

"I set it up last night. You've already gained two hundred followers. That's a cool start. Here's one I did for Sensation Cajun." She showed him. "It's Sunday Suppers, showing some of his dishes. We do different ones every week."

"Along with waiting tables, you're doing social media for Bastien?"

"I have been for a while."

"Then why didn't you use him as your project?" Despite scoring high on IQ tests and being an HFA (a nonmedical term for high-functioning autism), Jim was still having difficulty sorting all this out. Not that he didn't spend a great deal of time on the internet, but that was on message boards with other people working with plant genomes. Not looking at videos of Sunday dinners, which, for him, was always a grilled cheese sandwich and Campbell's tomato soup made with water, not milk.

"Because he's doing everything right. He already had his account up to twenty-five thousand. I've just added a polish to the posts, stories and reels he was already doing. You, on the other hand, are a blank slate. I mean, your social media presence," she assured him. "Not you, personally."

"Do you have to get permission from the people in this reel to put them online?" he asked, hitting the key to replay the wedding photo. The bride was carrying a bouquet of peach peonies, which Sage had to know he grew because she'd seen them at the market. But he couldn't remember delivering them to a wedding lately.

"Don't worry. It's a stock video I bought. I edited it so it focuses on the bouquet as she walks down the aisle, hands it to her maid of honor, then throws it after the happy couple has been proclaimed man and wife."

"I've been to some friends' weddings," he said, relieved

to have something to say that wasn't another question. "And I've never understood that tradition."

"The belief is that the woman who catches the bouquet will be the next to get married."

"So I've been told," Jim said. "But that's not logical. Or realistic. Even if the woman who catches it turns out to be the next to marry, her odds of winning would involve a probability sampling method utilizing some form of random selection."

"You know what?" she asked.

"What?"

"I love watching your mind work. But sampling methods aside, it remains a popular superstition, and since I know you prefer facts, it started back in ancient England when female guests at the wedding would tear off pieces of the bride's dress or flowers in order to get good luck."

"That sounds very rude. And chaotic."

"It does, doesn't it? That's why brides started throwing their bouquets as far as they could to send the other women running after it."

"Then she could run in the other direction." Jim found that a very sensible solution to such foolish behavior.

Sage beamed like the sun. "Exactly. This reel is just a trial run. I figured with the June wedding season almost upon us, it would be good to open with a wedding theme. And point out that Blue House Farm is *the* place to get your wedding flowers on the peninsula."

"We are not the only farm selling flowers on the peninsula."

"True. And I'm sure the others are wonderful places, run by very nice people, but they don't have the media presence you're going to have.

"Don't worry." She placed a hand on his arm. "I'm also

sure that they have a loyal customer base, the same way you do. What we're mainly looking for is brides who are planning a wedding in Honeymoon Harbor, assuring them that we can provide the same stellar service any city can give them."

"That sounds reasonable," he said, noting that she'd used *we* instead of *you* as if they were partners in this enterprise.

"Thank you. We're also going to feature the market booth for locals. Which brings up another point. I can work the booth on my time off, but the restaurant's going to be picking up, which means that Bastien may need me for more hours. And I'm going to be spending time working on this. I was thinking that maybe we could hire someone to handle it two of the four days the market is open. I went through the financial record books you gave me to check out, and we—I mean, *you*—can afford it."

"You were correct the first time," Jim said. "When you said *we*. I realize that I'm a class project for you, but after all the plans you suggested at the lake, I do feel as if we've become a team. Until Jessie got married and became busy with her children and lavender garden, we were partners. She did the books and arranged the flowers, and I planned out the gardens. And began the hybrid and herbal business."

"Which was a great idea. But another thing about the booth…" Her voice trailed off. He'd noticed that she talked with her hands a great deal. Now they were clasped so tightly together at her waist, her knuckles were going pale.

"What about it?"

She inhaled deeply, then blew out a long breath. "I'm sorry. But it's boring."

"It's a farmers market booth. I'm not selling the booth. I'm selling flowers and herbs."

"Exactly. But you can't see that until you get right up to

it. You're lucky that you have an outside-facing one rather than having it stuck in those narrow aisles in the interior."

"My parents chose the spot when the market opened when I was young. They were two of the founders and on the board. It was much smaller then. Just a few local farmers. Now they accept vendors as far away as Yakima. And Grant County."

"On the other side of the Cascades? Where the apples come from."

"Yes. The oceanic climate here on the peninsula is unsatisfactory for commercial apple cultivation. But settlers in the early nineteenth century discovered the east side of the mountains' soil has a rich lava-ash and that its Mediterranean climate received far more sunshine than here on the west. Also, eastern arid climate means fewer insect and disease problems."

"Giving a better quality apple."

"Exactly. And there are many streams that serve as irrigation. Do you like the movie *Casablanca*?"

She blinked at his sudden turn in topic. "Of course. It's a classic. I can't count the number of times I've seen it."

"Would you like to see it again? It's playing Wednesday evening at the Olympic theater."

"Are you asking me on a date?"

Jim could feel the tips of his ears heating. "That was my intention. But if you feel that I'm harassing you in any way, like the 'hashtag Me Too' movement, I apologize for possibly crossing the line."

This time her smile lit up her eyes. "You'd never harass anyone," she said. "And yes, I'd enjoy seeing the movie again with you."

"Gabe Mannion and I were talking about it, and he suggested we go to Luca's Kitchen afterwards for dinner. They have a private room. But it wouldn't be just us. He suggested he and Chelsea attend, as well as Burke and Lily Carpenter."

"Lily is dating Burke Mannion, the football star?"

"So it appears."

"I had no idea he was back in town."

"He returned after his mother's accident."

"Hmm. I wonder how he knows Lily."

"He didn't say, and it didn't occur to me to ask." His mind had been focused on asking Sage out on a date. And to be truthful, he didn't have that much interest in other people's social lives.

"Well, I think that's a lovely plan. What time should I be ready?"

For a moment, Jim was tongue-tied. He'd stumbled into asking her in a very poor segue from apple growing, but despite his nerves being so tangled, he'd managed to get the words out. Having braced himself for rejection, he was surprised by her immediate acceptance.

"The film begins at six. If we arrive at five thirty, that will give us time to buy our tickets and find our seats. I'm told it's a very popular movie. It runs an hour and forty-two minutes, so with the restaurant right down the street, we shouldn't have any problem with our dinner reservation at eight."

With the movie being so popular, it meant that the theater could be very crowded. Yet on the drive back to the farm from Gabe's boat shop, Jim had assured himself that it would be all right. Because they'd mostly be in the dark, and people were not supposed to talk during movies, so there wouldn't be a loud buzz of conversation until when they were leaving the theater with the crowd. Which would be a challenge. But one he was willing to subject himself to in order to go on a date with Sage Fletcher.

"It's one of the best movies ever made," she said. "Thank you for asking. I haven't been on a date since the jerk took off to Bali with the wedding planner. I'm looking forward to it. And now that we've settled that, let's get back to the booth."

As she began suggesting putting the type of plastic advertising wrap that was done on cars and even buses on the booth, or at least painting it in bright colors so it would stand out against the more gray-brown weatherworn ones, Jim tried to concentrate on her words, but she could have been speaking in Klingon. He set his face in an attentive appearance, nodding at what seemed the appropriate times, while inside, he was feeling as if he'd just won an Olympic gold medal.

Jim knew that his parents and sister loved him. He also knew that they worried he might never have what most people considered a "normal" life. He'd begun to think they might be correct and was all right with that idea. He had big plans with his hybrids. That was enough to keep him busy. But every so often, when picking up his grocery order—he'd always call it in on Monday mornings, then pick it up at three o'clock sharp—he'd see people strolling down the street, or out on the pier, or getting married in the lacy white gazebo at the park, all looking as happy as he knew he'd be when he finally managed to create that blue rose.

He wasn't expecting to fall in love the way people did in the Hallmark movies, be loved in return, then live happily ever after. That was, perhaps, too much of a reach. But right now, he was going to enjoy the heady anticipation of having a movie and dinner date with the pretty, intelligent Sage Fletcher.

CLEARWATER COMMUNITY COLLEGE was located in a heavily wooded area of town, and Burke got lost on the winding, one-way roads more than once before finally locating the administration building that housed Lily's office. Newer than most in town, it had been painted a deep brown to blend in with its surroundings, and the soaring front of it, which was mostly glass, reminded him of the bow of the old clipper sailing ships that had once populated the harbor. Contrasting with the more modern architectural style, a sixteen-foot-tall totem pole, carved from red cedar, depicting a bear holding a pair of salmon and topped by an eagle with outstretched wings, greeted visitors in a garden beside the door.

A friendly young woman sitting behind a counter in the foyer gave him a visitor's badge and directed him to an office on the third floor. When he entered, a young man, whose desk name plaque read Paul Kallappa, was on the phone. He smiled, and held up a finger, suggesting he'd be just a moment, quickly finished the call, then said, "Good afternoon. I'm sorry. Things are a little hectic right now while we're planning the school's entry in the Heritage Day parade. How may I help you, Mr. Mannion?"

Having gotten used to being recognized, Burke simply asked if Lily was in. "She just got back from a meeting with the diversity committee," the young man said. "Let me tell her you're here."

Burke would have preferred to have just walked in, given that he wasn't sure she'd see him here at the office—in public—but agreed to wait while the young man got on the phone again and announced him. A moment later, the door to the adjoining office opened.

"Good afternoon, Mr. Mannion," she greeted him professionally, as if he didn't know what she looked like beneath those business clothes. She was wearing a slim black skirt, a white tuxedo-style shirt with a pleated front beneath a little black ribbon tied around the neck, and flats. And a pair of black-framed glasses he'd never seen her wearing. Her long hair was pulled into a ponytail she'd tied at the base of her neck. "Why don't you come in and tell me why you're here? Would you like some coffee?"

"I'm fine, thanks," Burke said.

"Fine," she echoed, moving aside and gesturing him in. After she'd shut the door, she folded her arms and asked, "What are you doing here?"

"That should be obvious. I came to talk to you about our date."

"I told you, I need more time."

"That's why I'm here. To ask you out Wednesday night. For a movie and dinner. It's classics night at the Olympic, and they're showing *Casablanca*."

"I love that movie. But again, I need time."

"I understand that. But something unexpected turned up. Jim Olson stopped by Gabe's boat shop yesterday afternoon. He wanted to ask Gabe about how to ask a girl on a date. Seems he's smitten with someone named Sage."

"Oh, that's so sweet. I sent her out to his farm to ask if he'd let her help with her semester marketing project. She's taking a course from me. I have to admit I hadn't foreseen that happening."

"Jim called Gabe, who called me, and told me she'd accepted."

"I'm happy for him. And her. He's very sweet." Lily sat behind the desk, gesturing him to the chair on the other side, effectively using the desk as a barrier between them. "But what does that have to do with me?"

"Well, I was already there, visiting Gabe, so we got to

talking with Jim, and one thing sort of led to another, and after Gabe suggested they double-date at Luca's because it has a private room—"

"Which would be less stressful for Jim because he hates crowds."

"Exactly." Burke flashed his best smile. The one he used while being interviewed on camera after a winning game. "Like I said, one thing led to another, and I heard myself suggesting that we make it a triple date. That'll make it easier on Jim. Because with Burke and Chelsea, and you and me, along with Sage, there'd be more people to help keep the conversation going if Jim gets nervous."

She put her elbows on the table, laced her fingers together, rested her chin on them and gave him a look that told him she'd spotted the admittedly obvious quarterback sneak play. "You're using Jim to get me to go out with you."

"No, I'm helping the guy have a social life. Which you can't deny he's entitled to, even though it's not all that easy for him to connect with people. But they've already had burgers from the pub out at the lake, so—"

"Wait a minute." She held up a hand. "They had lunch at the lake? And that wasn't a date?"

"Jim said they were talking about business. About her working on a marketing plan."

"Right. But there's no reason they couldn't have had that discussion at the farm. Hmm. She didn't mention anything about going out to the lake. I wonder if it was her idea."

"That'd be my guess. But it also seems to have gotten him interested in raising things to a more personal level. And yes, I'll readily admit that going out for a movie and dinner with you, even if we won't be alone, would not only be a new experience, but the icing on the cake."

She gave him another long look. "Let me make some

calls before I answer. You didn't give me much time to fix things."

"Like I said, the opportunity unexpectedly arose, so I grabbed it. I realize I should apologize, but my only excuse is that despite how we ended things, I've missed you. It also occurred to me that having us be seen out with others first makes it appear more casual. Not so much a date, but friends and family getting together."

"It's not a bad idea," she admitted. "But, again, you didn't give me much time. Did you tell Gabe about us?"

"No. So far, only Quinn knows. Gabe is obviously wondering, but I left before Jim did, so he didn't get a chance to grill me."

She leaned back and folded her arms again, which, rather than intimidating him, only drew his attention to those pearl buttons running down the center of that pleated blouse. "You do realize life isn't a football game, and you don't get to call all the plays, don't you?"

Her question shattered a vision of unfastening those buttons, one by one. But it didn't stop him from wondering what, exactly, she was wearing beneath that tidy white blouse.

"Of course I do," he said. "But for the record, you spent three months calling all the plays when we were together. Seems I should be allowed to call an audible once in a while."

She shook her head. He might not have known her backstory until now, but he'd learned to read her well. Although she was trying to hide it, he saw repressed humor in her gaze. "Get out of here," she said. "I've got to try to gather everyone up before Wednesday night."

"I'm on my way." He stood up and began to leave, pausing at the door to look back at her. "May I ask one question?"

"Just one. I really am busy."

"Could you wear that outfit Wednesday night?"

"This?" She glanced down at herself. "Why?"

"Because, I was thinking, just maybe, if you were up for it, after dinner we could go to your place and play stern boss and sexy secretary."

Instead of throwing that glass paperweight on her desk at his head, she laughed. Which he found encouraging. "Go," she said, waving her hand toward the door.

"I'm going. But just keep the idea in mind, okay?"

Just as he was reaching for the doorknob, she called out to him. "Burke?"

He glanced back over his shoulder.

"I've missed you, too."

"Thanks for sharing that," he said. "I'll see you Wednesday night." Then he left while he was still apparently, hopefully, ahead.

CHAPTER FIFTEEN

DRIVING BACK TO his parents' house from the college, as Burke passed Blue House Farm, a thought occurred to him. Since the farm's truck was in the driveway, he pulled up next to it. Then, after not getting any answer at the door, went around back to the greenhouse, where he found Jim.

"Hey," he greeted him. "I just realized that there was something Gabe and I should have told you. If Sage likes the movie, you do, too."

"She has already said she like it."

"Good. But if you don't, don't argue with her."

"I don't enjoy arguments," Jim said.

"Great. Things are easier if you just go along with whatever she says on a first date. That is, if you want a second one."

"I do," Jim said. "I'll agree with whatever she thinks of the movie."

"Okay. And while this may be hard, remember that the story is fiction. Not real life. Try not to point out all the things that are illogical. Because it's best just to go with the flow."

"What if she brings up something illogical?"

Knowing how difficult keeping silent would be for Jim, Burke backpedaled a bit. "Then you'll have something to discuss. You can carefully make your point without being pedantic, because no one enjoys being lectured to. And don't insist on being right. Sometimes you have to agree to disagree."

"Dating sounds very complicated."

Burke laughed. "You're not going to get any argument from me on that."

LILY SAT AT her desk, staring out over the wooded campus. She'd hadn't expected to tell Burke that she'd missed him, but now that the words had been said, it was too late to take them back. Also, Wednesday night wasn't actually a date, but merely a dinner out with friends. It wasn't a big deal. They were both single. After all, she was close friends with Gabe's wife, Chelsea, as well as friendly with Jim, and Sage was one of her students. Even if they did continue to see each other while he was here, it didn't have to mean anything. Lots of people had summer flings. That's what vacations were for. Like Gabe and Chelsea, but they were undoubtedly in the minority.

As for her past, as the therapist she'd seen after changing her name had told her, she didn't have anything to be ashamed or embarrassed about. It was her parents, her grandmother, and all those lawyers who should have been ashamed, using an innocent child as a weapon.

Picking up the phone, she called Chelsea first. "Hi," she said when her friend answered. "I heard we're triple-dating Wednesday night."

"Gabe just called me," Chelsea said. "I'm looking forward to it. Brianna told me that you and Burke had known each other in New York."

"We met at a fundraiser I'd organized."

"Small world. That you'd both end up here."

Lily heard the question in her friend's voice. "That's why I'm calling. I was wondering if you could come over tonight. Maybe for drinks and some conversation."

"I'd love that. We've both been so busy with Heritage

Day preparations, we haven't had any real girl talk in a long time."

"I thought I'd make it a group night," Lily said. "I'm also calling Brianna, Kylee, Mai and Jolene. I was thinking about stopping by Don Diego's and picking up dinner."

Diego Chavez had started his business with Taco the Town, a popular food truck that he'd kept for special events after having established a full-service restaurant that was not only a play on his first name, but also an homage to Don Diego de la Vega, aka Zorro. Various posters of the many movies made about the fictional Mexican hero had been framed on the walls, going back to the 1920 silent classic starring Douglas Fairbanks. In the center of the main dining room, he'd had a replica of his Taco the Town truck built, with seating for a dozen that had proven especially popular with Honeymoon Harbor children.

"That sounds like fun. I'll bring the tequila and limes for margaritas. What time?"

"About six thirty?"

"Works for me. I'll see you then."

Despite the lack of advance notice, all the others immediately agreed to show up, making Lily wonder if there'd already been some discussions about her and Burke. "Well, if there were, they'll definitely be answered tonight," she said to herself as she hung up from her last call and took her jacket from the coat tree.

"I'm off," she said to her assistant, who was currently working on a list of suggested food items the culinary students might make for the Heritage Day celebration. Paul, a member of the Olympic Peninsula's Jamestown S'Klallam tribe, had suggested serving oysters from the tribal seafood company. After surviving on local seafood and shellfish for ten thousand years in the area, the tribe's oysters were now being served at some of the top restaurants throughout the country. He'd also suggested cooking salmon over wood in a firepit. Which would probably require town council approval, given that the spring had been unusually dry.

"Have a good evening."

His tone suggested he assumed she was going out with Burke. There was no way to keep any relationship they might have a secret in Honeymoon Harbor. Perhaps influenced by the name of their town, or the fact that like all small towns, they needed to keep their population growing, it seemed a large part of the community was invested in everyone else's romances.

"Thanks," she said. "Have a good one yourself."

"I hope to. I'm taking my girlfriend to your brother's pub for a sunset dinner. We have a table reserved in the raised view section. Anna loves Quinn's sweet chili lime wings."

"He's been making those for home cookouts since he was a kid. Brianna told me that Burke used to take them to team meetings. Have a great time."

"Thanks." He paused, as if planning for a way to say something else. Hoping it wasn't some fire she'd have to put out, she managed not to look at her watch, but instead asked, "Is there a problem with our entry?"

"No. That's fine. It's nothing," he said, not quite meeting her eyes. He glanced down at his desk drawer.

"Okay." She blew out a breath. "What's up?"

He didn't immediately answer, but instead opened the drawer and pulled out a small black velvet bag. Untying the gilt ribbon drawstring, he took out a small royal-blue box, then opened it. "What do you think?" he asked, nerves making his voice higher than the usual baritone that sounded so good in the school a cappella group.

Lily felt her eyes moisten as she looked down at the small, round cut diamond surrounded by smaller ones.

"The jeweler told me that it's a halo cut," Paul said. "Those little diamonds are called *melee*. He suggested them to add more sparkle."

"It's beautiful. And it definitely sparkles." She blinked away tears and covered her heart with her crossed hands. "Oh, Paul, Anna is going to love it."

He'd worked for her for the two years he'd been attending school, and on top of keeping a straight four-point average, last month he'd received a job offer to work as a phlebotomist at Honeymoon Harbor General Hospital, where his soon-to-be fiancée was already working as an RN in the family birthing center.

"I hope she says yes."

"Of course she will." Lily had met Anna Garcia at several school functions, and she was an intelligent, sweet woman whose eyes sparkled like that diamond whenever she looked at Paul. "You two are going to have the best life. I couldn't be happier for you."

"Do you think I should ask her after dinner? Or before?"

"It depends. How nervous are you going to be?"

"I think super nervous. Although I'm pretty sure she'll say yes, because we've been talking about marriage, it's still a major decision."

"Here's an idea. Why don't you get there a little early? I'll call and have the hostess tell you that it'll be another fifteen or twenty minutes, but you're welcome to wait at the bar. It's going to be a beautiful evening, so you can suggest walking out on the pier instead. Then you won't have an audience for your proposal. When you get back, you can celebrate with champagne. On me. Dinner, too. So order whatever you want. Quinn and I will work it out. Meanwhile, does she have a favorite dessert?"

"She likes the chocolate raspberry cheesecake."

"Great. That's always on the menu, but I'll make sure they don't allow it to sell out. So, put the phone on voice mail and we'll both leave early."

"But—"

"How many times are you going to propose in your life?"

"Only one," he said with a certainty Lily found herself envying. Some people found love so easily. To her, it was the equivalent of going white water rafting after climbing Mount Rainier.

"Then go home. Get ready. And relax. You've got this."

"Thanks, Lily. I'm going to miss working for you."

Damn. Those stupid tears were threatening again. "I'm going to miss you, too," she said truthfully. "But it's not like either of us is going far. I only ask one thing."

"What?"

"An invitation to the wedding."

"You're definitely on the list."

"Thank you. Oh, and be sure to take tissues with you," she said.

The brows above those doe-brown eyes lowered with concern. "Do you think she'll cry?"

"Sweetie, you almost made *me* cry. Of course she will. But happy tears are the best."

As she left the building, she called Quinn and told him about the impending engagement. "Don't worry, I'll take care of it," he said. "Though you do realize that ever since Jarle gave his heart to Ashley, he's such a fan of love, I'm probably going to have a giant Viking cook crying in the kitchen."

Despite being on edge from her looming confession, Lily laughed.

As she headed toward Don Diego's, Paul's news had her feeling much more positive about life in general. How bad could things be if nice people like Jarle and Ashley, and now Paul and Anna, continued to fall in love?

THE GREAT CONFESSION that she'd been fearing since Burke's arrival went easier than Lily could have hoped for. She'd picked up three platters of Taste of the Truck, a tasting menu featuring the most popular dishes Diego had sold from his Taco the Town truck. The platters had samples of something for everyone: nachos with the best guacamole she'd ever tasted; cheesy tomato, corn, and black bean empanadas; street tacos made with fresh Pacific cod; local Dungeness crab tostada triangles; flank steak fajitas; and fudge brownies made with what Diego had told her were the important three Cs—chocolate, cinnamon and cayenne.

Since margaritas were also on the menu, not wanting to risk anyone driving tipsy, she'd arranged for a limo to pick everyone up and bring them to the cottage and back home. Lonnie Weaver, the son of now retired longtime cabdriver Earl Weaver, had returned home from eastern Washington's Gonzaga College with a degree in business administration, bought his dad out, and immediately purchased several more vehicles to expand the town's only taxi business. The newly named Honeymoon Harbor Limousine Service had proven popular with the local wedding business as well as tourist trips to the national park and coastal towns.

It wasn't often the entire group of friends was all together, so the dinner part of the evening was a freewheeling discussion about Sarah Mannion's accident and Jim Olson, who was nearly agoraphobic when it came to leaving the farm, being seen in town with Sage Fletcher. After everyone oohed and aahed over recent photos of Kylee and Mai's daughter, Clara, the conversation moved to plans for the Heritage Day celebration to this year's Library Adventurers, which Chelsea had created as part reading summer program, part field trips around the area to learn firsthand what the kids were reading about. She'd met Gabe when she'd been struggling to talk him into letting the adventurers visit his boat shop while he'd been building his faering.

Both Kylee, who took wedding photos, and Jolene, who did hair and makeup for many of the bridal parties, were expecting a busy summer. A mama orca had been seen nearby with her calf, the first of the year. Which wasn't all that unusual, given that Honeymoon Harbor was on the "whale trail," a part of the state where orcas, humpbacks, and gray whales were a common sight, but the first baby of the season was always a reason to celebrate.

Finally, while the others moved from the kitchen into the front room, Lily whipped up glasses of *carajillo*—an espresso-and-brandy after-dinner drink—on the espresso machine Sarah had surprised her with when her friends had helped her move into the first house she'd ever owned.

Having made *her* drink with more brandy than the others—liquid courage, she'd thought as she'd prepared them—Lily sat down and took a sip and a deep breath. Then, feeling as if she was standing on one of the beach cliffs, she dove straight into the topic.

After finishing the story she'd finally shared with Burke, there wasn't a dry eye in a room. And it wasn't resentment for her having essentially lied to them about her identity she saw in their shiny wet eyes. It was sympathy.

"So," she said, "that's my story, and I'm sorry that I wasn't forthright about who I was."

"You showed us who you were every day," Kylee said. "The woman we've all come to love."

"I'm amazed you went through all that abuse and managed to come out such a normal, warm and caring person." This came from Chelsea, who'd survived losing her younger sister to cancer. As far as Lily was concerned, that was harder than what she'd experienced.

"I don't think any of us know what we can endure until we have to," Mai said. Lily had heard the story of how she'd never known her grandfather, who'd died too young in a forest in France, fighting the Germans in World War II while her family had been in a Japanese internment camp back home in Hawaii.

"I thought you'd be angry at me for not being truthful."

"We all have things we want to keep to ourselves," Brianna said.

"Like when you and Seth believed you were keeping your affair secret, while everyone in town knew," Jolene said.

"Not one person in town said anything," Brianna said.

"Oh, honey, everyone was talking, just not to either of you. But because we all loved you both and had seen how hard Zoe's death had been on Seth..." Kylee said. "Being a widower had nearly crushed him. But when you came home, we could see him coming back to life. Which is why we all left you two alone. To work things out."

"I don't know if I can work things out with Burke," Lily said.

"What?" every woman in the room asked, except for Brianna and Chelsea, who was part of the triple date. But even Chelsea appeared openly curious, which suggested that Burke hadn't told Gabe about their history.

"What does Burke have to do with this?" Jolene asked.

"What could have happened between him arriving in town and tonight?" Kylee asked.

"You and he had a thing, didn't you?" Brianna asked. "I knew the story of you two meeting at that fundraiser wasn't the whole explanation. The electricity in the hospital waiting room was off the charts."

"It was complicated." Lily was starting to sound like a broken record to her own ears. She sighed. Ran her hands through her hair. While working for that charity in New York, she'd put on a legal poker tournament, and the winner had taught her about *tells*, gestures that give away emotions. She'd realized at the time that running her hands through her hair was hers, and as nervous as she'd been the past few days, it was a wonder she hadn't gone bald.

"We really did meet at that fundraiser. And I know it sounds bad, but we left together and went to my apartment."

"Like none of us haven't had a hookup," Kylee said. "And good move going to your place. That way you weren't the one doing the walk of shame."

"It's worse." Now that she was getting the truth out, Lily went all the way and told them about the restrictions she'd put on their relationship in trying to keep it a secret.

Rather than being judgmental, Brianna laughed. "I'd have paid to see my brother in a Jets jacket and cap."

"As he's belatedly pointed out to me, that photo would've not only made the photographer a lot of money but would have hurt him terribly with his fan base and especially other team members."

"Not being a football fan, you wouldn't have understood the intensity of fandom," Brianna said. "Though, nothing against you, but I am a bit surprised he was willing to do that."

"It says a man in love to me," Jolene said.

"I agree," Mai said. "So, it wasn't just a brief fling?"

"No. We were together for three months."

"And no one found out?" Kylee asked.

"I don't think so. Maybe my doorman recognized him, but if he'd gotten caught calling any reporters, he'd have been fired. One thing I loved about my building was that the doormen were very discreet. Burke told me that he wants to spend at least part of the summer while he's home, maybe until training camp, reconnecting. But I don't know if we can overcome what I did." Lily felt her eyes tearing up again. "Especially since I broke up with him by text as I left New York."

"Ouch," Chelsea said. "But I can understand how, after your childhood, you'd want to avoid conflict."

"Of course you can move on," Brianna said soothingly. "Admittedly, you wounded his pride. Taking off without any warning and dumping him with that text. But I know my brother. He'll get past that."

"We're triple-dating Wednesday night," Chelsea announced. "Burke and Lily, Jim Olson and Sage Fletcher, and Gabe and me."

"Jim has a date?" Brianna asked, clearly surprised by this development.

"He and Sage are working together on a marketing plan for the farm," Lily said. "It's her semester project. They had one business meeting, but apparently he stopped by Gabe's boat shop for advice on how to ask her out, and the plan formed from there."

She'd survived her confession with far more ease than she'd expected, but still, Lily was pleased when the conversation turned to speculation about Jim and Sage's possibly budding relationship.

CHAPTER SIXTEEN

TUESDAY MORNING, since Sage had classes and wouldn't be coming by the greenhouse, instead of getting right to work, Jim called Thairapy. Jolene's mother's salon and spa, which Seth Harper had remodeled, was located in the old lighthouse keeper's house. Jolene had joined the business after returning from Los Angeles.

Ten minutes later, she greeted him with a wide, friendly smile. "I was glad to get your call," she said. "Even though I had you booked for the first of the month." Jim always had a haircut on the first day of the month. Unless it fell on a Sunday. Then it was moved forward to Monday.

"My schedule changed," he said as he sat down in the chair she'd swung around for him. "I'm grateful for you fitting me into your work schedule."

"Oh, it's no big deal. I had some time before my next client. Also, I would've fit you in anyway, so you'll look all spiffed up for your date tomorrow."

"You know about that?" he asked as she put a black cape around his shoulders.

"This is Honeymoon Harbor," she reminded him. "But I didn't hear it through the grapevine. I had a girls' night dinner last night at Lily's, and she said that she and Burke and Chelsea and Gabe are going out with you and Sage."

"On a triple date," he said as he followed her over to the shampoo sink. "Gabe thought it would be a good way to break the ice. We're going to see *Casablanca*, then have dinner at Luca's."

"That sounds like a lot of fun. I love that movie, although I always cry at the end. You might want to take some tissues, in case Sage doesn't bring any with her. And don't worry, when you're done, I'll have you looking as hot as Nick Jonas, whose hair I cut once when he and his brothers did a concert in LA."

Jim didn't have any idea who Nick Jonas was, but he trusted Jolene not to do anything crazy. One nice thing about getting a haircut from her was that he wasn't forced to participate in the conversation, because she always talked while she snipped away at his hair. Today she chatted about the scented candles she and her mother were making to sell for the Heritage Day celebration, and filled him in on other local news, including her mother dating Mike Mannion, Burke's artist uncle.

"I swear," she said, grinning at him in the mirror, "you'd think she was sixteen again. She had such a tough life until a few years ago, especially after the cancer scare, that she really deserves to be happy. She went there with some book club friends for his wine and art night."

"Wine and art?"

"They drink wine while he teaches them to paint. From what she's told me, it's grand fun." She pointed the scissors at a watercolor of the mountain meadows in full bloom framed on the wall. "This is one of her works. Mike says she's very talented, and they've been spending a lot of time together while he helps her explore her artistic horizons." Another grin. "I suspect they're exploring more, but right now Mom and I are in 'don't ask, don't tell' mode. From the not-so-subtle questions he asks when I cut his hair, I suspect he might even have a future in mind."

"I hope it turns out well for her," Jim responded, having found that was usually an appropriate response for any situation in flux. He was also thinking that Jolene's outgoing personality was very similar to that of Kylee and Sage. His monthly haircut was always an enjoyable experience.

"Thanks. I do, too." She brushed some stray hairs off the back of his neck, whipped off the cape, and ran some sort of gel through his hair.

"This cut is called a classic taper," she said. "It's Nick's classic gentleman look, which goes really well with your face." She picked up a comb, ran it through his hair, then turned the chair around so he was facing the mirror again. "So…what do you think?"

"It's very different," he said.

She was standing behind him, and he saw her brows furrow in her reflection. "Different good? Or bad?"

"Different good."

"I'm glad you approve." Giving him a hand mirror, she turned him so that he could see the very much shorter back and sides she'd blended into the top, which was also shorter than he was accustomed to. "I look like me. But better." Less nerdy.

That earned a dazzling grin. "I told you, you're a dead ringer for Nick Jonas." She went over to a magazine rack, pulled out a copy of *People*, flipped through some pages and showed him a photo. "See?"

Other than the haircut, Jim couldn't see a resemblance to the man he now knew was a pop superstar.

"You both have the same shaped face. You, my friend, look really hot. This will be super easy to style," she assured him. "Just run a tiny bit of this gel through your hair after drying, comb it, and it's set for the day. Would you like some spray?"

"No, thank you."

As he paid at the counter, he saw some bottles of after-shave next to a display of cosmetics. He'd noticed in many of the movies he'd watched, women would talk about how good their boyfriends smelled. As soon as she'd seen the direction of his gaze, before she swiped his card, Jolene chose a bottle, opened it, took his hand and then spritzed a bit on his wrist. "Smell," she said.

Jim had been afraid it would be a strong perfumed smell. It wasn't. "I like it."

"It's woodsy, with a bit of spice, but light enough that you won't overpower any scent Sage or the others might be wearing—or bother anyone else in the theater or res-taurant. It's a scent my mother and I created."

"I'll take it. And the gel." The way she blinked suggested she was as surprised as he was by his impulsive response.

"Terrific." She put them in a recycled brown paper bag with a lighthouse on the front, then rang up his card and had him sign the screen.

"You forgot the aftershave and gel," he pointed out.

"They're on the house," she said. "My good luck gift."

Jim had learned to accept gifts because gift giving was an act of kindness, like the flowers he'd taken over to the Mannions' farm after Sarah had returned home from the hospital. Even if it wasn't something the recipient would have chosen for themselves, it was proper to pretend other-wise to make the giver happy. From Jolene's dazzling smile, it appeared that this gift had pleased them both.

"Thank you," he said.

"You're very welcome. Oh! Should I move your next ap-pointment to a month from today?"

"That would be a good idea," he agreed. And with yet another life change to his strictly planned monthly ritual,

Jim began to feel more and more like the *Star Trek* crew members must have felt, heading off to a new frontier.

"IF I'D KNOWN I was going to be eating so well, I would've gotten in an accident years ago," Sarah said over a dinner of Dungeness crab étouffée with a fresh spring greens salad from Sensation Cajun. Overcoming resistance from John, who'd wanted her to stay in bed despite receiving the okay from Dr. Kim, she was sitting at the kitchen table with her husband, Burke, and her parents, who lived in a cozy single-level house Seth had built for them on the property.

John's parents had moved to a waterfront house on Lake Washington, adjacent to Seattle, after his father had sold the bank his family had established during the town's boom days. Though it wasn't a topic of open discussion, Burke had heard that it had taken the senior Mannion a few years to forgive his son for deciding to grow Christmas trees rather than take over the bank. The rift had ended with Quinn's birth, but they still weren't as close as they were with his mom's parents.

"Don't even joke about that," John said. "You scared us all half to death."

"Amen to that," Harriet, Burke's grandmother, said. "I nearly wore my rosary beads down to a nub."

"We stopped by the church to light a candle," Jerome, her husband of over half a century, said. "She insisted on lighting so many, I was afraid we'd set off the smoke alarm."

"I wanted to make sure I had God's attention," Harriet said. "And it wasn't that many."

"Two rows' worth," he countered.

"So? It's not as if I took them all." She stabbed a piece of crab with her fork. "I left three rows for others."

"I appreciate the gesture, Mama," Sarah said.

"I just wanted to remind God that it wasn't your time," Harriet said briskly. "That having a child go before a parent is not the way it's supposed to work. So if he had to work a miracle, that was the time to do it."

Burke exchanged a look with his dad and could tell they were thinking the same thing. That they weren't sure even the big guy would want to cross Harriet Harper when she put her mind to something.

"It's lovely that everyone has been so generous," Sarah said. "We probably have enough food in the freezer for a month."

"You're the heart of the town, love," John said. "Everyone wants to help. You're supposed to be resting. Though I could've made the meals, I'll have to admit that it's nice to have such a variety of choices."

"Your father used to cook seduction dinners for his roommates," Sarah revealed.

"Why have I never heard that story?" Burke asked.

"Because your mother exaggerates. The real story is that my senior year at UW, I moved into an apartment with three other guys. None of us could cook. The most any of us had ever done was burn hot dogs and s'mores over a fire, or boil ramen. But that can get old after a while. So does take-out Chinese, pizza, and fried chicken, which we couldn't afford all that often anyway."

"Especially since he was saving money to fly back East to see me," Sarah said.

"Which you didn't happen to mention to us," Harriet said.

"True," Sarah admitted. "But look how well it worked out." Burke had to bite his lip when his grandmother rolled her eyes like a teenage girl.

"I'm not going to deny that," Harriet said.

"I'll have to admit John turned out to be good enough for her," Jerome allowed.

Burke and his father exchanged another look. "Thank you, Jerome," John said. "I've tried my best."

"Get back to the seduction story," Burke said.

"It's not a seduction story," John insisted. "Finally deciding one of us needed to learn to cook, I bought a couple books, watched reruns of *The Galloping Gourmet*, and picked up enough skills to feed myself and the other guys, who chipped in for groceries. Then they got the idea to pay me to cook dinners they could heat up and pretend that they'd made. Because apparently girls find guys who can cook sexy."

"Thus the term 'seduction dinners,'" his mother said in a teasing way that suggested this was a conversation they still enjoyed after all these years. "And, I have to admit, it works. I accepted your father's proposal after we'd both ended up on the same plane back to SeaTac. He was returning from Nepal, and I was coming from Japan." Her brow furrowed. "You know, I'd never thought of it before, but that seems like an amazing coincidence."

"It was kismet," John insisted. "No way could I have arranged for something that complicated to happen. I will admit that I'd spent a lot of nights staring up at the wide starry Himalayan sky, pondering different scenarios to win you back. But there weren't any phones where I was living, and I'd already spent twenty-nine hours in the air on two different flights when I landed in LAX. I didn't know if us flying together on the same plane back to SeaTac was a crazy coincidence, luck or fate. But whatever it was, I sure as hell wasn't going to question it."

"We didn't exactly fly together," she told Burke. "Your father was in first class. I was in coach."

"The Peace Corps paid for first class?" That was a surprise.

"No," John said. "But, by another fortunate coincidence, when I checked in for the flight, the woman behind the counter told me that her mother, who'd married a Peace Corps worker, was from Nepal. Since a seat was available, she upgraded me."

"That's always been his story," Sarah pointed out. "But he'd obviously used his superpower on her."

"I have a superpower?" John asked.

"You do," she said. "And you're well aware of it. It's your manly charm."

"I thought the boy was a bit too cocky for his britches," Jerome said gruffly.

"As you claimed, many times," Sarah agreed. "Yet he eventually won you over."

"That's because he promised to be good to you. And kept his word."

"I meant it," John said. "But even if I hadn't, I wouldn't have had much choice, since you'd threatened to cut me up into little pieces and use me for fish bait if I ever hurt your daughter."

Burke had heard that story many times over the years. But it still made him laugh. The funny thing was, as tough as the wiry old fisherman was even now, Burke wasn't entirely certain the threat hadn't had some truth to it.

"You charmed the ticket agent the same way you charmed the flight attendant," Sarah said. "The one who put her C cups in your face when she bent down to serve you breakfast."

"I didn't think you were watching," he said. "Every time I glanced back, before they pulled the curtain shut, I saw you reading a book."

"I've always been an exceptional multitasker. Which was important, being a high school teacher, then principal, along with being the mother to five children."

"You're stellar," John told her, his heart in his Irish blue eyes. "But I definitely didn't encourage her. And she undoubtedly got the message that I wasn't interested when I sent that drink back to you."

"A mimosa," Sarah remembered.

"Which you accepted."

"Only because you'd caused such a stir, everyone around me was watching. There were two elderly ladies who, by the end of the flight, undoubtedly had us engaged."

John's smile was slow. And Burke thought, his grandfather was right. It *was* a bit cocky. Then again, as Aiden had pointed out after he'd become police chief, Honeymoon Harbor's mayor could talk just about anyone into anything. "That took another day."

"When you kidnapped me to take me to your family's coast house instead of mine."

"We needed to talk things out. Set some misunderstandings straight."

"I'm not going to argue that." She sighed. "Love is so different when you're young and afraid of taking a misstep that will mess things up."

"True." John reached out, took her hand, and after tracing a heart in the center of her palm, pressed a light kiss on it. "But we were always meant to be together, so fate gave us a second chance. No way was I not going to take advantage of the opportunity."

"Your father had it all planned out," Sarah said, something Burke hadn't known. "He called from the airport and had your uncle take some wine and food out to the house. After we arrived, he grilled me a steak with a baked potato. And served Boston cream pie for dessert. Mike, being Mike, had failed to include anything green, but it was still a lovely dinner. He also plied me with wine."

"Now that's an exaggeration," John defended himself. "You may have been a bit mellow."

"And jet-lagged," she reminded him.

"We both were. But you were a long way from even being buzzed."

"True. But only because I wanted to keep a clear head so I could remember everything single detail of that night." They exchanged a warm look that once again had Burke thinking that's what he wanted for himself. A partnership based on love that could stand the test of time. The trick was, he had to figure out how to convince Lily such a thing was possible.

"So, speaking of dinners," his mother said, briskly segueing from his parents' life to Burke's, "I hear you have a dinner date with Lily Carpenter tomorrow evening."

"Wow, that got around fast." People might use the term "New York minute" as a description of fast, but gossip traveled at supersonic speeds in Honeymoon Harbor.

"Mia had this afternoon's assignment to keep me from doing anything I wasn't supposed to—"

"We're only watching out for you," John said, for what Burke guessed to be the millionth time since his mom had gotten home from the hospital.

"I know." Sarah sighed. "Anyway, Mia got a call from Gabe, who'd asked her and Kylee to allow Hannah and Hailey to stay at their house while he and Chelsea went out on a triple date with Jim and Sage and Burke and Lily."

"It was Gabe's idea," Burke said when all heads turned his way. "Because Jim Olson showed up at the boat shop to get instructions on how to ask Sage out on a date, and what he should do. I was hanging out there, so we suggested dinner and a movie. Then Gabe got the idea to make it a double date, so Jim wouldn't have to experience those dreaded drawn-out silences that can happen on first dates."

"And you suggested going along, too?" John asked as he took another sip of coffee. There was no wine with this dinner while Burke's mom was continuing to have a hopefully uneventful recovery.

"The more the merrier," Burke's grandfather said.

"I didn't realize you knew Lily Carpenter." His mom's tone was easily casual, but Burke had no trouble hearing the question in it.

"We met in New York," he said. "I was one of the 'celebrities' at an event she put on for a food hunger foundation." He'd put the word *celebrities* in air quotes, because while he couldn't deny enjoying some of the fame that came with being a pro quarterback with the largest media audience in the country, with family, it felt a bit like when he'd been a full-of-himself top high school player in the state.

"That's quite a coincidence that you'd meet again on the opposite side of the country," Sarah said.

"I saw her at the hospital." Someone was bound to tell her, so he figured he should get ahead of speculation.

She smiled, as if reading his mind, which, when they were kids, they all thought she could do. Along with those eyes-in-the-back-of-her-head thing. "I heard. Nurses can be very chatty. You caused quite a stir. And of course, the two of you having coffee together in the cafeteria created some interest."

"We didn't have coffee together." That was the absolute truth. "She was down getting coffee for everyone. I saw her and stopped to talk for a minute. She told me she'd gotten the idea to come here because of the way I'd spoken about it. She was getting burned out on the pace of New York life and thought she'd give Honeymoon Harbor a try."

"She's lived all over the world," John said. "I've heard she has money."

"Yeah, I heard that, too." He decided not to mention how recent that had been.

"You couldn't tell it from how she acts," Jerome said. "She's a real nice girl."

"Sweet as pie," his grandmother agreed. "Though I wonder if she'll stick. Lots of people think they're going to escape a former life, living in a small town. From what I've seen over my eighty-some years, many of them discover not even Honeymoon Harbor has any magic elixir to make problems vanish. If anything, without the distraction of a busy city life, you have more time to think about things. And if you brought unhappiness with you, it won't make a difference where you settle down."

After his talk with Lily at Hurricane Ridge, Burke decided his gram had it right.

"However, she's always seemed like a happy girl," Harriet continued. "Perky. And she's got enough energy for three people, doing all she does at the college, not to mention her volunteer work. I hope she stays, because Honeymoon Harbor is lucky to have her living here."

"She told me she's staying," Burke said.

"Well, isn't that nice." His mother smiled at him over the rim of her cup. He knew, from watching his siblings pair off, that she probably wouldn't be fully satisfied until she got all her children settled down and married. "You'll have to invite her to the barbecue."

"What barbecue?"

"The one your father's cooking for our anniversary party."

"Our thirty-seventh," John said.

She turned toward him. "You remembered."

He gave her a slow, sexy smile that, having grown up watching it, didn't surprise Burke. But it did make him just a little envious of his dad. "I remember everything."

As a soft color rose in cheeks that had been ghostly pale when he'd first seen her, Burke decided to up his game plan. After all, he'd learned early in life that if you wanted to win, you needed to follow in the footsteps of those who'd played the game before you.

CHAPTER SEVENTEEN

LATE WEDNESDAY AFTERNOON, Jim had analyzed the upcoming situation while he'd been in the shower, washing off the sweet, earthy scent of potting soil. He usually never quit work this early in the day, but then again, it wasn't just any day he had a date. It might be a first date with Sage, but it wasn't his first ever date.

His first had been when he'd taken Kylee to the prom their junior year. She hadn't come out yet, so he'd acted as a cover so she could get to dance with her secret girlfriend before the night was over.

He still remembered Kylee spending Christmas vacation at the Mannions' because her father had cut her out of his life when she announced she was a lesbian. At the time, Jim had considered himself highly fortunate that his parents had not only accepted him having been born with a brain that was wired differently , but they'd also celebrated that difference, and made him feel every bit as loved as his older sister.

None of his college dates had been the least bit romantic, despite studies showing that personal relationships of people on the spectrum worked better when they matched up with like-minded people.

Somehow, although it took him very far out of his comfort zone, he'd always been more attracted to people whose brains were wired differently than his own. People like extroverted Kylee, whose personality burned as brightly as her flame-red curls.

Sage affected him in much the same way. Her enthusiasm was contagious. And despite taking a risk, he reminded himself that attempting to mix a personal relationship with a working one had apparently worked out very well for Marie and Pierre Curie. Then again, they were like-minded. Which brought him back to those studies.

When his watch alarm rang, set to remind him that he should be getting dressed to pick Sage up at one of the large Victorians that had been turned into an apartment building, he realized the more he thought about the problem, the more variables he could come up with, possibly ending with a polynomial equation that could not be solved. Which could, in turn, trigger his OCD, which he'd managed to overcome in order to have burgers at the lake with Sage.

So the current objective was to concentrate on tonight's mission. To survive the dinner without making an inappropriate comment.

He stood in front of his closet, trying to decide what to wear. His mind, which was jumping all over the place, went back to his first trip to visit his parents in Arizona. Taking one look at him getting off the plane wearing his favorite T-shirt, printed with the periodic table and the caption "I wear this shirt periodically," his mother had said that she was not taking him to a nice restaurant in that. As yet another indication that Arizona had changed her, she'd turned out to be a speed shopper. Driving straight to Nordstrom, she'd marched him into the men's department and within twenty minutes had purchased a week's worth of clothes he'd doubted he'd ever have reason to wear again.

He'd been wrong. While Honeymoon Harbor was a casual town, he felt a dinner of such social importance required more of an effort than his usual T-shirts and jeans, which were faded and torn—not due to any attempt to look cool.

On the other hand, the dark suit, tie, and white shirt he'd bought from a helpful man named Joel at Port Angeles's Men's Wearhouse to wear to Seth Harper's wife Zoe's funeral felt too formal for this occasion.

Finally, since the clock was ticking away, he made a decision. Then, just to be sure, he called Burke for confirmation.

"Perfect," Burke assured him when he said that he was considering a pair of slim, dark-wash jeans, a navy-and-white-checked collared shirt, and polished low dress boots that Jessie had bought him two years ago for Christmas. "Just don't wear a hoodie."

That would eliminate several items in any Olympic Peninsula closet. Fortunately, his weather app had forecast clear skies and a temperature of seventy-seven degrees. Although high for this time of year, it was appreciated tonight, with only a one-percent chance of rain.

Before leaving the house, he ran a comb through his new Nick Jonas haircut.

Then headed out the door.

As LILY STUDIED her closet, trying to decide what to wear to dinner, Burke's comment about her playing sexy secretary to his stern boss was doing exactly what he'd expected it to do. Reminding her of all those stolen, secret nights of the best sex of her life.

"Relationships are about more than just sex," she told herself firmly. Look at Aiden and Jolene. Each had overcome past difficulties and found each other. As had Brianna and Seth and Gabe and Chelsea. And they'd found happiness together by starting over. Which could only happen when they surrendered what had been holding them back, leaving themselves open for a new future. A future they each were sharing with a person they loved.

She was also belatedly starting to realize that Shakespeare's quote from *The Tempest*, about past being prologue, didn't necessarily mean that *her* past controlled the rest of her life. The realization had her finally accepting what her therapist had meant when she accused her of dragging her past with her. A prologue wasn't the story. It only set the stage for the story.

"Like a blank page," she said.

Which brought up a Buddha quote she'd learned while taking a college comparative religion class. "Today is the most important day of your life, for today is the first day of the rest of your life."

So, the trick was to treat each day as if it were the first day of her life. And each new day offered an opportunity to change her life. If she was brave enough.

Since Jim had told them he'd be at the theater at five thirty. Gabe and Burke had decided they should all be there by the same time, so as not to make him feel uncomfortable.

Since she didn't live far from downtown, Burke arrived at exactly five fifteen, as hot as ever in a black lightweight sweater she recognized as cashmere, black jeans, and low black boots that looked buttery soft. Just as his running clothes had the other day, the black only highlighted his blue eyes.

He took in the messy bun she'd created, leaving a few tendrils trailing down. "You do realize that I'm going to spend the entire dinner thinking about pulling out those pins?" A blue flame flared in his eyes. His smile was slow, wicked, and rife with sensual promise.

Backing up just a bit, he skimmed a slow look over the cropped dark blue denim jacket she was wearing over a crisp white shirt with light-wash jeans. Her shoes were white leather with red baseball stitching and fire-engine-red heels. "It's not exactly naughty secretary, and the shoes are the wrong sport, but I do like the look." His gaze returned to linger on the buttons running down the front of the shirt. "Fortunately, I have a very good imagination."

And didn't she know that? He'd taught her things about her body, about how it could respond to every touch, that she'd never experienced before. Her mind flashed back to when he'd been telling her, as his fingers skimmed over her warming flesh, exactly how he placed his fingers on the laces of the football. Through the sensual haze clouding her mind, she'd thought that was an odd topic to bring up while making love.

Until his hand moved between her legs, and he'd told her that each finger had more than three thousand touch receptors. And every one of them loved the feel of her. Everywhere.

"I told you," he said. "I remember everything."

His eyes held hers, holding her as captive as that time he'd used the silk tie he'd arrived wearing from a press event to secure her hands to the headboard of her bed. As he watched her remember that night, it wasn't only her cheeks that were burning up.

Then, just as quickly, he broke that sensual spell.

"We'd better leave," he said, glancing down at the black calfskin-banded Cartier watch that she knew cost more than several cars. "To make sure we're there when Jim and Sage arrive."

They drove the short distance to the art deco theater that dated back to the late 1920s, just as "talkies" were taking over the earlier silent movies. Gradually replaced by drive-in theaters, the ability to see movies at home on television, and megaplexes, the theater had fallen into disrepair in the 1960s. Over the years, various nonprofit groups would attempt to bring it back for stage productions and classic theaters.

None of the attempts lasted very long until one of the twelve thousand employees who'd been given stock as part of their early Microsoft salaries and become millionaires when the company went public had built a vacation house on the lake. A longtime film buff, he'd used some of that money to restore the theater, which now mostly showed new releases, but had a classics night twice a month.

"You came up with this triple date idea on purpose," she accused him as they drove around the block twice in order to arrive at the same precise time as the other two couples. "Because you knew I wouldn't refuse to help Jim."

Burke didn't bother to deny it. "All's fair in love and war," he said mildly.

When he'd first arrived in the cafeteria, Lily had thought they were at war. Now she wasn't sure what to think. If these feelings did end up being love, she'd definitely have some decisions to make.

"I adore your shoes!" Sage said as they greeted them on the sidewalk outside the door.

"And I love your dress!" Lily said. It was a blue-and-white-checked mini with a puckered bodice and puffy sleeves. She'd paired it with white platform sneakers.

"Thank you." Her face, surrounded by all those curls, lit up. "We honestly didn't plan it, but Jim and I match."

Which was true. And if Jim was at all uneasy at suddenly being the center of attention, it certainly didn't show, because all his attention was directed at Sage. He was, Lily thought, looking at her as if she were that blue rose he was determined to create. Which wouldn't normally have been a surprise, because she looked darling, but she couldn't remember Jim ever showing his feelings so openly.

One advantage of the Olympic was that you could reserve seats ahead of time, which Gabe had already done. They were in the first row of the balcony, and as the curtains opened and the room darkened, Burke took Lily's hand, linking their fingers together. It felt so right. She felt a twinge of regret for all that she'd cost them. Then, as the image of the spinning globe appeared on the screen, accompanied by "La Marseillaise," the French national anthem, she allowed herself to become lost in one of Hollywood's most memorable love stories.

"That was a very entertaining film," Jim said as they walked out of the theater. "Captain Renault was meant to be hypocritical when he said that he was shocked—*shocked*—that there was gambling going on, wasn't he?"

"He was," Chelsea said. "It's something people will still say to describe a variety of situations. Although, like so many movie lines, it's morphed into a cliché."

"Still, it is a good line. There were many good lines in that movie."

"'We'll always have Paris' makes me cry every time," Sage said.

"That is why Jolene instructed me to bring tissues for you," Jim responded. "I was told it was a common response when watching the film. Even when someone has seen it several times."

"Because it's so sad," Chelsea said. "There really couldn't be any other ending, though, which is odd because it's still one of the most emotional love stories ever made. I took a film class in college and learned that, amazingly, no one knew how it was going to end because they were making it up as they went along. That scene was written only a few days before it was shot."

"My favorite line is, 'Here's looking at you, kid.'" Lily sighed. "It's one of the most romantic lines ever. I may be in the minority, but I believe it's even more romantic than 'We'll always have Paris.'"

"I didn't understand why Rick said that," Jim admitted. "Because it was obvious that he was looking at Ilsa."

"Bogart reportedly ad-libbed it, but most people take it to mean that even if they never see each other again, he'll be looking after Ilsa forever. Maybe not physically following her around, or anything," Lily said, not wanting Jim to take it literally. "But that he'll never forget her. And he's acknowledging that whatever happens, they'll always have that special connection between them."

"And that," Chelsea said as they entered the restaurant, "is what makes it still so romantic. Even with that sad but inevitable ending."

"I'm beginning to think romance is even more complex than dating," Jim murmured to Burke while Lily, Chelsea and Sage were all animatedly talking about the movie to Luca, who'd greeted them as they arrived at the restaurant.

"Join the club," Burke agreed as they followed Luca through the dining room that was an easy blend of formal and casual.

The tablecloths were a crisp white, rather than the red-and-white check often seen in casual Italian restaurants. In the center of each table was a cut crystal glass with a single red flower from Blue House Farm. The brick wall of what had once been a lumber warehouse had been painted a rich gold. Cut into it, between the bar and the swinging door to the kitchen, was a large redbrick wood-burning pizza oven.

Rather than a clichéd mural on the wall, photographs of family, going back what appeared to be at least three generations, hung on display. All showed people cooking, serving, or standing in front of a restaurant. White bulb lights hung from the high, open ceiling rafters.

The private dining room was much the same, except instead of the two- and four-top tables and the long red leather booth against the wall in the main room, the white draped table was circular, inviting conversation. As in the outer dining room, a single red flower in a crystal vase sat in the middle. The napkins were red, white and green, echoing the Italian flag that flew next to the restaurant's door. More family photos adorned the walls.

"This is the original restaurant that goes back to the early 1900s," Luca pointed out one of the more faded ones after seating them. "It's still in business, located near the Vatican. The family joke is that it was established there in case the pope ever decided to drop in for dinner or to order out."

"Has one ever done that?" Lily asked.

Luca flashed a grin, having obviously set up the question. "Every one since they opened the doors, from Pope Pius X, who died a month after the beginning of World War I, to Pope Francis. Pope John the Twenty-Third told my great-grandmother that her spaghettini alla carbonara was Rome on a plate and sure to guarantee her a place in heaven. Family legend has her attempting to bargain for future members of the family to get free entry on her pass."

Burke laughed. "She'd have gotten along great with my grandmother, who apparently was instructing God on why he had to keep Mom alive after her accident."

"That's very admirable of your grandmother," Jim said, after their glasses of water had been filled, menus delivered. "Without any scientific proof that the outcome would be assured, her faith must be very strong."

"I suspect faith is helpful when you spend so many years married to a man who grew up working on his family's fishing boats," Gabe suggested.

"Fishing is the second most deadly occupation after logging," Jim said. "So it's very understandable that she would feel that way."

After looking at the extensive menu, Burke said, "I think you've sold me on the carbonara. Over a century of popes couldn't be wrong."

Everyone else at the table immediately agreed to have the same and an antipasto to share. Although Jim seemed a bit hesitant, he went along with the majority. They'd no sooner had their glasses filled when a server brought out plates of toasted slices of bruschetta, drizzled with olive oil.

"I watched all your last season's games at your brother's pub," Sage told Burke. "The Knights are a great team, but if you don't mind me saying so, you really need a stronger offensive line."

"You're certainly not the first person to suggest that," Burke said.

"Sage's brother is a high school football coach," Jim volunteered. "In Boston. She was a cheerleader while in high school there."

"That would make you a Patriots fan," Burke said.

"I was," Sage agreed. "But now that I'm here, like most everyone in town, I'm a Knights fan first, with the Seahawks coming in a close second."

"Which is why Quinn has two flat-screens in the pub," Gabe revealed. "For those days they both play at the same time. Fortunately, being in different leagues, you'd only end up playing against each other in the Super Bowl."

"When even the most ardent Seahawks fan would root for our hometown hero," Lily said.

"The fans are very ardent," Jim said. "They're in the *Guinness World Records* for causing an earthquake."

"Surely not an actual earthquake?" Sage asked, her amber eyes widening.

"It's true," he answered. "I watched it with my dad on television. The Seahawks were playing in the 2011 NFC Wild Card playoff game against the New Orleans Saints—who were the reigning Super Bowl champions—when, with only four minutes remaining in the game, running back Marshawn Lynch shook off nine defenders to make a sixty-seven-yard touchdown. When the Hawks won, the fans' celebration was so loud it registered on a nearby seismograph."

"That was an iconic run," Gabe said. "It's still making NFL highlight reels."

"It was the day the term 'Beast Mode' was born," Jim said, demonstrating that his eidetic memory did not merely relate to his own genome work.

Burke was accustomed to football being a main topic whenever he went out. Not that he brought it up, but it was what he was known for. Now, for the first time in his life, it wasn't his favorite topic, so he welcomed Luca's arrival with a platter of antipasto so artfully arranged it could have been taken from a Renaissance painting.

As they passed the platter around, he changed the topic to the upcoming Heritage Day, which had both Chelsea and Lily describing the floats the library and college were making.

"My dad was cast as Teddy Roosevelt in a play about the history of the town," he said. "Back when he got home from Nepal."

"I didn't know that," Gabe said.

"Neither did I until it came up at dinner last night. He and Mom were coincidentally reunited at LAX when he was returning home from Nepal at the same time she was coming from Japan, so before the plane to SeaTac took off, he called Uncle Mike and asked him to take out some groceries to our family's coast house. Mike agreed to do that if Dad would take over the role, which, apparently our uncle had gotten stuck with. Which was only a few lines telling the newly married king and queen of Montacroix about the wonders of the peninsula, which had them adding this town to their honeymoon trip across America."

"Which caused the town's name change," Chelsea said.

"Exactly. So, instead of taking Mom to her parents' house when they got back to town, while she'd fallen asleep from jet lag, he kidnapped her and drove to the coast house, where he proposed to her over what she insists was a seduction meal."

"Go, Dad," Gabe said.

"John kidnapped Sarah?" Lily asked.

"That's so romantic," Sage said, crossing her hands over her heart as she sighed.

"Kidnapping is against the law," Jim pointed out.

"It wasn't an actual kidnapping," Burke clarified. "If she'd asked him to take her home, he would have. But they'd been apart for two years, and he said he wanted some time to catch up and talk to her alone."

"That makes sense," Gabe said. "Since nothing is private in Honeymoon Harbor."

"As much as I've come to love this town, that's definitely true," Lily agreed.

"I'm not so sure about that," Burke suggested mildly. "I suspect it's still possible to keep some things private.

Even secret, if you're determined enough." He slanted a look at Lily.

"Like your father taking your mother to the coast," Jim said.

"Exactly," Burke agreed. "Mike was the only person in his family who knew he was home. He wanted to try to fix things with Mom before he told his father that he wasn't going to work at the bank."

"I can't picture your father stuck working in a bank," Lily said.

"Neither could he. There was also the fact that her parents didn't approve of their relationship. They felt he'd hold her back."

"I'd like to see anyone try," Gabe said.

"I'm with you there. Also, apparently Gramps thought he was too cocky." That drew a laugh.

"As it turned out," Burke continued, "Dad still had the engagement ring he'd intended to give Mom during a visit to her college back East. But there was a misunderstanding that had them separating for those two years. She went to Oxford, then taught English in Japan, while he was in Nepal, teaching the farmers tree rotation so all their trees didn't bear fruit at the same time."

"Which would extend their season and help prevent diseases wiping out a season," Jim said.

"So Dad explained to us when we were growing up."

"He's right. I'd like to talk with him about that someday."

"He'd love nothing more," Burke said.

As they discussed the surprise that John and Sarah Mannion's romance had been more complicated than any of them could have suspected, a busser came in to sweep away their empty antipasto plates. She was followed by Luca and a server, both carrying trays with their pasta, which they placed on the table with fresh silverware. Then they left the group to their meal.

The carbonara was simply and perfectly made with spaghettini—a thin pasta that landed between spaghetti and angel hair—mixed with parmesan cheese, and pancetta.

"Oh, my God. I think the pope called it," Lily said after taking a bite of the creamy dish. "Because this is absolutely heavenly."

"It is much superior to canned," Jim agreed.

Sage was visibly shocked. "That's a joke, isn't it? You do *not* eat canned spaghetti."

"It's very simple and only uses one pan, which makes for less cleanup."

"It's also undoubtedly a cardinal food sin," she said. "Please tell me that you've never said that to Luca when you deliver his flower orders."

"The topic has not come up."

"Good." She nodded decisively. "Next time I come to the farm, I'm teaching you a basic red sauce that you can freeze in portions. Then all you'll have to do is nuke it and cook some pasta, which I have no doubt a man with your higher-than-average intellect can figure out by following the instructions on the box."

"Along with being very social-media-savvy, and pretty, Sage can be very strong-minded," Jim informed the others.

As color rose in Sage's cheeks, Lily suspected that it was not caused by his comment about her being media-savvy or strong-minded, but him announcing to the others that he found her pretty. One thing Lily enjoyed about Jim was that although he didn't speak all that much, when he did, he lacked filters. Since his personality was so very kind, and she'd never heard him say a negative word, she found it refreshing. Which, in turn, had her wondering if Burke felt the same. Because if he did and compared Jim's openness with her having kept so many secrets during their time together, she'd definitely be lacking.

As the conversation turned to what projects Sage was working on for Blue House Farm, Lily put away the worry. For now.

"They're wonderfully eye-catching," Chelsea said as she glanced through the photos on the other woman's phone.

"And ambitious," Gabe added, leaning over to check them out before passing the phone around to the others, who agreed.

"Sage is very ambitious," Jim offered. "I believe she thinks nearly as much about social media as I do plant genomes."

"What's that old saying?" Chelsea said. "That if you love what you're doing, it's never work?"

"I think that's a bit overstated," Gabe suggested. "Because work is still work. But I enjoy making boats a lot more than I did moving money around."

"Brianna says she's happier with Herons Landing than she ever was at any high-end hotel she worked at," Chelsea said. "And Quinn claims he enjoys all those hours spent at the pub more than he did practicing law. I know Aiden is much better off being chief of police than he was in Los Angeles, where he lost his partner and was almost killed."

"Looks as if Burke's the only Mannion who didn't have to come home to live his best life," Chelsea said.

"It would be impossible for him to come here to play football," Jim pointed out. "Other than the high school, we have no football teams in Honeymoon Harbor. Although he could move to Seattle, where he'd be closer to home."

"I'm sure the Seahawks are very happy with their quarterback," Burke said.

His tone was easy, but Lily saw a shadow move across his eyes and thought about how he'd hedged about his plans. She also noticed that he'd change the subject whenever the topic of football came up. Perhaps because of what she'd told him about his fame having been problematic for her?

Remembering what he'd said about his contract currently being negotiated and thinking about all the social media speculation about where he'd be playing this coming season, she wondered if he planned to leave New York for another city. If they did find a way to have a more normal relationship, it would definitely be easier if he were here in Washington State. Which, as he'd pointed out, was highly unlikely.

Though anywhere on the West Coast could work. Heaven knows he spent weeks a year traveling for the games from August into January, and airlines flew out of SeaTac to any city he might end up.

Not that she should even be thinking about the future on their first date. Especially one with four other people. Their relationship was so strange. Physically, they knew everything about each other, but they'd never experienced anything close to real life. How did she know if they were truly compatible outside of bed?

Realizing she'd definitely jumped ahead several steps along this other road he'd suggested, Lily decided to just let matters play out, and what would be would be. She knew that Sage's mother believed in messages from the universe. As an admitted skeptic, as well as a control freak, she put all those questions aside for now.

Instead of her usual tiramisu, which everyone else at the table had ordered, she'd opted to try the zabaglione, a simple but decadent Italian dish made of egg yolks, sugar and marsala wine, somewhere between a custard and a sauce. During her time in Florence, she'd learned that it had been invented in the city in the court of the Medici in the sixteenth century. Luca served it warmed, topped with strawberries sourced from Blue House Farm.

"I nearly became addicted to zabaglione during the six months I lived in Florence," she confessed when he returned to the room to ensure that they'd enjoyed their meal. "I've had it warm, cold, whipped with cream, frozen. Even for breakfast. But this is hands down the most delicious I've ever had."

"Every family has their own recipe," he said. "I can share mine if you'd like to make it at home." She suspected, like most chefs, he didn't do that very often.

"That's a lovely offer, but I think it'll be more special if I save it for a treat here."

"I'd be honored if you would. And desserts are on the house."

"All in all, I think it was a success," Burke told her after they'd said goodbye to the others.

"It was," she agreed. "Sage certainly seems to bring Jim out of his shell."

"She definitely does," he agreed. "Which was a nice surprise. And the haircut is new."

"Jolene called and told me about that. She said he looked like Nick Jonas when he left the salon."

"I'm not sure I saw that, but it was definitely an improvement over the days when he looked as if he'd cut his own hair at home with a Weedwacker." Spring could always be iffy, especially in this part of the country, but the night was unseasonably warm with a full moon rising. "What would you say to walking the two blocks to the pier before I take you back to your house?"

She smiled up at him. "I'd say yes."

CHAPTER EIGHTEEN

When he took her hand in his, it felt so right, so natural, Lily wasn't about to worry who saw them. "I was thinking during dinner that that there are so many wonderful chefs in town, perhaps I could come up with a series of regional cooking lessons, using the college's culinary class's kitchen. We could sell tickets and have someone demonstrate how to cook a dish. Or maybe even make it a hands-on lesson. We'd have to charge more to cover the ingredients, but that way people would have something to take home. Money could go to the school's food bank."

"There's a food bank at the school?"

"You'd be surprised how many students' families run out of money at the end of the month, making grocery buying difficult. This could not only bring in some much-needed funds, but also draw attention to the food bank and hopefully bring in more donations."

"You weren't kidding about settling down here, were you?"

"No. I understand why you might doubt me, but every single thing I've told you, since we spoke in the hospital cafeteria, has been the absolute truth. I'll admit I came here because I was curious and too jaded to believe a town like Mayberry, or Stars Hollow from *Gilmore Girls*, actually existed. When I discovered it was even better than you'd described it, I still only planned to stay a few months, although I didn't choose the best time of year to arrive.

"Late January, early February, is not an ideal time to get to know this part of the country," he agreed.

"True. But the summers definitely make up for it."

"We never did this," he said as they walked to the end of the pier. "Hold hands in public."

"That's on me." She drew in a deep breath. Exhaled. "I've been thinking a lot about what you said. Which is, by the way, also what everyone told me during the great confession night over many margaritas."

"And what was that?"

"That I've been allowing my past to follow me wherever I went. Dragging it along like an anchor. And since I've proven myself a strong, capable woman, I should just let it go."

"How's that working for you?"

At the nearby ferry dock, pedestrians and people in cars were lining up for the short ride to Whidbey Island, from where they could drive to other Puget Sound cities. Others were strolling down the street, illuminated by the original old-fashioned streetlights that had been long ago electrified. Enjoying the lovely evening, for the first time, she didn't care who might see them.

"Since we're starting over, how about I show you?"

She went up on her toes, and lightly brushed her lips against his. As always, from the very first touch, heat flared instantly, like a lightning bolt to dry tinder, the kind that started the forest fires that were getting hotter every year. *Here there be danger*, she thought even as she played with that fire, pouring herself into the kiss that deepened, grew hotter. Just when she was on the verge of imploding, he put his hands on her shoulders and broke the kiss.

"That was a damn good start," he said. His voice was rough, as if he'd swallowed some of that smoke from the flames she'd imagined having surrounded them. Showing far more self-control than she was feeling at the moment, he brushed a kiss, as soft as thistledown, against her temple. "I think this is where I take you home."

They strolled hand in hand back to the car and drove the few blocks to her house, where he walked her up the moss-and-stone path to her door. "Would you like to come in?" Every part of her body that had always responded to his taste, his touch, had awakened.

The invitation in her voice was unmistakable. "I would. But if we're starting over, I have to tell you that I'm typically not one of those guys who have sex on the first date."

"But—"

"I know. Waiting is hard. Though, believe it or not, since I never knew whether a woman was going out with the star quarterback or me, the guy, I developed a rule about that. A rule that I knew would be shattered the moment we met."

Just the memory caused a warmth to flow through her veins. "That was a rule worth breaking."

"True. But this time, we're going to slow things down."

"That could be difficult," she said. "Given that I kept wanting to jump you during dinner."

His smile was slow and decidedly wicked, punishing those parts of her too long denied pleasure as they were yelling that they wanted him. *Now.*

"Says the woman who wanted to keep us a secret," he pointed out.

"That was then. This is now."

"They say patience is a virtue." As he twirled a tendril of her hair around his finger, his eyes turned hot and hungry. Then, as he'd said he'd wanted to do earlier, when he'd picked her up to take her to dinner, he plucked out a pin and slipped it into the pocket of his jeans. Then another. A third. And continued until her hair had tumbled over her shoulders. They stood there, him looking down at her as she was looking back up at him.

"Tell me all this this isn't some sort of payback," she said.

"Never." He brushed a finger over her swollen, still tingling lips. "I want you, Lily Carpenter. That's the God's honest truth, but—"

"Good evening, Lily, dear," a voice called out, interrupting him. Lily could have screamed when her neighbor, an elderly retired chemistry teacher, came by, taking her Pekingese for one last walk before turning in as she did every night around this time.

"Good evening," Lily called back, the moment lost.

Adjusting her glasses, the woman looked closer. "Burke Mannion, is that you?" she asked.

"Yes, ma'am. Uh, Mrs. Davidson."

"I'd heard you were back in town. How's your mother?"

"Except for a concussion and fractured ribs, which her surgeon says will heal by themselves, and bruising, she's doing well. Thank you for asking."

"That's good to hear. I've enjoyed watching your games at your brother's pub. I always tell people that I had you in my class." She chuckled. "It's my brush with celebrity. Of course, I never tell them that you nearly blew up my chemistry lab."

"Thank you, Mrs. Davidson. I appreciate that."

"No problem. Those damn tabloids have already written enough trash about you. I didn't want to add to it by having them tell the world that you were my first pyromaniac." Another chuckle. "It's all fun and games until you forget the Bunsen burner. You all have yourselves a good evening."

She was walking away, but suddenly turned back. "And for heavens' sakes, tell your coach that you need a better offensive line."

"Yes, ma'am," Burke replied.

"That seems to be a theme," Lily said.

"You think? But they're right. Which is one of the things that are part of the negotiation talks."

"So, the social media posts that say you're leaving New York may be true?"

He shrugged. "I honestly, at this moment, have no idea what I'm going to be doing next year. But I do know what I'm going to be doing right now." He threaded his fingers through her tumbled hair, gathering it together at the nape of her neck, as he lightly tilted her face up. In contrast to that earlier kiss, this time Burke's lips barely brushed against hers. Tasting. Teasing. Tempting, as their breaths mingled.

"What are you doing tomorrow?" he asked against her lips.

"Working." She managed to get that single word out, even as she wanted to drag him into her house. Into her bed. No. She didn't want to wait that long. She wanted him to take her against the door. On the floor. Hard and fast so she didn't have time to think any of this through. "I have a lot going on right now."

"Understood. Quinn's letting me bunk on his boat while I'm here. I thought maybe we could take it out and watch the sun set."

"I'd love that." Except for that memorable Christmas Eve, they'd never done anything romantic. Having told herself that their relationship would not, could not, ever go anywhere, she hadn't wanted romance back then. But she'd been wrong. About that and so many other things.

"Great. What time do you get home from work?"

"About five thirty. But I'll need time to change."

"I guess the naughty secretary outfit isn't exactly suitable for an evening on the lake," he said with an exaggerated sigh that made her laugh. And also made her wish she'd been up front with him from the beginning. Now that she'd been forced to face her fears, she realized they'd been merely ghosts that she'd let follow her along for far too many years.

"I've been told patience is a virtue," she said, tilting her head and fluttering her lashes at him in a way she'd never done in her life, as she threw his words back at him.

"Whoever told you that is an idiot."

She laughed. "I'll see you tomorrow."

"Tomorrow," he agreed. "Meanwhile, I'll have to be satisfied with seeing you in my dreams. As I have been every night." He framed her face with his palms. "Maybe tomorrow evening, I can tell you a few of the more interesting ones. Or even show you. If you ask nicely."

"That's definitely payback," she accused.

His smile was wickedly sexy. "Maybe. Just a little. But I promise it'll be one we both enjoy. Now you'd better go in before we end up giving Mrs. Davidson something more exciting than a chemistry lab explosion to talk about."

She took her keys out of her bag and, although it wasn't her first choice, let herself into the house alone. She could sense him waiting until she clicked the lock before he walked back to the truck.

Chance jumped around her, welcoming her home, while Zendaya lifted her head and meowed a complaint, then turned her back and ignored her. After patting the dog and giving him a cookie from the lidded jar on a nearby table, Lily stood at the front window, watching Burke walk—no, *swagger*—away, with his hands shoved in his pockets. She remembered what he'd said at dinner about his grandfather having thought John Mannion was cocky.

Like father, like son.

LILY WAS RELIEVED when Thursday proved too busy to dwell on that night's date. But as she juggled calls from the alumni association, the boosters, the Heritage Day committee, the scholarship committee who'd been collecting applications for the fall semester, and the committee for Open House Week in August, she kept glancing at her watch.

By the time five o'clock rolled around, a very strong part of her just wanted to go home, put on her pajamas, climb into bed, and sleep until tomorrow morning. A stronger part couldn't wait to see Burke. Being back with him felt like denying herself chocolate during the forty days of Lent, only to eat an entire box of truffles for breakfast on Easter morning. Not that she'd ever done that.

Liar.

One of the first things she'd learned when moving here was the importance of layering. Especially during the temperamental spring when a capricious Mother Nature would tease you with a friendly warm sunshine, only to send in steely rain clouds ten minutes later. She'd literally seen it rain on her house while the sun was shining on Mrs. Davidson's next door. And it could be even more changeable out on the water. After a quick shower, she opted for a navy-and-green argyle sweater with a crocheted Peter Pan collar over a white blouse, jeans, and a pair of waterproof navy sneakers with white rubber soles that wouldn't scratch the deck of Quinn's boat. Because it could be windy on the water, she plaited her hair into a single braid.

Forgoing full makeup, she put on some lightly tinted moisturizer and used a rosy crayon on her lips. A brush of waterproof mascara and she was done right before he rang the bell. Which had Chance charging at the door, barking his fool head off in an earsplitting half bark, half howl.

"Hi," she greeted Burke, telling herself that she was only breathless because she'd chased after the dog, who, until the doorbell had rung, had been lying on the bed, curled up with the cat, watching her get ready. She grabbed hold of his collar and told herself that once Heritage Day and the school semester were over, she was going to take him to training classes. "I'm sorry. Every time the doorbell rings, Chance feels the need to sing the visitor the song of his people."

"And a damn fine song it is." Burke reached down to scratch the dog between the ears. On cue, Chance dropped down on the floor and rolled over. "I miss having a dog. My mom and dad have two."

"Mulder and Scully," Lily said.

"They're very smart. And loyal. Dad tells me they haven't left Mom alone since she got home from the hospital. He says they'd go in the shower with her if she let them."

He skimmed a look over her in a way that felt intimately familiar, warming her to the core. "I've tried to tell myself that my memory had exaggerated how just looking at you made me feel." He framed her face with his hands, and slowly, holding her gaze with his, he lowered his mouth to hers. "But I was wrong."

He took his time, brushing soft butterfly kisses from one corner of her mouth to the other. As his lips caressed hers,

Lily, beguiled, was drawn into the mist. "I never forgot how you tasted," he murmured. "Not even in my dreams."

She twined her arms around his neck, melting into the kiss, allowing her mind to empty. As Burke's lips skimmed over her face, her world tilted on its axis, seemingly suspended in time. She nearly cried out as he ended the kiss, then bent down, touching his forehead to hers. "I was wrong," he said. Those words, spoken with what sounded like regret, broke the spell. "We can't start over." His tone and face were so grave, she nearly looked down to see the pieces of her heart lying in shatters all over the floor. "Because we never really quit. You feel so perfect in my arms, Lily. So familiar."

"It's the same for me." Surely that trembling voice couldn't be hers. Concerned for his mistress, Chance began to whine. Was this when Burke would tell her that he couldn't start over because he couldn't put what she'd done behind them?

"Besides talent, and hard work, there's this thing athletes who make it to the top need," Burke said.

He was talking about football? Now? Annoyance that he seemed to have been playing her after all, to lure her back, only to dump her, filled her mind.

"What's that?" She. Would. Not. Cry.

"The ability to forget the past. Like when you throw an interception, if you let that stay in your mind, it'll screw up the rest of your game. You have to wipe your mind clear, like glass. I developed that ability in JV ball."

"And that's relevant to our situation, how?"

"I can't do that with you." He shook his head. "I can't forget how it felt to be with you. To hold you. Those soft little sounds you made when I'd touch you. All over. The way you'd scream when you came."

This time it was Lily who backed away and folded her arms. "I did not scream."

"Yes, you did. We were just lucky you lived in a ritzy place with concrete firewalls between the apartments or we could have had your neighbors calling 911 on us."

How could he smile at a time like this? Lily wondered.

"Here's the thing." He cupped his hands over her shoulders again. "I don't want to forget any of that. Because that was the only time you let those damn walls down. When you showed me who you were. And let me know the real you. The other day, at first, I was admittedly pissed that you hadn't been honest with me up front. That you thought I couldn't understand and hadn't given me a chance to try to help figure out how we could deal with what, for you, was a very real problem. But you were always honest in bed. Unless you were faking."

"I wasn't! How could you even think such a thing?"

"I didn't, really. Which is why I just decided to change the game plan."

"Again with the football," she muttered.

"Football has been the most constant thing in my life. Actually, it's been the focus of my life since I was five or six years old. Mom says earlier than that, back to my crib days when I wouldn't go to sleep without my plush football. It's how I've viewed most situations since. So, how about you give me a break and let me try to tell you, in my own fucked-up way, what I mean about not going back?"

"Okay. I'm listening." She waved her hand in a slight *go ahead* gesture.

"I *do* want to move forward with you. But I also want to hold on to this part. The part that connected us from the moment we met. We fit, Lily. What do you say we just move forward from here, one day at a time, and try not to overthink things? Or look back on mistakes, or worry about the future?"

"I'm not all that good about staying in the present."

"I understand your need to plan things out. But right now, there's so much in the air on my end, I can't tell you where I'll be or what I'll be doing after July 21st. I realize that's not fair to you, and truthfully, I'm not real happy about it, either, which is partly why I think just enjoying one day at a time together is the best way for now. I don't want to dump my problems onto you, but I will promise that when I do make a decision, it'll be something that we can both live with."

"I've always felt that sharing problems should be an important part of a relationship." Lily may have grown up in a take-no-prisoners, ongoing War of the Roses family, but she'd witnessed enough solid marriages among the Mannions and Harpers, along with Kylee and Mai, to want the same for herself.

"I agree. And whatever happens, if we're going to be together, I'm not going to decide unilaterally."

"Why do I feel as if we're negotiating a contract?" she asked.

"It does feel like it," he agreed. "Which is precisely why we need to live in the moment right now. Because we're dealing with too many variables."

"Only on your part. Because, as I told you, I'm happily settled down here."

"I could make you happier."

"You could also break my heart." Too late she remembered what he'd told her about going through the stages of grief, because she'd inadvertently done exactly that to him. She shook her head. "I'm sorry—"

"It's okay. We've moved beyond that." He held out a hand. "Ready to go?"

"Let me just get a jacket." She took a light rain shell from the closet to wear over the sweater, just in case the clear skies in the forecast turned out to be a lie. "And speaking of jackets, don't you own anything that isn't black or charcoal?" He was wearing a black leather jacket and a black sweater with a zipper at the neck over a silk charcoal T-shirt. His jeans were black and his sneakers black with gray rubber soles.

"I travel a lot. Black and gray make it easier to get dressed because I don't have to make choices and can't screw things up. It's like the Garanimals Mom bought us when we were kids."

"I recall Garanimals having bright colors and prints that made it easy for children to mix and match."

He shrugged. "I've improved upon the concept."

Despite the earlier seriousness of their conversation, he'd made her laugh again. And as they left the house and headed to the marina, he'd opened her up to thinking of a future she'd never allowed herself to imagine during those months together.

CHAPTER NINETEEN

QUINN'S BOAT WAS BEAUTIFUL, as Lily expected, having come out of Gabriel Mannion's boat shop. The hull was a gleaming red mahogany while the water-resistant slip-proof deck had been made with strips of burnished gold teak. "The Southeast Asian teak market is stable and under strict conservation laws," Burke told her when she'd commented on its beauty. "Gabe told me that you need documents reflecting a 'chain of custody' back to its original point of harvest in order to be legally sourced. Let me show you the cabin."

It was compact, but perfectly arranged. A dark gray leather bench curved around a table that he showed her could be folded up into a berth. There was a glass stove top, microwave, a black granite sink, and cherry storage cabinets with fasteners that would prevent them from coming open during rough seas.

Behind a sliding door was a sink and toilet with a separate shower, and, impossible to miss at the back, a raised double bed in its own alcove with draw curtains.

"You definitely have all the comforts of home," she said, knowing that as high-end as it was, with the beautiful leather, wood, and shiny fixtures, it was a far cry from that penthouse he'd never talked her into visiting. "You can even cook."

"I could. But being a good citizen who cares about contributing to the local economy and small businesses, my plan is to either stick to takeout, eat at the farm, which is also currently takeout, or enjoy the occasional meal from Brianna. Which is what I brought along tonight." He bent his head and brushed a quick kiss against her lips. "Wait here. I'll be right back."

He went out to the truck and returned with a wicker basket. "Although she doesn't serve lunch, or dinner, Bri occasionally makes up baskets for guests who want to take a picnic lunch out with them."

"It seems you've thought of everything," she said, wondering if he was following in John Mannion's footsteps and planned for this to be *his* seduction dinner. If he was out to seduce, he'd get no argument from her.

"I try. I thought we'd go out to Pirates' Cove, drop anchor, and have a light supper."

"That sounds perfect."

Tales of rum-swigging pirates plying the waters, hiding out, and burying their treasure in the cove had been invalidated when a University of Washington historian discovered the cove had initially been named by an ambitious land developer in the 1800s, hoping to become wealthy off the railroad that never arrived.

Nevertheless, although it might not appear on any official geographical map, the name Pirates' Cove had stuck, conjuring up visions of swashbuckling pirates sailing on tall-masted ships flying black Jolly Roger flags.

With all the work events she'd been dealing with, Lily had been feeling stressed out even before Burke had come home. Yet now, as she stood beside him, enjoying the mist on her face and breathing in the tang of salt water along with the sharp scent of the fir trees, she felt her mind calm and the tension that had taken over her body begin to relax.

"Thank you," she said. "I needed this."

He smiled down at her. "Me, too."

The smile was a warm, intimate one that Lily had thought, when she'd first left New York, she'd never see again. Although she couldn't see his eyes from the sunglasses he'd put on, she could feel them smiling.

Both the sky and the deep blue water were turning shades of brilliant orange, pink and lilac as a golden sun was lowering when Burke pulled into the hidden cove, which, Lily considered, would have been too small to hide any pirate ships. A sandy beach curved around its shore, and fir, cedar, and Western hemlock, the state's official tree, created a thick green curtain between them and the rest of the world. After dropping anchor, Burke asked, "Do you want to eat in the cabin, or here on the deck?"

There were comfortable chairs, with striped sailcloth cushions she suspected were usually stored inside out of the weather, along with a table bolted to the deck. "Definitely out here." The air was cooling, making her glad she'd layered her sweater and jacket over her shirt, but so far, the sky, as promised, showed no sign of rain.

"I'll be right back." He kissed her, and as he climbed down the ladder into the cabin to retrieve Brianna's basket, she could feel her head spinning.

"This is some picnic," she said as he laid plates with the Herons Landing Victorian house printed on them on the table. In the basket were containers of fat green grapes, bright red-and-yellow Rainier cherries, candied pecans, and a smoked salmon spread with a choice of either water or sesame seed crackers.

"This is Brianna's version of a caprese sandwich," he said, unwrapping two sandwiches from the foil that had kept them warm. "She told me that it's pesto, made with fresh basil from her kitchen garden, mozzarella cheese from a local dairy, and tomatoes from Blue House Farm, since hers haven't quite ripened yet." The ingredients had been layered onto whole wheat bread, then grilled in a panini press.

"It looks delicious," Lily said.

"To be honest, green isn't my favorite food group, but I taste-tested the pesto, and it's excellent." He pulled a bottle of sparkling wine from Oregon's Chateau de Madeleine out of the basket, along with white pottery plates, silver utensils, linen place mats and matching napkins.

"If this is the type of pampering guests get at breakfast and in their rooms, I can see why she's booked through the summer," Lily said.

"She's never believed in not being the best at what she does," he said as he peeled the foil off the bottle. When he pushed the cork out with his thumbs, a whisper of vapor rose.

"That appears to be a family trait," she noted as he poured the sparkling wine into two flutes Brianna had packed and handed her one.

"I suppose so," he said thoughtfully. "And, as I said, there was competition between Gabe and Quinn, but being younger, Aiden, Bri and I were pretty much left out of it and were encouraged to choose our own paths."

What must it be like, she wondered with a bit of envy, to grow up in a family where everyone was encouraged to strive in their chosen fields, knowing that all the others were there to cheer you on and have your back?

They created their plates from the abundance Brianna had provided, content to appreciate the stillness. There were only the sounds of water lapping against the boat, and the breeze sighing through the trees.

"When we were kids, we'd dig in the sand here, looking for pirate coins," Burke said, breaking the comfortable silence.

"Did you ever find any?"

"We did." A slight reminiscent smile curved his lips. "It was a really big deal. By the time I was in middle school, I discovered that Mom and Dad bought fake coins and buried them for us to find."

"I love that story. That your parents would do that." She felt her eyes moistening as she imagined what adventurous fun that must have been. Like a Tom Sawyer and Huckleberry Finn existence.

"I'm sorry," he said quickly, his eyes echoing his words. "You know I didn't mean to hurt you—"

"It's okay. You're living proof that happy families really do exist."

"I lucked out," he said. "It occurred to me this afternoon that this boat ride is partly to get to know one another." He lifted a cluster of grapes, holding it out to her.

"I thought that's what we're doing," she said after she'd bitten into a fat green grape and tasted the explosion of sweet yet tart juice.

"True. But to help things along, and just cut to the chase, while I was running at the lake this morning, I thought of some questions to test our compatibility." He pulled a folded piece of paper from his pocket.

"You can't be serious."

"You never know. We could be, like you suggested, only a dynamite match in bed... So, here goes. Cat or dog?"

"That's obvious. Both."

"Good answer. Chocolate or vanilla?"

"No contest. Chocolate. With fudge sauce."

"We're on a roll. Movies at home or in a theater?"

"It depends. Am I alone, with friends, or are we talking about a 'Netflix and chill' evening?"

"That's for you to decide."

"As much as I enjoyed our date night movie, home, if I'm

alone or with friends. With messy, buttered popcorn. 'Net-flix and chill' is defined by watching at home. And I'd still go for the popcorn." She paused. "But we'd probably miss a lot of the movie because we'd be too busy making out."

He ran his finger around the rim of his glass, his eyes on hers, letting her know that he was remembering nights they'd never made it to the end of a movie. "A woman after my own heart... Meat or vegetables?"

Lily had been so transfixed by that finger now running slowly down the stem of that glass, then back up, that she'd missed the question.

"I'm sorry." She lifted her gaze back to his. "What was that again?"

"Meat," he repeated as she struggled not to be distracted again by those dark, stroking fingers. Although they'd experienced that immediate, initial spark at the charity event, and the sex had always been off the charts, something had changed tonight. *He* had changed as the air between them was becoming charged in an unfamiliar way. "Or vegetables?"

"Both." Trembling beneath her skin, with effort, she lifted her chin and met that steady blue gaze. "Steak with mushrooms and roasted asparagus."

"Good compromise." His lips, which she could still taste in her sleep, quirked in a slight smile that gave her the impression he knew exactly the effect he was having on her. She also now fully understood why he'd been voted offensive team captain during all those NFL seasons. Burke Mannion possessed a quiet yet commanding alpha male presence that caused her to surrender the tightly held control that had served as her lifeline for as long as she could remember.

"We continue to be a perfect match... Name the happiest time in your life."

That was an easy one. "My previous one was ice skating with you at Rockefeller Center," she admitted.

He nodded approvingly. "I like that response. What surpassed it?"

The sun sank into the gilded water with a burst of fiery colors. "Here. Now." Her voice was soft. A bit shaky. But sure. "In this moment."

"We crushed it." His voice deepened. "Final question for the win. There are still two slices of Brianna's famous key lime pie in the basket for dessert. Do you want to eat yours now?" He trailed the back of his hand down the side of her face. "Or later?"

There was no need for him to have asked. She met his steady gaze and polished off the last of the champagne in her glass. "Later."

"I told you that we were a perfect match," he said with satisfaction. He stood up and held his hand down, pulling her to her feet and kissing her again. "Did I give you a tour of the cabin?"

"You did. But I wouldn't mind another. In case I missed something the first time."

His answering grin was quick, deeply creasing those dimples. His gaze was wickedly satisfied. "A perfect match," he repeated as, her hand still in his, he led her down the ladder into the cabin.

All day long, as Lily had attempted to concentrate on her work, her thoughts had been like spindrift, sea spray blown around by the wind, while waves of memories she'd tried so hard to forget kept tumbling through her mind. Fortunately, having gotten engaged to Anna didn't seem to have affected Paul's brain nearly as badly as hers had been by merely anticipating this evening. Every time she stumbled over a question from one of the many committees she'd met with, he'd jumped in with facts and figures to save her.

She hadn't dated during her time in Honeymoon Harbor. Not because she hadn't been asked, but because none of those men had been the one standing before her. She took off her jacket, hanging it on a wall hook.

When she turned around, she found him still standing there, his face serious. "Although this risks breaking the mood, you need to know that although I admittedly went batshit crazy for a while, I always used a condom, and after I'd passed that stage, I had a clear STD test. And I haven't had sex—well, except solo—since," he admitted. "But if it'll make you feel safer, I brought protection with me."

"I haven't been with anyone since you," she said. "And the birth control implant I had when we were together lasts for three years, so we're good there."

"Okay." He blew out a long breath. "So…now that we've gotten that out of the way, moving on to the good stuff, did I tell you that I like that sweater?"

"No, but that's okay." The wool knit sweater wasn't the sexiest thing in her closet, but she'd chosen it to keep warm on deck; it wasn't as if she'd expected to be wearing it for that long.

"I was remiss. I do like it, especially that cute little collar. But let's start with you taking it off." His earlier conversational voice turned deeper, and, like a tuning fork, sent vibrations through her.

After she'd taken off the sweater, putting it on the leather bench seat, he tugged her blouse free of her jeans and unfastened the buttons, pressing his mouth against each new bit of revealed skin. When done, he slid the blouse off her shoulders and down her arms, leaving the last two remaining buttons at her wrists still fastened, effectively keeping her hands from being able to reach out and touch him.

His gaze heated as he took in the lacy white bra. Then he trailed one of those long, ultrasensitive fingers that had had her so transfixed over the crest of her breasts, leaving a trail of sparks. "Nice," he murmured. "Do you have any idea how long I've fantasized about being this way again with you?"

"No," she whispered.

"Since the last morning in Manhattan, when I left your apartment to go on that road trip. Whenever we were apart, except for those four quarters every week when my mind autofocused on the game, I'd look forward to getting back to you. To be with you, skin to skin, buried deep inside you, with your long, smooth legs wrapped around my hips…"

"Even after that text," he answered the question she didn't dare ask.

There was a wicked gleam in eyes that had darkened to the deep blue of a storm-tossed sea. "I did imagine ways to pay you back after reading it," he said. "I imagined touching you, branding every inch of your body with my hands." He skimmed a thumb from the lacy band at the bottom of the bra to her waist. Glancing down, she could see the faint pink trail his neatly trimmed nail had left behind.

He bent his head again, and when she'd expected another of those deep, dark kisses, he merely skimmed the tip of his tongue over her lips.

"After I imagined being done with my hands," he continued, breaking off the light touch, "I'd picture tasting all those places my hands had been. Like here."

He pressed his mouth against where her pulse was hammering in that hollow of her throat, then lower, over her breasts. Having planned for sex, she'd worn a bra with a front clasp, which he undid with the easy touch of a man who definitely knew his way around women's lingerie. Cupping each breast in his hands, his thumbs skimmed over nipples that pebbled beneath his touch. Then, lifting her up onto her toes with one arm, he took them, one at a time, into his mouth, wetting them with his tongue before nipping, ever so lightly, on her ultrasensitive nipples.

Lily heard a ragged, needy sound escape her lips. "Burke. Please."

"Shhh." He pressed a finger against her lips. "Do you know what I'd imagine doing next?"

Unable to answer, she merely shook her head.

"When I had you desperate for release, I'd make you beg."

She'd do that. Now. If begging was what it took, she wouldn't hesitate tonight.

"The thing is," he continued, "now that the occasion has actually arisen, I find myself reconsidering." His gravelly voice revealed that she wasn't the only one affected by his words. And the visions they conjured up. "Turn around."

None of this had been in today's fantasies, but trusting Burke, knowing that he'd never hurt her, Lily did as instructed. She then felt him lifting her braid to blow a soft, hot breath at the nape of her neck. Next, she felt an open-mouthed kiss at the warmed place that, like her tightened nipples, apparently had a direct connection to the hot, dampening place between her thighs.

She felt him pull off her stretchy hair tie. Then his fingers went to work. After he'd undone the plait she'd so carefully interwoven, he gathered her loosened hair in his fist, using it to turn her back around to face him.

Again he paused. "It wouldn't have worked," he said as he yanked his sweater over his head, tossing it onto the floor.

"What wouldn't have worked?" she asked. "And not to

break the mood, but that's a terrible way to treat a Brunello Cucinelli sweater."

"Getting revenge by making you beg isn't really me. I'd rather a woman be equal, in life and in bed. And you have a good eye."

"When I lived in Florence, I went to Milan during Fashion Week. Admittedly mostly for the shoes, but Cucinelli isn't called the cashmere fashion czar for nothing. You'd also make me very happy if you'd ditched that silk jersey T-shirt." The dark gray shirt fit his body like a glove, clinging to his biceps and rock-hard eight-pack she'd once loved to map with her mouth. "And I'd appreciate you unfastening my wrists. Because it's not fair that you get to touch and I don't."

"Point taken." When he yanked his shirt over his head, then tossed it on top of the sweater, Lily had to remind herself not to drool. "I've always liked the way you touch me. Which, by the way, you were doing exceptionally well in last night's dream." After unfastening those last two wrist buttons, he pushed the blouse the rest of the way off, where it joined their other discarded clothes on the floor.

Then they stood there, facing each other, both naked from the waist up. "You're still wearing too many clothes," Lily complained.

"Great minds." His lips quirked. "I was about to say the same thing about you."

Before Burke, she'd been more comfortable having sex with the lights turned off. At the very most, a candle or two. But although he might have been reluctantly willing to stay hidden away in her apartment, he'd insisted on watching her during sex.

"We could do rock, paper, scissors to see who goes first," he suggested finally. "Or we could just get the rest of our damn clothes off and have boat sex."

"Which I've never experienced." When he didn't say

anything, his silence spoke volumes. "And of course, you have." For some reason, although Lily had no claims whatsoever on Burke Mannion, the fact that she wasn't the first stung. Just a little.

"I was sixteen. And Gabe had built a sloop for Seth. Which I borrowed to take Peggy Ann Robbins out one summer day. If it makes you feel any better, a fast thunderstorm that hadn't been on the radar when we'd left the marina came sweeping over the mountains from the coast, and we nearly capsized. Wrapping up, we both managed to make it home safely, with our virginity intact. She's now a dental hygienist, with three kids, living in Portland with her orthodontist husband."

"You both could have drowned."

"Now you're sounding like our parents. Who grounded each of us for two weeks. For the rest of the summer, we did our best to avoid each other because that humiliating afternoon will never show up on either one of our best moments highlight reels. So you'll be my first successful sex on a boat. Could we just move on and talk later? Because I've got to tell you, Lily, this is getting downright painful."

She told herself not to look. But she couldn't resist. And she felt her knees weaken.

"First one in bed gets to be on top," she said, the metal teeth on her jeans rasping as she quickly unzipped them while toeing off her sneakers.

Although she beat him onto the sheets, being a generous woman, Lily let him have his turn, too.

Much, much, later, as they lay together, gazing up at the dazzling diamond stars through the skylight Gabe had installed overhead, Lily slipped out of his embrace. Although he'd said that he wouldn't make her beg, she went up on her knees, folded her hands together in supplication and said, "Please, sir. May I have some more?"

CHAPTER TWENTY

BECAUSE THE NEXT day was a workday for Lily, Burke got her home by midnight.

"Like Cinderella," he said as he took her face in his hands and kissed her at her door. Despite the way they'd spent the past few hours, which should have left them both sexually sated, he felt her faint tremor. Her lips were full and swollen, but that didn't stop him from nipping at the bottom one.

"We could change the storyline," she suggested, looking up at him through thick lashes. Although he might have been taking too much for granted, he suspected he was the only person who knew Lily Carpenter could flirt. She trailed her fingers down the front of his sweater. "Why did it have to be midnight, anyway?" she asked, toying with his belt buckle. "Why not one o'clock? Or two?"

When she appeared inclined to take that stroking touch lower, he caught her hands. "Because all the magic disappears at midnight."

"But how does she know that for sure if she doesn't test it?" she argued. "That deadline is merely an example of the patriarchal mandate of obedience. Emphasized by a threat that if Cinderella doesn't return to domesticity and remain docile, she'll risk losing her chance at ever nabbing the prince. The entire message of fairy tales, instilled during childhood, is to keep women in their place."

As the memory of Lily naked and on her knees flashed through Burke's mind, a far corner of his male brain, which had apparently not yet fully evolved, momentarily considered that a very fine place for her to be.

She'd proven herself to be even more sexually eager than she'd been in that sterile apartment in New York. He shoved his hands into his pockets to keep from dragging her inside the house and giving in to what they both wanted. Unfortunately, the gesture caused yet another problem, as it pulled the denim of his jeans taut, outlining a renewed erection. From the glint of satisfaction in her eyes, he knew that she'd noticed it, too.

"Have I ever given you the impression I want to keep you in your place?" he asked. "Which, as you've already proven, is impossible anyway?"

"I've already apologized for running away," she said. "And no, you always treated me like an equal. Even in bed."

"Which is where you always wanted to keep me."

Her lips quirked. "Touché."

"Remember when I suggested going up to the Lodge at Lake Quinault for dinner?"

"Of course."

"How about tomorrow?"

"I'd love that." She went up on her toes, threaded her hands through his hair, and kissed him. "Text me with the time," she murmured against his lips.

"I'll do that." And then, as he waited for her to go into the house and close the door behind her, Burke began making plans.

JIM HADN'T ATTENDED the Heritage Day festival since he'd freaked out during the parade when he'd been nine years old. At the time, having already been diagnosed with what was then called Asperger's syndrome, his parents, only wanting the best for him, had reacted in a way that had seemed logical at the time. They'd avoided putting him in situations where he'd feel overwhelmed and stressed out. Elementary school had proven challenging, but he'd been fortunate to have mostly caring teachers who'd encouraged him.

Later, a therapist his mother had taken him to for six weeks when he'd been in middle school had added a diagnosis of social anxiety disorder, and assigned him tasks. Like asking a different student a question each day, which was designed to result in a brief conversation. He'd kept a journal, and after he'd gone a month, the task had become two questions a day. Then three. Then five.

"Fake it 'til you make it," his dad had always said. Meaning that if he pretended he could carry on a conversation with others, he'd eventually be able to. Tom Olson had not been a psychologist or therapist, but he'd turned out to have a good idea of human nature, because practicing that advice began to help. Many kids had laughed at him. Others had simply walked away. But day by day, month by month, he'd developed the ability to survive middle school, which his dad had assured him was a chaotic period for everyone.

By the time he was in high school, he'd collected a small circle of friends. There'd been all the Mannions, even Aiden, who'd spent so much time in detention he could have been one of the students in *The Breakfast Club*, which Jim had watched the summer before he'd gone to high school to help prepare for that new experience. Then there was Seth Harper and his girlfriend, Zoe, along with Kylee. Also, Jolene. Having had a father in prison, and a mother who was rumored to be a prostitute—which wasn't remotely true—made her another outcast. Like him.

He'd been doing well enough that by his junior year, he'd been able to take Kylee to the prom. And although she'd spent most of the time dancing with her secret girlfriend, leaving him standing against the wall with the parent and teacher chaperones, he'd survived.

But over time, his friends had left Honeymoon Harbor, and his social sphere gradually narrowed. It had gotten even smaller once his parents had left for Arizona. One of the more difficult parts of social anxiety was that it could be a very private battle if you didn't have anyone to share your problems with. Or, as Gabe and Burke had called themselves, wingmen.

Then Sage had suddenly appeared in his greenhouse and had pulled him out of his narrowing comfort zone. Her enthusiasm proved so contagious, he'd searched for internet message boards populated with people like him and was surprised by how many there were. One group in Port Townsend, led by a very friendly licensed psycho-therapist, held monthly in-person meetings to reportedly keep people from sliding into agoraphobia. Jim was intelligent and self-aware enough to realize that could become a very real risk for him.

The monthly meetings were held in the woman's home, in a room with a small indoor fountain and many pots filled with plants. Brightly colored posters on the wall featured encouraging messages such as *Life is not waiting out the storm, but learning to dance in the rain.* And *I Am Calm. I Am Capable. I Am Strong.* Which were very encouraging, but Jim identified most with a T-shirt one man wore that read, *I came. I saw. I had anxiety. I left.*

Members were encouraged to share both problems and achievements. One young man coded from home, only having to connect with his boss and coworkers by email or texts. It sounded as if he had a perfect life. Until he shared how isolated and lonely he'd become. Which was why he'd attended the meeting. After welcoming Jim, the friendly therapist congratulated him on choosing to find change but pointed out that she didn't have a magic solution. He could go to all the therapists in the world, even take prescribed drugs to quiet the anxiety caused by heightened flight response. But at the end of the day, if he wanted to change—which Jim certainly did—he'd have to take responsibility for those changes and pick up the reins of his own life.

At that point, a woman stood and shared that she'd spent years trying to do the simple household task of buying groceries, but the minute she'd walk into the store, she'd envision the aisles as tunnels where monsters would hide, waiting to attack. Hiring someone to do the shopping and delivery for her solved the problem of acquiring food but had only isolated her more. Then, two months ago, she'd sought help from a volunteer group where people would do different tasks for you. In her case, someone would accompany her to the market each week and walk her through the shopping. Six weeks later, not only was she able to shop on her own, she'd made friends with the cashier who, like her, turned out to be a knitter and even invited her to a knitting circle. Digging into a canvas bag of yarn at her side, she held up a tiny pink sweater and cap that she'd just finished for her first grandchild, who was due to be born next month.

After everyone had applauded her success story, she said that she'd learned to think of any goal as a journey, and if you didn't take that all-important first step, then a second, and a third, you'd never reach it.

Taking the messages of the meeting to heart, Jim left feeling encouraged. After all, having survived the trip with Sage to eat burgers at the lake, thanks to Gabe and Burke

Mannion's help, he'd even initiated a date, a successful one, during which he'd eaten a very good meal and had enjoyed talking with the others about the movie and hearing about John and Sarah's romance.

Emboldened, he put down the petri dish he'd been working on, took his phone out of his pocket, and called the number Sage had put in it before having him put his in hers. He'd seen people doing that on the movies he'd been watching for research for his date.

"Hi," she said, answering right away. "I was just working on an Instagram story letting people know Blue House Farm was going to be at the Heritage Day festival." She'd already ordered canvas shopping bags with a logo of the house she'd created herself and ceramic coffee mugs and stainless steel travel mugs with that same farm logo in an oval surrounded by bright flowers, which she assured him would help build his brand. "What's up?"

"I'm calling about the farm's booth at the festival," Jim said.

"Oh, you don't have to worry. I got one and I promise not to wrap it in vinyl. I did paint it, though. Like I did the one at the market."

She'd gone along with his firm belief that the farmers market booth should blend in more with the rest of the rustic ones at the market. But she had painted bright herbs and flowers all over it, which had proven more eye-catching to people walking by than the bare wood. She'd taken him to see it after the market had closed.

"I'm not worried." That was a partial truth. He wasn't concerned about her being able to handle sales and draw passersby in with her sunshine personality, but he was worried about whether or not this latest plan would work. "I'm calling to tell you that I'll be there, too."

"You're going to the festival?"

"I thought I would. I haven't attended in a very long time."

Not since Saturday, May 23, 1998. The day of the infamous meltdown.

"Are you sure?" He could hear the concern in her voice.

"Not really," he admitted, remembering the advice from his group that if you tried to stuff your fears inside, they'd only grow and smother you. "I have concerns, but I'm feeling surprisingly confident that I can do it." And he reminded himself that he'd come a very long way since the meltdown.

"Any man who can create a blue rose should be able to accept compliments on his flowers from everyone who'll be buying them."

It did not escape his notice that she'd said *can*. As if it were a foregone conclusion. Except for his father's *fake it until you make it* advice, and Gabe and Burke reassuring him that his dating worries were normal, no one had ever stated such confidence in him before. After agreeing on a time for her to come out to the farm the day before the festival to pack up the flowers and herbs they'd be selling, he hung up. As he started to put his phone back into his pocket, he realized that the muscles in his face felt strangely different. Holding up the phone, Jim took his first ever selfie and saw that he was smiling.

"I DON'T KNOW why it took me so long to get up here," Lily said as she gazed out over the expansive lawn leading to the spectacular lake surrounded by towering trees. The ninety-six-year-old cedar-sided resort was both grand and rustic at the same time. Guests included a who's who of old-time robber barons like the family she'd been born into, movie stars going back to the 1920s, and President Franklin Roosevelt. "I kept planning to, but something always seemed to take precedence."

"Eight of the largest trees in the US, some of the largest in the world, are in this little rain forest corner of the peninsula," Burke said. "Six of them right around this lake, and all of them over a thousand years old. We'd come up here a lot when I was a kid, and I'll admit we took them for granted. But now, thinking about it, it really puts life in perspective. The world's largest gigantic cedar is right down a trail from here. If you weren't dressed in those fancy, spindly high heels, I'd take you to see it."

"Next time," Lily said, accepting that there'd be a next time. Their conversation over dinner—clam chowder, grilled king salmon for her, what was billed as Roosevelt classic pot roast for him, and marionberry pie—had been easy and comfortable. No one watching them would have known that only days ago, there'd been so much negative energy sparking between them that Brianna had immediately picked up on it.

"Besides, I'm not that dressed up." She wore a black wrap dress with a deep V-neck that she hadn't donned since leaving New York. "Okay," she admitted when he slanted a significant glance at the leopard-print pumps she'd had to carry to keep from sinking into the lawn, "it might be overkill for here, but my only excuse is that whenever a hot pro quarterback takes me out on a date, it's only natural to want to knock his socks off."

"Been out on dates with a lot of quarterbacks, have you?"

"Only one. And only two dates. Wednesday night doesn't count because it was a triple date. And if you want to get technical, last night's boat date wasn't one, either, because the deal was these dates are supposed to be for learning new things about each other. Which I suppose we did because of your questionnaire. But sex is the one thing we learned early on that we're really, really good at."

"Together," he agreed. "It's only that good with you. And in the future, sweetheart, know that anytime you want to knock any piece of my clothing off, you won't need a designer dress and snazzy high heels to do it. I'll take off whatever you want, whenever you want." He flashed those dual dimples she'd never thought she'd see again when she'd left New York. All the Mannion men, from John and his artist brother, Mike, along with Burke and his three brothers, should have come with warning labels.

"That would be most of the time," she admitted.

"Only most?"

"I can't remember any prohibition being stated in my personnel manual, but I suspect that having sex in my office at the college might be frowned on."

"You could be right." He thoughtfully chewed on that thumbnail that had trailed down her body last night. "Do you have a key to the building?"

"It works by a coded number on a keypad," she said.

"Which you know."

"Of course. Because I work a lot of nights and weekends when the building is closed." The gleam in his eyes had her getting his drift. "No. We are not going to have desk sex in my office."

Heaven help her, she was drowning in his eyes as he leaned closer, slipping a hand into the wrap dress's opening and skimming his fingers up her bare thigh.

"So, that's a no?" The fingers went higher even as he held her gaze with his.

"Yes. I mean, yes, that's a no. I couldn't. We couldn't." Her logical mind meant those words. But another, wilder, riskier part of her that only he had ever been able to release couldn't stop her from imagining it.

"I'll bet we could." His voice sounded all too reasonable for what they were discussing, "Like you said, sex is one of the things we do really, really well." The grin he shot her was deliberately provocative. "And it'd be one more thing I could take off my bucket list."

"Just because we *could* doesn't mean that we *should*." She needed to remember that. Even when she was wanting his mouth to follow that wicked path his fingers were making.

"Just keep it in mind." Stopping before they risked a ranger having to cite them for public indecency, he trailed those treacherous fingers back down to her knee and closed the gap in the black silk. As if, she thought as they walked back to where he'd parked the truck, she was going to be able to get that provocative image out of her mind.

"We'd better get back," she said as twilight began to settle over the lake. "I let Chance out before we left, but I don't want to risk him lifting his leg and marking everything in the house."

"We males do like to mark our territory." The teasing light dancing in his eyes told her that he was baiting her with that blatantly sexist remark, a bait she refused to bite at.

"That's why we women are a superior species. After all, Adam was merely a first draft."

He laughed and put his arm around her shoulder. "Don't take this the wrong way, but I always thought, when I finally got around to getting married, I was going to want a marriage like my folks'."

"Who wouldn't?" she asked as he unlocked her passenger door. "They've always seemed to be the perfect couple."

"They are. For them. But my grandparents are in their eighties, and Gramps still tries to get a rise from Gram. She'll shoot him right down." He walked around the front of the truck, climbed into the driver's seat, and fastened his seat belt. "It's not bickering like some elderly folks seem to do. They've been that way for as long as I can remember. It's just a game they play." As he drove out of the parking lot, he added, "I think we're going to be more like them."

Unable to think of an immediate response to the fact that he seemed to be taking for granted that they'd still be together fifty-some years from now, Lily didn't say anything.

Seeming comfortable with the silence surrounding them, he punched a button on the dash and had smooth jazz coming out of the truck speakers.

As they neared Honeymoon Harbor, he glanced over at her and asked, "Your place or mine?"

Lily momentarily wondered if he automatically expected to end the evening with sex. But being annoyed about that would be hypocritical; if she hadn't expected that herself, she wouldn't have dug out her sexiest lingerie.

"Mine," she decided. "The bed's bigger."

CHAPTER TWENTY-ONE

SATURDAY MORNING, since Lily professed the need to get some work done at her office, Burke was back on the boat, watching a replay of a forty-three-year-old Tom Brady dominate the Kansas City Chiefs 31 to 9 in the 2021 Super Bowl. Which secured Brady a seventh Lombardi Trophy, two more than any other player in NFL history. And he'd done it on two separate teams, a feat only he and a thirty-nine-year-old Peyton Manning had been able to pull off.

The game reminded Burke that he still had a lot of good playing years left to chase those records. He had not a single doubt that even if he did end up going to another team, like Brady to the Bucs, or Manning to the Broncos, he could win at least one more Super Bowl. Get a second Lombardi Trophy and another ring so ostentatious that he only wore it on special football occasions. Like awards dinners. Or when he was doing a charity event, like the night he'd met Lily. Who'd told him she didn't really watch football.

He could tell she hadn't been overly impressed by all the broken records the guy with the mike had read off while introducing him. In his line of work, he couldn't go to a club or even a hotel on the road without groupies, aka cleat chasers, hitting on him, offering all sorts of kink.

He remembered an older Pro Bowler warning him his rookie year that those women could be every young football player's dream. And every young football player's nightmare.

Though the attraction between Lily and him had been instantaneous, and they'd left together and ended up in bed, she was no groupie. That veteran player had warned him that when groupies came up to you, it was a good bet that nearly every other word out of their glossy red mouths was a flat-out lie. Lily hadn't been honest with him. But neither had she lied. While he understood her reasoning, and wished she'd told him earlier, they'd moved on.

But there were a lot of balls in the air right now. A lot of decisions to be made. Decisions that put more on the line than that day he'd walked into the Knights office, giving Sam Otterbein what they both knew was an ultimatum. Not helping were all the calls from his agent about other teams around the league asking if the rumors of him going on the market were true. And, if so, they wanted to get in on the bidding.

Now, whatever he chose to do, he'd have to figure out how he could make the situation fit into a life with Lily. And speaking of Lily, his phone began to buzz with her name on the screen.

"Hey," he answered. "Are you still at the office?"

"I'm afraid I am," she said. "But I was thinking, if you were interested, maybe you could pick up a pizza at Luca's, and I could take a break so we could have lunch together here in my office." She paused. "Unless you're too busy."

"No, I was just watching a Super Bowl game."

"I might not be all that up on football, but I do know that the Super Bowl is always in either late January or early February."

"True. This is an old game."

There was a long pause. "One you haven't seen?"

"I've watched it a few times," he said. And every time

he'd spotted another slight change in a play that he'd missed seeing the other times.

Silence. He wondered if the call had dropped.

"Lily, are you still there?"

"Yes. I was just trying to imagine watching a game when you already know the score."

"How many times did you say you've watched *Casablanca*? Even knowing how it ends?"

She sighed. "You win. Point taken… So, can you make lunch?"

"Give me thirty minutes. What do you want on it?"

"You choose. But no pineapple."

"Why the hell would anyone want pineapple on a pizza? That's just insane."

She laughed. "Once again, we're in perfect agreement. I'll see you'll in a bit." Then, after promising that he'd guard the code with his life, she gave him the numbers to the main door.

IT WASN'T THE way he would have preferred to spend a Saturday with Lily, but as he drove to the college, Burke thought of all the times she'd had to fit her life into his crazy road schedule, which she'd still have to do if he accepted the offer the Knights had put on the table. Or accepted an offer from some other team. So many decisions to make, and now that Lily was part of the equation, he had way more to weigh.

Remembering what he'd told her about living in the moment, despite the career pressure, Burke decided, for now, to take his own advice and enjoy having a pizza with his woman.

He put the numbers she'd given him into the keypad, which opened the outer door. It closed and locked behind him. The building seemed to be empty. He passed the reception desk, then took the elevator up to her floor. The outer office, where the young man had been busy at work, was empty, the door to Lily's office closed. He knocked once to let her know he was here, then walked in.

She was wearing that tidy white blouse with the little ribbon black tie, and that slender black pencil skirt again. His first thought was to wonder why she'd go to all the trouble to dress in office clothes on a Saturday. Then he took in her legs, which were clad in sheer black stockings. Her shoes were black stilettos, with thin suede ribbons that crisscrossed up to her slender ankles, ending in a bow that echoed the one worn at her neck.

"Oh, my goodness, Mr. Mannion," she said, her green eyes widening in apparent surprise as her hand flew to her throat. "I didn't realize you'd be coming into the office today. I was expecting my boyfriend, Dennis."

Lily initiating sexual role-play in her office was definitely not what he'd been expecting. But it sure as hell beat an old Super Bowl Game. He folded his arms. "I saw a guy, who I take was your boyfriend, trying to get into the building, and told him if he didn't leave right away, I was calling the cops."

"Oh, thank you," she said. "For not calling the police on Dennis. It's all my fault, sir. I was up late last night, then worked so hard this morning, I felt it would be all right to take a little break to have some pizza and some company."

"You know it's against the employee manual rules to use your office to entertain guests."

She lowered her eyes. "I'm sorry, sir." Her hands were now clasped at her waist as she twisted her fingers together. "It was only an impulse because I felt nervous being all alone in the building. I thought I'd be safer with a big, strong man here to protect me."

She took the pizza from his hands and bent over to place it onto the coffee table in front of the leather sofa, deliberately drawing his attention to her very fine ass.

Then she returned to stand in front of him and looked up at him through her lashes. "Please don't fire me, Mr. Mannion. I desperately need the money to pay for my dear granny's operation." She twined her arms around his neck and pressed her body against his. With those six-inch heels, she was at just the right height for all the good parts to line up. "Is there anything I can do to convince you to forget the whole thing?" she asked in a soft, breathy voice.

Burke slid his hand beneath her skirt, slowly lifting it up her legs. When he came to the lace top of the stockings, held up by a garter belt, he said, "I'm sure we can think of something."

MINUTES LATER, he stood over the desk, looking down at her. Her fair skin was glistening, her cheekbones flushed a soft pink. She was so beautiful. And she might not be ready to admit it yet, but she was his.

"Being a compassionate man, I suppose I can overlook your flaunting of the rules, Ms. Carpenter," he said in a gruff tone, returning to character to wrap up the role-playing scene she'd surprised him with. "I certainly wouldn't want to be responsible for your grandmother not receiving proper medical care." Unable to resist one last touch, he trailed a finger along the skin just above the top of those black stockings. "May I inquire as to what type of operation she's having?"

"A boob job," Lily said as she stood and began gathering up her clothes that had gone flying before she'd landed on the desk. "A new tenant moved into the apartment next to hers in the Cedar Lane Senior Residence Center, and she decided she needed to have her breasts fluffed up to have a better chance of nabbing him before the competition could."

"I thought you'd given up lying." Laughing, Burke drew her into his arms for a long, slow kiss.

After they'd come up for air, her smiling green eyes gleamed like finely polished emeralds. "I'm so sorry, Mr. Mannion," she said as she skimmed a pink fingernail down the front of his rumpled shirt. "It was an impulse."

INSTEAD OF RETURNING to the boat, Burke followed her back to her house, where Chance greeted him with his usual crazed dog welcome while Zendaya pretended disdain, which he knew was a lie, because when he woke the next morning in Lily's bed, the cat was sleeping, sprawled across his legs.

"She usually does that to me," Lily said. She was lying beside him, her elbow on the mattress, her head braced on her hand as she looked down at him. "Apparently I've been displaced, which just goes to prove your irresistible attraction."

Her smile was warm, and she looked more relaxed than usual. Like, he thought, a woman who'd been loved well and often. The sheet had pooled around her waist, causing his brain to flash back to the memory of when he'd been awakened sometime before dawn. The entire scene flashed like a high-definition movie on a screen in his mind, as real as if it were happening now.

At first, when he felt her fingers curve around his morning erection and begin to stroke it, he thought he'd been dreaming. Until her tongue swirled wetly around the tip.

Fully awakened, he rolled them over so she was beneath

him, her long, smooth legs wrapped around his hips. Covering her mouth with his, he kissed her slowly, deeply, slipping a bit inside her. He heard the catch of her breath. Then, when he paused, she arched, lifting herself, wanting more. Which was when he pulled out, rubbing against her heat, teasing her sensitive flesh. His eyes were on hers, watching her rising pleasure, along with a raw, naked need and vulnerability she'd only ever revealed in bed. He went deeper, pulling slightly back again, then deeper still, pulling out, keeping his thrusts slow and purposeful.

"Please, Burke," she gasped. "I want you. I *need* you."

She was not alone. He was aching but determined to give them both what they wanted. Needed. But not yet.

When she pressed her hands on his ass to hurry things along, he took them in his, linking their fingers, lifting them over her head. In. Out. In. Out. Each time pressing deeper, then pulling back while his mouth took hers, his tongue echoing the movement of his body. She was wet. Hot. And his.

He was thinking how she was the only woman who'd ever caused those caveman thoughts, when his control finally broke. He released her hands to grasp her hips. Lifted her up so he could plunge deeper, the way she liked it. This sex was no longer slow, sleepy, early-morning lovemaking. It was hard and fast until, with a ragged cry, she fell over the cliff, her orgasm pulsing around him as he followed.

"At first I thought I was dreaming," he said. "Because I'd been having a hot dream sex when you took me into your hands. Literally."

"Timing is everything," she said with a slow, satisfied smile. "I came back from the kitchen after getting a glass of water and saw you sprawled here in all your morning glory and couldn't resist."

"It sure as hell beats waking up to my phone alarm." The one he'd always had set for the dark of night, when she'd send him away.

"True. We've never had morning sex before. Which, I know, was entirely my fault, because except for that last day, when we left the house together, heading in different directions, I always made you leave right afterwards. Thinking about it, I'm sure that made you feel as if I was only using you for the sex."

"I knew, from that first time, that it was more than that, because I'd felt a connection I'd never experienced before with any other woman. What I couldn't understand at the time was why you had a problem with me staying over."

"It really was my concern over being found out. But also, I was afraid," she admitted. "Not of you, but of how you made me feel. It was so overwhelming."

"We fit." He ran a slow hand down her back, loving the way she arched in response. Despite the time apart, their connection was stronger than ever. "Now that we've hopefully put the ghosts of your insanely abusive family behind us, feel free to use me whenever or wherever you want."

"Be careful what you wish for," she warned. "As much as I'd be happy spending the rest of the day right here, I think I'll take a shower."

"Would you like company?" Another thing they'd never done together.

"It's important to save water these days. So by sharing, we'd be doing our part in saving our country's valuable resources." She gave him a quick kiss. "Let me just put Chance out and I'll join you."

The shower sex did not disappoint. The foamy soap she smoothed all over his body smelled like a piña colada, which, he knew if he got anywhere near his brothers, they'd give him a hard time about. It would be worth it to feel her wet, slick hands all over his body, then returning the favor.

The room steamed up as they took their time, dispensing with any excuse of saving water. The past few days had felt as if they were making up for lost time, and when neither of them was able to hold out any longer, he spun her around so that her hands were pressed against the white tile wall as he took her from behind. Including the desk sex, they'd set a new personal best for number of times in twenty-four hours.

As he indulged in tender afterplay, drying her with a fluffy white towel, he frowned as he took in her pink, beard-burned breasts and a bite mark starting to bruise on her shoulder. "I'm sorry," he said, gently touching the mark with a fingertip. "I hurt you."

"Don't apologize. I felt fabulously ravished. As if I was being taken by one of those marauding pirates that supposedly lived in that cove where you introduced me to boat sex. Besides, you should see your back."

Since it was the weekend, she dressed in a denim mini skirt and a tartan boyfriend shirt over a white tee. She'd discovered upon moving here that a plaid flannel shirt was practically a Pacific Northwest uniform, having been worn by both old-time loggers and Seattle bands Nirvana and Pearl Jam. Lily figured there were very few people in this part of the country who didn't have at least one plaid shirt in their closet. Today's was red, black and white, worn with simple, classic red Keds.

"I could make you eggs," she said, looking into a nearly empty refrigerator. "Or we could just go to Cops & Coffee. I've been craving one of their Boston cream doughnuts."

"Sounds good to me," Burke said. "Though I think I'll go with their apple bear claw."

"Those are good, too," she said, considering. "But mine is glazed with chocolate. And since we can walk there, I'll work off the calories."

"That's the same reasoning you gave for showers saving water."

She rewarded him with one of those dazzling smiles and a kiss. "Exactly."

THEY SPENT SUNDAY AFTERNOON at Mirror Lake, just outside of town, where Gabe, Chelsea and their daughters lived in a sprawling mansion Gabe had bought from a tech friend who'd initially had it built for weekends and vacations, belatedly realizing that peace and quiet got on his nerves. That night, they celebrated his parents' thirty-seventh anniversary at the home Burke had grown up in. Most years, the occasion grew to be a big, boisterous event including their many friends, who'd bring side dishes while John would grill steaks with potatoes in a re-creation of what their mother insisted was their father's "seduction dinner."

This year, not wanting Sarah to get too excited while her brain healed, they kept the party to just family. Plus Lily, who that night had made the unstated but obvious change from friend to family. Especially to Sarah, with whom Lily had shared a moment alone with in the kitchen.

"It's so wonderful that Burke's finally found his special someone," she said. "That it turned out to be you makes it even better. Have you made any plans?"

"Not really," Lily said. "We're pretty much living in the moment."

"That's a wonderful plan in itself. John and I never had what you could call an old-fashioned courtship. We were always having to steal whatever secret time we could. Then, when we both returned home, we just knew that it was time to begin the rest of our lives together."

"I knew the moment we met," Lily admitted. "But life proved complicated."

"It always is," Sarah said with a knowing nod. "But as long as you both remember that you love each other, things will work out."

Lily might have put away her discomfort about her past, but she still wasn't totally at ease discussing her feelings. "I'm not sure we're at that point yet," she said.

Sarah's eyes warmed. "Oh, darling, it was obvious the moment the two of you walked in the door. You both had that special golden glow around you."

Lily thought that sounded a bit surprising from the usually no-nonsense woman. It would more likely come from Sage's New Age self-named Wiccan mother, Willow, who'd come to Honeymoon Harbor to celebrate Yule with her daughter last winter. Not quite knowing how to respond, Lily managed a faint smile.

"It's like having another daughter," Sarah said happily. "And it was definitely worth having that accident to get you two back together. It was fate, although admittedly more dramatic than John and me finding ourselves at LAX coming back from different places in the world. Now if only Quinn would find *his* special someone," she said with a sigh.

Then, saving Lily from having to come up with a response to that, Sarah carried a platter of roasted Parmesan asparagus out to the dining room, leaving Lily to carry in her contribution to the dinner. She'd gotten the recipe for cheesy corn with bacon from Jolene, who'd been equally desperate for a side dish idea when she and her mother had been invited to the Mannions' for Thanksgiving. She'd gotten the recipe from her best friend, whose French chef husband had assured Jolene that not only was it easy, it had always sold out when he'd offered it at the food truck he'd run to fund his now insanely popular LA restaurant.

On Monday, Burke spent the day out on the lake on the boat, fishing with Quinn, trying to figure out how to make things work so he and Lily could be together.

"I know players who had long-distance relationships after they got traded, because their wives didn't want to make the kids move to another school. Or for those with short contracts, their wives would be tired of moving every few months. Sometimes she just liked the city they were in, better than the one he'd been traded to.

"They seemed to make it work, but there were times when there'd be some cheating going on. Mostly by the guy, because being away from home, he was less likely to get caught, but I've also seen marriages break up because of the wife."

"So Mom's right about you two being serious? I didn't realize you were talking marriage."

"I brought it up, casually suggesting we'd be more like Gram and Gramps than Mom and Dad."

"What did she say to that?"

"Nothing. But she didn't say no. So I'm taking it as a yes."

"You could just ask her flat-out."

"I told her I'd manage to work something out," Burke said. "I'm saving the actual marriage proposal for when I can figure out what I'm going to be doing. Where I'll be living. The one thing I know is that I don't want a long-distance relationship."

"Which complicates things, given that she's been putting down what appear to be pretty deep roots."

"While it was a helluva surprise, that's also obvious."

"For what it's worth," Quinn said as his line jerked, "my money's on the two of you to work it out."

As he watched his brother reel in a two-foot rainbow trout, its gills glistening in the spring sunshine, Burke knew there had to be a way. He just needed to come up with one.

WANTING TO TAKE advantage of whatever time they had together until Burke returned to training camp in New York, or whatever other city he might land in, Lily left work early Monday so they could take Chance to the recently established dog park. They stood side by side, watching him race around in circles on those short legs, attempting to herd all the other dogs, some nearly three times his size.

Not willing to be separated, Zendaya had gone along with them, wearing her pink harness and leash. Keeping an eye on her bonded brother, she'd hiss and swipe at any curious dog who dared come near to investigate what a cat was doing at a dog park.

That night, they went to a movie at the refurbished Harbor Drive-In Theater that had reopened for the vacation season the past weekend. It was a psychological thriller based on a popular novel. Parked in the back row, they kept losing the story thread because he was driving her to distraction with those wonderful, wicked hands.

"I never had a chance to make out in a car at a drive-in before this," she murmured.

"That's a teenage rite of passage." He nibbled on her neck. "I don't have a *Back to the Future* time machine, but I'll do my best to compensate for your loss."

"You're doing very well so far," she assured him.

"This has me thinking about how my parents would ride

the ferry just to be together secretly when they were in high school. Maybe we ought to try that next," he suggested.

"Since they were sneaking away to be alone, I suspect they stayed in the car," she said. "Which is too bad, because the view from the deck is amazing."

"I'd need to wash out my brain with bleach if I allow myself to imagine my parents having sex—"

"Which, they certainly did. At least five times," she pointed out.

"True. Thinking about their situation, locking the X-rated stuff away in a closet in my brain, I have a very strong suspicion that Dad would've preferred the view in the car."

He gave her a look that Lily had come to recognize well. He didn't need any words to tell her that he'd really like her to get naked. Again. He leaned over and brushed his lips against that little spot right behind her ear, which, before meeting Burke, Lily had never realized was an erogenous zone. "How much do you care about hanging around for the ending?" he asked, causing that internal tuning fork to vibrate yet again.

She turned her head to meet his lips. "We can always stream it at home later."

"Good plan."

CHAPTER TWENTY-TWO

FOR THE NEXT WEEK, despite so much happening with her festival preparations and his contract negotiations, Lily and Burke behaved like any other couple in love. Not worrying what his former chemistry teacher might think, the day after their dinner at the lake, Burke moved his things from Quinn's boat to Lily's house.

He'd hung his clothes up in the space she'd made for him in the closet and was putting his underwear away in a dresser drawer she'd emptied for him when he spotted the snow globe on top of her dresser. Picking it up, he pushed the button on the bottom, causing the miniature couple to begin skating around the tiny ice rink to "Let It Snow" while snow swirled around them.

"You kept it," he said.

"It was the most perfect night of my life for a very long time," Lily repeated what she'd told him at the lake. "In the beginning, I kept it away in a drawer because it made me sad given how we'd ended. Or more accurately, how I'd messed things up. Later, I got it out again because it reminded me how, right when you don't expect it, life can gift you with a perfect moment."

"Maybe we can repeat it this coming Christmas," he suggested.

"That would be nice."

Lily tried to sound positive, but knew he'd heard the

hesitation in her response. Because, as much as she wanted a long-term relationship, she still wasn't certain how they were going to work things out if they ended up living on opposite coasts. Even without money being a problem, neither one of them could afford the time all that back-and-forth traveling would entail.

"Hey." He put a finger beneath her chin and lifted her gaze to his. "We're living in the moment, right?"

Her eyes had moistened when her mind had veered onto that vexing side road. Trying to put the problem aside, she returned his patient, reassuring look with a watery smile. "Of course." Even if it was easier said than done. The adult in her knew that that he was right. The eight-year-old girl, who occasionally whispered in her ear, was still waiting for her life to turn upside down. Again.

DESPITE SPRING BEING the most unpredictable time of year, the skies were a bright blue dotted with fluffy white clouds without a hint of gray for the Heritage Day festival. The opening parade went off without a hitch, and people who'd been lining both sides of the street streamed into the park, where local crafters had set up booths and were selling a variety of items, including ceramics, knitwear, sea-glass jewelry, fused glass coasters and sun catchers. Mike Mannion had set up a gallery of his students' art, and both Sarah's and Jolene's mother's paintings had sold out within the first hour.

The pop-up food court featuring local restaurants was doing a brisk business. Diego Chavez had brought his Taco the Town food truck to the park. Members of Paul's S'Klallam tribe were grilling oysters and preparing freshly caught spring salmon the way they'd been doing for over fifteen thousand years. The only difference was that instead of building the fire on the ground, as many still did at home, they were using a portable firepit they'd brought to the park. Skewered onto long sticks, the filets were held in place by small horizontal sticks. Then the salmon was cooked upright until the skin was crisp.

Quinn's pub was serving wings with five sauces, and Jarle drew a crowd—mostly women—as he flipped burgers on the large grill, while next to him, Luca was cooking pizzas on that same grill. Bastien, from Sensation Cajun, served up plates of jambalaya and bowls of banana bread pudding with praline sauce, while Leaf offered a choice of grilled veggie and avocado wraps and vegetarian sushi rolls.

An always popular annual event was a tug-of-war between the town's fire and police departments, held over a long, three-foot-deep blow-up pool of water into which the contestants were often pulled. Although she loved being with Burke, Lily had to agree with all the cheering women that there was definitely something to be said for hot, wet guys dressed in bike shorts and running shoes.

She'd assigned four students, two working the morning hours, two the afternoon, to man the college booth, handing out brochures and answering questions as part of a real-world marketing class assignment. She'd selected them from a pool of student volunteers who led prospective students and their families on tours of the school. She knew they'd handle the assignment well.

As she and Burke made their way through the crowd, he was unexpectedly asked to pose for selfies and sign autographs. When a trio of teenage girls wanted him to sign his name on the fronts of their Honeymoon Harbor High cheer team shirts—while they were wearing them—he declined with his hundred-watt smile and suggested selfies instead.

"I'm sorry." He laced his fingers with Lily's as the giggling girls ran across the park to show off their photos to another group of teens who'd been watching. "This is exactly what you didn't want."

"You're a local hero," she said, her tone matter-of-fact. "I've moved on from worrying what people might think about us being together, and if I hadn't been prepared for all the attention, I wouldn't have come with you. Though I am wondering if you're planning to spend some of those millions the Knights paid you to buy your own island so we can sometimes have privacy."

"Like you said, it's a local crowd. No one bothered us at the lake inn."

"True. This feels nice," she said. "Being like this together. It makes me regret costing us all that time in New York."

He stopped and turned toward her, taking hold of both her hands. "No regrets," he reminded her. "That's one of the things we're leaving behind on that old bumpy road."

Loving this moment, loving this man, Lily went up on her toes and brushed a kiss against his lips. "No regrets," she agreed.

"Is that Jim Olson?" Burke asked, looking over her shoulder when the too-brief kiss ended.

Lily turned and saw Sage and Jim standing side by side, selling herbs and flowers at a booth that had been painted with bright blossoms. From the way she was waving her hands around, Sage was doing most of the talking, but they watched her occasionally turn to Jim, as if asking a question for him to answer.

"Wow," Lily said. "That can't be easy for him."

"He's not usually very animated, unless he's talking about plants."

"Which is what he enjoys most," she said as they strolled

toward the booth. "Sage is on one of the planning committees. I suspect she arranged to have their booth at the far end of the park, so he wouldn't be in the crazy, noisy middle of things."

"Makes sense," he agreed. "It was also a great idea to put the farm booth next to Amanda's." Amanda Barrow, owner of Wheel and Barrow, was a landscape architect Brianna had used for Herons Landing and Lily had hired to create her garden front yard.

Lily had heard stories of a peninsula-wide search—which included Aiden's police department, state troopers, the FBI, the US Marshals, and National Park rangers—for Amanda's abusive husband, who'd stolen sensitive government secrets from the National Reconnaissance Office where he'd worked. They'd divorced, with Amanda staying in Honeymoon Harbor, her former husband imprisoned in a federal correctional institution in Colorado.

Brianna told her that it had initially been hard on Amanda, who'd moved to town with him from California. He'd kept her from making friends. But the community had rallied behind her. While working with her on the yard, if Lily hadn't known the story, she never would have guessed what her talented landscaper had endured. And survived.

"Hi," Lily said as she and Burke reached their booths. "How's business?"

"Hello, Lily," Jim said. "Hello, Burke. It was very busy for a while, but it slowed down a few minutes ago."

"I suspect that's because the tug-of-war's so popular," Amanda suggested.

"I suspect you're right," Lily said. She turned to Sage. "That was clever, putting these two booths together."

"It's because we both sell plants," Jim volunteered. "Sage explained that it's called Hotelling's model of spatial competition, which is clustering, where competitors move near the center of their potential customer population to attract the greatest number of customers. It's like gas stations and fast-food businesses locating close to one another. When all the businesses have moved to the optimal location, it results in Nash equilibrium."

"It's nice to know that someone listens to my lectures," Lily said to Sage.

"I believe in learning from the best," Sage said. "It's always good to follow those who've been there before you."

"I've always believed the same thing," Burke said, thinking how his dad had worked out a way to be with the woman he'd loved.

"It helps that we have room back here to spread our plants out," Amanda said. "While some of our stock is the same, most of it isn't, and what I don't have, Jim might."

"And what I don't have, Amanda probably does," Jim said.

"Win-win," Sage, Amanda and Jim said together.

After buying a few small pots of herbs from Jim, and three-day lilies from Amanda, who promised to have them delivered to the house on Monday, Lily and Burke stopped by the Taco the Town truck and bought tacos, chips and guacamole to take up to Mirror Lake for a picnic before she had to head back to work the next day. At least, with the festival behind her, all she had to do was get through commencement, and her work would slow down for the summer.

As the sun brightened the impossibly blue water, a soft breeze whispering through the trees and birdsong filling the air, Lily realized she was putting off some hard decisions. But just then, in that very special moment, seated on a quilt, sharing tacos with the man she loved, she was living her best life.

BURKE LAY AWAKE much of the night, listening to Lily's

soft breathing. While he still had over a month before July 21st, while sitting out at the lake, sharing a perfect moment with the woman he loved, he'd decided that they'd already put their future on hold for too long. It was time to make a decision.

After kissing Lily goodbye and sending her off to her office, he made two calls—one to Gabe, the other to Quinn.

"What's up?" Gabe asked ten minutes later as they sat at a table in the empty pub. "If you're asking me to be your best man, I'm sure Quinn will be happy being an usher."

"Works for me. But I'd rather walk the bride down the aisle," Quinn said. "Seeing that she doesn't seem to have a dad in the picture, and I wouldn't have to worry about losing the ring."

"Her father died," Burke said.

"That's too bad," Quinn said.

"Yeah, I guess. She was young, and apparently he wasn't in the picture much to begin with." He shrugged. "But that's not what this is about. Well, not yet anyway. I can't propose to her until I can create a future that'll work for both of us. But I'll need your help."

He laid out his plan.

"I didn't see that coming," Gabe said, just as he had when he'd found out that Burke was taking Lily Carpenter on that triple date at Luca's Kitchen.

"Then you're blind," Quinn countered. "Though it's not playing out the way I figured it would, it's still a good plan. So long as you're sure."

"I've never been more certain of anything in my life," Burke said. "Well, except loving Lily."

"I think I'm missing some backstory," Gabe said. "You've only known her a couple weeks. Are you sure this is what you want to do?"

"Like I said, yeah, I'm sure. And you're missing a few chapters." He laid out only as much as he'd told Quinn. About their meeting, the secret three-month affair, then her breaking up with him by text.

"But we've put all that behind us," he said. "Now I just want to move on."

"She'll still have to go along with this," Quinn pointed out.

"She will." He hoped. "So, are you guys in? Or are you out?"

Gabe and Quinn exchanged a look. "Are you as offended as I am that the kid here even had to ask us that?" Gabe asked.

"Probably more," Quinn said. "Given that, as the eldest, I'm supposed to be the one handing out advice. It's part of the big brother code, the same as teaching you about sex."

"Which, while I appreciated it, I already knew all about," Gabe said.

"Reading *Penthouse Forum* letters about well-endowed fifteen-year-old pool boys giving libidinous, lonely house-wives the best ride of their lives, outwardly prim secretaries boinking the boss on the desk at lunchtime, or the mailman with women along his route who'd lick his stamps, did not give you anywhere near a realistic view of sex," Quinn said.

"Teaching us how to unhook a bra with one hand was helpful," Burke said, trying to keep a straight face after Quinn's reference to desk sex. He also didn't share that he'd used that bra technique with Lily at the drive-in.

Gabe's smile was slow and reminiscent. "Okay," he said. "I'll give him that."

"Getting back to the subject at hand," Burke said, "we're all on the same page?"

"We've got this," they both assured him.

"I really appreciate your offer," he said to Gabe, whom

he'd talked to last night. Although he already had an idea of what he was going to do, it turned out that his brother, who apparently knew everyone in the one-percent group of New Yorkers, had connections that could prove invaluable. It was a long shot, but long shots were his specialty.

"Just keep your phone free," he said to Quinn. "And when I call, stick to the script. Don't ad-lib, whatever they might say."

"You know," Quinn said, "as much as I'm in, you're starting to piss me off."

"You seem to have forgotten two important things," Gabe told Burke. "You're talking to the human sphinx, and only an idiot would dare piss off our deceptively mellow big brother."

"Sorry." Burke swiped a hand through his hair. "I just need this to go off as planned."

"Don't worry," Quinn said, reverting back to his even-tempered self.

"We've got your back," Gabe told him as they each layered a hand in unity. With that assurance, Burke headed to the college.

CHAPTER TWENTY-THREE

LILY WAS SEATED behind her desk when Burke walked in. She was wearing a cream silk blouse beneath a tidy beige suit that concealed the sexy woman beneath. Call him perverse, but he couldn't see her in business wear without the gruff boss, sexy secretary fantasy flashing through his mind.

"Hi." She stood up and came around the desk. "This is a nice surprise. Are you taking me to lunch? Because it's still a little early."

"I'm afraid not." The jacket nipped in at a waist he wanted to put his hands on. "I just dropped by to tell you that I'm leaving town for a couple days."

"Oh?" She paled for a split second, but then, managing to find the last vestige of wall he hadn't yet torn down, quickly recovered. "To New York?"

"Yeah. And like I promised, I'm not going to do anything without us talking it over first. But I figured there was no point in discussing details until I find out if what I have in mind works. Which it should, as long as Gabe and Quinn do their parts."

She folded her arms, pretending calm. But he saw the hurt in her eyes. "You've discussed this with your brothers? Before me?"

"Only because I needed their help."

"I see."

"No, you don't." He breached that remaining bit of wall

that had turned to ice, to wrap his arms around her waist. "You can't see because I haven't told you yet. But if plan A doesn't work, I promise I'll come up with a plan B."

"I'd prefer hearing plan A first. Unless you want me to track down your brothers. Quinn would never talk, but Chelsea could probably get Gabe to tell me what you're up to."

"Damn." He bent and leaned his forehead against hers. "Anyone ever tell you that you can be more than a little stubborn?"

"I prefer to think of it as tenacity." She slipped out of his arms, perched on the edge of her polished desk and crossed her legs. "So, tell me."

"Okay." He'd promised her that this relationship deal was up to her. She was right. "Except, first, do you think, just maybe, that you could sit somewhere, anywhere else? Because I'm having trouble keeping my thoughts straight."

"Good." She switched legs, crossing them again. "I'm enjoying seeing you be the one distracted for a change."

When she began to dangle a bark-brown, red-soled high heel from her toe, jiggling her leg up and down just enough to showcase it, he shook his head. She might as well have a flashing red *play this right, Mr. Hotshot football player, and you could get lucky* sign over her head. God, he loved Lily Carpenter!

"You are such a tease," he said. And it was working.

"Oh, I haven't even gotten started yet." With her eyes on his, she unfastened her top button. Then skimmed a finger slowly, provocatively, down the front of the silk blouse, reminding him of how he'd undressed her in this very office. And of what they'd done after.

"I don't suppose we could just lock the door—"

"No. Talk." Her shoe was back on, her leg still.

Surrendering, he jammed his hands in the back pockets of his jeans to keep him out of trouble, and talked. And when he was done, he could see her quick and clever mind running through his proposed scenario.

"That could actually work," she said finally.

"I'm going to do my best to make sure it does."

"Let me give you a bit more incentive." She slipped off the desk, glided toward him like a Victoria's Secret model on the runway, twined her arms around his neck, and purred, "Win this game for us, QB."

HAVING FLOWN AGAINST time zones, it was late when Burke arrived in New York, so he spent the night at his apartment. The next morning, as he walked through the door of 30 Rock, Burke was no longer that twenty-one-year-old, wet-behind-the-ears, first-round rookie draft pick. At that time, his life had changed. Now *he'd* changed. Having achieved a dream that he'd been working at for as long as he could remember, his life was no longer all about him—his wins, his stats, his highlight reels.

That was, as he'd continually reminded himself, the way you reached the elite level of any sport. Although they'd probably never admit it, most top-achieving athletes were self-absorbed, which was probably unavoidable when the majority of their lives revolved around the sport and both physical and mental training in order to perform game after game.

Looking back on it, the changes hadn't happened overnight. Except for that high school winning celebration when Quinn had caught him sneaking into the house, reeking of pot, he hadn't played around in high school or college. There were too many guys out there, all over the country, with the same dreams as his. Guys who might have equal, or even more, talent. But talent alone didn't get you to the top. He'd always believed that sacrifice was necessary in order to stay laser-focused.

But having had time to think about it, even what he'd viewed as sacrifice wasn't really that at all. No one was forcing him to skip a party on a Saturday night in order to watch old game videos, observing what to do or not do out on the field. Or spend a beautiful Pacific Northwest afternoon memorizing plays instead of going out to the lake with friends. Those weren't sacrifices. They were choices. Choices he'd made every day over many years. He hadn't done all the weight training, wind sprints, and running up and down the stadium bleachers because he'd enjoyed it. He'd forced himself to get up at dawn to run in rain, snow, sleet, and New York hellish summer humidity because somewhere out there, there was some other quarterback with dreams just as big as his own who might be getting ahead of him.

His mother's accident had given him a harsh wake-up call to the importance of the family he'd been neglecting while living his totally football-centered life. As Lily had pointed out, he hadn't been home for Thanksgiving or Christmas in years. And yeah, he could use the season schedule as an excuse. There were admittedly other days in the off-season when he could have returned. Hell, even when Gabe had lived in this very city, they'd been lucky if they'd gotten together once a month. And if he had to be brutally honest with himself, he'd admit that if he'd made Lily a priority back then, if he'd only fought for a real relationship the same way he'd fought to win all those games he'd left her for, they could have saved all that lost time.

Even as self-absorbed as he'd been, he'd realized winning took teamwork. Something he'd excelled at when it came to football. Unfortunately, it turned out, he'd sucked at it in every other aspect of his life. The trip home had reminded him that he and his family were a team. That he and his brothers were a team. Even all the people in town who'd jumped in to help his mother were part of that team. And most importantly, the thing he had to fix was that he and Lily Carpenter would be a team. Anything he had to do to ensure that they could someday be celebrating *their* thirty-seventh anniversary would be no sacrifice.

So entering through those doors created the same energy it always had. But today it was crackling with determination. As always, when he entered the suite of offices on the fifty-sixth floor, the receptionist greeted him with a chirpy "good morning." But apparently the office gossip machine had been working overtime, because nerves were showing behind that smile. Nerves that were echoed in today's minion's anxious eyes as he offered Burke his usual choice of beverages.

"How's your mom?" Sam Otterbein asked when Burke walked into his office. Which was not the opening line he'd been expecting from the Knights' general manager.

"Like I told you when you called, she fractured several ribs and had a concussion, but she's recovering well. Thanks for the flowers. She wrote you a note you should be getting any day." His dad had finally caved and, while holding the line against her working, had allowed her to write some thank-you notes. "I appreciate you asking."

"We care. All of us."

"I've always known that," Burke said. "Which is why I wanted to come here and talk to you myself."

The older man leaned back in his tall leather chair. "You're not signing a new contract, are you?"

"No, I'm not."

"I knew it," Sam said with a resignation that came from spending his entire career in the sport.

He'd worked his way up the team ladder starting as an overworked, underpaid scout who'd spent seven long years sitting in college players' living rooms with their parents, trying to convince them they belonged with a team that hadn't had a great winning percentage before head coach Vince Jones and QB Burke Mannion had arrived.

"So, what team are you going to?"

"None." Burke saw the surprise, then disbelief move across Sam's face.

"You've got to be kidding. You're still in negotiations, aren't you?" he asked. "And you can't tell me."

"I'm not." Burke held up a finger. "Just a minute. I need to make a call."

When Quinn picked up on the first ring, he said, "It's go time." Then he turned off his phone because he knew as soon as the news got out, calls, along with Twitter and Google alerts, would start flooding in like a tsunami.

"That was my brother, Quinn."

"The pub guy," Sam said.

"And former legal eagle. Also my agent for the day."

A gray brow, as furry as a caterpillar, climbed the furrowed forehead. "What happened to Phil?"

"I left his agency first thing this morning. Before I came over here. It wasn't like he was going to have another team contract to negotiate. Besides, we were never that good of a fit. The main reason I signed with him right before the draft was that he was all about the money."

Although his longtime agent had never admitted it, Burke had always suspected Phil Harris would rather go back to the days before concussion protocol, when a player could, and often would, lie about having gotten his bell rung on a tackle, just to get back on the field. Make more scores. Win more games. Earn more money. It wasn't like the guy was going to starve. According to *Sporting News*, he'd earned forty-six million dollars last year from commissions on one-point-five billion in negotiated deals.

"From what I heard through the grapevine, Denver and Miami offered more," Sam said.

"True. But they didn't have you." Burke blew out a breath. "I was more negative than I needed to be the last time I came in here, frustrated at how the season had turned out. I knew you were trying, and I knew that in the end, you weren't the one making the final call.

"We did some good things together, you, Vince and I. Even if, in a perfect life, I'd had a coach who wasn't so wedded to the running game, we've got a lot to be proud of, and I'm not regretting my decision to walk away.

"But I knew Phil would still try calling around to get an offer I couldn't refuse, just to keep me in the game, not even understanding that for me, it's no longer about the money. I had a talk with my brother Gabe when I was back home—"

"He's the gazillionaire who occasionally showed up in the box for games?"

"That's him. He used to be a hotshot trader venture capitalist. When I asked him why he'd quit Wall Street, he told me that money had only become a way of keeping score of who was on top. That's how I'd begun to feel. As we speak, Quinn is placing calls to teams that made offers, telling them that I'm off the market."

"So, what are you going to do? I sure as hell can't see you playing golf every day."

"You may remember me signing with CBS early in my career," Burke said. "It was open-ended, with the agreement that when I retired, they'd have a spot for me. Although they got first offer, I wasn't required to take it. They've kept in touch over the years to remind me that they're still interested.

"As it happens, Gabe invested in a sports management company that he advised to go public with an IPO three times what they'd been thinking they'd get. It's since grown exponentially, not just negotiating contracts, but it's opened up a side branch that's buying all sorts of online sports platforms, because a lot of people see that as where sports will be moving in the future.

"Don't ask me to explain, because my eyes blurred over about ten minutes into the conversation, but as it turns out, the president of the sports management place knows the president at CBS Sports. Gabe called him and told him that I might be on the market. The sports management guy, the CBS guy, and Gabe all ran some numbers yesterday and came up with an attractive offer.

"The details are fluid, but I had breakfast with the CBS president this morning, and he showed serious interest in my master's of science in sports management from Columbia. He knew of the program, having spoken there himself from time to time, so we had a personal connection.

"Even more so when I told him that one of the mentors in the program, a former CBS broadcaster, had stressed that not only was it important to make the story the center of any broadcast, it was equally important to know what was and wasn't a story."

"I know a lot of sports reporters who could learn that lesson," Sam muttered. As he was general manager, the negative press usually ended up on his desk.

"We'd started out with the idea of me rotating with a partner to be chosen later, as a game analyst, but by the time he was picking up the check, I had my own weekly show, with an agreement to do sports documentaries, which are really hot right now, especially since the Michael Jordan one."

"Sounds like you landed in high cotton," said Sam, who'd played college ball for Auburn and had kept many of his Southerisms.

"It gets better. I don't have to keep flying back here. Since I'm not going to be working with a partner except for guests I have on, I can broadcast from home."

"Like one of those Zoom things? Don't forget, I visited that bumfuck nowhere town before the draft. It had two stoplights and no TV station."

"Because I like you, I'm not going to take offense at that description," Burke said easily. "And we're getting a third stoplight. My dad's mayor, and he's using his pull with the town council to have one installed at the crossroads where my mom had her accident. As for the studio, my brother-in-law knows of a stand-alone law office building I can buy, and he can remodel it into a professional studio."

Sam scratched his head. "As much as I was hoping you'd stay, I have to admit that this sounds like a good deal for you. Are you sure you're not going to miss city life?"

"Nope. I am keeping my apartment here, at least for a time. My parents haven't had a real vacation in I don't know how long. I'd like them to be able to use it. And I figure I'll be coming back on a regular basis to talk with the CBS folk."

"Why don't you just stay here in the city?"

"Because I'm getting married to a woman who's lived here twice and didn't feel as comfortable as she does in Honeymoon Harbor. Also, I want more time to spend with my family, so doing it this way will work out. Lily—that's my fiancée's name—does enjoy the city. In small doses."

"Congratulations. On the job front and getting married. I married above myself, and I definitely recommend having someone you know will always be in your corner. Come hell or high water." Burke knew Sam had experienced his share of highs and lows and felt bad about throwing another problem on his plate, but he didn't have a single doubt that he was doing the right thing.

"Well, I'd say this calls for a drink," Sam said, knowing when it was the end of the fourth quarter and he'd lost the game. He reached into the bottom drawer of his desk and pulled out his bottle of bourbon. Although Burke was more a beer drinker, he understood that after so many years together, the end deserved to be observed.

"Henry McKenna came from Ireland, settled in Kentucky, and started making bourbon in 1837," Sam said. "And for my money, it's still the best bourbon made. Am I getting an invitation to the studio's grand opening?" he asked as he poured the bourbon into two glasses and handed one to Burke.

"If you want, you can be my first interview. If you're sure you want to come all the way out to bumfuck nowhere."

"Might as well," Sam drawled. "I wouldn't mind seeing a moose."

"We don't have moose. But we have elk. And whales."

"I had an elk steak once. In Jackson Hole. Before it became a billionaire wilderness. I was recruiting a kid from University of Wyoming, who ended up going to Green Bay, but the trip wasn't a total loss, partly because of that steak. There was this pretty young waitress…"

His voice trailed off, but his eyes turned reminiscent. "That was before I got married. I wouldn't mind seeing a whale. Marge has always wanted to see the West Coast.

She doesn't understand that after all my years on the road, I'd just as soon stay home."

"I'm sure not one to give any marriage advice, but after seeing how close my dad came to losing my mom, I think maybe you ought to consider taking her on a long vacation. Regrets are probably the hardest thing to live with."

Sam took a sip. "That's something to consider. When did you say you were getting married?"

"I haven't officially asked her yet. But I'd be up for as soon as possible."

"That might be a problem. Given that brides do like to put on a show."

"We'll send you an invitation," Burke said. "And first-class wagon train tickets."

"Anyone ever tell you that you can be a little cocky?"

Burke laughed. "That's what my gramps said about my dad."

"Seems the apple didn't fall far from the tree." Sam polished off the bourbon. "I guess I'd better go break the news to Mel. He's not going to be happy."

"Curt will be ready." Curt Long, the Knights' backup quarterback, had spent most of the past three seasons warming the bench.

"The kid lost that championship game."

"Because he wasn't confident enough. Coming off the bench after playing backup all season is a lot harder than starting."

Having begun his NFL career as a starter his rookie year, Burke had never personally been put in that position. But he knew it couldn't have been easy for a guy who'd won the Big Ten conference MVP award his senior year, been a Heisman Trophy finalist, and gotten drafted by the Knights in the first round. "Especially when it's a championship game. Show you have faith in him, have the QB coach put him out there to lead, and he'll surprise you."

"You wanna tell Mel that? Never mind." Sam waved him off. "Have a good flight back to bumfuck. And don't forget that invitation."

LILY WAS SEATED at her desk, checking her phone for the umpteenth time, as if she could force it to ring by the sheer power of her will, when there was a knock on her office door.

"Come in." Her heart skipped a beat, hoping Burke had returned, then settled back down when Sage entered. "Oh, hi."

"I can come back later if this is a bad time," Sage said, her hesitant tone revealing that she'd heard the disappointment in Lily's voice.

"No, it's not a bad time at all. I'm just waiting for a call." And going quietly insane.

"I just wanted to thank you for suggesting I work with Jim on my project."

"I read it last night. It's wonderful. Definitely an A-plus. And you both seemed to be having a great time working together when Burke and I saw you at the festival."

"We always have a wonderful time together," Sage said. "We went out to dinner afterwards. At Don Diego's."

"That sounds like fun." And definitely yet more proof that the extroverted Sage was bringing Jim out of his shell.

"It was. Afterwards we walked out onto the pier." She took a deep breath. "He asked me to be his girlfriend."

"Oh." Lily put down the pen she'd begun to fiddle with. "What did you say to that?"

"That if he hadn't hurried up and asked me, I was going to have to ask him."

Despite her nerves, Lily smiled. "I'm so happy for both of you." They seemed like a good couple. And definitely a case of opposites attracting, with Jim's yin to Sage's yang.

"Thanks. I'm moving into the farmhouse this coming weekend. Maybe it's soon, but sometimes you just know. And Jim's nothing like my cheating rat of fiancé. He's not only good to me, he's good for me. There's not a insincere bone in his body."

"That's true." They'd obviously have a period of adjustment. But wasn't that true in all relationships? "If you're moving in together, does that mean— Never mind." Lily waved off the inappropriate question that had sprung into her mind. "Your relationship is none of my business."

Soft color rose in Sage's face, and her eyes warmed. "Let's just say that Jim Olson's attention to detail doesn't solely apply to botany."

As they shared a laugh, for that moment, Lily felt her jangling nerves ease. They kicked in again after Sage left the office, to dash off to work in the greenhouse with her new boyfriend at Blue House Farm.

CHAPTER TWENTY-FOUR

FEELING AS IF a huge weight had been lifted off his chest, Burke called Lily on the way to the airport.

"It's about time," she said. "Not only did I not get any sleep, I've probably put ten miles on my Fitbit pacing."

"I'm sorry. The situation kept shifting."

"What happened to plan A?"

"That's not happening."

"Oh, I'm so sorry. Does that mean you're going to take one of the other offers?" Her concern didn't seem to be about him going back to New York or some other city. Although he knew she would've been disappointed if he was, but he could tell that right now, she was only thinking of him. They were a team. Just like his parents. And grandparents. Aiden and Jolene, Gabe and Chelsea, Brianna and Seth.

"No. Damn." He dragged his hand through his hair. "That came out all wrong. I didn't go with plan A because a new plan C came out of nowhere over breakfast this morning."

"What happened to plan B?"

"This is better."

Burke wasn't certain how he'd like broadcasting. But if he didn't, he could do something else. Like signing up for flying lessons and taking people on outdoor adventures around the state. Or talk Quinn's recipe for wings out of him and open up a restaurant. Maybe even franchise it, like people did on *Shark Tank*. Or there was this writer for *Sports Illustrated* who'd been wanting to write a book about him. A small-town-boy-makes-good type of story. Burke was savvy enough to know that walking away at the top of his game would make a good epilogue.

The thing was, it didn't really matter what he did with the hopefully forty to sixty years he'd have after his retirement from the pros. How he'd catch up with those former classmates who, while he'd been spending years out on the gridiron, had been out climbing the corporate ladder, making contracts, building careers.

Although he wouldn't be able to tap into his pension until he was forty-five, or his 401(k) plans until he was fifty-nine and a half, Gabe had taken a percentage of his salary and bonuses for the past ten years and invested the money well. Burke had seen too many players have their careers end in their early thirties and even twenties due to injuries who ended up bankrupt because they didn't have a backup plan.

However this retirement gig played out, it'd be perfect as long as he could spend those years with Lily.

"Burke?"

"I'm sorry. I was just thinking about stuff. Good stuff," he assured her. "But I want to tell you in person. Not here in a cab while you're all the way across the country."

"I'm going crazy with curiosity, but okay," she said, surprising him with her easy acquiescence. "We'll do it your way."

"There's something else I'd like you to do," he said.

"What's that?"

"Pack some clothes and let Gabe drive you out to the family's coast house. I know you said that you've overcome your press phobia, but things could get a little crazy over the next few days."

She paused less than a minute to think it through. "I

could do that. My workload's lessened now that Heritage Day is over, and although Paul can't help with commencement because he's graduating himself, I have another assistant who works on the scholarship foundation. She was doing my job along with her own until I showed up and got hired. I know she'll be willing to fill in for me for a few days. Especially since she reads a lot of romances, and we're definitely getting our requisite happy-ever-after ending.

"One question: Are you going to follow Mannion family tradition and cook me a seduction dinner while we're at the coast house?"

"Absolutely." As they spoke, Gabe was out doing the shopping, and unlike their uncle Mike had done all those years ago for his dad, he was going to pick up some asparagus. Burke might not be an Iron Chef, but he could manage a surf and turf with a farmers market steak and fresh Dungeness crab from Kira's Fish House. "But maybe you could give some thought to switching the order and having the dinner after the seduction?"

"I have another suggestion," she said, her voice turning all throaty in a way that he knew would still turn him on when he was one of those old guys they'd bring onto the field for the Super Bowl coin toss. The ones where people in the stands and at home watching TV would turn to each other and say, "Wow. I didn't know the guy was still alive."

"Anything." Burke felt like Jimmy Stewart, promising to lasso the moon for Donna Reed in that sappy Christmas movie his mom had always insisted they watch every year. There wasn't anything he wouldn't do for Lily Carpenter.

"What would you say to the seduction first, then dinner, then some more seduction for dessert?"

"I'd say that you're a beautiful, brilliant woman. And you've definitely got yourself a deal."

THE SUN WAS beginning to set over the water as Burke crossed the bridge over the creek. The house that had been in his family for generations was two stories, the cedar siding a silvery blue the hue of the ocean at twilight.

Because the house had originally been built for a whaling captain, there was a widow's walk around the top. When they were kids, Brianna used to make up romantic stories about the captain's wife standing up there all alone, pacing and watching for her husband to return from sea safely. In her tales, he always did.

Bad boy Aiden, unsurprisingly, would inject a darker ending to Bri's happy reunion stories by having a violent Pacific storm blow in and capsize the whaling boat in the turbulent waves, causing the ship, captain, and crew to all end up in Davy Jones's locker, consigned forever to the depths of the ocean.

The house was set back from the cliff far enough that erosion caused by wind and water wouldn't send it sliding off the edge, something that tended to happen occasionally on this coast, where the waters of the mighty Pacific—ill-named because there was nothing peaceful about it—warred with the land.

He'd kept Lily updated on his progress westward, the plane he'd chartered chasing the sun, and as he pulled up in front of the house, she opened the door and went racing out to throw her arms around him. "I've so missed you!"

"It's only been two days."

"Which included a night I was forced to sleep alone just when I'd gotten used to having you in my bed," she complained. "Zendaya wasn't all that happy, either. She's been very vocal about her displeasure, and poor Chance keeps looking around the house for you."

"I missed you, too."

He pulled her into his arms and kissed her. She kissed

him back, a hot tangling of tongues that had her moaning. Or maybe it was him. He couldn't tell because he was rapidly going brain-dead from all the blood rushing out of his head to below his belt. Lily shifted her legs apart, making room for him as she plastered herself against him.

The kiss was long, deep, and so hot he was surprised there wasn't smoke swirling around them. In another minute they'd be tearing off clothes, and fortunately, he still had enough brain cells to know that sex on all those fir needles, rocks, and fir cones dropped by careless squirrels wouldn't be a smart thing to do. Not when he knew there were plenty of beds inside the house.

Taking hold of her shoulders, he gently put some space between them. "That was quite a welcome. In fact, it was the best thing that's happened to me today."

"How about I open the bottle of champagne Gabe bought and let you tell me all about plan C?"

"I intend to do exactly that," he said. He was actually panting. And couldn't remember ever being this hard. "But first, I really want to go inside and take your clothes off."

"Another thing you can put on your compatibility test." She kissed him again with so much heat they were risking an appearance on the national news for being that couple who started Washington State's largest forest fire. And wouldn't that break the internet?

Deciding that he could get his bag out of the car later, Burke scooped her up into his arms. He carried her into the house and up the stairs, shutting both animals out of the first bedroom he came to.

Where he and Lily proceeded to take each other's clothes off.

When they came back to earth, the sun had set, and the dusk outside was deepening to lavender-blue as stars began to show themselves. They were lying together, arms and legs entangled, Lily's head on his chest, his hands playing in her hair, which was splayed over him.

He was thinking that he'd never felt so relaxed, so mellow in his life, and could easily stay just like that when she jumped up.

"The champagne!" She went running out of the room, giving him a very nice view of her heart-shaped ass. She returned carrying a green bottle and two flutes.

"Tell me about plan C," she said as she opened the bottle and poured two glasses before climbing back into bed.

So he told her.

After she'd professed to love it, he then shared plan D, which he'd seriously considered during the flight while drinking a very nice glass of wine from Passing Time, a winery owned in part by former QBs Damon Huard and Dan Marino.

Since Marino had been one of the players Burke had called for advice when he'd first started considering retirement, he'd been intrigued by how the two former players had marched down the football field into the Washington vineyards. As had former Patriots quarterback Drew Bledsoe, who owned Doubleback, another winery in the state.

"What would you think of owning a vineyard?" he asked her. "Growing grapes to make our own wine. Both Dan and Drew told me it's a great retirement gig, as long as we hire people who know the business to run it. Maybe we could do that along with plan C."

"Oh, I love that idea," she said, leaning over to give him a quick, happy kiss.

And as they lifted their glasses, toasting their future, Burke remembered what she'd professed to be the most romantic line from *Casablanca*.

"Here's looking at you, kid."

* * * * *

JUST ONE LOOK

CHAPTER ONE

Honeymoon Harbor Herald
Seen Around Town, by Mildred Mayhew

My GOODNESS, we've certainly had a busy summer here in Honeymoon Harbor! Two weddings—a glorious double ceremony between Brianna Mannion and Seth Harper, and Aiden Mannion and Jolene Wells—which took place at the Mannion family Christmas tree farm. The brides were both beautiful, the grooms handsome and, as a special touch that caused more than a few damp eyes, Jolene wore the sea-glass heart necklace Aiden had given her back in high school.

Proving that fate can, indeed, take us on unexpected journeys, Aiden Mannion is Honeymoon Harbor's new police chief (who would ever have seen that coming?) and not only was Jolene nominated for an Emmy for makeup on a Hollywood miniseries, she continues to work on the occasional film while building her organic skin-care line. It's available locally at Gloria Wells's Thairapy Salon and Day Spa, and if you haven't tried it, you must! And while you're there, be sure to get a facial and a stone massage that will melt all your cares away and leave you feeling like a new person!

Seth and Brianna Harper have opened Herons Landing, a delightful bed-and-breakfast in the Victorian man-

sion Seth restored to its original glory. And didn't we all sigh with pure happiness and reach for the tissues once again while watching those two receive their well-deserved happily-ever-after?

If all that weren't romantic enough, former Wall Street trader Gabriel Mannion, another of John and Sarah Mannion's sons and one of the most successful people to ever come out of Honeymoon Harbor, returned home from New York City this summer and got himself engaged to town librarian Chelsea Prescott. Even more wonderful, they're adopting two darling orphaned sisters Chelsea has been fostering.

The sight of the new family out on the water the other day, taking a smaller version of a Viking boat Gabriel built for its maiden sail before auctioning it off for charity at the festival, was guaranteed to warm your heart. I'll confess to tearing up again, and believe me, I was not alone.

For visitors new to the town, I invite you to drop in to our welcome center for a Honeymoon Harbor brochure, which, along with all the local news and a list of shops, restaurants and places to stay, tells the story of how our little Pacific Northwest hamlet changed its name in celebration of a honeymoon visit by European royalty. The name change caused a feud between the Mannion and Harper families for a time, however, that kerfuffle has been left in the past and is a story for another day.

Summer officially comes to an end with the boat festival, which brings in wooden boat enthusiasts from all around the globe. Other visitors come for the art and wine walk, featuring artists from all around our stunningly beautiful Olympic Peninsula. World-renowned artist Michael Mannion has returned home and is keeping company with Glo-

ria Wells, Jolene's mother, which has us all wondering if there'll be yet another wedding in the near future.

The Taste of Honeymoon Harbor, always a popular part of the festival, has gained several new restaurant booths for you to enjoy since last year. And, of course, the fireworks lighting up the sky over the water are always a glorious sight.

This year we're thrilled that the Lady Abigail, *a stunning, full-size replica of a US Naval warship that fought in the Barbary Wars, has honored us with a visit.*

And finally, if all that isn't enough (!), the festival committee has announced the first annual bachelor auction to raise funds for the food pantry and Honeymoon Harbor's animal shelter started by veterinarian Cameron Montgomery. I've heard through the grapevine that our very own Dr. McDreamy is planning a secret romantic surprise for some lucky Honeymoon Harbor bachelorette, and although Cameron's not talking, your intrepid Honeymoon Harbor Herald *social reporter will be on the scene and will share all the juicy details in next week's edition of "Seen Around Town."*

Meanwhile, I'll see all of you at the festival, and don't forget to check for updates on our Facebook page!

CHAPTER TWO

CAMERON MONTGOMERY WAS, by nature, a content person. He was doing exactly what he'd always wanted to do (despite his surgeon father not understanding why he'd want to have cats and dogs for patients rather than people, who paid better) and living exactly where he wanted to live, and he was especially happy on Wednesdays, which was when he spent his lunch hour with Megan Larson, owner and operator of the Clean Team. Not that he got to spend the entire hour with her. For the first twenty minutes or so, he enjoyed watching Emma, Megan's three-year-old daughter, play with the dogs and cats in the shelter he'd established on the property, while Megan bustled around the second floor of the old Italianate Victorian mansion where he'd established his clinic.

A neat person by nature—a necessity in the medical profession—he always took extra time to tidy up on Tuesday nights—enough so that Megan had told him more than once that although she wasn't about to turn down his business, she honestly wasn't sure he needed her. What she had no way of knowing, at least not yet, was that he'd had his eye on her ever since he'd arrived in town.

He'd learned from his staff that she'd grown up here, had married and divorced, and was not only a successful entrepreneur, but, as he already knew, also the mother of a three-year-old girl.

He'd also discovered the very first day she'd arrived for

her interview that just being in the same room with her triggered his hormones. But the attraction wasn't solely sexual. He'd come to look forward to those Wednesdays when she arrived to clean his house the same way children waited for Santa to arrive every Christmas Eve.

Her second week, he'd maneuvered her into having lunch with him, during which time they'd talked. She told him about how she'd attended Clearwater Community College at night after cleaning houses all day, finally earning an AA in business management, which had given her the skills to establish her own business, which had turned out to be successful enough that she was expanding into neighboring Sequim.

He'd told her about how he'd grown up on the peninsula in Port Angeles, gone to college and vet school at WSU, then took an offer to work for a large, multi-vet practice in Sacramento. But he'd missed the lush green Pacific Northwest, so when he'd seen an ad from Dr. Palmer, Honeymoon Harbor's retiring veterinarian, on an internet page listing practices for sale, he'd jumped on it. He'd also told her that he considered the day he'd come across the ad the luckiest of his life. But did not share that that was in large part because of her.

The lunches had turned into a standing weekly event. After trading brief biographies over that first meal, they'd spent the next few months talking about everyday things— like the leafy trees that had been planted all along Water Street, decreasing rainwater runoff and adding a natural element to the downtown that worked with the water view and refreshed everyone's moods. When some local business owners complained about the added cost of planting and maintaining the trees, John Mannion, Honeymoon Harbor's mayor, had produced a study showing that shoppers tended to spend more time and money in business districts where street trees had been planted, because trees provided a more appealing environment. And that had sealed the deal.

They laughed about the local gossip posted daily on the town's Facebook page, and Megan had informed him that his impending arrival had caused quite a stir after the *Honeymoon Harbor Herald* picked up a story, along with a photo, from the Sacramento veterinary hospital's website.

"You were, for a few weeks, the talk of nearly every single woman in town," she'd said on a laugh. "I'm surprised you didn't feel the flashing target on your back when you drove into town towing that U-Haul."

That had explained the initial rush of women bringing pets in for checkups. He'd also wondered, but did not ask, if Megan had been one of those interested women. Their lunches over the past months had become the best part of his week. So much so that he found it hard to remember what life had been like without Megan Larson in it. It also had him thinking that he'd like a lot more lunches and thought every day for the rest of their lives sounded just fine.

While he'd dated over the years, and stayed friends with most of the women, he'd never felt that special zing that told him this was the One. Until Megan walked into Mannion's with a group of girlfriends, and he'd known, in that instantaneous flash of recognition, that he'd found the woman he'd been waiting for.

WEDNESDAY WAS MEGAN LARSON'S favorite day of the week. And not just because of all the photos of hot hump-day guys that would show up on her Twitter and Facebook feeds, but because it was the day she had lunch with Cameron Montgomery.

Wednesdays were also the day that her mother, who

watched Emma during the day, had her Zumba class at the fitness center. Megan had grown up going on jobs with Brenda Larson, who'd taught her at a young age that cleaning houses was not only honest work, it was important work, and, if you had the right attitude, it could also be a job of joy.

She'd learned how taking care of a house, setting it to order, leaving even the humblest of homes looking like something out of a magazine, not only allowed her clients to live a calmer, easier life, it brought her a sense of pride and satisfaction of a job well done. Something she'd learned from both parents, who still laughed whenever her dad, a former Marine, told the story of how he'd attempted to perform a white-glove inspection of their marriage bed after a three-day honeymoon at Olympic National Park's Lake Quinault Lodge. Brenda, a tidy person, had informed him that if he'd wanted a maid, he could damn well hire one.

The irony was, that after he'd gotten out of the Marines and begun crabbing in Alaska as all the men in his family had done for generations, Brenda had begun cleaning for others to earn extra household money, which proved important those seasons when the crew didn't make its quota. Knowing how difficult and dangerous his job could be, and how each year had seemed to take a bit more out of him, Megan never ate crab without thinking of her father and the sacrifices he'd made for his family.

At first Brenda hadn't had many clients. After its boom days in the 1800s, Honeymoon Harbor's residents didn't embrace the concept of hiring someone else to do their housework. But Brenda's prices were reasonable, she left homes immaculate and gleaming, and as word spread, she'd developed a loyal clientele of working couples who discovered that not having to clean or even grocery shop, which she was also willing to do, allowed them more time to spend with their families.

Much later, when Megan began taking business classes at the local community college, she realized that rather than try to come up with a new start-up idea, the smartest thing to do would be to stick to what she knew. Which was how the Clean Team was born. And how her mother, now retired from housekeeping, had become her CFO. Which, in all honesty, was basically a bookkeeper, but they both enjoyed the official title. Brenda was also grandmother-in-chief, taking care of Emma while Megan took care of business.

Although there'd been times, out of necessity, that Megan would have to take her daughter on a job with her, her own days of cleaning were mostly in the past. Her company had now grown to the point that she could tend to the business end of the Clean Team while her employees did the actual cleaning. She'd even promoted one of her first and most meticulous hires to be the new team member trainer, ensuring their work would be up to the company's high standards. Megan did, however, continue to do a move-in cleaning for Seth Harper's completed remodels, because he'd been the first person in Honeymoon Harbor to hire her back when she was pregnant, newly divorced, living with her parents and cleaning houses while going to college at night.

She'd also taken on cleaning Cameron's home above his veterinarian office. Not because she didn't believe the crew she'd hired and trained could do just as good a job. But he hadn't minded her bringing Emma, who'd wanted a dog since she was in her stroller and loved playing with the shelter pups. The idea of letting her interact with the animals had been Cam's, and although Megan had worried that a three-year-old ball of energy who had turned into a chatterbox now that she'd learned to put words into sentences would interfere with Cam's job, he'd proven as patient with Emma as he was with the ill and injured pets he treated.

Whenever Megan glanced out one of the windows she was polishing to a glistening shine that sent rainbows dancing across the walls and saw her daughter romping on the fenced-in lawn with puppies, Cam playing with her and making her giggle, she'd occasionally drift into what-if land.

As she gave the gleaming quartz kitchen countertop one last swipe with her cleaning rag, she wondered if he'd ever felt the same attraction to her as she had him the moment their eyes had literally met across a crowded pub. She'd gone to Mannion's on a rare girls' night out, and although she hadn't yet taken a sip of the mojito she'd ordered, she'd suddenly felt as dizzy as if she'd been tossing back tequila shots.

Although she'd given up on men—having neither the time nor inclination to date, let alone remarry—when he'd called the next day to ask for a housekeeping quote, she'd managed to tamp down the burst of lust and suggest a meeting five days later. Not only did she not want to appear too eager, she needed time to weigh the pros and cons of taking this particular job.

She'd admittedly made her share of mistakes over the years. But as rocky and challenging as her marriage had been, Megan wouldn't change a thing. Because if her life hadn't played out the way it had, she wouldn't have Emma, who was the sparkling jewel in her admittedly tarnished crown.

The kitchen completed, she'd taken the clothes out of the dryer and was putting them away in the big pine chest. Like all home cleaners, she knew a great many personal things about her clients. It wasn't that she was snoopy, but when you found a vibrator and a blindfold while changing the sheets on Mr. and Mrs. Miller's bed on a day they'd been running late and rushing out of their house to open their CPA office on time, it didn't take Sherlock Holmes to figure out that the couple enjoyed spicing up their sex life.

While sorting out Jarle Bjornstad's apartment pantry, she'd discovered that the man who'd cooked for a crab boat crew in Alaska before going to work at Mannion's pub had a fondness for sugary kid's cereal. Given that he was six foot seven and, if spotted in a dark woods, might be mistaken for Sasquatch, she'd wondered how many boxes of Froot Loops it took to fill him up in the morning.

She also knew that Cam Montgomery had solved the boxers or briefs question with knit boxer briefs. All colored. As she rolled up a pair of red-as-sin ones, she wondered if he wore them to bed. Or if he slept naked. Although she knew it was horribly unprofessional, she couldn't deny that changing his sheets and pillowcases, which still carried his scent, had her imagining scenarios hotter than any of the Wednesday social media hump-day hunks. And in her male stripper fantasy, he wasn't wearing boxer briefs. Or anything else.

Stop that! she told her reckless mind. Unfortunately, more and more since that night at Mannion's, her rebellious body seemed to have taken over, fogging her brain.

She'd gathered up her supplies and equipment and was taking them out to the car when Emma came running up to her with what had to be the homeliest dog ever born in her arms. It had ears so large they looked as if it could take off flying at any minute, like Dumbo after those crows had given the baby elephant that feather. Its bottom teeth stuck out while patches of white fur were scattered like small icebergs across a sea of mottled pink skin.

"Look, Mommy," she said. "Somebody left this poor doggie in a box."

"A box?" Megan looked over at Cam, who was following Emma with his easy, long-legged stride.

"The guy clearing the ferry landing parking lot found her a few days ago. She doesn't have tags, though collars can get lost when a dog's on the loose. But I scanned her for an identification chip, which she also doesn't have. Good thing the sweeper had strong lights or there could've been a serious tragedy."

Megan didn't want to be judgmental, but the poor dog already looked like a tragedy.

"Who would do such a thing?"

"A bad person," Emma answered before Cam could. "Can we keep her, Mommy?"

"We've been over this before," Megan said with a sigh. "It wouldn't be fair to leave a dog alone at our house all day." Not to mention the puddles and other mistakes that she'd undoubtedly come home to.

Although her office was in her home, Megan still spent a good part of her day either visiting potential clients to give them quotes, or, more recently, driving to nearby Sequim, where she'd begun taking on additional clients. Although she trained all her team members to that same exacting standard she'd grown up with, she'd occasionally drop by a home unexpectedly to ensure things were going well. When she left the office for those occasions, Emma would spend the day at her grandparents.

"Mommy..." The whine had become one of Emma's favorite tools, although it was more effective with her grandmother than with Megan. Which was ironic, because Megan couldn't remember ever getting away with the ploy.

"Not now," she said. "We need to let Dr. Montgomery get back to work."

"I still have time for lunch," he said. "I have pizza and an antipasto from Luca's that I can't eat all by myself."

"Pizza!" Emma exclaimed, clapping her hands together. Then frowned. "But no 'shrooms."

Cam's lips quirked at that. "Don't worry, Your Majesty. I had your portion made with cheese and sauce."

"Yay!"

And so there Megan was again, sitting on the balcony of the bright blue Victorian, eating pizza and drinking iced tea. Their weekly lunches had begun one day four months ago seemingly by accident, when she'd finished her work and Cam had mentioned that he had too much leftover take-out spaghetti to eat alone, and maybe she and Emma would like to help him finish it so he wouldn't have to toss it out. The next week it was fried chicken. Then mac and cheese, which was when she figured out that all those leftovers were not coincidental.

And now, as she watched the white-and-green ferry chug up to the dock, its horn, which could be heard all over town, announcing its arrival, she wondered if he was just being friendly or if, just maybe, he'd been having those same naughty thoughts about her that she'd been having about him.

Of course, it could be that he simply enjoyed having company while he was eating. And perhaps she'd been alone in her feelings that day of the double wedding at the Mannion family farm. Having left Emma home with her mother, she'd danced with Cam to Usher's upbeat "Don't Look Down," which didn't involve any touching. But then that segued into "All of Me," John Legend's beautiful tribute to his wife, and when he'd taken her into his arms, one hand warming her back through her flowered sundress, it had taken all of Megan's restraint not to wrap around him like ivy.

"Are you going to the boat festival?" he asked, dragging her mind back from that afternoon when she'd been so lost in a gauzy, romantic world, she'd even missed the drama of Chelsea Prescott and Gabe Mannion's short-lived breakup.

"I wouldn't miss it."

She felt a little dip in her spirits as she remembered the year her ex-husband had been so stoned she'd stayed home from the festival rather than risk Jake embarrassing not just himself, but her and her family. It certainly wasn't any secret that their marriage had been less than ideal. What had seemed sexy and dangerous back in high school had turned out to be exhausting in a grown man. The first three years of their marriage, she'd followed him around the Pacific Northwest, drinking club soda at seedy bars where the audience was either too stoned or drunk to pay attention to the five-man rock band shouting their songs loud enough to wake the dead.

After the band had predictably broken up, not only had Jake, unable to keep a job because of his undependability, blown more than one unemployment check at the casino on the coast, he was always falling for a series of wildly improbable get-rich schemes that would flood into his email in-box, dressed up like the golden ticket. But they'd never paid off. Instead they'd depleted their bank account, which was usually bleeding red by the end of the month. When she realized she'd never be able to depend on her husband, Megan had started taking business classes at Clearwater Community College at night while cleaning houses during the day.

She'd been three months pregnant when Jake had left town with the female singer in the band, off on his latest venture—flipping houses—after wiping out their meager savings account and maxing out their credit cards for a seminar assuring him that he and his new lover would be the next stars of HGTV. Quinn Mannion had handled Megan's divorce pro bono and helped her change back to her maiden name.

"I'm sorry." She dragged her mind from those difficult days. "My mind was wandering."

"No problem." He plucked a stuffed olive from an antipasto plate so beautifully arranged, it should have been on the restaurant's Instagram account, and held it out to her. "I was just saying that after letting myself get talked into taking part in that charity bachelor auction, it'd be really embarrassing if no one bids on me."

Eating the olive from his fingers felt so very intimate. Although she hadn't had sex since the Ice Age, Megan did have a memory, and this felt a bit like foreplay. While she'd never, ever regretted having Emma, at this moment a part of her wished she'd left her daughter with her mother today so she and Cam could be alone. Not that she'd be able to get away with that. Emma would have to be in bed with the plague not to insist on coming here on her dogday Wednesdays.

"I doubt you'll have to worry about that," she said, somehow managing to sound calm while her hormones were exploding. "And you could never make a fool of yourself."

"Would you do me a favor? From one friend to another?"

Friends? Maybe it hadn't been foreplay. "Is that what we are?"

"Well, I like you. And you seem to like me."

"Of course I do." And wasn't that an understatement?

"And we're certainly friendly with each other. So, although I'm not a walking, talking dictionary like our town librarian Chelsea Prescott, I'd say that defines friends."

"I can always use another friend," she said mildly. Emma, having finished her piece of pizza, had gone back into the house to play tug-of-war with the dog and a small stuffed orca.

"I'm seriously dreading that auction," he admitted.

"Why?" She had no doubt that while the other Honeymoon Harbor men taking part were handsome and more than a little appealing, Cam would bring in the most money. And yes, she might be prejudiced, but not only was he super nice, she doubted any woman in town could resist that photo Kylee had taken of him for the auction brochures, posters and even a full-page ad in the *Honeymoon Harbor Herald*.

"Because it's embarrassing. And unprofessional."

"Says the man who posed shirtless holding a cocker spaniel puppy."

"Do you have any idea how impossible it is to argue with Kylee Campbell?"

"I do know. And am smart enough not to try." Though she'd worried Kylee had been serious when she'd suggested Megan wear a sexy French maid outfit for her Clean Team website photo. Kylee had found the idea outrageously funny. Megan had not. "And it's for two good causes."

"That's the only reason I agreed. There's another problem."

"Which would be?"

He dragged a hand through his summer sun–streaked chestnut hair. He had long fingers, which she decided would be helpful when he was performing delicate surgery on small dogs and kittens. His nails were also nicely trimmed, which not every guy, including her ex-husband, bothered to do. Which had her wondering what those hands would feel like on her body. All over. "What if no one bids on me?"

Megan almost choked on her iced tea. "You are kidding, right?"

"No. Did you see that photo of Flynn Farraday wearing those red suspenders?"

"He looked hot," she admitted. Flynn had also been shirtless, which seemed to be a theme with Kylee. As had Luca, in a black chef's apron, and all the other men Kylee had posed in varying tasteful stages of undress. Quinn Mannion had somehow managed to escape the auction. She suspected that was because, having been an attorney before returning home and opening a brew pub, he might be the one person on the planet able to hold his own against Kylee. "But everyone loves you."

"I've never saved anyone's life by carrying them out of a burning building," he muttered.

"No, but you have saved a lot of people's fur babies."

"It's not the same thing."

"You do realize that you're sexier than all of them put together." At least he was to her. As good-looking as those other bachelors were, he was the only one who, every Wednesday, had her lady parts pointing out how neglected they'd been.

"That's exactly what friends are supposed to say." As he swiped that hand through his hair again, she imagined them ripping open her green Clean Team T-shirt. Not that she actually believed such a thing was possible, but it certainly sounded sexy in romance novels. "Can I ask a favor? As a friend?"

"Of course."

"Would you start the bidding on me if no one else does?"

"Sure. Though I honestly don't believe that's going to be a problem." The problem would be having to think of him out on a romantic date with another woman.

"Have you decided what you're doing on your date?" she asked with forced casualness.

"If the winner, whoever she turns out to be, has something special she wants to do, I'm up for just about anything. But I do have my own secret idea in mind."

"Want to share?"

"Then it wouldn't be a secret, would it?"

"You already trust me in your house." And his underwear drawer. Which, dammit, had her thinking of those sexy red boxer briefs again. "Are you suggesting I'd tell?"

"No, I'm merely suggesting that if you win, I want to surprise you."

"Like that's going to happen," she said. "Unless I win the lottery or discover a money tree has sprouted in my backyard since I left the house this morning."

"You never know." He lifted one of those broad shoulders, undoubtedly capable of lifting a bull mastiff onto his operating table. Now *her* hand was practically itching with the desire to touch him. All over. Across those manly shoulders, down his sinewy arms—one of which had the veterinarian symbol he'd told her was an Aesculapius staff with a superimposed *V* inked on his rock-hard biceps—continuing over his chest, tracing a happy trail downward to...

Stop that!

As if he'd read her sex-crazed mind, he winked just before Emma came back out onto the balcony carrying that wretched-looking dog, which Megan assured herself must not have anything contagious, or Cameron wouldn't let her play with it.

"What kind of dog *is* that?" she asked.

"The best kind!" Emma pressed her case yet again.

"Your daughter's not far off. Mixes do have more going for them than purebreds. My guess, from the papillon ears—"

"That means butterfly," Emma broke in. Obviously she'd been asking Cam questions. "And I *love* butterflies."

"Who doesn't? They also don't need feeding and walking like a dog would."

"Mommy…"

"I have an idea," Megan said, trying to appease her daughter, who'd mostly outgrown her terrible twos, but there were still relapses. Like this was threatening to be. "Why don't we go over to Wheel and Barrow and ask Amanda Barrow what seeds or bulbs we can buy to make a butterfly garden? Then next spring when the plants flower, you can have all the butterflies you want. Maybe we'll even get migrating monarchs. I heard they eat milkweed, so we'll plant some of that. It'll be fun."

"Okay." Just when Megan thought she was off the hook, Emma said, "But I still want a dog. And not just any dog. I want Butterfly."

"We'll talk about it later." Megan wanted to shut this conversation down before it turned into a tantrum. "Right now I'm talking with Dr. Montgomery." Thinking perhaps a dog might be a nice addition to their little family, she turned back toward Cameron. "What else is she?"

"From that malocclusion, which is vet-speak for a misaligned underbite, I'd guess shih tzu, but her body and legs point to some Boston bull in the mix somewhere."

"So she's not going to grow to Great Dane size?"

"Signs, including the petite size of her feet, suggest that would be a no."

"What about that…" She waved her hand toward the unfortunate skin condition.

"That's not as bad as it looks. It's alopecia. I've done

all the blood tests and skin scrapings and wouldn't allow
Emma to play with her if there was a possibility she was
contagious, but all I could find was a thyroid problem that
can be fixed with medication. And, given that someone
dumped her suggests that she hasn't been well treated, so
it could also be stress caused. She's had puppies, but not
recently."

"Well, that's a plus. I'd hate to think of little puppies left
alone in boxes all over the peninsula. Will her fur grow
back?"

"Probably. With a possible caveat. I can't guarantee all
of it will."

Megan glanced over at the dog, who, if an animal could
look happy, appeared to be in seventh heaven being held
in Emma's arms.

"We might not get much snow here, but she'd get awfully cold come winter without a coat."

"Amy's dog wears sweaters," Emma broke in. Amy was
a friend Emma had made this summer on the playground.

Megan had never owned a dog. She'd wanted one and
had, probably, when she was Emma's age, lobbied for one,
but she had come to understand how impractical it would
have been. Her mother was allergic to cats, so kittens were
also out. As Megan studied the dog, she found herself being
drawn into those big round, brown puppy-dog eyes.

"As impossible as it is, I swear that dog knows what
we're talking about."

"She's a smart girl," Cam said. "Dogs have developed
the ability to read human behavior and expressions. Some
dogs can even raise their eyebrows to make their eyes look
bigger, which we unconsciously respond to. There have
been studies that show dogs with that ability are the most
likely to get rescued first in shelters."

"Seriously?"

"I've seen it in action. Just this past spring, a couple came in planning to adopt a cat and left with a fifty-pound bulldog they've named Winston. Who, by the way, now rides their son's skateboard."

"I've seen those competitions on *Animal Planet*. Now that I think about it, I've seen dogs with ears like this." But their coats had been white and flowing.

"Papillons are smart and take to agility training like play."

"I don't really have time to get into all that."

"No problem. They also enjoy lying around and handing out kisses. A daily walk is all that's needed to keep them in shape."

"I can walk her," Emma said, on cue.

"There aren't that many times I'm away from my home office all day," Megan mused. "Even my time in Sequim is usually half days. Most of my business comes from word of mouth, or people seeing the logo on the vans and cars, so it's not as if I'm out knocking on doors anymore."

"We can keep her?" Emma squealed.

Butterfly—heaven help her, Megan was already starting to think of the dog by that name—suddenly perked those oversize ears, looking as if she was going to take off like the Flying Nun at any moment.

"It means we'll see," she repeated. Then turned to Cam. "How likely is she to be adopted over the weekend?"

"I suspect everyone will be at the boat festival. Debbie, Marge and I will be there pitching the shelter with booklets of available adoptees, and although she's listed on the pages, she's up against some pretty stiff competition. Unfortunately, with her current appearance problems, I can't see people lining up to take her home, and if someone did happen to be interested, I could hold her back for a few days."

"I wouldn't want to prevent her from finding a home." Which she had to admit didn't seem likely, unless you were looking for a dog who was a shoo-in to win Honeymoon Harbor's Ugliest Dog competition.

"She's a sweet girl, Megan. And from what I've seen so far, she's smart enough that she'd be easy to train. She appears to be housebroken, and while she'll need some exercise, she isn't like a Lab or Aussie who needs a lot of activity. She'd also be a good TV-watching buddy."

"I'd have to get her stuff. Bowls, a leash, a bed—"

"She could sleep on my bed!" Emma shouted. "Amy's dog sleeps on hers."

Megan was getting a little tired of hearing about Amy and her wonderful, sweater-wearing dog.

"Mutts really are the best," Cam offered. "You're less likely to inherit genetic problems. And everyone I know who takes home a shelter dog swears it knows it's been rescued. They often bond quickly and are unrelentingly loyal."

"Why do I get the feeling that I'm being double-teamed?"

"I'd never send an animal home with a person who didn't really want it," Cam said mildly. "It makes for a bad situation for the new owners, and dogs that boomerang back to the shelter because they weren't a good fit become less likely to engage with other strangers. Which makes it more difficult for them to be adopted. And one last thought—beauty is in the eye of the beholder. She's a sweetheart, and I'll adopt her myself before letting her go to anyone who can't love her for her personality and not her looks."

He was such a good man. Not for the first Wednesday since she'd begun working here, Megan found herself drifting back into *if only* land.

CHAPTER THREE

ON THURSDAY, Cam left the clinic at noon, picked up a burrito from the Taco the Town food truck and, after shooting the breeze with Diego Chavez for a few minutes, headed to the library, where he found Chelsea Prescott, who'd recently gotten engaged to Gabriel Mannion, Honeymoon Harbor's very own billionaire. Despite the fortune he'd made since leaving town, Gabe sure didn't act like a really rich guy. Except for providing all those computers for schoolkids and building a children's trauma wing at Honeymoon Harbor General Hospital.

"Hey, you," she greeted him with her wide, Julia Roberts smile. "I haven't seen you for a while."

"You've been busy." Not only had she been taking care of library business, she'd been running all over town with her summer reader adventures group, had gotten engaged to Gabe and was in the process of adopting two foster daughters.

"Busy beats boredom."

"True enough. I came to ask you a question."

"Answering questions is my superpower." She pointed to the front of her navy blue T-shirt that read, *Librarians, the Original Search Engines*.

"This isn't exactly a library question. But, I guess, in a way it is. Are you open on Labor Day?"

"No. Labor Day is a closure holiday all over the state."

"Good. So, are you going to the boat festival?"

"Of course! Earlier in the day, the girls, Gabe and I are

taking the replica Viking boat he just finished building for a maiden sail before he auctions it off for Welcome Home." The charity built tiny homes and provided services for the area's homeless. "You undoubtedly know that since the committee sold so many tickets for the bachelor auction, it's been moved to the pavilion. Kylee, Mai, Jolene, Megan, Brianna and I bought a table. We asked Amanda Barrow to join us, but apparently Labor Day is a big bulb-buying day at the nursery. Who knew?"

"Not me. I had a houseplant once. The definitive word being *had*. Here's the thing… You know I'm going to be in the bachelor auction, right?"

"Uh, *yeah*. That poster of your manly chest and darling cocker spaniel are posted all over town."

Cam managed not to cringe. "That was Kylee's idea."

"And every woman in town thanks her for it. So, getting to the point—" She gave him a go-ahead wave.

"I want you all to bid on me."

"*All* of us?"

"Well, not Megan, because while she did agree to open the bidding, if necessary, she's not going to continue to bid, which I'm hoping is just because she's putting all her money into expanding her business these days and not that she doesn't want to go out with me. But, and I don't want you to take this the wrong way, I don't care who wins. As long as one of you does."

"As much as I'd love to help you out, my fiancé might have a problem with me going on a romantic date with you. The same way newlywed Aiden might feel about you dating Jolene. And Kylee and Mai are also married. To be honest, the only reason we're going is for the eye candy and the charitable aspect. So, as adorable as you are—"

"Adorable?" Cam glanced around to make sure no one was close enough to have overheard that.

"Are you telling me no woman has ever pointed out those

killer dimples? And then there's your yummy chocolate-brown eyes."

Okay. Before he died of embarrassment, Cam decided it was time to pivot back to the original conversation. "Labor Day is Megan's birthday."

"True, and Desiree is already making her a kick-ass cake for a girls' sleepover party at Herons Landing on the glorious birthday eve night. But how do you know it's her birthday?"

"It's on the Facebook post listing this month's anniversaries and birthdays."

"You read the town's Facebook page?"

"My amazing office manager and web goddess, Shelly, maintains the shelter's business page and shares on the town's Facebook page. So yeah, I see stuff.

"But here's the deal... I want whichever one of you who wins me to gift me to Megan as a birthday present. And I'll be paying."

"Oh!" Her eyes widened behind the lenses of her black-framed glasses, and she actually covered her heart with crossed hands. "That is one of the most romantic things I've ever heard! Of course we'll all do it. Are you going to tell me what the date is?"

Cam's first instinct had been to keep it a secret. But now he was wondering if maybe he should get a second opinion. One from a woman, who'd undoubtedly know a lot more about romance than he did. He leaned closer, kept his voice low and told her.

"Wow." She shook her head in a way that had him worrying he'd chosen wrong. "You have just set the bar for not only every other bachelor in that auction, but you'll be making every guy in town have to step up his game."

"So it's okay?"

She patted his cheek. "It's perfect. She's going to be blown away."

"I just want to give her a perfect time."

"It will be. Will you need someone to watch Emma?"

"Brenda's already signed on to having Emma spend the night, whenever it turns out to be."

Her bright, bluish-green eyes narrowed. "You've put a lot of thought into this."

"She's worth it."

"Megan deserves to be happy after everything her ex put her through. I admittedly didn't see it coming, but you're the perfect man for her. You can count on us. We won't let you down." Her brow furrowed. "Though, we're going to have to come up with an excuse as to why we're bidding with no intention of going out on a date."

"You could say it's for charity and that you're skipping the date part."

"We could. Though, knowing her, she'd feel bad that whoever lost the bidding would feel cheated."

"Good point."

She tapped a nail against a front tooth. "So I guess we'll have to admit that we're buying you for her birthday present."

"Which hopefully she won't turn down."

"Not going to happen. She's talked about you."

"Really?" That was a positive. Not wanting to sound like high school...okay, it was totally high school, but he had to ask. "What did she say?"

"That along with having a great butt, those killer dimples, melted chocolate-brown eyes and hair that has that cute Justin Bieber flop-over-the-forehead thing going, you're kind and sweet with Emma, and when it comes to your four-legged patients, you could be the reincarnation of St. Francis of Assisi.

"She did stop short of saying you walk on water, but I suspect a very strong part of her believes it. And if you tell her that I told you that, I'll call you a liar and say that our dog got fleas while being groomed there."

"It's our secret. And I appreciate you sharing." With the exception of the Bieber hair, she'd definitely boosted his confidence. "So, you don't think she'll turn me down?"

"I'm saying you're going to be the best birthday gift she's ever had, and I'm honored and excited to have a part in the plan."

"Super. When whoever wins goes up to pay, I'll be there with my credit card."

"What's our limit?"

"How high is the sky?"

Cam admittedly wasn't all that flush. Not anywhere near Chelsea's gazillionaire fiancé. But there wasn't that much discretionary money floating around Honeymoon Harbor. Even with school debts and his monthly payments to his predecessor, who was currently fishing for marlin off the coast of Florida, he should be able to cover the tab. And if worse came to worst, he could always pick up extra hours working weekends at the animal emergency and trauma center in Poulsbo.

"Super." She flashed him another of those sunny smiles. "This is going to be such grand fun!"

As he left the library, Cam could only hope so.

His positive attitude lasted the rest of the day, until right at closing, he got a call that sent him straight to Mannion's.

"You look like a guy whose dog just got run over," Quinn Mannion greeted him from behind the bar. "Although, considering your occupation, that probably isn't the best comparison."

"I just got a call. They've added a new twist to the auction."

"And that would be?"

"It's too humiliating to talk about."

"You're already dressing up in a tuxedo, strutting down a catwalk like some Victoria's Secret model and handing a long-stemmed red rose to some woman who pays for—"

"It's just a date," Cam said. "It's not like I'm going to be a damn gigolo. Besides, I've already got that part taken care of."

Of all the Mannion brothers, Quinn had always been the most levelheaded. Cam figured his ability to conceal his emotions had been handy in his previous job as a hotshot attorney and served him well now, listening to customers' stories behind the bar. But his arched brow revealed surprise when Cam told him his plan.

"You're going all in."

"Megan's the main reason I agreed to the auction in the first place," he said.

Quinn swished some pilsner glasses in the sudsy water of the bar sink. "You do realize that you could save yourself the public humiliation by just asking her out."

"I could. But she told me early on that she's given up on men. Apparently we're too high maintenance. I want to impress her enough to change her mind so she sees how perfect we'd be together."

"You're nothing like her ex. Besides, you two have spent every Wednesday together for months. You're a good guy who takes care of kittens and puppies, which, with the possible exception of Flynn Farraday, makes you about the most likely guy in town to get any woman you want. What's stopping you?"

"She works for me."

"She's a contract worker. Not an employee."

"But I still have the power to fire her, so I don't want to come off like a Me Too guy." And because, just in case he was the only one of them feeling that chemistry, Cam didn't want to risk making her so uncomfortable she'd give up their weekly lunches, or worse, start sending another cleaner to avoid him altogether.

"Have you considered that you might just be overthinking things?" Quinn asked.

"Maybe." Possibly. Probably. "But getting back to my current problem, along with the catwalk, the bidding and the stupid bachelor rose, the committee just added a talent section."

"It could be worse. It could be a swimsuit competition."

"Thanks for the sympathy. I still haven't figured out how you got out of it."

"I pointed out that it was more important to keep Mannion's open on festival day so people have somewhere besides the food carts to eat."

"My point is, having played basketball for Annapolis, Flynn Farraday is going to show off some Globetrotter ball moves."

"Thus showing off manly hands large enough to palm a basketball," Quinn said.

"And Cody Coulter can throw an ax."

"You're kidding."

"Would I kid about something like that? Apparently, when he was surveying for the forest service, he'd spend lunch breaks amusing himself and his crew by attacking innocent trees."

"That's kind of a cool thing. I can see women going for that."

"Thanks a bunch."

"I was merely stating the obvious."

"Nick Alexándras, who's opening his Taverna Limáni in time for the Christmas season, Latin dances and only missed getting a spot on the Greek *So You Think You Can Dance* because he was two months under the age limit. But they still showed the audition on national TV there. I looked up clips on YouTube, and he's really, really good."

"I had to learn some easy ballroom stuff for charity balls the firm wanted me to attend," Quinn said. "Latin dancing's admittedly sexy. Especially the tango. But it won't look the same alone."

"He's not doing it alone. He's got Julianna Hart partnering with him."

Quinn nodded. "She was a ballet dancer." One who'd danced professionally all over the world until an injury had her returning home to teach a future generation of tutu wearers.

"Apparently she's multitalented. But you're still not getting it. I doubt anyone would find neutering a dog onstage an appealing talent, so I've got nothing."

"Sure you do."

"No way," Cam said when Quinn suggested a stupid thing going back to skit night at Boy Scout camp at Mirror Lake, where Quinn had been a counselor.

"You'd bring the house down."

"Not doing it."

"I've seen YouTube clips of Ron Reagan Jr. at the White House doing an old *SNL* opener. If it's good enough for a president's son, it should be good enough for you."

"I don't care if President Reagan himself did it. No. Way."

"Then it looks like you're going to have to learn a magic trick."

"Also not an option."

"You'll come up with something."

"Or I could come down with Ebola." Which, at the moment, seemed preferable.

MOTHER NATURE WAS apparently feeling benevolent toward Honeymoon Harbor, because Labor Day dawned bright and sunny, and by noon, when Megan and Emma headed to the festival, the already warm temperature was predicted to reach seventy-five degrees. Last year, Emma had been too young to fully enjoy the festival atmosphere and had gotten cranky, but this year she couldn't wait to see and do everything.

She drove a kid-size red fire engine around in circles, flew in yet more circles on the back of a shiny green-and-purple dragon, rode a unicorn on the carousel, and after she'd passed the height test, she was strapped into the Ferris wheel.

"I see Gramma!" she said, pointing down at Brenda, who was at the long table waiting for a trio of judges to taste the apple pie she'd been taking to potlucks as long as Megan could remember. "Hi, Gramma," she called out, waving wildly. Amazingly, her grandmother heard her and waved back.

Scanning the crowd, Megan saw her father—who'd pitched for the Honeymoon Harbor High Sea Lions— throwing balls into apple baskets to win a stuffed animal. Apparently his eye and arm were as good as back when he was playing baseball, because, as she watched, the man behind the counter gave him a stuffed pink unicorn nearly as large as Emma.

Over the years, Labor Day in Honeymoon Harbor had escalated into part boat festival, part carnival and part county fair. And this year they'd added the bachelor auction. Where some lucky woman with a higher expendable income than Megan possessed would win a date with Cam.

Even if she had the money, she wondered if she'd have the nerve to bid on him. He had, after all, asked her to. But what if she won? Even a setup date like the auction would be bound to change the dynamics of their relationship. She'd hate it if somehow it made him uncomfortable enough to stop their Wednesday lunches.

Emma was chattering away about everything she could see, including the ferry out on the water, as they headed up for another spin. While she might be a talkative child, already speaking mostly in full sentences now, her thoughts were still simple enough that Megan was able to respond while her mind was still imagining dressing up and going on a romantic night with Cameron Montgomery. It didn't even need to be romantic. Just burgers at Mannion's Pub would be more of a date than she'd had in ages.

But now she was a mother who had no intention of bringing a man into her daughter's life unless he was going to stay. And despite all the Wednesday lunches they'd shared together, he still hadn't asked her out. So the attraction must only be on her side. Yet there seemed to be those moments when she'd caught him looking at her in a way that appeared to be more than merely friendship.

And speak of the devil, there he was, handing out those shelter leaflets featuring available rescues at a table next to the Big Dipper ice cream booth. The ride came to an end, and after getting off, Emma decided that she just *had* to have ice cream.

"Hi, Dr. Montgomery!" she greeted him cheerfully. "I drove a fire engine and rode a dragon. And then Mama and I went way, way up in the F-f-f—"

"Ferris wheel," Megan supplied.

"Yes." Emma's strawberry curls, the same color as her mother's, bounced as she nodded enthusiastically. "That's it! And I could see Gramma and the ferry. I like riding the ferry. Sometimes Mama takes me on it for fun. And I don't even have to pay."

"That's a good deal."

"It is!" Like Hailey, the five-year-old girl Chelsea and Gabe were adopting, Emma had begun speaking in exclamation points. As much as Megan enjoyed her daughter's enthusiasm, it could be exhausting. "We're going to get ice cream."

"Sounds like a plan," he said. "And, coincidentally, I was

thinking of closing down and doing the same thing before I have to go change into my penguin suit."

"You're going to wear a penguin suit? Really?"

"It's not really a penguin suit," Megan said. "That's what some people call a man's special dress suit."

"Dressy like to wear to a birthday party? I wore a new dress for Amy's birthday party. It had pink polka dots on it. And why do they call it a penguin suit?"

"Because it's black and white," Cameron said.

"Oh." Those curls bobbed again as she nodded. "Amy has a boyfriend," she offered, segueing on a dime as she so often did.

"She does?" *Dear God,* Megan thought, *don't let it start so soon!*

"Yep. His name is Peter. He's already four."

"An older man," Cam said.

"He's not an old man. He's a boy. And Amy turned four on her birthday. If you were Mommy's boyfriend, she could kiss you like Amy kissed Peter."

Megan felt the color burning in her cheeks as his glance moved from her little chatterbox to her. "There's an idea."

"Amy and Peter kissed?" Megan dared to ask, even as she'd love to change the topic of this conversation. For the first time, she understood why her parents had been so strict when she'd been growing up. And hadn't that turned out well?

"She kissed him on the playground. She chased him and caught him at the swings and kissed him. He said 'yuck' and ran away. But Amy's going to marry him. Then she can kiss him whenever she wants. I can't wait to go to school next week. Then maybe I'll have a boyfriend."

"She's going to school?" Cam asked as Emma ran over to the ice cream booth to choose her flavor.

"Preschool starts at three," Megan explained. "Half days. I don't know how that happened. It seems like just yesterday that she was born. On one hand, the speed at which she's maturing scares me to death. On the other hand, I get teary at the idea of my baby girl leaving home."

"It's only for half a day."

"I know. But next year it's full-time. And one of these days, I won't be her best friend. It sounds as if Amy's already moving me into second place."

He surprised her by taking her hand—in public, where anyone and everyone in Honeymoon Harbor could see them—and leading her to the booth next door, where Emma was torn between blueberry cobbler and chocolate chip.

"She'll make friends," he said. "But you'll never be second to anyone." The look he gave her, both fond and sizzling at the same time, could have melted all the ice cream in that display case.

Once they had their cones, Cameron suggested taking a ride on the Ferris wheel, which, as Emma reminded him, they'd already been on, but she wanted to ride again because "you can see everything!"

And after a brief stop at the ticket booth, they were all buckled in, Cameron and Megan on the outsides of the car with magpie Emma chattering away between them. As the wheel began its ascent, Megan realized that if you were a stranger, visiting Honeymoon Harbor for the festival, and happened to look up and see the threesome, you'd think they were a family.

And wasn't that dangerous thinking?

CHAPTER FOUR

THE RIDE WAS over way too soon. Cam wouldn't have minded if they'd stayed on that Ferris wheel forever. This, he thought, was the type of family he'd imagined himself having once he got a practice established. The one he might still have. No. Strike that. The one he *would* have. But for now, he was content to take whatever he could get.

Kylee, who'd arranged the auction in the first place, caught him as they were looking at the wooden boats where bidding for Gabe Mannion's faering was going through the roof. He had to admit that it was really cool, with its large, single red flag, and having Jarle Bjornstad standing in it, dressed like a Viking about to sail off to go marauding, was definitely marketing genius. Especially since it brought home the fact that this was not just any ordinary boat, but one built in the ancient Scandinavian tradition.

Elimination rounds of boat races had taken place early that morning when the tide was high. The final round would occur this evening, before the fireworks that, defying the calendar, would declare Honeymoon Harbor's summer officially over.

"Hey, Cam," Kylee said. "Time for you to get ready for the big show."

"Great." His tone said otherwise. "I guess I'll see you at the hall?" he asked Megan. Because if she'd changed her mind after their Wednesday conversation, he'd gotten himself in a damn mess.

"I'll be there. Mom and Dad are taking Emma home for a midday nap and bringing her back for the fireworks. And speaking of my parents..." They were headed down the midway, her dad, managing to walk without his cane today, half hidden by the enormous unicorn.

"Wow! Grandpa, did you buy this for me?"

"Nope," Joe Larson said.

"Oh." Her bottom lip came out in a pout.

"I won it at the baseball throwing booth. Do you happen to know any little girl who might want to take it home?"

"Me!" As she raced toward him, Megan reached for her too late, but her mother took the stuffed toy from Joe before he risked being knocked over by a three-year-old.

"She's been warned about being careful around Dad because of his MS, but despite the way she seems to be maturing more every day, she still doesn't fully understand the concept of illness beyond the sniffles or an ear infection," Megan murmured to Cam.

"Well, then," Joe said with a broad grin. "I guess you might as well give him a home."

"Thank you, Grandpa!"

"Careful," Megan warned as Emma went to throw her arms around him. She drew back just a little as he bent down so she could pat his cheek instead.

"You did good with her," Cam said quietly, just for Megan's ears.

"Thank you. I'm fortunate. Unlike her mother, Emma's been an easy child from the beginning."

That comment brought up thoughts of her supposedly reckless marriage, which, from what he'd heard, had surprised everyone, since she'd always been the perfectly behaved good girl. They were going to have to talk about it as they moved to the next stage of their relationship. But here, with nearly the entire town surging around them, was not the place. *Patience*, Cam reminded himself.

"Well, then," Megan's mother said, with a significant look between the two of them. "Give your mom a hug goodbye and then let's get you home for a little rest, Emma, dear. Then we'll have supper and come back here for the fireworks."

"I love fireworks," Emma said, giving Megan a noisy smack of a goodbye kiss right on her lips. Cam had never imagined ever being envious of a three-year-old child, but at this moment he was. "And cotton candy," she was saying as she pointed toward the booth selling the sugary treat. "Can I have one with all the colors?"

Her mother glanced back at Megan, who sighed and gave her a go-ahead sign. "She's going to be bouncing off the walls," she warned.

"My mom always said the same thing," Cam remembered.

"Now that we have all that settled," Kylee said, "you really do need to come with me, Cameron."

There was no way he was going to go through this again next year, Cam vowed as he changed in the men's room with the others. Though, the way the committee had gotten so many guys to agree to Kylee's plan, the only way Cam could see to escape his future fate was to get himself engaged like Gabe. Or married, like Aiden and Seth, who'd escaped the block.

He also never would have agreed if he'd known that the stupid talent show would be part of the circus. He still didn't know how the hell he'd let Quinn—and Jarle and every other guy sitting at the bar—talk him into what to do for that part, but since he didn't have a plan B, there was no turning back.

The format was for all the bachelors, wearing their tuxedos, to mingle for half an hour with the women who'd all paid twenty-five dollars for a ticket to participate in the auction. Margaritas and soft drinks were on the house, and although Cam had heard there'd been much discussion during a festival planning session about the cost of giving away the margaritas, the argument that the party was only for thirty minutes, the drinks would be weak and getting the bidders a little buzzed could up the bidding had won out.

Then, after everyone was seated, the bachelors would all go backstage and, one at a time, walk—no, they'd been instructed to *strut*—down the catwalk as they were introduced by name and occupation. That gave the women time to compare the photos in the program they'd been given with the actual bachelor.

Then would come the damn talent show, where the emcee, who happened to be Gloria Wells, the owner of Thairapy Salon and Day Spa, would give a longer, highly embellished introduction of the bachelor the women would be bidding on, after which the poor sucker would come out, smile like he was enjoying himself, perform his talent and then the bidding would begin.

Cam had survived the mixer part of the event, which, from the open sexual innuendos he received, gave him an even better idea of what women experienced, being hit on by guys when they were out with girlfriends. He doubted many of these women would have behaved that way under any other circumstances, but then again, this whole deal was supposed to be a fantasy. Like a smash-up of *The Bachelorette* and *The Price Is Right*. From Cam's point of view, it was more like *Survivor*.

He hadn't thought to ask, and no one had offered to tell him, what the auction's theme song would be. But when the hidden speakers began blaring out "It's Raining Men," and the women began screaming and shouting as if they were all at a bachelorette party visit to Chippendales, he seriously considered bolting for the fire exit.

Then, reminding himself that a third of the money raised would go toward his nonprofit, no-kill shelter—not to mention the date with Megan—he took a deep breath and walked through the curtain to take his turn on the catwalk.

"DOES ANYONE ELSE feel uncomfortable?" Megan asked, beginning to wish she hadn't come, but even though she hadn't planned to bid, Chelsea and the others had talked her into it. She hadn't expected an entire pavilion of women, most of whom she knew to be responsible adults, screaming like they were fourteen again and at a Justin Timberlake concert. "Now I fully understand the term *meat market*."

"They're not being treated like meat," Brianna, who'd left her B and B in the hands of her newly hired assistant for the event, said. "More like eye candy."

"Look at it this way," Kylee suggested. "We spend our entire lives being sexually objectified by men. Turnaround is only fair play."

"That's one advantage of growing older, I suppose," Jolene mused. "You get left alone."

Lily rolled her eyes at that. "Honey, I volunteer at Harbor Hill Home. You should hear some of those old geezers inviting women for sleepovers in their rooms. But for this one evening, twelve hot guys are going to have to strut their stuff for us. And I, for one, have come prepared to shop."

Megan couldn't decide whether or not she wanted Lily to bid on Cam. It wasn't as if she'd told anyone what she'd been feeling. Not that she didn't trust her friends. But saying it out loud would make it too real. And for now, since she and Cam would have to live in the same small town, constantly running into each other, she found it safer to dwell in fantasyland.

Brianna had casually mentioned hearing about those Wednesday lunches a time or two. To which Megan had not so truthfully answered it was merely a coincidence that she'd be cleaning during his lunch hour. And Emma did so love visiting the animals. She'd sensed at the time her friend hadn't exactly bought the story, but she didn't challenge it.

The bidding continued fast and furious, and as the excitement built, even the men, who'd looked a little uncomfortable in the beginning, got into the spirit. Megan was surprised at how many out-of-towners had shown up. All the motels, hotels, inns, and bed-and-breakfasts in not only Honeymoon Harbor, but neighboring towns as well, were filled to capacity.

"Wow, who knew Flynn had moves like that?" Kylee asked. After an afternoon of escalating bidding, the fire chief was the penultimate bachelor.

"Gloria introduced him as having played basketball at Annapolis and even won a gold medal with a team in the Olympics," Lily said. A bit of personal history that somehow hadn't made it onto the Facebook page when he'd moved up from Oregon to take the job last year.

"With a lot of guys, that would be the first thing they'd tell anyone," Brianna said.

"I like that about him," Jolene said. "It suggests he's modest. But as much as I love Aiden, I can't deny that the way he can palm that ball has me thinking wicked thoughts."

"I just wish basketball players still wore those old-time short shorts," Lily said, waving her paddle. "I'd like to get a look at those thighs."

"And you say it's not a meat market," Megan said.

Unsurprisingly, as hot as Nick Alexandras's tango had been, Flynn's still military-fit body, moving around that stage, long legs and arms looking as if they'd been sculpted by Michelangelo, shot to the top of the chart by two hundred dollars when Lily, who had been born into money and didn't have to worry about a budget, raised him two hundred dollars over Nick's tango.

EACH BACHELOR WAS assigned his own song. Since he was doing a tango, Nick's had been the song Al Pacino had tangoed to in *Scent of a Woman*, while Flynn's was "Anchors Aweigh," which had prompted Kara, owner of Rain and Shine Books, who was seated at the next table, to state that she certainly wouldn't mind sailing away with him.

Then there was one.

"And for our grand finale," Gloria Wells announced, "we have Dr. Cameron Montgomery, who grew up right here on the peninsula and attended WSU, where he also got his veterinary degree. He's been working in Sacramento the past few years, but having missed our beautiful Pacific Northwest, he has now settled in Honeymoon Harbor. And along with taking wonderful care of all our fur babies, he's established a nonprofit rescue shelter, which all of you who bought tickets have contributed to. I'm sure many of you have adopted dogs and cats from him since it opened.

"Now, I know you all have been waiting to hear about his date, which he's teased us by keeping a secret, but it's finally time for it—ta-da!—to be revealed. One very lucky woman will be taking a romantic, private starlit dinner cruise on the *Lady Abigail*, which is currently docked in our harbor.

"For those visitors who might not know her history, she's a full-size replica of the original US Navy tall ship that was named for Abigail Adams, first lady to John Adams, who is known as the father of the US Navy. She played a vital part in the Barbary Wars that put an end to the piracy and plundering of US ships and showed our navy to be one of the most powerful forces on the sea.

"So, without further ado, I give you Honeymoon Harbor's very own Dr. McDreamy, Cameron Montgomery!"

A collective scream went up as the loudspeakers started playing Bob Seger's "Old Time Rock and Roll," the song that had catapulted Tom Cruise to stardom in *Risky Business*.

"He wouldn't dare," Megan said on a gasp.

"Oh, wow. As much as I love Gabe, I certainly hope he does," Chelsea said.

"I don't even play on that team, but that dance was still one of the sexiest things ever. Even better, in my opinion, than *Dirty Dancing*, partly because it was so unexpected," Kylee said. "Though Swayze, being older, was hotter than Cruise."

Megan, who was holding her breath, couldn't respond.

When Cam suddenly burst from the wings at the left side of the stage, wearing white socks, a pink dress shirt and those red boxer briefs Megan had actually held in her hands a few days ago, lip-synching into a candlestick, the volume in the room nearly blew the pavilion's roof off.

"Oh. My. God." Megan couldn't believe it. Her hands flew to her lips to keep from screaming herself. The man had just turned her fantasies up to eleven.

"Cameron Montgomery is definitely proof there is a God," Kylee said. "And She sure scored perfection with him."

Women were jumping to their feet, already waving their paddles even before he'd ditched the candlestick for an air guitar. And in that last moment, when he slid across the stage floor on his knees—which, Megan thought, was going to leave him with a nasty floor burn—and the music stopped, he was looking directly at her.

"How old do you have to be for a hot flash?" Kylee asked as she fanned her face with her program.

"I don't know," Lily said. "But once again, you're not alone."

As they all looked from Megan's face to Cam, who'd gotten to his feet, back to Megan, she felt her cheeks flaming. And those were just the parts that showed. She took a long sip of the ice water she'd taken from the tray instead of a margarita, hoping it would cool her off. It didn't.

"We'll begin the bidding at two hundred and fifty dollars," Gloria announced.

That bid was instantly matched by bookseller Kara.

Lily raised her paddle. "Three hundred dollars."

"You just bought Flynn," Megan reminded her.

"True. But I'm a generous woman. If I win, I'll give him to one of you."

"You and Megan are the only ones who're single," Chelsea said.

"Yeah," Lily agreed with a wink. "Funny how that works out, isn't it?"

He looked so good. So gorgeous. So damn self-confident. If Megan hadn't known how much he'd been dreading this auction, she would have believed he was enjoying himself.

"Three fifty!" This from a brunette out-of-towner at the back of the room.

Chelsea jumped up. "Four hundred."

"Four twenty-five," another out-of-towner, this one a blonde from the neighboring table who was painted into a pair of leopard-print pants and wearing enough makeup to stock every makeup counter in the Seattle Nordstrom, called out.

"Five hundred," Jolene countered.

"Five fifty," the earlier brunette called out.

"Six hundred," Brianna, who no one had ever heard raise her voice, shouted.

"What are you guys doing?" Megan asked.

"It's for a good cause," Lily reminded her. "We're bidding him up."

"But what if you win him?"

"I already told you. I'm giving him to you… Seven hundred," she countered after a new bidder in the back of the room topped Brianna.

"Seven fifty," the determined blonde jumped back in.

"Eight hundred," Chelsea shouted out.

"I doubt Gabe would be all that thrilled to have you going on a starlit cruise with Cameron," Megan warned as the brunette jumped back in.

"He wouldn't care. Neither would Aiden." Jolene raised it to an even one thousand. "And don't worry about us. We're all pitching in to give him to you for a birthday present."

"You're seriously giving me a man for my birthday?"

"Not any man," Brianna said, shooting a very uncharacteristic glare at the blonde who was refusing to surrender. "This is Cameron Montgomery we're talking about. Twelve hundred!"

As the bidding continued, Megan tried to do the division in her head to figure out how much each of her friends' share of the final amount would be if they did win. At the pace it was climbing, she was afraid only Chelsea, who could get the money from gazillionaire Gabe, and Lily, with her robber-baron ancestor trust fund, could afford what they'd have to chip in.

"This is really generous," she said. "But you have to stop, because it's going to cost you all a fortune."

The other women shared a look. Chelsea shrugged and added another fifty dollars to the total.

"Don't worry," Brianna said. "It's supposed to be a secret, but it won't be any fun if you're worried about us. Cam's paying."

"What? Why?"

"That should be obvious," Jolene said as the blonde stayed in.

"He doesn't want anyone but you to win him. And damn, would she drop the hell out?" Lily tossed up yet another bid. "So, because we all think you'd be perfect together, we collaborated in the conspiracy to make this date happen."

Megan was stunned into silence as Brianna stood up and walked over to the blonde.

"Just in case you're wondering, the sky's our limit," she said in the calm, polite tone that she might have used during her years as a high-end hotel concierge. "So I'd advise you to sit down now, because it's bound to eventually get painful standing on those five-inch stilettos."

"What do you mean, 'the sky's the limit'?" Megan asked as Brianna sat back down at their table.

"Exactly that."

"But Cam's still paying off student loans."

"Which only shows that he believes you're worth busting his budget for," Chelsea said.

"Which is *so* romantic," Kylee and Mai said in unison.

"It needs to be a movie," Jolene decided. "I'm still doing makeup for Hallmark films. I'll call a producer friend tomorrow and pitch the idea to her."

"Set it at Christmas," Lily suggested. "Those are like chocolate truffles. You can never have too many."

"Exactly," Jolene agreed, shooting a withering, warning look at the blonde. Having overcome bullying when she'd been younger, she was the most outwardly tough woman of their group. "My mother would eat it up. Me, too, actually."

"You're all crazy," Megan said as the blonde surrendered, sank to her seat and motioned to the young man wandering the room with a tray for another margarita. "Most of all Cameron." But didn't it warm her from the inside out, just thinking that he'd go to such extremes when he could've simply asked her out to a movie and burger at Mannion's?

"We're all varying levels of crazy in our own way," Chelsea said. "But I've got to tell you, Megan, Cameron Montgomery is head-over-heels crazy about you."

"I'm going to get to help plan another wedding!" Brianna actually clapped her hands. Knowing that her friend had once coordinated a Las Vegas wedding for a pair of King Charles spaniels, Megan decided that event planning must be in her genes. Which might also explain why all the rooms at Herons Landing were idyllic, Hallmark-movie-set cozy.

"You're getting ahead of yourself," Megan said.

"Possibly," Brianna said. "But in case you haven't noticed, even after he went to stand next to Gloria for the bidding, the man hasn't taken his eyes off you."

"He's definitely serious," Chelsea agreed.

As every other woman at the table nodded, although she wasn't looking to get married again—been there, done that, and had been left with a pile of debt to prove it—Megan had to admit that she hoped they were right. Because no man had ever made her feel the way Cameron Montgomery did.

The bidding finally stopped. After her going-once, going-twice warning, Gloria declared Lily the winner. At which time, Lily stood up and announced that she was gifting Honeymoon Harbor's veterinarian to her dear friend Megan Larson for a birthday present, which caused a murmured wave of surprise and mostly delight, save for the losing bidders.

"Give me your car key," Lily said.

"Why?"

"Because Jolene and I are going to take care of getting your car to your house. Cam can drive you home. Unless you want to spend the night together. I'd bet your mom would be happy to have Emma stay over."

"I'm not spending the night with him." But oh, how that idea sent warmth flooding through her blood. "The military could've used you all when they were planning the Normandy invasion." Megan took her key ring from her bag and handed it over. "You can leave it in the window box on the right-hand side of the door."

"My husband—and by the way, I do love saying that word, so expect to hear it a lot—who happens to be Honeymoon Harbor's police chief, would not approve of you hiding your keys in such an obvious place," Jolene said.

"What he doesn't know won't hurt him, just this once," Lily said.

Still shaking her head at what had just transpired, as Megan wove her way through the tables toward the front of the room to claim her gift (which still had her stunned), she felt as if she were looking through the close-up lens of a camera. With her gaze focused directly on Cam, everything and everyone in the pavilion faded away.

There was only her. Only him and, amazingly, his look toward her mirrored her feelings.

As she stood in front of him, he took her hands in his. "Happy birthday." Then he bent his head and kissed her. A light, sweet kiss that had the room bursting into applause as the traditional "Happy Birthday" song started playing, an indication that Gloria had also been in on the subterfuge.

"You shouldn't have spent all that money," she chided as nearly everyone in the banquet room began to sing along. Dammit, now she was tearing up. It was all too, too much.

"Money's not important. I was willing to spend whatever it took to make sure that you'd be the one I'd be having that dinner with. I'm yours, Megan Larson." He held out his arms, offering himself to her, which, now that the song had ended, caused a united sigh from most of the women in the room. "Use me as you will."

Whoever was working the sound system, had, instead of turning the loudspeakers off after the birthday song, somehow let the mic go hot just as he'd said that. At any other time, Megan might have wanted the floor to open and swallow her up. But this entire situation was so fantastical, she couldn't feel embarrassed. Not while feeling like Cinderella.

Taking her hand again, Cam thanked Gloria, blew a kiss to her friends who'd made this happen, then walked off the stage with Megan to a round of applause.

CHAPTER FIVE

"I can't believe you did that," Megan said as they left the pavilion to the sound of a calliope from the midway.

"It was Quinn's idea. I had no idea there'd be a talent aspect to the show. Unfortunately, I don't have any talents."

"Try telling that to all those women back there," she said. "It was as if Gloria had thrown you into a tank of piranhas. Brianna actually threatened that blonde."

"You're kidding." He'd laced their fingers together, and as they walked past the dock where the *Lady Abigail* was towering over all the pleasure boats, Megan couldn't help thinking how right it felt. How easy.

"No. You were amazing, and so is your date idea."

"I got the idea from that old movie *Romancing the Stone*. The final scene when Michael Douglas shows up on the street outside Kathleen Turner's apartment with that gleaming white yacht on a trailer to take her away. Since I couldn't bring the *Lady Abigail* to your house, I decided to bring you to the *Lady Abigail*."

"Adding to the surrealism of this day is discovering that you actually know that movie."

He shrugged. "I dated a woman in Sacramento for a while who must have watched it at an impressionable age, because she had me watch the video, then informed me that was the type of romance she wanted from the man she married. Knowing I couldn't live up to that fictionalized ideal, we agreed to go our own ways. But stayed friends. After a couple years, she married a guy who put on those mystery dinner theaters and was into grand gestures, so all ended well."

"For a man who doesn't do grand gestures, booking a tall ship, especially one as famous as this, for a private dinner sail is awfully grand."

"That's what Quinn said. Here's the thing… I hadn't ever met a woman I wanted to do something over-the-top romantic for. Until you."

"Oh, wow." Megan had to remind herself to breathe. "For the record, I certainly don't expect gestures like that every day." She'd already fallen in love with him because of the way he'd planned those weekly lunches, the way he was so wonderful with Emma and, yes, because just thinking about him had butterflies fluttering their wings inside her. That light kiss when she'd claimed him had left her as breathless as she'd always imagined Cam kissing her would be. It had also left her wanting more.

"Truthfully, I don't really want to wait for tomorrow," he said.

"Me, neither," Megan admitted. After all he'd gone through for this date, there was no way she was going to play coy.

"But here's the deal. You've been on my mind for months, ever since you first walked into Mannion's—"

"Really?"

"Really, which is why I called and asked you for a quote."

She laughed. "I felt the same way. It was like being hit by lightning. Which was why I agreed to clean your house, which I don't do for anyone but Seth these days."

"Yet you made me wait five days for the appointment."

"I needed to think about the consequences if we were

still attracted to each other once we'd spent some time together. I'm a mother, Cam. I can't bring a man into my daughter's life because I'm attracted to him."

"I'm glad you decided to take the risk. Because I've been obsessing about this day for weeks, enough so that I even let Quinn talk me into doing that damn dance."

"Not only was it very sexy, think how much more you earned, not just for the food bank, but for the shelter."

"There is that. But we don't have to wait until tomorrow to be together. How about picking up something to eat at the food booths? By the time we finish eating, your parents will be back with Emma, and we'll all watch the fireworks together. Then I'll take you both home and return to my very clean but lonely house and dream of you."

"I'm ahead of you. Because I've been dreaming of you for months."

"Me, too. And I'm kicking myself for waiting so long. So, we'll just have to make up for lost time."

They ordered the wings Quinn was famous for from Mannion's booth, and hummus and pita bread from the booth Nick Alexandras had rented to advertise his upcoming restaurant.

"Now to find a place to sit," Megan said, looking around at the crush of people.

"I've got that covered. Come with me." He led her through the crowd to the pier, where a white hardtop cabin cruiser bobbed on the water. "Seth offered me his sloop, but it was too small for you, Emma, your parents and me, so I rented this one so we could watch the fireworks from the water."

This was so much better than Cinderella's pumpkin coach, Megan thought. But still… "I can't imagine what this, the auction and our date is costing you."

"It's not a problem and nothing you need to worry about. I've watched you, Megan. All you do is work and be a mom to Emma. Which is admirable, but when was the last time you just stopped worrying about doing everything perfectly and had some fun?"

"Now you sound like Lily. And Jolene. And," she admitted on a sigh, "all my other friends. And my mom."

"See?" He flashed her a smile. Although he'd smiled a lot over the past months, this one was sexy as sin. "You're well overdue." She was well overdue for a lot of things, especially one she'd been thinking of far too much lately.

They sat side by side on a padded bench seat sharing the meal with bottles of Quinn's Good Vibrations summer craft beer as the lighted Ferris wheel kept turning.

Megan felt as if her mind had gone into some sort of freeze. She literally could not have a normal conversation after such an extraordinary day. Finally, after a period of silence, Cam put his empty plate down on the bench beside him, then took her face in his hands.

Megan was glad she was sitting down, because she was already trembling with anticipation. His lips were smiling as they kissed hers, clouding her mind again, fogging out the crowd, the barkers from the midway, a country band playing Dierks Bentley cover songs. Still holding on to her plate, she couldn't move, even to put her arms around him as he angled his head, deepening the kiss, while at the same time keeping it gentle, which still made her head spin and stars burst behind her closed eyes.

His fingers trailed down her neck, his thumb pausing at that hollow in her throat where she knew he could feel the blood pounding.

Just as the beam of the Honeymoon Harbor lighthouse

flashed across them like a spotlight, she heard a familiar high voice.

"We get to go on a boat?"

Cam raised his head as Emma came running down the dock toward them. "We have company."

"Surprise, surprise." As they drew apart, she touched his cheek. "Thank you. For everything."

His dimples creased again. "Believe me, it's been my pleasure."

Apparently the nap had restored Emma's energy, because she talked a mile a minute, her words falling over each other, making them difficult to interpret. "I don't remember seeing fireworks," she explained to Cam. "Gramma says that was because the first year I was a baby and they didn't take me because they didn't want me to be scared and cry. Then last year, I was just a toddler. But now I'm a big girl, so this is like my very first time."

"These you'll remember," Cam promised as he buckled a life vest on her. "Want to go out on the water?"

"Yes!" She jumped up and down, clapping her hands as Megan's father unfastened the ropes and Cam started the engine.

"My parents knew all about this, didn't they?" Megan asked beneath her breath as they pulled away from the pier to join the other boats already anchored around the harbor.

"I had to tell them so they'd know where to find us when they came back."

"That makes sense. But I'm getting the feeling that half of Honeymoon Harbor was involved in this."

"Not everyone," he said. "But if I were you, I'd stay away from the town's Facebook page for a few days."

Emma had settled onto Megan's lap just as the first red, gold and purple fireworks lit up the night sky. Booms echoed, and shrill whistles screamed as a rocket shot high into the sky, exploding into blue spirals following by a rain of flashing silver.

For the next thirty minutes, oohs and aahs floated over the water as the sky lit up with more complex blasts of color than previous years. Megan had heard that was due to Gabe Mannion throwing some of his gazillions into the town's budget to create an extravaganza. Which he'd definitely pulled off. The colors were brighter, the bursts, which were set to music for the first time, continuing to explode inside each other, not allowing a moment for viewers to catch their breaths before the next explosion. And there were shapes: red hearts, blue and silver stars, and bright yellow smiley faces.

"Oh! Those smiley faces are my favorite!" Emma shouted, clapping her hands.

The finale was a dazzling display of all the colors, all the sparkles that kept going on and on, saturating the sky. Just when it seemed it was over, more rockets were sent into the smoky sky, creating a wide silver-and-white waterfall that tumbled down, disappearing into the water.

"Wow," Megan said. "That was really something."

"It was amazing!" Emma turned toward Cam. "You're right, Dr. Montgomery. I'm going to remember this forever and ever!"

"Me, too." As he reached out and ruffled the little girl's curls, Cam knew he'd never forget how Megan's face had lit up beneath that bright sky. She was always cheerful and friendly, but behind the smiles, he could see the serious seeds of responsibility. But tonight, caught up in the moment, she'd looked as awed and happy as her daughter. He knew he'd still be remembering that on their golden anniversary. Now all he had to do was convince her to marry him.

NOT KNOWING WHAT to expect, but reading on the ship's website that it was suggested guests dress warmly, in layers, Megan had dressed for her dinner in a long black skirt over opaque black tights, a turtleneck sweater and calf-high boots with low heels, because she suspected the deck of a ship was no place for heels. Looking at herself in the mirror, she liked the way the black contrasted with her strawberry-red hair, which she'd pulled back into a loose braid that should survive any winds.

"But the sweater's all wrong." Remembering Cam's touch on her throat, she pulled off the turtleneck and exchanged it for an angora sweater with sequins embellishing the lower, scooped neckline. And, because a girl could always be hopeful, she'd stopped by the Dancing Deer Dress Shop and bought some seduction underwear in their lingerie section. Gratefully, Dorothy and Dottie acted as if she bought black lace demi bras and barely there panties every day, yet as she left the store with her underwear wrapped in tissue in the store bag, Dottie, the more cheerful of the twin sisters, called out, "Have a wonderful, special date, dear."

She'd dropped Emma off at her parents' early in the afternoon, which gave her time to give herself a facial with peach-scented cream Jolene had assured her was the line's bestseller. Then, pouring a small glass of wine, she spent the next luxurious half hour lounging in a bubble bath—again courtesy of Jolene's skin care—feeling every bone in her body nearly melting with a relaxation she couldn't remember experiencing for a long, long time.

Although she usually just stuck with a light face cream and lip balm, tonight she was going all out with actual makeup, following the detailed chart that Jolene had created when she'd stopped by the salon and spa. Both Jolene and her mother had refused to let her pay, telling her that it was their contribution to her special evening.

Brianna had also dropped in with a black wool jacket cut like a classic military peacoat from her own closet. "For walking on the deck," she'd said.

"I have a coat."

"You have a bulky, hooded rain parka that's perfect for everyday. But not for the first date you've had in forever. This is a special night, Megan. You need to go all in. And you don't need a rain hood, because the forecast is for clear skies tonight. But here's a cute knit hat to cover your ears because it'll probably be windy and chilly out on the water. And you know what they say about heat escaping through the top of your head."

Because her body thermostat turned to blaze whenever she was around Cam, Megan wasn't certain all this was necessary, but the hat did look cute with the coat, and Brianna was being so generous, she wasn't going to argue.

Finally, although she stabbed herself in the eye with an evil killer mascara wand, she was ready half an hour before Cam was due to pick her up. The ship was going to leave right before sundown so they could enjoy that golden hour between daylight and dusk. She'd put forty-two hundred steps on her Fitbit when she finally heard him pulling up outside her house. After pausing to give herself one last check in the mirror on the wall of the small entry, she opened the door the instant he rang the bell. Not that she wanted to let him know how anxious she was or anything.

"Wow." His dark eyes widened. "You look amazing."

"Meaning I clean up well," she said dryly as she opened the door wider to invite him in.

"That's not what I meant at all. You're always beautiful. But I've got to admit, Megan, you're kind of scary right now."

"Scary?"

Jolene had assured her that if she just followed the chart showing how to do a smoky eye, she wouldn't have any problem. "Makeup is supposed to be fun," her friend said. "Like playing with Barbie. But this time you're Barbie."

Having always thought Barbie was a bit overdone, especially when dressed as an astronaut, Megan had applied the makeup with a light hand. But now she was worried she'd ended up looking like RuPaul.

"Scary, because you're intimidating. But in a good way. Natural," he assured her. "But more city sophisticated. And why don't you just kill me now before I get in deeper?"

Her quick laugh eased the tension that had, despite the bath and wine, been building in her all day. "Thank you," she said. "This just feels awkward. I haven't dated since high school."

"I promise I'll do my best to make it painless." He picked up her coat from the back of a chair. "Ready to go?"

For one suspended instant, she almost chickened out. Which was ridiculous. They got along perfectly on Wednesdays and had shared a wonderful time before and after the auction. Why was she putting so much pressure on one night?

"Maybe I just should've chosen bowling," he suggested, as if reading her mind again. More likely her body language, given that she'd turned as stiff as the Tin Man before Dorothy had saved him with that oilcan.

"I'd be okay with bowling," she said. "My dad and I used to go every Saturday afternoon when he wasn't fishing. That was before his MS. But you paid a lot for this evening, and I know it's going to be wonderful."

Which it was…

As if they were visiting royalty, they were piped aboard by a sailor in a uniform dating back to the 1800s. The captain, who was waiting at the top of the ramp, welcomed them before turning them over to another sailor, who led them up three flights to the upper gun deck.

"Welcome to the admiral's quarters," he said as he opened the door to a room furnished in period antiques. In the center of the room was a round dining table covered with a white tablecloth. The gilt- and cobalt-rimmed china and heavy sterling flatware reminded Megan of the old photos from when Herons Landing had hosted the newly married king and queen of Montacroix, whose visit had resulted in the town's name changing from Port Vancouver to Honeymoon Harbor in their honor.

"I feel as if I should be wearing a formal dinner gown," Megan murmured as a steward arrived with a silver tray holding a bottle of champagne and two martini glasses filled with Oregon pink shrimp and Dungeness crab cocktail that he set on the table, then discreetly left the room.

"The whole idea of this evening is to relax," Cam, who was wearing a Shetland sweater a few shades lighter than his eyes with a dark indigo pair of jeans, said as he pulled out her chair. "If you were to get all formal, I'd have to put that penguin suit back on."

"But you looked so handsome in it," she said as he poured the champagne into one of the stemmed flutes embossed with the ship's silhouette in frosted glass and handed it to her. "But I have to admit that there was a lot to be said for that *Risky Business* outfit. Though you'd changed up the underwear."

"I'd do nearly anything for you." Pouring his own glass,

he lifted it toward hers for a toast. "But wearing tighty-whities in public would push the limit."

"I liked the red ones better," she admitted as they touched the rims of their glasses. No way would she admit that on more than one Wednesday over the past months she'd fantasized about him wearing them.

As the ship pulled away from port, they sat on couches on that high deck, looking out the expansive windows as Honeymoon Harbor grew smaller and they moved out onto the Salish Sea, where islands dotted the gilded sapphire water like scattered emeralds.

"I love this," Megan said with a long, happy sigh. "Sometimes I take a ferry to escape for an hour or so. Getting out on the water, looking at green trees lining the banks, drinking in the fresh salty air, gives me a new lease on life."

"Emma said you two sometimes ride the ferry for fun. She made sure to point out that she got to ride for free."

Megan laughed. "That's always a big deal for her. Which makes me wonder sometimes if I put too much emphasis on money."

"From what I hear, you've had a lot of reason to focus on it. And it doesn't hurt for kids to learn that money doesn't grow on that tree that hasn't magically popped up in your backyard."

"A lesson I certainly learned early… The admiral lived well, I see," she murmured, taking a sip of the sparkling wine. Soft instrumental music was playing through hidden speakers.

"With rank comes privilege," Cam said. "Though I expect, if we wanted the true experience, we'd be drinking a flagon of rum—I strongly doubt that the crew lived anything like this."

"True. I imagine their circumstances were far grimmer. But when you think about the wars back then—and granted, I don't know anything about it other than watching the *Pirates of the Caribbean* movies—it doesn't seem as if rank, even on a magnificent ship like this, could keep you from getting killed. Or dying from disease."

"Probably not."

"I wish Dad could see this," she murmured. "After all those years working on crab boats in the Bering Sea and Bristol Harbor, it would probably blow his mind."

"Your dad's a tough guy. I'm sorry about the MS."

"Me, too. But, as bad as it sounds, he was fortunate to get relapsing-remitting MS, which is the most common kind. There will always be flare-ups, but also periods where it doesn't manifest itself or progress. Doctors have assured him that his life expectancy is pretty much the same as any other male his age. Although the inconvenience will admittedly progress. He's only started using the cane this past year."

"Still, that's got to be hard on his ego."

"I suppose it was, but he and Mom seem to have a happy life since he retired. I took it hard when he was first diagnosed. He'd always been so strong, I couldn't imagine him as an invalid and overreacted."

"But you were, what? Sixteen?"

"Seventeen. And I won't lie. I think it hit me harder than it did either of my parents."

"You were at an emotional age."

"True." She sighed. "I'd grown up being taught that God was all-knowing and benevolent. That sustained me a lot when I could see my mother was worried about some storm in Alaska when he was out crabbing. Surely God would protect him. Then suddenly, after having become more fatigued than usual on his last trip, he was diagnosed. And my life, at least in my self-absorbed teenage mind, changed. Instead of going to Friday night football games and buying prom dresses, I turned angry and rebellious and started hanging out with a different crowd. My boyfriend, Jake, played in a band. He wore lots of black leather and chains, had piercings and a lot of tattoos. But while he might have looked like a gangbanger, deep down, he was a nice guy. When I told him I was pregnant, instead of running for the hills or trying to talk me into an abortion, he was actually excited about the baby."

"Wait a minute. You were seventeen, but Emma is—"

"Three. She's my second child. I miscarried during my first trimester."

He reached across the table and took her hand. "I'm sorry."

"I was, too. Nobody talked much about those things back then. While lots of mommy groups were starting up, there weren't any support groups for mothers who'd lost their children before birth—at least not around here. There wasn't any prescribed way to grieve. My mother tried to help, assured me I'd have more babies. And, of course, I did eventually have Emma. But as much as I love her, that doesn't mean that I don't still grieve for the baby who should have been her big brother or sister."

"That would be hard on any woman," Cam said. "But at your age you couldn't have possibly been prepared."

"I wasn't." Her laugh was without humor. "What I knew about sex back then could have been written on the head of a pin and still had room for a thousand dancing angels. I was scared to death when that pregnancy test proved positive. But then, when Jake got all excited, I started looking forward to being a mother, and even started planning a nursery." She shook her head. "I was so young and naive,

I had no clue that approximately fifty percent of pregnancies end in miscarriages."

"I'm an adult who's had my share of biology classes, but I had no idea that percentage was that high."

"Well, you're a guy. It's probably not a topic that comes up a lot over beers at Mannion's."

She fell silent as the steward returned to take their empty cocktail glasses away and bring a plate of freshly baked bread with honey-thyme butter and bowls of silky fennel and potato soup.

"Anyway," she said, "life eventually moved on. Though the marriage turned out to be pretty much a disaster."

"He wasn't abusive?"

"No, not verbally or physically. But I came to realize that I'd married Peter Pan, that Jake would never grow up. So, although I'd be the first person in my family ever to get divorced, when I got pregnant again, with Emma, I'd already decided to leave Jake. Then he left me first. But I have Emma, so if I could go back in time, I wouldn't change a thing."

"She's a gem."

"She is, indeed. And this is really great soup."

It was too lovely an evening for such a serious discussion. But they weren't alone that often, and if she wanted to move forward with Cameron, which she did, she needed to share her story, then leave it in the past where it belonged.

Having dispensed with the topic of her ill-fated marriage, over an entrée of grilled Alaskan salmon, a chilled salad of finely chopped parsley, cherry tomatoes, mint, onion and couscous, seasoned with olive oil, lemon juice, salt and pepper, and roasted seasonal vegetables paired with a smooth red pinot noir from a winery on one of the San Juan islands, the conversation moved on to more enjoyable topics—the upcoming harvest celebration, the town Halloween party where children would trick-or-treat at various businesses, Thanksgiving and, of course, Christmas.

"This time of year seems to have been created for children," Megan said. "Emma's already insisting on going through the corn maze at Blue House Farm. And, of course, she's going to be a princess for Halloween."

"She'll make a good one. She already has the attitude."

Megan laughed, agreeing entirely.

They'd just finished a light, lemony cheesecake topped with berries when "Just One Look" came up on the ship's playlist.

"They're playing our song." Cam stood up and held out a hand. As she stood, he deftly turned her into his arms. She'd already discovered at the wedding how well he'd danced. How well they fit together. "Last night was fun," he murmured against her temple as they swayed to the music drifting through the speakers.

"It was. I think my daughter is in love with you."

"That makes it mutual, then," he said, spinning her out, then bringing her back against him. Closer this time.

She nestled her cheek against his broad shoulder as they swayed to the music drifting through the speaker.

Those long fingers she'd imagined on her body so many times rested at the base of her back, pressing her close enough to feel his need. Her pulse quickened.

"Just one look," he sang softly along with the song, his breath a warm breeze against her hair. "And I knew."

The words floated away. She shut her eyes and twined her arms around his neck as the songs—all slow, all romantic— changed. Megan was just thinking that she could happily stay like this forever, when the steward discreetly knocked on the door to let them know that they'd returned and were approaching the dock.

After Cam helped her into Brianna's coat, they went out on the deck and watched as Honeymoon Harbor came into view. "Although I've lived here all my life, I've never seen the town from the water at night," she said. "With all the lights reflected in the cloud cover, it looks as if it's wearing strings of jewels. Or," she reconsidered, "like I imagine Brigadoon must look."

"It's a special place," he agreed. "I'm glad I found it." He drew her close as the sailors around them prepared to dock. "Because if I hadn't, I wouldn't have found you."

It was magic, decided Megan, who'd been brought up to be practical and not encouraged to daydream. This place, this night, this man.

After thanking both the steward and the captain for the very special hospitality, they were piped off the tall ship like visiting admirals.

"That was," she said, as they strolled along the deck to the parking lot, "the very best date night ever."

"I'd hoped you'd enjoy it."

"It was even better than having a white yacht show up outside my door. And you were a hundred times more handsome and sexier than Michael Douglas. I probably should feel sorry for her."

"Kathleen Turner?"

"No. That woman who didn't think you could be romantic." She paused long enough to lift her lips to his. "She has no idea what she missed out on."

"And just think," Cam said, "the night isn't over yet."

CHAPTER SIX

MEGAN HAD WORRIED that she'd end up ruining a perfect evening with an imperfect night. It had been ages since she'd had sex with a partner. Her first time had been a fumbling, inexperienced event in the back seat of a car parked out at the lake that had resulted in the conception of the baby whose gender she'd never know, whom she'd never hold to her breast and whose chubby little feet she'd never play this-little-piggy with, the baby she'd loved from the moment she'd seen that positive line on the pregnancy test, the baby that a part of her would always grieve.

In the first year of her marriage, she'd wondered if the reason she couldn't climax wasn't due to her husband's quick, self-satisfying technique that never changed since that first teenage night, but because depression had taken her to a very dark place for a very long time. Her ever-practical mother, in an attempt to bring Megan back into the light, began taking her on cleaning jobs, which had given her a sense of purpose. She might not be able to go back in time and change the past, she might not ever stop missing her lost child, but she could clean bathrooms until they sparkled, organize a messy, jumbled pantry, make crisp, tight beds her father could have bounced a quarter off and leave perfectly straight vacuum lines in a carpet. Her work might not save the world, but it had certainly saved her life.

All those thoughts were tumbling around in her mind as

she stood in the middle of her living room, Cameron looking down at her, her looking up at him.

"We don't have to do this," he said, his hands smoothing over her shoulders. "I don't want to rush you."

"I do want to. But... I'm a little out of practice."

His lips curved in a slow smile. His dark eyes, which she'd seen blaze, turned tender as he ran the backs of his fingers down the side of her cheek. "It's like riding a bicycle. It'll come back to you."

"I was never very good at that, either," she admitted. "It's some sort of balance problem. My pediatrician said it was an inner-ear thing that I might outgrow."

"And did you?"

"I don't know." She shrugged. "I didn't try again after that."

"I think I hear a metaphor there," he said. "Next weekend, we'll rent one of those bicycles built for two and we'll take it for a spin around the harbor. Meanwhile, I'd very much like to top this date off by making love to you. The same way I have in my dreams since that first night I saw you at Mannion's."

"I'd like that, too."

His strong arms went around her, gathering her close as he lowered his head and touched his mouth to hers. Gently, softly pulling her back into those mists where she'd been floating while they'd danced.

When her lips parted on a soft sigh, he deepened the kiss and pulled her closer. His body was hard as granite, and very much aroused. She did that to him, Megan told herself as her blood turned warm and golden. Without breaking contact, lightly humming their song against her lips, he danced her, turning in smooth circles, down the hall. She was grateful her house was small, allowing him to easily find her bedroom without her having to break contact to tell him.

He placed her on the bed she'd optimistically made with fresh sheets this morning, then the mattress sighed as he lay down beside her. Exploring her with his gaze and his hands. When she would have rushed, he took his time, slowly undressing her, even managing to pull those tights off, which wasn't an easy feat. When he'd gotten down to the skimpy black panties and bra that had been engineered to make her B-cup breasts appear almost voluptuous, his eyes deepened to nearly black as they licked a slow, hot kiss over her almost-naked body.

"You are beautiful."

"It's the packaging."

"No, it's you. Although I'm not going to deny the packaging is pretty damn fine."

"I'm glad. Since I bought it for you."

"I'm looking forward to showing my appreciation." He stood up and stripped much more quickly than he'd undressed her. When she first saw those black boxer briefs, the idea that they'd matched underwear colors almost made her laugh. Until he bent down and stripped them off.

He was, in a word, magnificent. And he was hers. At least for tonight. "You are," she said breathlessly, "the best birthday present I've ever received."

Megan was no virgin. She'd lost one child and given birth to a daughter. But she'd never known, until now, how mere words could have such a direct effect on a man's body. Cameron Montgomery had been born in the wrong time. If he'd lived during the Renaissance, he would have been immortalized in marble, and David, who'd always set the standard for male beauty, would have had to settle for second place.

As Cam's gaze swept over her, his eyes somehow managed to be both sleepy and hot at the same time. For the very first time in her life, Megan understood what all those authors meant when they wrote about "bedroom eyes."

"Now we're going to get you back up on that bicycle," he said in his low, rough voice. "And ride all night long."

By the time the sun was filtering through her blinds and the long sound of the incoming morning ferry's horn blast sounded from the water, Cam had definitely proven to be a man of his word.

FALL HAD ALWAYS been Megan's favorite season, and this year was even better with Cam in it. Even as the weather cooled down during the two weeks after Labor Day, the sun seemed to have a warmer glow to it, a glow that matched her emotions.

The morning after her date with Cam on the *Lady Abigail*, she'd taken Emma to her first day of preschool, preparing for a possible meltdown as they arrived to find other first timers in tears. But Emma allowed only a quick kiss before rushing into her classroom, immediately disappearing into a group of three-year-olds digging into a big chest of Legos. As Megan drove out of the school's parking lot, the first-day tears were her own.

She and Cam continued their Wednesday lunches, which he'd moved up a half hour due to Emma's half day at school that allowed her to play with Butterfly, who unsurprisingly hadn't yet found a home. But she had grown a bit more fur. What Emma didn't know yet was that the dog would be coming home for her fourth birthday before the end of the month.

Proving that no life could remain perfectly rosy, Megan

and Cam had their first argument when she told him that she was no longer charging him for cleaning.

"It's your business," Cam had pointed out. "You and Brianna are friends. Yet I see the Clean Team van out in front of Herons Landing every day with your crew taking care of the guest rooms."

"I'm not sleeping with Brianna. Now that we've had sex—"

"Made love," he corrected.

"Now that we've *made love*," she continued, "I'd feel like a prostitute."

He raked a hand through his hair, and as frustrated as Megan was that he either couldn't or refused to see her point, she couldn't help getting turned on by the way it flipped back down. Not the Bieberish full-bang teen thing. Just a bit on the left side of his brow that called attention to his too-sexy eyes.

"I wouldn't be paying you for that," he insisted. "Just cleaning."

"There's not that much to do. I'd be doing it anyway if we were living together—"

"Which I wouldn't mind," he uncharacteristically interrupted her again, showing how equally frustrated he was. "I'd also chip in, which I already do before you show up. But I do realize that you wouldn't want to move in with Emma."

No. She wouldn't. She didn't want to cause her daughter heartache if things went wrong. Also, perhaps she was old-fashioned, but she didn't want her daughter to grow up thinking that moving in with guys was necessarily a good thing. And didn't she hate having to even consider right and wrong in these types of situations? No wonder her mother had those gray hairs.

"You've already been paying for the lunches," she said. "And that rental boat for the fireworks, the date, even Emma's ice cream cone at the festival. I refuse to be a kept woman, Cameron." Okay, now, perhaps she'd been reading too much historical romance.

"Hell." He threw up his hands. "Do whatever you want."

"Thank you." She crossed what had become a Grand Canyon between them, went up on her toes, linked her hands together behind his neck and rewarded him with a long, deep kiss that would've ended up in his bedroom if Emma hadn't been downstairs helping Debbie, one of the techs, give Butterfly a bath.

Having missed most of her dating years, she got a thrill from kissing Cam in the back row of the Olympic Theater, basked in the afternoon she went sailing with him on Seth's sloop while her parents took Emma to a Dora the Explorer movie with pizza afterward, and loved shopping with him at the family market, where along with a bounty of fresh vegetables, Emma had gotten a blue balloon dog she'd promptly named Butterfly, just in case her mother hadn't gotten the hint yet.

And then, two weeks after Labor Day, after hearing that she and Cam had planned a weekend trip to the coast, her mother invited Megan, Emma and Cam to dinner.

"I think," Cam told Megan, "that we've just hit a milestone in our relationship. The dreaded *Meet the Parents* moment."

"You already know my parents."

"True. But until recently, I'd just been the town vet. Now I'm the guy sleeping with their only daughter, which is why I've been invited to an inquisition."

"It's only a roast chicken dinner. Not an inquisition." She hoped.

CHAPTER SEVEN

CAMERON HAD SURVIVED the roast chicken dinner, which, he'd assured Brenda Larson, was the best he'd ever eaten. Which was true. His mother had many attributes. Cooking had never been one of them. The conversation had remained casual, everyone sticking to safe topics like Emma's upcoming birthday, which was when she made a pitch for Butterfly again, openly frustrated when she only got a "We'll see" from Megan, who already had food dishes and a dog bed hiding in a closet at Cam's. Her plan was for Megan and Cam to take her shopping for toys and a coat for the dog after her party.

The next event on the calendar was the harvest festival, where Emma would be going through her first corn maze out at Blue House Farm and choosing a pumpkin, which Cam had volunteered to carve into a jack-o'-lantern. She was, unsurprisingly, wearing a princess costume for the downtown merchants' trick-or-treat street party.

"How are your parents doing in Tucson, Cameron?" Megan's mother asked as she picked up the empty dessert plates that had held pieces of warm, home-baked apple pie topped with vanilla bean ice cream Joe Larson had made that morning.

"They seem to be enjoying retirement." Cameron's dad had been a general surgeon in Port Angeles, while his mom ran his medical office. "Mom's even taken up golf."

"Well, doesn't that sound nice," Brenda said.

"I'm not sure it's her favorite thing to do, but she says she prefers it to becoming a golf widow."

"I can understand that. And isn't it nice that after all those years working together, they still enjoy each other's company?"

"Dad's always said he fell for her his first week as an intern. She was an ER nurse, who informed him that he was doing nearly everything wrong, which made her wonder what type of doctors medical schools were churning out those days."

"That could have gone the other way," Megan said as she wiped a bit of ice cream from Emma's cheek. "Not all men, especially doctors, I suspect, would be happy to be criticized by a woman."

"We Montgomery males come from strong Highlander stock. We like equally strong women." He'd looked directly into Megan's eyes while making that assertion. Meanwhile, his hand traced what felt like an infinity design on her thigh beneath the table, causing a familiar heat to rise in her cheeks. She couldn't remember ever blushing before meeting Cameron Montgomery. It was as if even being within touching distance had her internal temperature rising.

"Megan, dear, why don't you and Emma come upstairs and help me choose some quilt material while your father and Cameron watch the football game?"

"I thought I'd help do the dishes."

"There aren't that many. I took care of most of them as I cooked. They can always wait." Megan had never heard her mother say that before. Which, she feared, hinted at a planned inquisition after all. "I thought Emma would enjoy looking at all the material."

"I would!" Emma said, sealing the deal.

"I didn't know you quilted," Megan said as they climbed the stairs to her mother's craft room.

"I don't. Yet. But I thought I'd take it up to make blankets for Project Linus, so I went online, watched a bunch of those YouTube videos, then went to Port Townsend and bought myself some tools and material. I probably bought too much."

As they entered the room and Megan viewed the stacks of fabric piled high on a craft table, she laughed. "You think so?"

"Well, hopefully it won't be the first and last one I make," her mother said a little huffily, as if being accused of being a spendthrift, when the very opposite was true.

Brenda Larson was the most frugal person Megan had ever met, which had been frustrating when she'd been younger and was continually told that *want* and *need* were two very different things. But as she'd become an adult with a child to support and a business to run, she'd been grateful for those early lessons in making—and sticking to—a budget.

"You deserve to spend some money on fun after all the years you've worked. Everyone needs a hobby. And this is for a good cause."

"True." Her mother gave her a sideways glance as she began plucking a few sample squares from the piles she'd sorted by color. "What hobby do you have?"

"I've been a little busy with Emma and establishing my business." One with primary-colored planes, trains and cars caught her eye. "This would be cute for a boy."

"I was thinking the same thing. I'd guess more people make quilts for girls, just because they'd be prettier. Which is why I liked that pattern. And good try changing the topic."

"You might want to try these multicolored stripes with it," Megan said, not walking into that conversational trap. Her mother was a fine one to talk. She'd worked full-time while keeping the house up and taking care of her own daughter for years.

"I like unicorns," Emma said. "If you make a quilt for a girl, Gramma, you should make a unicorn. Or a princess. That would be good, too."

"Those are both very good suggestions," Brenda said. "Why don't you take these pink squares over to the sofa and see if you can find some that a little girl would like?"

"I'll find the best ones!"

"Of course you will." Once Emma had settled down, Megan's mother turned to her. "So, how serious is it with you and Cameron?"

"It's serious," she admitted. "At least on my part. And I think his. Which, to be honest, scares me."

"Love can often be scary." Brenda placed some rainbow-striped material next to the car-patterned one. "Especially once you've had an unfortunate experience. Or when the man you love has an incurable disease."

Like her father's MS. "How's Dad doing? He seems well." Except for that cane.

"He has his good days and bad." Brenda switched the pattern out for a solid Christmas red. "Today's one of the good ones. He does get tired more often and uses his cane more, but the doctors all say that he's doing better than most of the patients they see, considering how long ago he was diagnosed. They suspect that it's partly because he was so fit from all the years of physical labor on those boats."

"Does he miss crabbing?"

Her mom laughed at that. "I asked him that a few months ago, and he asked me why the hell I thought he'd miss freezing his ass off in drenching rain and icy waves that washed over the side of the boat onto the deck. He also lost friends out there. Friends with families. I know that always worried him, but we never talked about it." She shrugged. "Because there wasn't any point, and why borrow trouble?"

"After I watched *The Deadliest Catch* and saw what Dad had actually been doing all those years he was away, I can't imagine what you went through."

"Fortunately, I hadn't even heard of that show until recently, when he started streaming the reruns, which terrify me. Sometimes I suspect that while he doesn't miss all that miserable weather, he does miss the male bonding that's so obvious on board those boats. But he seems content to play cards with his friends at the VFW and watch football. Sometimes, on good days, he plays darts at Mannion's.

"And getting back to your heart, Cameron doesn't seem at all the sort of man who'd ever hurt you. If he weren't a nurturer by nature, he would have chosen another profession."

"True. And he's amazing with Emma."

"Well, then. I think you ought to stop worrying about the future, enjoy the moment and follow your heart wherever it leads you."

Which was easier said than done, especially as she'd already risked her heart by going out with Cameron in the first place. Then by making love with him. If something did happen between them, while it would be difficult to break up in a town as small as this, especially if she had to watch him dating someone else, at least she'd always have this special time to look back on.

"I found some!" Emma came running back waving two squares of pastel colors. One featured a unicorn, the other a Disney princess.

"Those are great," Megan said.

"They'll be perfect." Brenda took the two squares and held them up. "I can use one for the front, then the other for the back to make it reversible."

"Good idea!" Emma dived into the squares of material, scattering the carefully separated colors. "Let's find some more. This is fun!"

As she watched her mother and daughter trying out different possible quilt combinations, Megan decided that she wasn't going to think about those pesky if-onlys or, as she was prone to do, think too far ahead. For this special time, she was going to take her mother's advice to try to relax and just go with the flow.

"THE SEAHAWKS COULD USE more passing," Joe muttered.

"They're gaining good yardage on the ground."

"I know. But I get frequent flier miles for every yard they pass during the regular season."

"You do?"

"Yeah. And before you point out that I never go anywhere, I donate the miles to veterans so they can travel home and visit their families."

"That's really generous of you."

Megan's father shrugged massive shoulders, almost as large as Jarle's down at the pub. Cam figured that it must take a helluva lot of strength to pull wire cages teaming with crawling, snapping crabs out of a roiling ocean. "It was easy to sign up. And, like you said, I'm not going to use them, so I might as well pass them on to those who need them more... What are your intentions toward my daughter?"

Despite the abrupt change of subject, Cam had seen this coming from the hard looks Joe had been giving him across the table during dinner. Having anticipated "the talk," he'd come to the house today with a response already worked

out. What had him suddenly feeling like a teenager coming to pick up the man's daughter to take her to the prom
was the fear that Joe might not get on board with the plan.

Which wasn't going to deter Cam. But it would make
their situation more difficult.

"I'm glad you asked that question, Mr. Larson." His voice
was the same calm, self-assured tone he used when assuring that nervous cat owner this morning that Mittens would
survive her spaying. He was grateful they were sitting down
so Megan's father couldn't tell that nerves had his knees
shaking. "I'd like to ask your permission to marry Megan."

"I didn't know guys still do that."

"It's probably not a typical thing anymore. But Megan is
different. In this case, it seemed appropriate. Sir."

"I appreciate that. I asked for my Brenda's hand, but like
Dylan said, times, they are a-changing."

"You listen to Dylan?"

"What did you think? That we all sat around on the boat
at night drinking rum and singing sea shanties? One of the
crew was a roadie for Dylan for a while. He told some great
stories. Other guys were into Springsteen, then, every once
in a while, you even got one of those Deadheads. All in all,
there was usually a pretty good mix. Johnny Cash was one
guy everyone could agree on.

"Whenever we wanted to piss off the captain, we'd play
'Don't Stop the Music' and 'We Are Family.' He flat out
hated disco. If he was in a real suckfest mood after a cold,
wet day of pulling up empty traps, we'd all line up and
dance to the Village People." Joe grinned at a memory
that Cam was nearly breaking his mind trying to imagine.

"You've lived an interesting life."

Joe shrugged. "It was a job like any other. But it had its
moments," he allowed. "The hardest part was being away

from family. I missed out on a helluva lot of reunions and weddings over the years. My sister-in-law's son just got engaged. We're going to their wedding in Portland come spring."

"That's nice."

"Yeah. Though Brenda tells me I have to wear a suit."

"And you're complaining to a man who had to wear a penguin suit to get a date with your daughter?"

Joe barked out a laugh. "Good point," he agreed. "From the chemistry you two have, even Stevie Wonder could tell Megan loves you."

"And I love her."

"Yeah, like I said, that's obvious enough."

Joe turned back to the game just as the Seahawks QB took a hard hit. "They could also use some stronger line defense," he muttered. Then rubbed a jaw bisected by an ugly, raised scar undoubtedly from his years doing one of the most dangerous jobs in the world.

"Emma never knew her dad. He took off soon after Meggie got pregnant."

"So she told me. And I swear that I couldn't love that little girl any more if she were my own daughter. And, if Megan and I have other children, they'll all be treated the same."

"I believe that. I've kept my eye on you since Megan started cleaning at your place, which was a giveaway since she'd quit personally cleaning for anyone but Harper Construction last year. When you two started having those Wednesday lunches, I figured that this moment would eventually come. Though I didn't expect you to go old-school and ask me for my daughter's hand." His eyes narrowed. "What would you have done if I'd said no?"

"Married her anyway, then won you over by treating your

daughter and granddaughter as if they were the most important people in the world. Which, to me, they already are."

Joe blew out a breath. "Can't ask for much more than that. I guess all that's left for me to do is welcome you to the family."

He held out a bear paw of a hand lined with calluses and scars. Cam was extremely grateful Megan's father didn't object to him marrying Megan, because he figured that if he ever pissed Joe off, he'd be pounded to a pulp then thrown into the sea for crab bait.

They were shaking hands as Megan and her mother came downstairs. While Brenda showed not a scintilla of surprise, Megan's gaze went back and forth between them, obviously trying to read what had gone on while she'd been upstairs.

"Your fella here thinks the Hawks will beat the spread," Joe lied deftly. "I just bet him that he's overly optimistic. Winner has to buy the loser a beer at halftime."

"Which, given that it would come from your refrigerator, wouldn't be that much of a loss," Cam said.

He hated even hedging at the truth, especially having heard stories of her ex's behavior. But he also understood why her father had come up with that phony explanation for the handshake. Because there was no way Cam wanted to propose to Megan with the blare of the halftime show in the background while her parents and daughter looked on.

Especially since he'd already come up with another plan. It might not be as crazy romantic as Michael Douglas showing up with that yacht, or Richard Gere climbing up a fire escape with a red rose, but Chelsea, who'd become his go-to Dear Abby on all things Megan, had assured him that she'd love it.

CHAPTER EIGHT

THE PICTURESQUE BEACH town of Lucky Harbor, Washington, was much like others scattered around the peninsula, while still keeping its own individual vibe. The Victorian houses were painted in brighter colors than those in Honeymoon Harbor, and Megan's hometown pier, while popular with the shiny boats the summer people would arrive in every Memorial Day, was also more commercial, being home to a fleet of fishermen, a large boatyard and the wooden boat–building school.

"We came here once between crabbing seasons when I was growing up," Megan said as she and Cam walked hand in hand down the pier. "It wasn't often we got away for a family vacation, so it was a big deal." Cam's family owned a beach cottage where they'd be staying while in town.

The evening had grown cool, making her glad she'd brought a light fleece hoodie. Which might not be as cute as a lacy cardigan sweater or one of those cute little shrugs so many city visitors would show up in Honeymoon Harbor wearing, but hoodies were a practical western Washington uniform.

While Lily had suggested she take at least one cute date dress, Megan instead opted for jeans—though these were tighter than usual and she'd taken time to iron a crease into them—and a long-sleeved red V-neck T-shirt. A date dress felt like too much pressure. Taking a weekend away together was definitely adding a new dimension to a relationship that had become so natural and easy, she didn't want to risk ruining it with making it seem like a big deal.

She was also mindful of that ex-girlfriend he'd told her about, the one who'd wanted every day to be like the ending of *Romancing the Stone*. While Megan knew that she'd remember their *Lady Abigail* date for the rest of her life, she couldn't imagine how exhausting it would be to live a life of constant high drama. Jake had been like that. Every time he'd screw up, which was often, he'd go out and buy her some extravagant apology gift they couldn't afford and she didn't want.

The huge Ferris wheel was lit with strings of light that shone brightly against the deepening purple sky. Cam bought two tickets from the operator, who looked to have two inches on Jarle's six foot seven. But while Jarle could be intimidating to those who didn't know he had a marshmallow heart inside that giant body, this guy, with his head-to-toe black leather and studs, looked like a badass Hell's Angel.

"You two lucked out tonight," he said, sounding a lot less fearsome than he appeared. "You can't see it now, but you're going to have a helluva surprise when you get to the top."

He shut the bar, handed them a plaid Pendleton blanket, then shoved a lever that had the wheel jerking to a start.

"How tall is this thing?" Megan said as they went higher and higher. Then higher still, giving her a bird's-eye view of the town. If they went any higher, it might begin to look like miniature buildings on a train set.

"Five stories. I didn't think to ask if you were afraid of heights because you went on the one at the festival."

"This is a lot taller than that."

"Maybe you ought to snuggle a little closer," Cam suggested.

"Yes, that will help if the car suddenly falls from the sky."

"You're right. It undoubtedly wouldn't. But the ride would be more fun in the meantime."

Since Megan couldn't deny that, she leaned into the curve of his outstretched arm that gathered her close against him as he pulled the red-and-black blanket more tightly around them.

When they'd finally reached the top, the wheel came to a sudden halt. And stayed stopped.

"Please don't tell me it's broken." She'd seen news videos of people stuck on top of amusement park rides. Sometimes for hours. Trying to find a silver lining to what she hoped weren't going to be the last minutes of her life, she told herself that at least they weren't hanging upside down.

"I'd guess, since we're the only ones on the ride, he's giving us time to enjoy the view."

The ocean, lit by a floating galleon of a full moon, seemed to go on forever. It was a perfect fall night, and as she listened to the sound of the surf, she was thinking that Biker Dude had definitely been right about them being lucky. It was a beautiful view.

And then, suddenly, she saw it. A bright, almost neon-blue glow, looking like twinkling stars suspended in the water, cutting across the silver trail of moonlight.

"Oh, wow!" Bioluminescent tides, usually caused by algae in the water, were a very rare, very unpredictable sight. Once, when she'd been about ten, they'd appeared off a beach near the ferry landing, and her dad had made them start dancing like fireflies with a stroke of his finger. "This may be worth risking death for."

"I promise I won't let you die."

"So if we do fall, you'll swoop down and catch me in your manly arms of steel like Superman did Lois Lane?"

"If I have to."

"Which would be impossible."

"So is the concept of the situation in the first place. Not only can man not fly, given the speed of a falling object, if Superman had caught Lois, the impact of the sudden stop would have killed her. Unless he had a malleable force field around him that he could dump her kinetic energy into and soften the blow."

She stared at him. "What science class did you learn that in?"

"I read a lot of DC comic books growing up. Flash's energy field is what allows him to avoid friction and not cause sonic booms. It's the only way that Lois could've survived at the end of that scene."

"You do realize that you've taken us way off topic."

"I do. And do you realize that I distracted you from being afraid of falling? Suggesting, perhaps, that diversion is *my* superpower."

She laughed, deciding that his wry humor was only one reason she'd fallen in love with him. She'd been, by necessity, so serious for so many years, until their weekly Wednesday lunches, she couldn't remember how it felt to be silly and just have fun for fun's sake.

"Life with you certainly wouldn't be boring," she said.

"About that..." Her breath caught as he reached into his pocket and pulled out a deep blue velvet box. "Megan Larson, will you marry me and be my beloved wife forever and ever?"

The solitaire ring, lying on the bed of ivory satin, gleamed in the moonlight as bright as any star. But...

"Cameron Montgomery, are you crazy? What if you

drop that box? You'd lose that beautiful ring in the ocean forever." A fish or orca could swallow it. Or it could end up on the beach for a seagull to snatch up.

"We can avoid that possibility if you let me put it on your finger."

"Crazy," she said again, even as she held out her left hand.

"Crazy about you," he agreed, slipping the ring onto her fourth finger. "So, are you just trying to save me an insurance loss? Or saying yes?"

"You lied," she said.

"About what?"

"About not being into grand gestures." How many men, she wondered, would propose marriage at what felt like the top of the world, beneath a full moon, as the ocean below them sparkled like sapphire? "And yes, absolutely, positively, my answer is yes. Forever and ever."

She lifted her lips, and as he kissed her, Megan felt as if she were falling. But that was all right. Because she knew that Cameron Montgomery would always be there to catch her.

* * * * *